Wild Irish Yenta

by

Joyce Sanderly

Cover Art by *Lisa Dawn MacDonald*

The Wild Rose Press, Inc.
PO Box 708
Adams Basin, NY 14410-0708
Visit us at www.thewildrosepress.com

Publishing History
First Edition, 2024
Trade Paperback ISBN 978-1-5092-5093-6
Digital ISBN 978-1-5092-5094-3

Published in the United States of America

Patricia owed it to Roberto to try to figure out exactly what happened the night he died. She felt a kinship with him. Like her, he had been an outsider trying to fit in. While she was trying to gain acceptance into the Jewish faith, the temple, and her husband's family, for Roberto the stakes had been much higher. He was struggling to be adopted by a new country, learn a language, and hold down a job to support his family. He'd described to her how he left his home and many of his relatives in El Salvador, because of gang violence perpetrated against innocent people. He'd worried the MS-13 gang would try to recruit his son to sell drugs. Anyone refusing or complaining to the police could be subject to retaliation.

Patricia's paternal grandfather had told her how he emigrated from Ireland in the middle of an economic panic that devastated the family farm. He fought for a longshoreman's job and a decent place to live in Boston. Neither of Patricia's parents had earned college degrees, and Patricia could see she had taken a leap upon arriving on the shores of Potomac Pines. Roberto had a much higher bar to clear but he was on his way, improving his English fluency and learning computer skills.

The blare of her cellphone's Real Detective ringtone made her jump. It was Michael.

"Just checking in. I was worried—that hit and run—your friend Roberto's death. What a waste. Did you park close to the entrance?"

Praise for Wild Irish Yenta

"Wild Irish Yenta lives up to its title—this keenly-observed, funny mystery features a plucky heroine who converts to Judaism and throws herself into synagogue life, only to discover a corpse in the temple parking lot. And so begins this whimsical cozy that combines an insightful look at interfaith marriage, the complexities of friendship, and the politics of religious institutions."

~Susan Coll, author of Bookish People

~*~

"Debut novelist Sanderly has written an inventive mystery that satirizes the modern Jewish suburban experience. In Wild Irish Yenta, Philip Roth meets Agatha Christie, and the result is a page-turner that also explores the interlocking dynamics that exist within an interfaith marriage, a family, and a Maryland synagogue."

~Michelle Brafman, author of Swimming With Ghosts

Dedication

To Alan

Chapter One

Saturday, May 9; Sunday, May 10

Patricia Weiss nee Reilly nearly choked on a sip of steaming espresso as she leaned over her kitchen counter and skimmed the morning's *Washington Post*. She wanted to finish the paper before her family stirred awake, but a familiar name caught her eye. She abruptly let out a low cry.

Rockville, MD: The identity of the body found Friday morning in the back parking lot of Temple Israel has been confirmed as Roberto Gomez, a custodian at the Temple. Carol Plotsky, the Temple's administrative assistant who discovered the body, stated that Gomez "was a hard worker and exhausted himself. He maybe napped a minute against the dumpster, the garbage truck barreled in, and bam he's hit. What a tragedy for his family." Gomez was the married father of two children.

How could this be? Patricia groaned. She had just seen Roberto the night before last. With her umbrella and four-year-old son Danny in tow, she'd driven to the temple that humid Thursday evening to pick up the syllabus for her upcoming adult b'nai mitzvah class. A storm loomed in the overcast sky, and she arrived later than she intended. Aside from her minivan, only a few cars occupied parking spaces. The lot seemed hauntingly empty compared to the usual frenzy of circling cars and jay-walking parents and children.

Roberto unlocked the wide glass door to the temple foyer, warning them not to slip where he had been mopping the ceramic floor. Danny ran over to the full trash bags leaning against the door, spilling open with papers tinted red, blue, and green, like Joseph's coat of many colors.

"Hey, Danny, why don't you help yourself to the paper. There's lots." Roberto smiled. "I might take some sheets home to my kids for art projects."

Patricia pulled out the crayons she always carried in her tote just in case. While Danny scribbled on a discarded page, Patricia and Roberto had talked about the vocabulary assignment she gave him as homework for their weekly English language tutoring sessions. While he described the Excel computer course he was taking at the local community college, they had surveyed the foyer's bursting garbage bags and laughed about the virtues of the "paperless office."

Now in her cozy kitchen, as the fragrant espresso cooled in its mug, Patricia heard the light patter of footsteps overhead. Danny was awake, running out of his upstairs bedroom and calling for her. She quickly closed the paper as if turning the page would make the bad news go away and wished there was a way to protect her son from the world's cruelty.

If only the dead could schmooze and share what they'd belatedly learned about tricking fate and delaying life's universal yet mysterious destination.

****

That Sunday evening as she rinsed the dinner dishes, Patricia looked across the granite countertop at her graying, curly-haired prince. Dr. Michael Weiss, M.D., Board Certified in Cardiology, sat at the glass kitchen table. He examined the congealed pasta bake on his dinner plate, gently prodding the remains as if probing for diseased tissue. Danny, who had inherited his father's adorable curls, sat next to Michael and imitated his father's poking motion.

She recognized that skeptical expression on Michael's face, his lips twisted into a half grin/half grimace. Okay, her pasta bake wasn't as tasty as the General Tso's chicken from Shanghai Gardens that Michael's family had eaten every Sunday night when he was growing up in Great Neck, New York. But broccoli, ground meat, and noodles were surely healthier than an orgy of artery-hardening fat and sodium. Maybe pasta bake wasn't the most creative dish. She wasn't her mother's daughter when it came to cooking. Although her mother, Maria, had worked as a nurse, she still managed to concoct dynamite Italian dishes for supper without even using a recipe. Unfortunately Patricia had failed to inherit the cooking gene. So it was a challenge to come up with nutritious meals on a daily basis to serve her picky husband and equally finicky four-year-old son.

She scrubbed at the pan in the sink, then gave up scouring the charred bottom and left it to soak. "Michael, honey, can you take over here? Then Danny needs a bath and stories. I have to leave in a minute for my b'nai mitzvah class. Rabbi Deborah's email asked that everyone be on time."

"Mommy, I want you to read to me."

"See, Danny doesn't want you to go," Michael replied. "Besides, is it a good idea for you to drive to

3

the temple alone? Look what happened to that poor janitor."

Forgetting her son's radar ears, she blurted, "Roberto Gomez. I can't believe it. I just saw him. There's no way he would have fallen asleep on the job. Carol's comment to the newspaper reporter about his napping was absurd."

"Mommy, why can't you read to me?" Danny whined. "What happened to Roberto? He's nice."

Patricia knelt down in front of her son and took his hands in hers. Trying to sound comforting, she explained, "I'm so sorry, Danny. Roberto was in a bad accident." She gave Michael a pleading look for help. He only shrugged. "We can talk more about it tomorrow. Right now I have to go to my class."

Patricia hoped her answer would satisfy Danny's curiosity until she could read up on how to discuss death with a young child. She'd been dreading this conversation.

Standing, she addressed Michael. "Danny and I saw Roberto on Thursday evening when I picked up the b'nai mitzvah syllabus from the temple. He's the one I'd been helping with English language skills on Tuesday mornings at the temple library. He emigrated from El Salvador ten years ago and then brought over his family."

"Yeah, now I remember. I didn't realize he was the one you were tutoring. The temple was okay with your tutoring while he was on the job?"

Flushing with annoyance at Michael's presumptuousness, Patricia tried to keep her voice calm. "Rabbi Deborah approved the arrangement. Roberto worked overtime, and since I have free hours while Danny's in pre-school, I thought I could support someone else who was trying to become fluent in a new language. Sort of like me and Hebrew. Roberto wanted to improve his English, so he could help his ten-year-old son with homework."

"It was a nice idea. Don't get upset."

Silently accepting his implicit apology, Patricia moved to more neutral territory. "You should see the books that fifth graders are reading now—Greek myths, Wrinkle in Time, Philip Pullman's fantasy tales—way advanced beyond my schooldays. And now nothing more will come from all Roberto's diligence. His wife and two kids left alone. I feel so bad for them."

"What a shame, that accident. The parking situation at the temple is a disaster, with all those old farts and aggressive drivers fighting over the closest spaces," Michael observed. "Everyone has handicapped stickers, even if they're able-bodied. And that back parking lot where they found him is so poorly lit—it was an accident waiting to happen." He shook his head as if trying to clear the image of a bleeding body in need of delayed medical assistance. "All the more reason to avoid the lot. Why don't you take an Uber?"

"You're overreacting!" Putting her hands on her slim hips, Patricia straightened to her full height and glared at her husband. "I'm a good driver and I need to leave right now so I can get to class on time." She grabbed her sweater and stuffed the class syllabus into her big black fake designer tote, the bargain she'd bought in Boston on the advice of her sisters.

"Okay, okay, I'll finish cleaning up. But if you leave now, you're going to miss the call to my mother again." Michael's face took on that familiar dismayed look, the corners of his shapely lips and deep brown eyes pulling downward.

"Daddy, can I talk to Grandma?"

Patricia would not let herself be swayed into a delayed departure. "Seriously? I asked you to phone your mother earlier." She held up her hands in frustration, feeling both guilt and relief at missing the weekly call. "And yes, Danny, I'm sure Grandma Lilly would love to talk to you." There was no correct course for a daughter-in-law. "You know, Michael, my class starts at 7:30."

"Well, you know my mother has her bridge game on Sunday afternoons. And then she naps, and then she has to eat or her blood sugar drops."

"Inform her I went to the temple for the adult b'nai mitzvah class. Her Catholic daughter-in-law studying to have a bat mitzvah should make her happy."

"She thinks it's strange."

"Strange? Why? Danny, please bring Mommy your plate so I can put it in the dishwasher."

"She says there's a conspiracy. The non-Jews will take over the temple." Michael rubbed his forehead as if trying to divine an answer that would satisfy both his determined wife and his crotchety mother.

Patricia was aware of how sensitive Michael remained to his mother's opinion. An only child, he'd never outgrown the need for parental approval. "Remind your mother I converted. I'm a member of the tribe now."

As Danny handed over his plastic plate to Patricia, his brown eyes opened wide. "Mommy, are you in a tribe like Pocahontas? Can we read that book again?"

"Oh, thank you, Danny, what a big boy four-year-old you are. No, tribe's a way of saying someone belongs to a special group. We'll read tomorrow. Daddy's doing bedtime tonight."

A puzzled expression crossed Danny's face. "Mommy, Mrs. Rubin says I'm a member of the Dan tribe and it's lost."

Patricia smiled and bent over to kiss her son's forehead. "Good remembering. Dan is the name of one of the twelve tribes of Israel. The legend is…"

"When will you be back?" Michael sounded anxious. "Danny wants to know too, right Danny? I'm on call tonight although I don't expect any emergencies."

"Don't worry. I'll be home by 9:30. I'll keep my cell on vibrate. Put Danny on the phone with your mother. She won't realize I'm not here until after you're off the call."

Patricia knelt to give Danny a hug, and slipped out the front door, her black tote hanging heavily on her shoulder. She hoped scenes like this wouldn't be repeated every Sunday night. They lived ten minutes from Temple Israel, and she'd likely be the last one to class.

The front floodlights spontaneously turned on and shined a path as she hurried down the stone walkway to the minivan parked in the semi-circular drive. God showing her the way? Or suburban wizardry casting a spell over their five-bedroom, white brick colonial?

The McMansion in Potomac, Maryland was Michael's dream house. Although her own fantasy consisted of a shingled cottage on Nantucket Sound with her own bathroom and study, she enjoyed the elegant ease of her suburban home. She loved the brick façade, oak floors, and screened deck.

The house was much bigger than her modest childhood home in Randolph, Massachusetts, south of Boston—more spacious than any other place she'd lived or had expected to live. They bought the house two years ago, based on borrowed future earnings from Michael's cardiology practice—their sole source of income since Patricia had given up her job as a nurse at Shady Brook Hospital. She was ambivalent about no longer being employed outside the home. She had less independence and no external source of income. But she was happy to have more family time. For Danny. And for many a nurse's dream husband—the distinguished doctor. And in her particular case, after some soul searching and family confrontations, "the Jewish Cardiologist". He didn't drink, he didn't smoke, he just whined.

****

Patricia strapped on her seat belt and drove like a mad woman. She stopped impatiently at a traffic light as it turned yellow, fighting the temptation to cruise through the caution signal. With hidden cameras everywhere, she'd better not risk it. She got a speeding ticket on Wootton Parkway last month and had intercepted the mail to collect the envelope before Michael saw it. The crumpled ticket was safely buried in her tote, away from prying eyes. But the fine was due soon. She would have to dig out the ticket from the mess of receipts, shopping lists, Kleenex, coupons, metro farecard, and paperback mystery swimming in the tote's depths. If she wrote a check, Michael would grumble when he saw the entry. She'd try to pay on-line and pray he wouldn't notice.

Her neck felt stiff, and her shoulders ached – the weight of her heavy tote and the weekend's worries about Roberto's death and her husband's expectations. Patricia drummed her trimmed unpolished fingernails on the steering wheel. She still kept nurse's nails, as she referred to them, even though she was a cardiologist's stay-at-home wife. She checked her reflection in the rearview mirror. Thank goodness no broccoli stuck in her teeth. Could she pass for younger than her thirty-six years? Maybe. She tilted her head. Her shoulder-length auburn hair fell thick and straight and hid most of the wiry gray strands that were starting to sprout. Faint wrinkles winged her hazel eyes. Her fair skin, inherited from the paternal Irish side, was mostly smooth.

Fortunately, she'd been religious about sun block since the age of twenty-five. As a teenager, Patricia had spent summers waitressing on Cape Cod. On her days off, she and her two older sisters had smoothed on baby oil and fried at the public beach. None of them had the vision to anticipate ten years into the future. Except for the expectation that they'd all have good Catholic husbands and lots of babies.

The light turned green, and Patricia accelerated—nine miles above the speed limit—just slow enough to avoid a photo-enforced ticket. What would her father have said if he could see her racing toward the temple for a b'nai mitzvah class?

Dennis Reilly had been a cop on the Randolph police force and helped solve at least one of the more notorious cases – a rape at a bar in his precinct. He died of a sudden heart attack at the racetrack three months after his retirement and six months after Patricia's marriage to a Jew from Long Island. Coincidence? Her sister Teresa lamely joked that Dad had been cheering for his horse to come in but he never made it to the finish line.

As her minivan approached the temple, Patricia's shoulders tensed again. She remembered Roberto telling her that as soon as he finished another year of computer courses, he might earn an IT certificate and look for part-time coding work to supplement his temple job. He'd been so optimistic about his kids' future in this country. His ten-year-old son and seven-year-old daughter wouldn't only play soccer. They would go to college, become teachers or doctors like Patricia's husband.

Her stomach churned at the unfairness of Roberto's tragic end. The circumstances were odd. Could Roberto have gotten sick or fallen down by the garbage dumpster and then been run over? He seemed fine when she spoke with him earlier that evening.

Patricia couldn't stop obsessing about the accident. She couldn't help herself. Figuring out mysteries was an itch she had to scratch. Like her dad, she was good at solving puzzles – even when there was no picture on the box. Whether she was unraveling the convoluted logic of an Old Testament conundrum or analyzing the complicated plot of a crime novel, she became totally consumed. Blame her cop father.

If she'd been a boy, Patricia might've followed her father into the police force, become a detective. Instead she was encouraged to choose between the two "N" professions that had traditionally been popular among nice Catholic girls of a certain era: nun or nurse. While she heard about women of her generation pursuing law and medical careers, none of them seemed to live in

Randolph. Patricia followed her mother's path into the nursing profession.

She was an RN at Boston's Beth Israel Hospital when she met Michael during his cardiology fellowship—over the sunken chest of Larry Sheinmetz whose heart had briefly arrested. After assisting Dr. Michael in reviving the patient, she felt her own heart fluttering as she gazed at the handsome cardiologist. Mr. Sheinmetz survived his heart attack. She and Michael joked they should invite him to their wedding.

The glare of the setting sun angled directly into Patricia's line of vision. She squinted and slowed down. God forbid she should run into someone or something in her rush to class. Temple Israel finally rose ahead, an oasis of study and worship amidst the suburban desert of sterile office buildings, strip malls, and undeveloped land. She pulled into the temple's front lot and squeezed between a metallic SUV and a low-slung emerald green sports car with vanity plates: *TnnsChk*.

Ugh, that must mean Susan Hoffman, officious president of the Temple Sisterhood, was taking time out from her hectic tennis schedule for the class. The Sisterhood hadn't always welcomed the likes of Patricia, the convert. The slights could be subtle. When she'd volunteered for the Sisterhood's Hanukah Mart last November, her name was mysteriously left off the phone tree. She feared taking the class was a mistake. Would she be ostracized, snubbed?

"Ready or not, here I come – social rejection be damned." She whispered words of encouragement to herself.

A beat-up blue compact pulled into the empty space across from Patricia's minivan. She glimpsed a sticker on one side of the compact's rusty front bumper, a leftover from last fall's presidential election. Another sticker reading *Caregivers Must Care For Themselves— Unionize!* wrapped around the bumper's other side.

The compact's driver-side door opened, and a petite dark-haired woman dressed in a black long-sleeved dress stepped out. A lacy scarf covered the thickly coiled bun at the nape of her neck. Her skin was a deep almond shade. Not recognizing her, Patricia guessed she might be Hispanic, in her mid-thirties. Could she be here for the b'nai mitzvah class? The class could certainly use more diversity. Was the attractive woman related to Roberto—his wife, Bertilla? Patricia had never met her, but Roberto talked about how his wife worked full time at an assisted living facility in Rockville, taking care of elderly residents, while her sister took care of the two Gomez children.

The woman walked rapidly toward the temple entrance. Patricia tried to follow but needed a minute to gather up her stuff. She slammed the door shut with her free hand and hurried toward the temple entrance, but the mystery woman was no longer in sight. Patricia was late, too late to pursue the mystery woman now.

Alice in Vunderland she was. But was she ready to chase a tennis ball down the b'nai mitzvah rabbit hole?

Chapter Two

Later Sunday, May 10

Temple Israel's sandstone façade glowed in the last rays of sun and emanated a warmth that embraced Patricia as she hurried through the main entrance. The low, two-story building hugged the ground in a crescent of connected modules decorated with arched windows and engraved designs. Patricia imagined a caravan of Israelites crossing Jerusalem to worship at the ancient Temple. She'd love to travel to Israel someday with Michael and Danny and see the Western Wall. Perhaps for Danny's bar mitzvah. But that was far in the future.

A new custodian quickly unlocked the doors. Except for his pencil mustache, he resembled Roberto with his black hair and narrow physique. Same crinkling eyes, same brisk walk. She introduced herself and held out her hand.

Only an inch or two taller than her, the thin man shook hands and smiled. "I'm Jorge, Roberto's cousin."

"I am so sorry. Please give your family my condolences. I knew Roberto. He was a very nice man, very hardworking."

"Yeah, he was. We grew up together in the same village in El Salvador. Beautiful, in the mountains. We left because of the gangs and drug wars, to make a safe home for our families in this country. Now look what happens. We feel bad about Roberto, Miss, but what can we do except go on and pray for his children. My wife and I, we will help Roberto's family as much as we can." Jorge shrugged helplessly while fingering the crucifix around his neck.

"I was tutoring Roberto in English. He was making great progress. Roberto was teaching me the rules of soccer, because he knew my son was going to play."

"Yes, Roberto told me about his English lessons. Nice to meet you." Jorge quickly relocked the doors behind Patricia.

Recently, the temple officials had tightened security precautions after events on the West Bank had intensified. Israeli soldiers and Palestinians had clashed repeatedly in Hebron over expanding settlement boundaries, inadequate services to Palestinian neighborhoods, and attacks on Jewish civilians. Two months earlier, vandals had scrawled swastikas and various expletives in red paint on the temple's exterior walls. The temple bigshots had tried to keep the desecration quiet to avoid panic among the congregants. They called the sandblasters immediately. Now all three entrances were locked at four o'clock p.m. unless a service or other event was scheduled. Otherwise you were required to ring the bell that had been installed by the main entrance to gain access to God's sanctuary.

Class was about to start in the social hall. Rabbi Deborah Zalman, Temple Israel's Assistant Rabbi, stood at a small podium, shuffling through her syllabus. She looked up and smiled at Patricia, who waved.

Patricia had studied with Rabbi Deborah to prepare for the conversion process. They had become friends, and now met weekly at Java Junction on the Pike where Patricia could buy a decent shot of espresso—her guilty pleasure—as opposed to the dishwater caffeine provided by the temple. Patricia wasn't a foodie but she had acquired a penchant for good coffee, in particular high-octane espresso. The zero-calorie shots gave her an energy boost and kept her mind alert. At least that's what she wanted to believe.

Alas, no espresso tonight. Patricia stopped at the hot water urn in an effort to fix herself a drinkable cup of instant coffee. No real cream, only artificial powdery stuff that never dissolved and tasted like talcum powder. She'd drink it black and bitter, or just inhale the acrid scent.

She surveyed the blue carpeted room with white movable walls that allowed the space to expand or contract to meet every need of the temple's congregation: classes, bar mitzvah parties, holiday services. That's what she loved about the way Reform Judaism was practiced at Temple Israel—it was so adaptable. And debating doctrine was considered a virtue in contrast with traditional Catholicism where faith, the virgin birth, and papal infallibility—even in the face of sex abuse scandals—were nonnegotiable gospel.

Patricia glanced around for the dark-haired stranger but saw no sign of her. About twenty people, all women, were in attendance. The way they sat at the tables in their usual cliques reminded her of junior high. The women all knew each other from sisterhood activities, congregational committees, kids, or the neighborhood. She supposed the temple social scene was no different than her old church, the same people complaining about the status quo but refusing to support change and making it hard for newcomers to break in and feel accepted.

Rabbi Deborah had encouraged her to take the adult b'nai mitzvah class. Along with the rest of the students who completed the class and participated in the ceremony, Patricia would then officially be recognized as a full-fledged member of the Jewish community. She would be able to lead prayers and read from the Jewish Bible, what Patricia used to call the Old Testament. Now she tried to use the Hebrew term, Torah, to describe the five books of Moses, the much-interpreted holy text that provided the foundation for the Jewish religion.

Rabbi Deborah explained to Patricia that many women brought up in the Jewish faith had skipped the bat mitzvah coming of age ritual usually performed at age thirteen. Thirty years ago Orthodox and more traditional Conservative synagogues did not allow girls to be bat mitzvahed. But watching their own children become b'nai mitzvahed had awakened a longing among these thirty- and forty-year-old women, a silent urge to participate in the beautiful ceremony on their own behalves.

Patricia knew that Rabbi Deborah was smart and very articulate, so the class was bound to be interesting. But would this whole bat mitzvah effort be a fiasco, at least as far as her being welcomed into the temple community as a full-fledged member?

She slid into the seat beside Brenda Gottlieb, her best buddy at the temple. Brenda had taken Patricia under her generous—in all senses—wing when the two met at one of the temple's Friday night dinners. The fact that Patricia's husband was a respected cardiologist may have been Brenda's initial incentive to befriend her. Everyone in the congregation worshiped doctors second only to a divine being. But she and Brenda had now bonded over prayer and pastry. Brenda had become her interpreter of cultural Judaism, a topic she desperately needed help understanding, given her previous lack of close Jewish friends.

Brenda described herself as a born-again Jew from Jersey. Though her parents were both Jewish, the family had never joined a temple, and she never had a bat mitzvah ceremony. She got religion when her two sons kept asking what they should tell their friends. After her kids were grown and her now ex-husband had moved on to blonder pastures, she decided to pursue her bat mitzvah credential along with her eternal quest to become a lifelong Weight Watchers member.

For the moment, Brenda appeared not to be following the program. She was squeezed into a chair against the wall, positioning herself so as to be in charge of distribution of the table's chocolate chip cookie platter. Several cookies were already piled on a napkin in front of Brenda's well-endowed chest. In response to Patricia's questioning look, Brenda held up her plump hands as if in surrender and swallowed. "Classes make me anxious. I need a comfort nosh."

Struggling to get the women's attention, Rabbi Deborah coughed loudly. She was short and rounded. Zaftig was the Yiddish word Brenda used to describe the Rabbi as well as herself. The Rabbi's brown unruly hair was shoulder-length. She pulled her curls into a lop-sided bun, probably in an attempt to appear more ministerial. A *hamsa*, the silver filigreed hand symbolizing good luck, hung from a chain around her neck. Her plum-colored, scoop-necked dress of a stretchy material clung a bit too tightly to her body, revealing more cleavage and thigh than some older congregants considered appropriate—fodder for their whispered criticism that women shouldn't be ordained as rabbis in the first place.

The esteemed Senior Rabbi Saul Weinstein would undoubtedly consider the present class of all women to be nothing more than a coffee klatch of middle-aged busybodies in various states of wedded bliss, overly worried about their own and everyone else's marital status, including that of both rabbis. Rabbi Deborah was still single at the age of thirty-one, an old maid according to the busybodies' timeline, and there were rumors about the state of Rabbi Weinstein's marriage.

Rabbi Deborah's pale blue eyes surveyed her flock. "Ladies, ladies, and I see we are all ladies, I would like to start class."

Conversations quieted.

"I guess none of us single ladies are going to meet our soulmates in this class," Brenda opined dryly. "I'll have to keep supporting myself as a party planner."

The Rabbi smiled and shook her head. "Perhaps that's a good thing. We can concentrate on our own studies and souls. Tonight we begin our year-long course toward becoming what for women is the bat mitzvah. The Hebrew term literally means daughter of the commandment. The bat mitzvah ritual signifies becoming a member of the Jewish community."

She patted wild strands of hair that had come loose from her bun, and her face became grave. She teared up. "Before we begin tonight's session, please join me in reciting the Kaddish in memory of Roberto Gomez. I assume most of you have heard that he died this past Thursday in a tragic incident at the temple. He was our custodian for many years. Our prayers go out to his family. Please rise."

The Rabbi led the solemn chant for the mourner's prayer honoring the dead: "*Yis'gadal v'yiskadash shmay rabbo*—Exalted and hallowed be God's name." Everyone including Patricia knew the words by heart since the Aramaic chant was intoned at virtually every service. She tried to take comfort from the ritual.

At the prayer's end, murmurings of sympathy and disbelief filled the room. Several women at another table, including Benita Schwartz, who practiced law, began debating whether Roberto bore some blame for the accident, putting himself in the way of the garbage truck. Patricia felt herself flushing, her temper rising. The assumption Roberto had fallen asleep was not only ludicrous but ethnic stereotyping.

Before Patricia could "get into it" with her classmates, Rabbi Deborah cut off the debate with a strong "Enough! Let's all sit down. The police are investigating the accident. Please do not indulge in speculation. The temple will plan a memorial service in the next month. For those of you who can attend, the funeral service for Roberto Gomez will be held tomorrow at St. Rose's Church in Rockville, ten o'clock a.m. If you need directions, see me after class."

The Rabbi paused and looked down at her sheaf of notes atop the class syllabus. "Let's focus on the task at hand tonight. To whet your appetite for the rich texts we will be studying, we begin with a discussion of one of the great biblical romances. The story of Jacob and

Rachel is found in Genesis, the first book of the Torah. The tale involves first wives, second wives, mistresses and may give us insight into the nature of contemporary marriage."

"Yeah right, what does she know, that little *pisher*?" Brenda whispered to Patricia. "She doesn't even have a boyfriend, let alone a fiancé. I should be giving this talk, after one divorce, two kids, and an alimony award that my divorce lawyer brags about."

Patricia smiled at Brenda but put a finger to her lips.

"Jacob tricks his blind father, Isaac, into giving him the blessing intended for his older firstborn brother, Esau," Rabbi Deborah continued over Brenda's whispers. "To escape his brother's wrath, Jacob flees to his Uncle Laban's house, where he meets Laban's two daughters, Rachel and Leah. Jacob falls in love with the beautiful younger daughter, Rachel."

Patricia thought of the intense rivalry between her two older sisters, especially over boyfriends. As the youngest of the three Reilly daughters by five years, Patricia disqualified herself from the competition. Resting her cheek in the palm of her hand, Patricia stared away and recalled how she played the role of mediator, when both her sisters were interested in the same guy. There'd been the infamous beer throwing incident at her twenty-first birthday celebration. Her next oldest sister, Teresa, age twenty-four, returned from the ladies' at O'Leary's Pub to discover her date had bought a beer for Jeanne, the oldest Reilly sister. At twenty-six, Jeanne was the beauty of the bunch. Teresa promptly picked up the bottle of beer and threw it at Jeanne, who ducked. Luckily the bottle missed and hit the wall, but not before beer splashed the couple at the next table. Patricia had to drag Teresa out of the bar and promise to pay the dry-cleaning bills. Happy twenty-first birthday.

Brenda bumped Patricia's arm. "Listen up, Rabbi Deborah could be getting to a good part."

Rabbi Deborah laughed. "Jacob arranges with his Uncle Laban to marry beautiful Rachel after seven years of labor for his uncle. However, Laban tricks Jacob into first marrying weak-eyed Leah by substituting Leah under a heavy veil in Rachel's place on the wedding day. As Jacob deceived his father, so he is deceived."

Brenda raised her hand but didn't wait to be called on. "You mean to tell me Jacob really couldn't tell it was Leah even after they were in bed together?" The women in the class tittered.

Marcia Kraus frantically waved her arm as if class participation was going to be graded, then blurted out her expert opinion. "Perhaps he had a dissociative identity disorder?" Marcia was a social worker with her own practice. Always empathetic, she was ready to offer advice for the dysfunctional.

"Some biblical scholars believe Jacob did recognize Leah at that point and decided either it was too late to do anything or in fact was attracted to her," explained Rabbi Deborah. "Given he and Leah eventually had eight children together, there's support for this latter view."

"But Rachel must have realized what was happening," Patricia said. "My sisters and I could never have hidden that kind of juicy secret from each other."

"You may be right," confirmed Rabbi Deborah.

"Rachel may have participated in the deception—hidden under the wedding bed—to get Leah married off first. Jacob eventually marries Rachel after seven more years of hard work for Laban. Jacob's marriages represent two models for matrimony. With Rachel, love precedes marriage. With Leah, love comes after marriage. Only after Leah bears Jacob four sons while Rachel is infertile, does the rivalry develop between the two sisters that begins to destroy their relationship."

"Imagine your sister sleeping with your husband," huffed petite Susan Hoffman, she of the vanity plates pronouncing her the tanned, tennis-playing queen of Potomac. She shook her smooth cap of straightened ebony hair and pointed her French-polished, acrylic-nailed index finger at Rabbi Deborah as if the Rabbi were responsible. "Our Biblical forefathers should have shown more control. It's embarrassing."

"Oh, my sister deserves my ex-husband," snorted Brenda. "Ever since she stole my boyfriend in tenth grade, I've waited for revenge."

"Thank you, Brenda, for sharing," joked the Rabbi. "Rachel, however, takes out her frustration over her infertility by giving Jacob her handmaid Bilhah, who bears Jacob two sons. In retaliation, Leah gives Jacob her handmaid Zilpah who also bears Jacob two sons."

"Wait a minute. All this is okay? Doesn't the Bible or anyone else consider this fooling around and partner swapping unhealthy?" Marcia's normally calm social worker voice rose in pitch as she sputtered out her unprofessional outrage. A drop of spit frothed at the corner of her mouth.

"It offends us now," responded Rabbi Deborah, "but these practices were accepted social customs of the time. Eventually Rachel does bear two sons with Jacob. Leah and Jacob also have two more sons and a daughter. So despite all his marital problems, Jacob produces twelve sons. The twelve tribes of Israel descend from Jacob's male children, not only the sons of Rachel and Leah, but also the sons of the handmaids, Bilhah and Zilpah."

"You mean to say that the sons of the slaves were treated the same as the sons of Leah and Rachel? Boy, those two sisters needed a good lawyer. Too bad I wasn't around to recommend one," opined Brenda as she bit into a cookie from her pile.

"Yes, those sons fathered with the "handmaids" were given equal status with the ones Jacob fathered with Leah and Rachel, although it's doubtful that Bilhah or Zilpah practiced Judaism. In fact, Jacob's relationships with these two handmaids can be considered early examples of unions between people of different faiths. Informal intermarriages so to speak. As you can see, our patriarch Jacob was not a perfect man."

"So let me know when you find one." Brenda whispered sotto voce and the class laughed.

"Nor were these the only examples of Biblical intermarriage," added Rabbi Deborah.

"After Sarah's death, Abraham married Keturah, a woman from outside his tribe. Following in his father's footsteps, Jacob's son Joseph had an Egyptian wife. Later on, Moses married Tziporah, a Midianite. Intermarriage has existed for millennia."

"That's way longer than my marriage lasted," Brenda proclaimed.

"Ah, I can see you ladies are going to make this a

fun class. Since it's the first one, we'll end early," said Rabbi Deborah. "Please check the assignment sheet and read the noted chapters in Genesis. We'll start at the beginning next session with the creation story – more forbidden sex and sin. I'll see you in two weeks. There's no class next Sunday night because we will be observing the Shavuot holiday."

Patricia helped the Rabbi clear the tables. "I got a babysitter for Danny, so I'll see you at Roberto's funeral tomorrow. Can you still do Tuesday, ten o'clock a.m., coffee with Brenda and me?" For the past two months, Brenda had joined Patricia and Rabbi Deborah for their weekly Java Junction coffee at the Pike Center.

"Can we do coffee at nine o'clock? I have a meeting at ten o'clock with Rabbi Weinstein."

"No problem. I'll tell Brenda we're getting together at…."

A commotion of Spanish voices in the hall interrupted Patricia in mid-sentence. She and the Rabbi turned to the open door. Jorge, the new janitor, was patting the woman from the parking lot on the shoulder. She seemed on the verge of tears. They both moved toward Rabbi Deborah.

"Sorry to bother you. This is Bertilla Gomez, Roberto's wife," Jorge introduced her. "She wants to talk to you, Rabbi. She says Roberto never sleeps on the job. She doesn't understand how the garbage truck could not have seen him. She's afraid. She says there are phone calls to her house from an insurance company. They say the accident maybe was Roberto's fault. Bertilla's English isn't so good."

Rabbi Deborah took Bertilla's arm and walked her toward the Rabbi's study. They were virtually the same height, and both wore their hair pulled into buns. But the Rabbi's short clingy purple dress provided a contrast to Bertilla's calf-length black mourning outfit. Jorge trailed behind. Rabbi Deborah nodded at Patricia and mouthed "See you Tuesday."

Hurrying out, Patricia was annoyed with herself. Why couldn't she remember more details from Thursday evening? Who else had been around that night when she stopped by the temple before the accident? Had there been lights on in the office, in the Rabbis' studies? What other cars were in the parking lot? Had Roberto acted tired or nervous or afraid? She must have been one of the last people to see him alive. She vowed to be more observant. And good for Bertilla for challenging the assumption that Roberto fell asleep on the job. Carol's offhanded remark in the newspaper about Roberto's napping only served to reinforce ethnic bias. Who knows—Roberto could have had a heart attack or blown an aneurysm.

Patricia owed it to Roberto to try to figure out exactly what happened the night he died. She felt a kinship with him. Like her, he had been an outsider trying to fit in. While she was trying to gain acceptance into the Jewish faith, the temple, and her husband's family, for Roberto the stakes had been much higher. He was struggling to be adopted by a new country, learn a language, and hold down a job to support his family. He'd described to her how he left his home and many of his relatives in El Salvador, because of gang violence perpetrated against innocent people. He'd worried the MS-13 gang would try to recruit his son to sell drugs. Anyone refusing or complaining to the police could be subject to retaliation.

Patricia's paternal grandfather had told her how he emigrated from Ireland in the middle of an economic panic that devastated the family farm. He fought for a longshoreman's job and a decent place to live in Boston. Neither of Patricia's parents had earned college degrees, and Patricia could see she had taken a leap upon arriving on the shores of Potomac Pines. Roberto had a much higher bar to clear but he was on his way, improving his English fluency and learning computer skills.

The blare of her cellphone's Real Detective ringtone made her jump. It was Michael.

"Just checking in. I was worried—that hit and run—your friend Roberto's death. What a waste. Did you park close to the entrance?"

"I'm fine. I'm about to leave."

"Good. Please, use the phone flashlight to get to the car? You can never be too careful. Danny and I are hoping for good night kisses."

Patricia smiled at the plaintive note in Michael's voice. "Be there in ten minutes."

Home in time for bed check and kisses—what more could she desire? Nice to feel her presence was missed. Coming from a big family, that had not frequently been the case. She appreciated Michael's concern, but his protectiveness could be overbearing. Like having her own personal Jewish mother.

On the other hand, their contrasting backgrounds might be what contributed to that mysterious *jeu ne sais quoi*— her high school French was pathetic—the irresistible magnetism that attracted her to him physically and intellectually. She was drawn in by his deep eyes, abundant curls, forthright opinions, intellectual prowess. And considering prowess, when it came to sex, his caring and tenderness were great assets. No denying that appeal. The old myth about relationships being based on having lots in common was dubious. More important, they were able to relate to each other and navigate life together. Admittedly they did need to work on their problem-solving abilities.

Plus Michael was a good provider. His cardiology practice gave her the freedom not to work, at least for a few years. But was nursemaid the only role she wanted? She sighed. She would have to consider what choices lay ahead, especially with Danny in preschool and then next year all-day kindergarten. But tonight she was tired. She couldn't wait to hug and kiss her warm boys before they fell asleep.

Chapter Three

Tuesday, May 12

The Pike Center strip mall was a regular estrogen alley with all the essentials for female survival in suburbia: caffeine oasis, nail and hair salon, bakery, taco takeout, drug store, ATM machine. As usual, Patricia was the first to arrive at Java Junction. With her double espresso in hand, she sat at a wooden table near the window overlooking the parking lot and waited for Brenda and Rabbi Deborah. The sky was overcast but bright, the forecast uncertain.

Since Danny had started preschool, she enjoyed these morning hours for solitary contemplation or conversation with her adult friends. Normally she looked forward to a little *kibitzing*, as Brenda described the threesome's wide-ranging and supportive discussions. *Kibitz*— another term Patricia had added to her Yiddish vocabulary.

Today she forced herself to focus on whether she observed anyone suspicious at Roberto's funeral at St. Rose's yesterday. She and the temple clergy had attended along with a few temple bigshots, although not Susan Hoffman. There was a big crowd of what must have been friends and family. No one seemed out of place or acted strangely. The Catholic service was familiar enough. Thankfully the casket had been closed. Roberto's son Javier's eulogy had brought her to tears. Recalling his words, her eyes welled up again. She'd try to calm herself by reading a couple pages of her mystery novel. Rummaging through her tote, she pulled out keys, wallet, phone, sunblock, checkbook, comb, lip gloss, crumpled ticket, all the usual suspects except her paperback. Oh well, she must have left the book on the washer when she did laundry earlier.

She gazed out the window to see if she could catch a glimpse of Brenda's SUV or the Rabbi's sunny yellow hybrid. It had been four years since Deborah Zalman had been hired as Temple Israel's assistant rabbi at the age of twenty-seven, then a new graduate from theological seminary in New York City. Since her arrival, she had taken on all the responsibilities that Rabbi Weinstein preferred not to deal with, including conversion and adult b'nai mitzvah classes. Patricia had been impressed by Rabbi Deborah's enthusiastic inclusion of non-Jews in congregational activities. Although Patricia and Michael had joined the liberal temple six years ago, she hadn't really felt welcomed until Rabbi Deborah's arrival.

Patricia initially considered conversion to make Michael and his mother happy. After long conversations with Rabbi Deborah, she realized she needed to decide for herself if conversion was the right path. Besides, she had learned that making her mother-in-law happy was an impossible task.

Her two-year course of study with Rabbi Deborah confirmed for Patricia that she was drawn to Judaism not only because of Michael. She admired Judaism's strong intellectual traditions and the Old Testament's emphasis on justice. As one of the final steps of her conversion process, Patricia appeared before a Beit Din, a rabbinical court of three Reform rabbis, who interviewed her to ensure she understood the importance of the decision to convert. The rabbis asked her to tell of her journey to Judaism. She gave a rational explanation of her attraction to Judaism's principles for a just world, to its essence as summarized by the famous rabbinical scholar Hillel: "That which is hateful to you, do not do to your fellow. That is the whole Torah. All the rest is commentary."

Thank God she passed. She felt a spiritual connection to Judaism in her gut that she couldn't completely explain. She didn't feel pressured to believe, to take things on faith. Perhaps it was Judaism's encouragement of inquiry, rather than accepting answers, that was so appealing.

As Patricia sipped her espresso, she saw the highlighted bronzed curls of Brenda's carefully moussed shag coming her way. "I'm dying for my grande decaf skim vanilla latte with a bit of whip. Wanna start the day being healthy," Brenda gasped, slightly out of breath, as she rushed by. Three minutes later, gripping her steaming cup, she joined Patricia.

"So tell me if it's me or Michael's mother who's paranoid." Patricia took a deep breath to calm herself and recounted her Sunday night conversation with Michael. "Can you believe his mother claims it's suspicious that I'm studying to be bat mitzvahed? When is she going to accept the fact that I'm a convert, that I'm *really* Jewish?"

"Patricia, you are never going to pass as a Jew – it's your legs, they're too good. No matter how much tennis these JAPPY women play at the club, their legs will never look as long and lean as yours. Maybe their arms, but never the legs. Not in the Jewish gene pool."

Patricia laughed although she wondered if Brenda was right. Patricia had heard Brenda use the term JAP before. Brenda said the acronym for Jewish American Princess originally described privileged Jewish women who belonged to the class of royal gentry on Long Island where Jews were finally allowed to buy choice plots of land. Now the acronym was generally applied to any entitled woman of the tribe, especially one with straightened hair and nose. Brenda could be outrageous, but Patricia admired her forthrightness. Patricia should use her as a role model.

"At least you have breasts."

"Had is the operative word," Brenda said. "My boobs have a slow leak. They're deflating. Sinking an inch every year since I passed my forty-fifth birthday."

"We're already talking bodily endowments at nine in the morning?" Rabbi Deborah, cupping a grande coffee, plopped down at the table. Patricia observed the Rabbi had forgone the bun and blow dryer today. Her naturally curly hair was frizzing, and her flowered skirt was crawling up her thighs. She seemed stressed.

Although Rabbi Deborah looked young for her now thirty-one years, Patricia worried she was lonely. The Rabbi worked so hard and rarely socialized with single people her own age. Maybe the older congregants would be less critical if the Rabbi met a nice guy to help her live up to the Jewish ideal of wife and mother. According to Patricia's mother-in-law, marriage and children came first. Having a profession, even as clergy, was not sufficient achievement for a

Jewess.

"Sorry I'm late. I can't stay long. I wanted to imbibe caffeine before my ten o'clock meeting with Rabbi Weinstein. We're trying to process Roberto's death and decide what kind of memorial service would be appropriate. We'll definitely be establishing a memorial fund for his family. Patricia, I'm glad you and Rabbi Weinstein were with me at St. Rose's yesterday morning for the funeral. So tragic for his family especially with two young children. At least they have cousins in the area. If my Spanish was better, I could've offered more comforting words of condolence."

Patricia shook her head and sighed. "I should be studying Spanish but I'm still struggling with Hebrew. I'm sure his family appreciated our being there even if we couldn't express our sympathies in fluent Spanish. You know, for Catholics, death isn't exactly the end. The soul passes to the afterlife, preferably heaven."

"Yes, heaven's a comforting concept for the bereaved. Judaism's interpretation of heaven is not nearly so reassuring," Rabbi Deborah replied. "It was nice that the Gomez family passed out funeral prayer cards describing Roberto as a dedicated family man, a fan of soccer and baseball, and a computer whiz in training. Good to remember Roberto by how he lived and not by how his life ended."

"Yeah," Patricia affirmed. "I saved the card from my dad's funeral. It offers a bit of consolation." Repressing the old urge to cross herself, she clasped her cup of espresso more tightly.

"I nearly broke down when Roberto's son Javier gave his eulogy—that his dad wanted him to play baseball and soccer, to be a son of both America and El Salvador, and how his dad was learning the rules of baseball since he hadn't grown up with the game and how they were supposed to go to a Nationals' game." Rabbi Deborah swiped at her eyes. "Rabbi Weinstein and I plan to arrange to trip to Nationals' Park for Javier and his sister Anna. You and Michael and Danny are welcome to join us."

"Let me know when."

"What about me? I'm happy to join in," said Brenda. "I'm a big Nats fan. I love watching those young players swing at the ball. Plus the new stadium has a great burger and shake joint. I could take everyone in my SUV."

"The memorial fund's a great idea too. Roberto's family must be worried about finances." Patricia took a sip of espresso and let the bitter taste linger in her mouth. Recalling her frustrations with the temple's mixed welcome of those not born Jewish, she felt compelled to ask, "Is Roberto's wife okay with having a memorial service at the temple?"

"Yes, we checked. Bertilla likes the idea of the community honoring Roberto's memory. Plus she is asking us to investigate further." The Rabbi tugged at her short skirt with one hand and pushed frizz away from her forehead with the other. "The temple has an insurance policy that covers its employees in case of accidental death while on the job. The insurance company has been calling Bertilla, questioning her about Roberto's lifestyle—whether he drank, stayed out late, gambled, was depressed."

"Typical!" Patricia fumed. "The company must be nosing around to see if there was contributory negligence and avoid a big payout. No wonder Bertilla's upset."

She recalled overhearing her father talk about a firefighter who died after his car crashed into a tree on a rainy night on the way home from the fire station. The insurance agent had contacted her dad to find out if the police investigation had revealed whether the firefighter had been drunk and/or depressed. Her dad complained to her mother that the insurance company was pressuring him to say the guy committed suicide. But her dad refused to speculate and followed his own advice – just stick to the facts.

"She doesn't trust the insurance company or the police," Rabbi Deborah continued, "for good reason. They seem to be implying that all Hispanic men are lazy and sleep on the job."

"You aren't kidding. Are we the only ones who've noticed the implicit bias in the napping presumption? Is there a way to follow up with the cops and ensure they're investigating all possibilities?"

"I'm not sure. I'll call Officer O'Donnell," Rabbi Deborah replied. "I don't want to worry Rabbi Weinstein any more than he already is. Roberto's death has hit us all hard. But Saul feels responsible. He helped hire Roberto seven years ago, met his wife and two kids at the temple picnic, and encouraged Roberto's computer studies."

Patricia nodded. "I was there that Thursday evening to pick up the bat mitzvah class packet. Roberto didn't seem tired and was looking forward to his classes. I keep wondering whether I could have done or said anything…"

"Please, don't go down that path. You'll drive

yourself crazy. You sound like Rabbi Weinstein," said Rabbi Deborah as she reached out and touched Patricia's hand. "We need a deep meditation session or at least a group hug. Plus, Saul told me he's aggravated about the quality of care being provided to his younger son, Ethan. Although Ethan's been diagnosed as autistic, he aged out of state-subsidized special needs services after he turned twenty-two last year."

"Yeah, Rabbi Weinstein's been looking kind of worn down lately," Brenda interrupted. "I assumed it was all the complaints he gets: services too crowded; dues too high; cantor can't carry a tune; wives complaining their ex's shouldn't be allowed to join, or if the ex-husbands join, they should pay all the dues."

Rabbi Deborah acknowledged these constant complaints were part of the problem. "But the temple also has budget concerns. We're the largest Reform congregation in Maryland. We need more support personnel, enhanced security, updated computers. But there's one benefit for me. Because Rabbi Weinstein hasn't been feeling well, he's allowing me to give the sermon this coming Friday for the first night of Shavuot."

"Remind me, what are we celebrating on Shavuot?" Brenda slipped in her question, seeming embarrassed to reveal her ignorance. "Do I have to fast? As I informed you, Patricia, Jewish holidays are divided between days on which we must starve and days on which we pig out. Of course never any ham."

"Shavuot is the holiday that commemorates the giving of the Old Testament and the Ten Commandments to Moses at Mount Sinai, isn't that right?" Patricia replied with a fair amount of pride.

"Yes," confirmed Rabbi Deborah. "To be precise, God gave Moses and the Israelites the Torah. We also celebrate the spring harvest and read from the Book of Ruth. I'd really appreciate you two coming to the service."

"Of course Brenda and I will be there." Patricia knew that Rabbi Weinstein rarely deferred to Rabbi Deborah when it came to holiday services, so this was a big deal. "Should we invite Roberto's wife, Bertilla—I mean Mrs. Gomez—to the service? Maybe she'd like to say something about Roberto?"

"We definitely have Roberto on the list of recent deaths. Either Rabbi Weinstein or I will recite the Kaddish blessing to honor his memory. I'll ask Bertilla if she'd like to attend, but I'm not sure the Shavuot service would be the best occasion for her participation. Too big, too much going on." The Rabbi glanced down at her watch. "Oh dear, it's almost ten o'clock. I have to go. Please don't repeat my comments about Rabbi Weinstein looking stressed." She pushed back her chair and quickly rose.

Rabbi Deborah was probably right, especially if the temple was planning a separate memorial service. Patricia wondered if Roberto's wife blamed the temple for his death or did she suspect otherwise? Was it an accident? Or was he a target?

Chapter Four

Friday, May 15

Patricia pulled into the temple's front lot at 7:00 p.m. sharp as drivers madly fought for parking. A crimson foreign-looking coupe—probably some guy's midlife crisis—and an oversized topaz SUV were vying for the same space. So much for the harmonious spirit of Shabbat. As there was no point in waiting around to see who would win, she drove to a less congested lane a few rows away.

As she entered the lobby, Patricia waved to Rabbi Deborah who was walking into the sanctuary with Rabbi Weinstein. Attired in their flowing white robes, both rabbis looked solemn, almost priestly. Rabbi Deborah nodded to Patricia.

Rabbi Saul Weinstein had been the Senior Rabbi at Temple Israel for the last twenty-five years and took his position very seriously. He had that dignified presence that congregants found so comforting with his substantial frame, graying but still full head of hair, and sonorous voice. Close to sixty-five, he remained an attractive man, although he looked fatigued tonight.

Rabbi Weinstein's wife Lenore stood at the back of the sanctuary, greeting congregants. A shapely brunette in her mid-fifties, she'd probably been a beauty in her youth. She was pretty in that worked-on way of wealthy women of a certain age. Her face was meticulously made-up and probably lifted or at least Botoxed. Her hair was tinted to a natural brown shade, and her body looked toned in a slimming suit of navy silk. Impressive since she'd birthed two children. Noah, the older of their two sons, practiced law at a big New York City firm. According to what Rabbi Deborah said, their younger son, Ethan, was on the autism spectrum and lived in a group home in Rockville.

Patricia and Michael had met with Rabbi Weinstein when they first joined the temple. Rabbi Weinstein assured them the congregation welcomed intermarried couples. Patricia now had her doubts about whether his representation was true, given the cold shoulders she'd been subjected to from the temple "Sisterhood." And Rabbi Weinstein continued to refuse to officiate at any interfaith marriages, because the Association of Reform Congregations had not affirmatively approved the practice.

She looked around for Brenda, late as usual. Seeing no one she knew, Patricia filed into the sanctuary to save seats in front of the lectern where Rabbi Deborah would give her sermon. She tried to convince Michael to come. They could've found a sitter for Danny, but Michael claimed he was too tired and would rather stay home for quality time with his son. His idea of quality time probably meant fifteen minutes of block building, then sticking Danny in front of the television or the family laptop to play learning games, while Michael went online with his iPad to check e-mails.

It seemed the more active she became in the temple, the less involved Michael became. The balance had somehow shifted. Was Michael using her to express rebellion and anger at his overbearing mother? He had been able to distance himself from his mother physically but not so much emotionally. Patricia's conversion only complicated the situation.

As she surveyed the sanctuary, she was impressed again with its amalgam of symbols. The sanctuary was renovated three years ago to accommodate the temple's growing membership. The arched ceiling drew the eye toward the pulpit also known as the bimah. The sacred ark stood at the center of the bimah and contained the Torah scrolls. The ark was covered with a gold latticework of carvings representing the burning bush where God revealed himself to Moses.

Hanging brazenly behind the latticework was what members of the congregation now commonly referred to as *the shower curtain*, a rainbow-hued piece of material intended to represent Joseph's coat of many colors. The controversial gift to Joseph from his father Jacob led to much rivalry among Joseph's brothers. The shower curtain had also sparked an uproar at the temple. The curtain was despised by congregants, such as Lois Kaplan, who considered themselves to have more refined aesthetic tastes. In addition to taking the adult bat mitzvah class, Lois managed the temple gift shop—when she wasn't redecorating her condo in Boca and running her Judaica art gallery. She started a petition to have the curtain removed. But the art committee responsible for selecting the curtain was co-chaired by the rabbi's wife Lenore and Sisterhood President Susan Hoffman. Few congregants were willing to put their opposition in writing.

In any event, the curtain became a focus of

discontent within the temple. Huge sums of money had been spent on the temple renovation. Now it was rumored the temple had a serious budget deficit, too much borrowing to fund the addition and too little capital to repay the loan. Temple membership was already pricey. No one would be happy with a dues increase or a special assessment to cure the deficit.

As she turned around to look for Brenda, Patricia noticed Susan Hoffman and Lois Kaplan enter the sanctuary, their spouses in tow. Although she waved to them, they took seats well behind her. Blushing in embarrassment, Patricia faced forward. Did they not want to sit next to her and/or be associated with a convert? Or did they not want to sit up front? Was she being paranoid?

Brenda's cooing interrupted Patricia's self-chastising. "I love your earrings. How did you finally convince Michael to buy you diamond studs?" Brenda loomed over Patricia in an indigo two-piece outfit decorated with swatches of glittery fabric. Her lips shined in glossy fuchsia. A chunky jade choker collared her neckline. She resembled an imposing piece of abstract art.

"They're cubic zirconia. I bought them at the mall."

"I should have known Michael wouldn't ante up for diamonds. Too cheap."

"He's a practical guy. And I don't need real diamonds. I fooled you. Your necklace is beautiful. Where's it from?"

"Thanks. I bought it online. Figured it would take people's minds off my wrinkled neck. Do we have to sit so close? How will we be able to talk about who's here? What if I doze off?"

"Brenda, we're here to support Rabbi Deborah. We're supposed to actually listen to the sermon."

"Okay, okay. Look, there's Susan Hoffman. I can't believe she's wearing that slinky sleeveless black dress."

"Yeah, she declined to sit up here. Is it appropriate for her to wear a sleeveless dress in the sanctuary even if we are a Reform congregation?" Patricia asked. "I'm never sure."

"It's not verboten nowadays, especially if you have her tennis muscled biceps, not flying squirrel arms like mine. Who's she sitting with—the new boyfriend or her husband?"

"Shh. It's her husband. He may have darkened his hair."

"I guess when you're a successful developer it's socially acceptable for a guy to dye his hair. Looks like he baked in the same tanning salon as Susan. Or did they just return from Boca? Let's sit next to the Milcheks two rows back. He's a successful stockbroker. We can get some hot tips. Or how about Dr. Kahn, the podiatrist on their left. I can ask him about my inflamed bunion."

"Brenda, there's Marcia from our class. She's by herself. Let's ask her to sit with us."

"Fine with me. I hear part of her social work practice is intimate relations therapy. You guys need help?"

"Enough." Brenda could go overboard. What happened to marital privacy, although Patricia supposed she already opened that door. She waved to Marcia. "We have a seat over here."

The sanctuary was nearly full now. The two rabbis stood up to indicate the beginning of the service. The rotund cantor, Max Snyder, started singing the opening hymn, *Ma Tovu*, How Lovely Are Your Tents, O Jacob, and the congregation hushed. Patricia tried to follow along in the prayer book as the service proceeded with the lighting of the Sabbath candles and the Shema, affirming God is one and reminding Jews that God is to be worshipped, not idols, wealth, prestige, or other false gods. How especially fitting for this wealthy congregation. This was not the milieu in which she'd grown up. On the other hand she appreciated the community's high level of education, willingness to contribute to charitable causes, and support for the arts. Was she becoming a member of the espresso-drinking, *Washington Post*-reading, SUV-driving elite?

Patricia listened with admiration as Brenda sang the prayerful melodies in a sweet alto voice. Despite claiming she'd been brought up with the abridged version of Judaism, Brenda easily followed the service. Patricia supposed the religion in which you were raised, even the condensed version, was the equivalent of your native language. A child absorbs vocabulary, grammar, and oral traditions without trying and then reacts appropriately. Studying a new religion was like learning a second language. Would practicing Judaism ever come as naturally to her as to Brenda? Not that she had been all that comfortable with her Catholic faith. Someday Patricia would dream as a Jewess but not yet.

Rabbi Weinstein returned to his seat on the pulpit after announcing it was time for silent meditation when congregants prayed without words to express private thoughts in their heart. A few snores echoed in the sanctuary. Behind Patricia, a female voice loudly whispered where she'd bought her bargain of a designer suit. Off to the side of the sanctuary, a father and son were staring at a silenced iPhone. From afar, she glimpsed the screen showing what appeared to be a baseball game. She wanted to admonish them to power off the phone, that they were being disrespectful. But she hesitated. It wasn't her place.

Rabbi Deborah stood up and walked to the podium. She looked nervous. Patricia sat up and elbowed Brenda to attention. Rabbi Deborah's petite frame barely rose above the lectern. With a practiced move, she lowered the microphone to her level. Her firm voice resonated through the sanctuary.

"Tonight we celebrate Shavuot, the holiday that commemorates the day God gave the Torah to the Jewish people at Mount Sinai. The Torah is the guide for how we are to live a just life in this world. Shavuot is also a celebration of the spring harvest. On this holiday, we read from the Book of Ruth where the two themes of Shavuot—harvest and revelation—come together.

"A famine has struck Israel. Naomi and her husband, along with their two sons, leave for the nearby nation of Moab. In Moab, Naomi's husband dies, and her two sons eventually take Moabite wives, Orpah and Ruth. After ten years of marriage, both young men die. Naomi hears the famine has subsided in Israel and decides to return home. Her devoted daughter-in-law Ruth insists on leaving with her even though Naomi tries to discourage her.

"In one of the Torah's most moving passages, Ruth responds to Naomi, 'Do not urge me to leave you. For

Joyce Sanderly

wherever you go, I will go; your people shall be my people, your God shall be my God.' Although under no obligation to do so, Ruth accepts responsibility to care for her mother-in-law. At the same time Ruth chooses to accept the values of the Israelite people although she realizes she will probably remain an outsider in Naomi's world."

Patricia and Brenda simultaneously turned to each other and shook their heads. "Wow," whispered Brenda, "Imagine being so attached to your mother-in-law. That should count as a miracle."

"Ruth should be sainted—patron saint of daughters-in-law," Patricia whispered. "Faithful young wives could pray to her for intervention with their mothers-in-law." As she joked, Patricia felt a twinge of guilt about her criticism of Michael's mother. Maybe she should be more accepting.

Marcia leaned over and murmured her social worker's insight. "Two women—the wife, the mother—loving the same man creates an inherently conflicted situation. Family therapy can ease tensions."

Patricia whispered dubious thanks. Brenda snorted. Rabbi Deborah cleared her throat and looked in their direction. The chastised threesome fell silent as the Rabbi continued.

"Naomi and Ruth arrive penniless in Israel. Ruth goes into the fields to collect barley left over for the poor. The fields belong to Boaz, a generous Israelite businessman. When he sees Ruth, he falls in love with her, impressed both by her beauty and her loyalty to her mother-in-law. Boaz and Ruth eventually marry."

Patricia sighed and glanced over to see Brenda raptly listening. Hard to resist such a romantic story.

Rabbi Deborah raised the volume of her voice and delivered her punch line. "The Ruth story reveals how accepting the early Israelites were of intermarriage. We know from Biblical sources that there were many among the Israelite tribes who participated in the community but were not members. Several of Jacob's wives, from whom the twelve tribes of Israel descend, were not born of the Jewish faith. But the children of Israel loved them and treated them fairly."

Brenda nudged Patricia with her elbow. "We discussed this in bat mitzvah class. See, I've been listening." She beamed and smiled up at the Rabbi.

"After her marriage, Ruth gives birth to a boy who becomes the grandfather of King David. According to Jewish tradition, the Messiah will descend from King David. So the Messiah will be a direct descendant of Ruth—quite an honor to bestow upon a Moabite convert to Judaism. Clearly Ruth's virtuous behavior mattered more to the Biblical authors than her ancestry."

Patricia nodded in silent agreement with the Rabbi. She aspired to follow Ruth's path and be welcomed into the community, but life was more complicated now. Torah study and good deeds were not the contemporary measure of a person's worth or popularity.

Loud whispers bubbled around Patricia as if to confirm her doubts. Seated on the pulpit, Rabbi Weinstein was flushing red. Rabbi Deborah plowed on, refusing to acknowledge the intensifying rumble.

"As the story of Ruth demonstrates, falling in love with a Jewish person can be the first step in an affiliation with the Jewish people. I attribute part of the attraction not only to the individual of Jewish faith, but to the beauty of the Jewish traditions and values shining through the beloved. We must support both Jews and non-Jews in the creation and celebration of their loving unions. The non-Jewish partner frequently would like to participate in the traditions of the Jewish family they are marrying into. But they do not want to be subjected to ultimatums before taking their marriage vows. We all know non-Jewish parents who are helping to raise Jewish children without having expressly stated their intent to do so prior to marriage, or officially converting to Judaism themselves."

Rabbi Deborah caught her breath before rushing on as if afraid she might lose her nerve. "The Book of Exodus, Chapter 23, reminds us that we know how it feels to be a stranger, because we were strangers in the land of Egypt. Regardless of the religion practiced by the non-Jewish partner, the message is clear. We should welcome the non-Jewish partner, whether Christian, Muslim, Hindu or Buddhist, into the temple community for the full cycle of Jewish rituals, not only marriage. The non-Jewish partner should be allowed to recite blessings, to read the weekly Torah portion at services, and to be buried with the Jewish partner in the temple's cemetery."

Did Rabbi Deborah have Patricia and Michael's situation in mind? Patricia wondered. According to the news surveys, there were tons of intermarried couples. So where were they all? Why did she feel so isolated? And she hadn't realized that burial with Michael in a Jewish cemetery might be problematic if she hadn't converted. Stranger in a strange land. She imagined how Roberto must have felt.

Mutterings—"Really, is this necessary?" and "How

inappropriate!"—filled the sanctuary. Patricia observed Rabbi Weinstein's complexion darken to crimson. She was concerned. His deep flush could be a symptom of sky-high blood pressure. She wished Michael was with her.

Rabbi Deborah persisted in a louder voice. "Any two people sharing their lives together will experience difficult times. Certainly couples who intermarry will have differences to work out. Our goal as clergy and as a congregation should be to give the couple a positive experience with Judaism so they will feel comfortable participating in a full Jewish life. This is good for Jews, for the people who love them, and for the future of the Jewish people. Amen."

Rabbi Deborah slowly walked to her seat on the pulpit. The cantor rose to lead the next hymn. The voices of the congregants, however, had erupted into a dull roar of debate, not a sonorous melody.

Patricia noticed Rabbi Weinstein squirming in his seat. He stood and looked as if he was about to interrupt the cantor. But no, he sat down until it was time to honor the memory of those who had died in the last month. Rabbi Weinstein rose again. In a strong voice, despite his unhealthy color, he recited the names of congregants, as well as Roberto Gomez, U.S. troops, and other community members who had recently passed away. The cantor sang the *Kaddish*, the mourners' prayer, and most congregants joined in.

Patricia was reassured by Rabbi Weinstein's recognition of Roberto's death in front of the whole congregation. Hopefully the temple would come through for his family. Too bad Bertilla Gomez wasn't there. But now Patricia understood why Rabbi Deborah had steered away from inviting her. This sermon would cause trouble for Rabbi Deborah.

Patricia remembered all too well the hostility she and Michael experienced when they tried to find a rabbi and a priest to co-officiate at their marriage ceremony. After contacting the most liberal Reform rabbis in the Boston area and being repeatedly rejected, she gave up the hunt. To preempt conflict between their families, she and Michael married in a neutral zone—a banquet hall in Hyannis. A justice of the peace, a friend of Patricia's father, officiated. They exchanged vows under a trellis decorated with roses and lilies, the flowery arch resembling the traditional Jewish marriage *chuppah*. Perhaps that trellis had been a portent for her conversion.

The temple president, Howard Strauss, scurried to the pulpit and announced the upcoming activities at the temple: the Torah study session and bar mitzvah for the next morning, Sunday afternoon mahjong mania, Wednesday morning Weight Watchers meeting, next month's art auction fund raiser. He hesitated and then started to stridently disclaim: "Please note that Rabbi Zalman's sermon tonight does not necessarily reflect the temple's…"

Rabbi Weinstein abruptly rose and began to chant the closing blessings before Strauss could finish his sentence. "May God bless you and keep you. May God's presence shine upon you and be gracious unto you. May God reach out to you in tenderness and give you peace. Amen and *Shabbat shalom*," the Rabbi intoned.

The service concluded and, as if on cue, the entire congregation stood, air-kissed the closest cheeks, and pushed through the open doors to the social hall for the Oneg Shabbat. Brenda described the Oneg as the treat rewarded for sitting through services. Patricia and Brenda made their way through the buzzing throngs. Rabbi Deborah was besieged by a coterie of congregants all talking at once. Rabbi Weinstein strode through the crowd who parted way before him and briefly conversed with Rabbi Deborah. Perhaps it was the gossamer white of their silk robes, but both rabbis now appeared pale and anxious.

Pulling Brenda along, Patricia reached Rabbi Deborah, as Rabbi Weinstein was walking away. Rabbi Deborah seemed relieved to see them. "Was I too scandalous?" she asked in a whisper. "Rabbi Weinstein has already insisted on meeting first thing Monday morning to discuss *matters*."

"You were very brave." Patricia smiled encouragingly. "The temple needs to face these issues."

"So it would appear," Rabbi Deborah murmured. "Half the congregants are complaining I'm destroying the Jewish religion. The other half want to know if I'll perform a wedding ceremony for their children and/or grandchildren who are dating non-Jewish significant others."

"You were great," Brenda seconded Patricia. "Besides, available Jewish men are scarce out there, especially once you exclude the ones who only want to date a blonde *shiksa*. That's Yiddish for non-Jewish girl. Sorry, Patricia, but you're not a blonde and you're a Jew now. Anyways we should all be free to get involved with whomever we want. As long as they're willing to share fifty-fifty. That's what my mother always said."

"You know my view," added Patricia. "The temple should welcome interfaith couples with open arms. How else to convince them to raise Jewish children?"

"Let's pray Rabbi Weinstein can be flexible enough to see my point of view even if he doesn't totally agree." Rabbi Deborah glanced toward a chair. "I need to sit."

Brenda offered to get her punch and veered off toward the dessert table laden with cookies, brownies, and rugelach. She expeditiously loaded a plateful, balanced punch in her other hand, and returned to present her harvest to the Rabbi and Patricia. "We can share," she offered as she bit into a brownie.

Patricia peered toward the dessert table hoping to spy fruit, nuts or some other healthful snack. The back of a dark-haired man dressed in a custodian's uniform blocked her view. As he cleared away paper plates and cups, her stomach twinged. Was she imagining things? His hands full, he turned and then nodded in response to Patricia's stare.

Of course, it was Roberto's cousin, Jorge. Patricia laughed weakly and headed toward the coffee urn. Caffeine, even the temple's weak version, might clear her head of phantoms.

Chapter Five

Monday, May 18

At ten-thirty on Monday morning, Patricia received a panicked call from Rabbi Deborah. "The temple is surrounded by protesters, and we're stuck inside. Tell me what's happening out there so I know the world hasn't gone totally insane."

With her phone nestled between her ear and shoulder, Patricia sat next to Danny at the kitchen table, holding a spoonful of plain yogurt in front of his mouth. The yogurt was the brand recommended by a parents' advice blog as kid-friendly, but Danny's lips glued shut. After pleas of "try it, you'll like it" were decisively ignored, she gave up and handed him his favorite truck book.

She took the phone firmly in hand and asked, "What's going on?"

"I guess everyone heard about the sermon I gave on Friday night. The Orthodox Coalition for Preservation of World Jewry, along with the Central Conference of Conservative Rabbis, have organized a demonstration on temple grounds. It looks like every other religious, fringe, and lunatic political group has joined the party. Could you check your Twitter newsfeed?"

"Oh my, I don't have a Twitter account. Should I

switch on Channel 5 to see if there's any news coverage?"

"Yes, but I have to get off the phone and to the conference room. We are discussing emergency procedures and exit strategies."

"Have you called the police?"

"Of course. The cops are on the way," Rabbi Deborah reassured her. "I'm worried Rabbi Weinstein and the Executive Director may end up pushing me out the door as a peace offering to these crazies. Who knows what these *meshugge* demonstrators might do—carry me off and throw me into a volcano as a sacrifice to any and all gods and political parties."

"I'm a witness. I heard you live at ten-thirty-five. Besides, I don't think there are any volcanoes around here."

"Assuming I get out of here, are we on for tomorrow at Java Junction? I need something to look forward to. Gotta go."

"Definitely." Patricia put down the phone and looked at Danny with a combination of concern and determination. So many horrible things going on in the world—poverty, disease, terrorism—and people decided to protest intermarriage. Ridiculous! She had to see this event. Intermarriage was her issue. "Danny, you and Mommy are going for a ride to the temple."

With Danny buckled in and still entertained by the truck book, she headed out, accelerating as usual until she neared the photo-enforced speed traps. Too bad it wasn't Tuesday when Danny was in preschool. But it wasn't, and, for the love of God, she really had to witness the protest.

The weather was sunny and mild, the kind of day

that encouraged the crazies to come out. As they approached the temple, she slowed down. Placards blocked her view. Buses parked in rigid lines throughout the shopping center across the street from the temple. She pulled in next to a bus with a neon logo of six Jewish stars on the side. The parking space was as close as she could get to the sidewalk. With effort, she lifted Danny out of his car seat. He was growing so fast. She set him down quickly, grasped his hand, and crossed the street toward the temple.

The police had arrived. The crowd was boisterous and did not seem intimidated. As demonstrators pushed closer to the temple, the cops attempted to move in front of the crowd to form a holding line.

"Mommy, how come nobody's listening to the policemen? Can I look at the police cars?"

"Good questions. Let's try to walk closer. We can check out all the police cruisers on our way."

There were at least ten uniformed officers, all men. They looked determined but didn't seem able to establish control. Demonstrators kept pushing in between and in front of the cops. Patricia was used to her father's gruff certainty about how to handle a crime scene. On the other hand, she doubted the Rockville police force had much experience dealing with demonstrations. In addition to good schools, the Potomac-Rockville area boasted a low crime rate, two of the reasons why she and Michael chose to buy a house in the area. These cops had their hands full, given the importance of political correctness in the liberal suburb. They'd have to prevent physical injuries while at the same time avoiding emotional offense.

Although she hadn't seen any coverage on the

morning news shows, word must have traveled fast. A reporter from a local TV station stood by the main temple entrance while one of her crew adjusted a mike. Another bus offloaded a group of twenty-something protesters carrying make-shift placards and posters. There weren't many occasions for a political free-for-all in Rockville, and everyone seemed to want a piece of the action. Or had there been misleading Twitter feeds about the nature of the gathering? One good reason not to engage in Twittering.

People standing behind a banner labeled The Central Conference of Conservative Rabbis held up signs: "Safeguard the Covenant of Marriage."

Another group wore large buttons identifying themselves as "Messianic Jews For Intermarriage." They waved a banner proclaiming, "Jesus Blesses Intermarriage."

A contingent of elderly men raised a placard declaring "The Orthodox Coalition for Preservation of World Jewry Warns DO NOT Let Your Children Be Led Astray—Deuteronomy 7:3."

Black hats bobbed on a sea of dark waves. All of Hasidic Brooklyn, sideburns and beards flying, seemed to have organized over the weekend and traveled down on that cheap bus service run by Orthodox Jews. A noisy gaggle of Chabad *Lubavitchers*, recognizable by their brimmed hats, chanted, "No Strange Gods, No Strange Children."

The Williamsburg Kabbalah Center set up a card table pasted with the organization's name and covered with flyers listing services for couples' dream interpretation, recovered memory assistance, and personalized numerology analyses to test for compatibility.

At another table labeled "JScreen For Prevention of Genetic Disease," representatives offered sign-ups for free genetic testing and gave away promotional mints with the group's name on the wrappers.

Patricia noticed members of the ultra-orthodox groups giving the evil eye to several couples walking under a Mormons for Multiple Marriage signboard and handing out leaflets for marriage counseling to all takers.

Patricia could barely see the temple among the multitude of posters and placards from The Catholic Family Community for Pro Life/Pro Faith, Baptists for Abstention, Methodists for Peace in the Middle East, African-American Fellowship for Cultural Preservation, and The Federalist Society Against the Marriage Tax.

Palestinians for Peace waved green and white flags with red lettering claiming, "All Children are Mohammed's Children." Several attractive women in dress suits, heels, and beautiful head scarves, held a banner that said, "Muslim Women for Moderation."

The Rabbinic Center for Research and Counseling was actually distributing pamphlets on the issue of the day, "Interfaith marriage: Pros and Cons." However, they were engulfed by The Gay Judeo-Christian Coalition, picketing in support of same sex marriage and ordination of gay/bi clergy and a group of students wearing University of Maryland T-shirts plastered with the motto "Boycott Divest Sanction Israel."

Directly across from Patricia, a middle-aged woman draped in a worn looking sari held up a sign "The Buddhist Temple of Greater Washington Cares." Patricia recognized the woman as a former congregant who had been invited to Temple Israel to give a lecture on diversity. The woman said she converted to Buddhism because Judaism did not have all the answers. What religion did?

A van plastered with stickers reading Mothers Against GMOs tried to pull up closer to the demonstration. What did genetically modified organisms have to do with interfaith marriage or any kind of marriage for that matter?

A line of women, mostly non-Caucasian, followed in the van's wake on foot. Their arms were linked, and they held a banner reading "Domestic Work Is An Act of Love—Domestic Workers Alliance Supports A Living Wage."

Among the faces, Patricia thought she recognized Bertilla Gomez. It made sense that Bertilla would demonstrate for higher wages now that she was a single parent and head of the household. But why here? To prod the temple about its responsibility for Roberto's death? To spur a settlement? Or simply to get news coverage for the Alliance's cause? She could see the TV cameras panning the crowd of demonstrators. Bertilla's presence was haunting, like a vision of a nudging angel.

Patricia felt a tug on her hand, and she refocused her attention down on Danny. He was staring with apparent fascination at the crowd, so absorbed he hadn't been his usual wiggly self. "Mommy, why are all these people standing in front of our temple? Do they want to go in? Is everybody Jewish?"

"It's complicated, honey. People of many faiths are here. Everybody wants to tell everybody else what they believe about certain things like—well—"

"Why are they yelling? It's so loud."

"Not everyone agrees with each other. Some people are trying to convince other people that they are right. You know how you and your friend Nathan fight over the fire engine at school, and Mrs. Levy tells you to share and take turns? These people aren't being very good at taking turns or listening to each other. Let's see if we can get a better view." How could she possibly explain the reasons for the demonstration to Danny? Luckily, he was distracted by the chaos.

Keeping a tight grasp on his hand, Patricia tried to move closer to the temple and get a better view. But the crowd stopped them. From afar she glimpsed Rabbi Weinstein and Rabbi Deborah sneaking peeks around the main door. Rabbi Weinstein looked as though he wanted to address the demonstrators, but the police barred his way.

"Mommy, do you see your rabbi teacher?" Danny pointed to the temple with his free hand, so small and vulnerable. "Is she inside? Is she hiding? Why doesn't she come out?"

"I can see Rabbi Deborah by the entrance. And Rabbi Weinstein, too." Patricia was unsure how much to explain without worrying her son. "They are talking inside, because so many people are crowded outside and making noise."

"Are the rabbis afraid? Does someone want to hurt them?"

"No, no. The police are here to make sure everyone is safe." Patricia tried to sound more certain than she felt.

Just then, one of the policemen took out an electric megaphone and stepped forward. He announced that most groups did not have the required permits to demonstrate. Although the coalition that had organized the rally may have done so legally, the logistics of separating out representatives from the various groups could not be practically implemented without safety risks. Therefore the police would clear the grounds by noon, in thirty minutes. Anyone remaining on temple property would be arrested for trespassing. Patricia looked down at Danny. Now was the time to go.

Not until after she'd strapped Danny into his car seat did she let herself acknowledge the seriousness of the situation. The demonstrators were getting louder and more unruly. She hoped that the police would be successful in dispersing the protestors without violence breaking out.

Not caring about the speed limit, Patricia raced away from the temple. She'd have to phone Brenda to catch her up.

****

Much later that afternoon, Patricia spoke to both Brenda and Rabbi Deborah. The police had successfully convinced the demonstrators to leave without incident although the temple grounds weren't completely cleared until two p.m.

Brenda was sorry she had missed it all. "Were there any cute guys?"

"Believe me, Brenda, they were all Hasids and barely out of adolescence. By the way, Rabbi Deborah texted. She prefers not to meet at Java Junction tomorrow. Too public, too exposed after all this commotion. She suggested we meet at Swain's Lock down at the Canal because it will be peaceful and calming."

"Swain's Lock? Are you serious? I haven't been since my younger son was a Cub Scout. What's there? A bunch of trees, dirt, mosquitos, and that mucky canal? How will we get coffee?"

"We can take out coffee from Java Junction on the way."

"What if I have to go to the bathroom? Where will I go?"

"I'm sure they have porta potties."

"Porta potties? Oh, you mean an outhouse. They stink."

"Brenda, we can do this for Rabbi Deborah."

"Okay, I'll pick you up tomorrow after you drop Danny off at school. But I'm going to bring my own toilet paper."

Chapter Six

Monday, May 18

Michael arrived home after seven, too late for the family dinner. An old story. It wasn't fair for him to criticize her cooking when the food was always cold by the time he ate. He did look tired tonight. Contrary to his usual erect posture that stretched his frame to just over six feet, he stooped over. His hair was plastered against his sweaty forehead and seemed to be peppered with more silver. To Patricia, the silvery highlights only made him look more distinguished. Men were lucky in that regard.

"Sorry I'm so late again."

"Honey, you must have had a rough day." Patricia kissed his cheek and brushed curls off his forehead. At least he sounded contrite.

"A long-time patient, Roger, came in today. He's been with me for three years, and I've advised him to lose weight. When we weighed him today, he'd gained fifteen pounds." Michael scratched at the shadow of beard grazing his strong jaw. "I told him nicely but firmly to make lifestyle changes, modify his eating habits, exercise. I want him to have a carotid artery screening but he's refusing. He argues what's the point, he's taking his statin and blood pressure pills and enjoys a good pastrami sandwich. You and Danny probably had dinner?"

"Yes, we've eaten, but I made meatloaf. I used low-fat ground turkey."

Michael nodded in approval. Patricia knew he watched his weight. At thirty-nine, he'd never been thin, but his square body remained muscular and solid. He maintained the same weight since she met him thirteen years earlier. Five early mornings a week, he worked out with weights in the basement or jogged five miles around the neighborhood.

As Danny ran in and hugged Michael, Patricia prayed her son had forgotten all about the drive to the temple that morning. It would have been useless to warn him not to say anything. The warning would only serve to highlight their excursion and make it the first thing Danny remembered to tell Daddy. Michael undoubtedly would not approve. His cautious physician's approach to life did not easily yield to spontaneous exploratory adventures.

Without complaint, Michael took his plate of micro-waved meatloaf and green beans into the family room along with his laptop and turned on the sixty-inch flat screen television. Patricia followed Michael into the airy room with the arched ceiling, oak beams, and skylight. Ivory walls set off the oak-planked floor covered with an indigo and aquamarine rug. She picked out the rug at Macy's home goods sale last year, and Michael was happy to go along with one of her rare attempts at decorating. The rug's shades reminded her of childhood summers at the ocean.

The family room had been a big selling point when they bought the house. On warm spring evenings after

Joyce Sanderly

dinner clean-up, Patricia enjoyed curling up on the overstuffed couch with Danny before his bedtime or with Michael after. The room could be drafty in the winter even when she managed to convince Michael to light a fire in the stone hearth. Actually Patricia was the one who usually made the fire, a skill she acquired hanging out at beach bonfires on the Cape.

The spaciousness of her family room contrasted sharply with the cramped living room of the bungalow where she'd grown up. Her entire family had squeezed around the small television set and argued over which shows to watch. Her mother preferred sit coms or cooking demos. Her dad wanted the nightly news hour. Her sisters adored prime time soap operas, and Patricia pined for the female detective series. She loved how the lady detectives joined jigsaw pieces until everything fell into place by the end of the show. Her father grumbled that wasn't what happened in real life detective work, but he watched with her. Maybe he got a vicarious thrill at how the truth unambiguously appeared, and the TV crime was always solved.

A portrait of President John F. Kennedy hung prominently over the fireplace in the Reilly living room. Kennedy's picture had been a requirement for every Catholic home in the Boston area, at least until the full extent of his womanizing had been disclosed in the last decades. Framed commendations awarded to her father from the Randolph police department were displayed on either side of Kennedy. Department store portraits of the girls taken every five years or so littered the bookshelves filled with World Encyclopedia volumes.

Her mother's collection of nativity figures and

saints covered the tops of cabinets and the upright piano, mostly unused after each daughter's short-lived attempt at lessons. Her dad was the only musical member of the family with his melodious Irish tenor.

Patricia tried to keep her Potomac family room uncluttered with knickknacks—what Brenda referred to as tchotchkes. Patricia wanted Danny to have as much space as possible to build his Lego cities, drive his cars and trucks, and play imaginary games of good guy/bad guy. The only decorations on the family room walls were a couple of abstract oils, gifts from Michael's parents. She had never heard of the artists and could never remember their names. But she appreciated how the paintings brightened the room. Michael's mother had repeatedly told her that the works were quite valuable and should be specially insured, another task on Patricia's list.

The mantelpiece over the fireplace held Patricia and Michael's wedding portrait. After the ceremony, the photographer posed the couple under shady elm trees behind the banquet hall. Ocean glimmered in the background. To economize, Patricia wore a wedding gown borrowed from a second cousin. Once the dress was altered, its lacey quarter-length sleeves, heart-shaped neck, and trim bodice fit her to a tee. Michael wore an elegant black tuxedo. They gazed intently into each other's eyes. The photo was corny but captured an idyllic moment, with family conflicts at a distance and hard compromises in the future.

Neither set of parents had been happy about the wedding. Michael's parents wanted him to marry a nice Jewess from a professional family. Patricia's parents expected her to marry a good Catholic boy with a reliable job who could support lots of kids. At least the two fathers found a shared interest in poker and beer. They were quicker to accept the marriage than their wives. The mothers seemed to be holding out for a broken engagement.

In any event, a Kennedy wedding it was not. On the other hand, neither side considered the other to have won. For the reception, Patricia and Michael financed a supplement to the menu that ensured a plentiful supply of lobster Newburg, shrimp in black bean sauce, and bacon-wrapped scallops to satisfy Michael's parents' and their friends' appetites. Clearly the wedding was not a kosher affair, to the relief of both Patricia's Irish-Italian family and Michael's liberal foodie family.

After the event took place, both mothers eventually resigned themselves to the marriage, especially once Danny was born. Patricia's mother didn't believe in divorce, and both grandmothers must have already learned the closely held secret that Patricia was gradually discovering: there was no perfect "happily ever after" marriage.

The mantel also held candid photos of Danny from infancy through his fourth year. After Danny's birth, Michael bought a digital SLR camera to record his new son's life. Michael didn't end up having much time to shoot photos, but Patricia made a point of learning how to use the complex new camera. Not wanting to be limited to the posed department store portraits that her parents had insisted upon, she studied the camera's instructions. Michael explained what she couldn't figure out on her own. He learned photography as a kid from his dad. He patiently showed her how to focus the camera manually, adjust the exposure, and use interchangeable lenses. Unlike her cellphone, the SLR had a great zoom, and Patricia became skilled at taking action shots and close-ups of Danny. Her goal was to create a family history that they would all appreciate in years to come.

Low mutterings of "damn it" interrupted Patricia's recollections. Michael's laptop had slipped to the rug as he tried to arrange himself and his meatloaf into the black leather recliner. After Patricia came to his rescue, Michael sunk into the chair with an exhausted sigh. They bought the recliner last year from the pricey Steady Posture Store as their tenth anniversary present to each other. The recliner had become Michael's throne at home. As he settled in with his dinner and patient charts to update, Danny moved his bin of Legos across the rug so he could play at Michael's feet. With Patricia's encouragement, Michael tried for quality time each night with his son. She knew he considered this multi-tasking half hour to be his quality time with Danny, but for once she didn't care. Hopefully, the evening would pass with Patricia cleaning up in the kitchen, Michael distracted by his patients' problems, and Danny building a fort without mentioning their temple adventure.

Ah, but for the seven-thirty news update: "And today at Temple Israel in Rockville, demonstrators gathered to protest a statement by temple clergy last Friday night supporting interfaith marriage."

"Patricia," Michael called excitedly. "Stop washing dishes. Come see this. There was a demonstration at the temple today! These Jews, they're crazy. Look at those Hasids with their sausage sideburns, screaming at the top of their lungs, fulfilling every anti-Semite's stereotype." Michael, cocooned all day in his office, knew nothing about the demonstration.

"Mommy and I saw them."

Patricia cringed.

"On the TV?" His eyebrows raised in a question, Michael shifted to face Patricia.

"No. Mommy and I drove to temple. We saw people dressed in funny hats and dresses. They were yelling with their outdoor voices. The policemen told everyone to go home."

Michael closed his laptop and sat up. "What—are you kidding? You took Danny to the temple with all those fanatics? Do you know how dangerous that was?"

"It wasn't dangerous. Rabbi Deborah called to tell us about the demonstration." Patricia moved directly in front of Michael in his reclining throne. "I didn't realize how big the crowd was going to get, and we left as soon as the police announced they were clearing the area. Danny was next to me the whole time." She stared down at Michael with a defiant gaze. She did nothing wrong.

Michael's velvety brown eyes deepened to opacity. So much for windows into the soul.

"What were you thinking?" he exclaimed, thrusting open his arms as if drawing a giant question mark.

"I needed to observe what was happening at the temple on an issue I feel very strongly about. After all, we began as an intermarried couple."

"You exposed Danny to a potentially explosive situation!" Michael stood up, careful not to dislodge Danny who was curled at his feet. "Just because your father was a cop doesn't mean you should be taking risks with our family. There could have been a riot, people getting beat up!"

"It was a peaceful demonstration; no one got beat up." Behind her, Patricia heard the TV promoting the benefits of a popular erectile dysfunction drug that seemed to be advertised everywhere. She grabbed the remote from the table and switched off the set.

"And look where it got your father— to the track where he lost a chunk of his retirement pension." Michael's tawny complexion darkened to a burn. "Maybe my mother was right."

"What's that supposed to mean? And leave my father out of this." Patricia flushed with anger. Michael was pulling out the big guns, his mother and her father.

"No Jewish woman ever goes to a demonstration," he countered. "She'd be too paranoid."

"What an outrageous thing to say! That's not true. There have been plenty of politically active Jewish women, Emma Goldman, Betty Friedan, Bella Abzug, Golda Meir." Patricia had been reading a history of Jewish women in politics.

"They certainly would not have risked taking a four-year-old child to a danger zone!"

"First, I'm Jewish. Second, I held Danny's hand the whole time. We were not in a danger zone."

"You should have called me."

"What would be the point of calling your office when you're never available, even when I tell your receptionist it's important?"

"Of course I would be available for a real emergency," Michael lectured as if he were preaching to a noncompliant patient.

"How can you call yourself a Jew?" Patricia shot back. "The Torah tells us to welcome people from

67

inside and outside the community regardless of whether we agree with them. And engage with them in peaceful debate. Exodus, Leviticus, the Book of Ruth all say we should offer hospitality to strangers, not hole ourselves up in Potomac McMansions!"

"You don't have to make such derogatory remarks when I'm trying to have a rational discussion."

"And you accuse me of insulting you?" Tears began to course down Patricia's cheeks. "Who do you think you are—Micah the prophet? Let me tell you—you are no saint!"

"Mommy, why are you crying? Daddy, why is Mommy crying? Why is everyone using outdoor voices?" Danny started to sniffle and rub his eyes.

Patricia raced out of the room before exposing Danny to more argument. She heard Michael calling after her, saying he was stressed about work, he overreacted.

Too bad. Too little too late.

She knew she should go back and defend herself in a reasonable tone of voice so as not to upset Danny. Explain how careful she was and how she could evaluate the risks of the situation. How it was a learning experience for Danny to see how ultra-orthodox Jews and Muslim women dressed.

But she had the urge to scream: "You bastard—why did you marry me if you wanted a "nice Jewish girl?" He should have listened to his mother, and she should have followed her sisters.

Chapter Seven

Tuesday, May 19, Wednesday, May 20

From the passenger seat, Patricia watched Brenda ease her SUV into the muddy parking lot at Swain's Lock. Brenda had run late picking up Patricia but was taking an inordinate amount of time maneuvering her huge vehicle into a narrow space between the rocks.

"I am not about to ruin my wheel alignment on this crummy road just because we agreed to meet in the park," Brenda whined. She was shod in strappy wedge sandals under tight ochre-colored Capri pants. Hoisting herself down from the SUV, she walked slowly, balancing a large coffee cup in her right hand and a roll of toilet paper in her left.

Patricia, in jeans and tennis shoes, moved quickly ahead of Brenda toward the shed where the old caretaker rented canoes and fishing rods. Patricia held a tray with her own espresso and a chai tea for Rabbi Deborah. The May sun was low in the sky, and the temperature was cool under the ancient oak trees. But humidity was starting to build and press down on the day.

Rabbi Deborah waited on a log bench. She looked relaxed in her khakis and V-necked shirt as she watched a mother duck and four ducklings waddle away. "Thanks for meeting me here. I needed to get away from all the publicity. I fed stale challah to the ducks. Aren't they adorable?"

"I suppose it's good not to be at Java Junction. At least I can't be tempted to buy a muffin with my latte." Brenda swiveled her head around. "Yeah, the duckies are cute but look at all the poop they leave. Speaking of which, I gotta find the porta-potty."

"Don't panic, Brenda. I see one on the other side of the canal over the bridge." Patricia pointed to a wooden hut. "And this morning will be much better exercise if we rent a canoe. Reminds me of Cape Cod summers with my sisters. What say you, Rabbi Deborah? Are you up for a canoe ride?"

Rabbi Deborah stood and stretched. "Great idea."

"A canoe? Will the three of us fit in one canoe? I'm going to use the porta potty first, although I have to say, it's not exactly the ladies lounge at the mall. I hope you both appreciate the sacrifice I'm making to be here enjoying nature with you. All this humidity is going to make my hair frizz. Not your problem, Ms. Patricia, with your unconverted Catholic hair, smooth and straight. Here, hold my latte."

Sticking the latte in her tray, Patricia walked to the rental shed. A grizzled elderly man with a head of unkempt white hair leaned on the counter. "We'd like to rent a canoe for the morning."

"Ten bucks an hour, special for you ladies." Mr. Swain, or at least that's who Patricia assumed he was, looked as if he had lived in that shed for the last forty years and would have to peel off several layers of gray clothing if he ever took a bath. "Help yourselves to a canoe and paddles. Push off under the bridge. Head west. There are pretty spots along the way where you can admire the river."

"Thanks. We won't be gone too long." Putting the caffeine array down on a rock, she motioned to Rabbi Deborah. The two women grabbed hold of the closest canoe and dragged it down to the canal's edge, then went back for paddles.

"Choose an oar that reaches to your chin," Patricia suggested to Rabbi Deborah. "Here comes Brenda."

"At least the potty already had toilet paper and hand wipes. What's going on?"

"Grab a paddle, about chin height."

"Paddle? Me?" Brenda held out her hands tipped with long nails polished to a high magenta gloss. "I'll sit in the middle and direct."

Patricia rolled her eyes and held up her hands with their bare nails. "Much simpler to go au natural."

Rabbi Deborah laughed. "Brenda, you can be the captain."

The three women walked down to the beached canoe. Patricia suggested Rabbi Deborah climb into the bow and Brenda take the center seat for non-paddlers. "Climb in, Brenda, and I'll hand you your latte. Grab both sides of the canoe and step in the middle." She would reward Brenda with the coffee, like encouraging Danny's manners with ice cream.

"*Oy veh*, I am too old for this. Okay, I'm in. You get in quick before this boat takes off."

Patricia made a motion as if she might shove the canoe into the water but then grabbed the caffeine tray and hopped in at the last minute. She positioned herself at the stern so she could steer. Kneeling on the canoe bottom with her back braced against the rear seat, she gently pushed off from shore with her paddle. She could hear her oldest sister Jeanne admonishing her that she'd chip the paddle by launching that way.

The threesome glided along the canal under budding leaves and chirping birds. "This isn't so bad. I feel like Miriam in the bulrushes." Brenda sniffed. "Although you have to agree, the canal stinks. What is it – leftover picnics, trash, a couple of dead bodies?"

"You watch too much TV," Patricia responded. "All this water makes me feel spiritual, reminds me of the ritual bath I took as part of my conversion process."

"Yes, this does feel like a purification rite. The quiet is wonderful, no phones, no reporters." Rabbi Deborah sighed. "I recognize what I said about intermarriage was controversial, but protests? Did I go too far?"

Patricia shook her head. "No way. You wouldn't believe how many times the sisterhood has snubbed me or not included me in the phone tree. Or how bat mitzvah classmates avoid sitting next to me at services."

"Yeah, as far as I'm concerned this community needs shaking up," Brenda agreed. "These Jewish men expect their wives will put them through med school, raise their kids, and keep dinner warm until the guy decides his younger blonde receptionist makes a hotter wife. Then he may decide to have a second family and actually spend time with them, since he's realized what he missed with the first set. No offense to the present doctor's wife, Patricia. Besides your skinny Catholic ass did not put Michael through med school."

"Brenda, you're bad. All this stereotyping might lead a person who didn't know you to think you're an anti-Semite," observed Patricia.

"What was that old Woody Allen joke?" Brenda scrunched up her face. "Oh yeah, 'I only want to be a member of the club I'm not allowed to join.' That was from one of his movies. I don't remember which one."

"That's a paraphrase of an older Groucho Marx joke." Rabbi Deborah chuckled. "I don't care to belong to any club that accepts people like me as members." I assume, Brenda, you *are* joking."

"I'm impressed, Rabbi. You know your comics."

"Thanks. I'm a Marx Brothers buff. Unfortunately, it's not a funny joke, given the resurgence of Neo-Nazism and hostility toward Israel."

"Even in our supposedly enlightened community, how do you account for the swastikas plastered on the temple wall two months ago?" said Patricia. She slowed her steady paddling and let the canoe drift for a minute. Morning light refracted off the water's smooth surface. A shimmer of silver minnows darted around the canoe.

"Listen to the birds," observed Rabbi Deborah as she stuck her paddle inside the canoe and pivoted to face her companions. "I'm afraid I may have put my job in jeopardy. My aprés- sermon meeting with Rabbi Weinstein scheduled for yesterday was derailed by the demonstration. Now the meeting's rescheduled for tomorrow—to address fallout and damage control." Despite her light tone, Rabbi Deborah had tears in her eyes, or else she was allergic to something in the air. "I may have to campaign to keep my job, ask all my supporters, at least you guys, to call and confirm you agree with my position."

With a shake of her head, Rabbi Deborah flicked drops from her eyes and gazed directly at Patricia. "On another complicated subject, how are things with

Michael? Has he been helping out more?"

"They could be better." Patricia rested her paddle on the edge of the canoe and shrugged. "Despite eleven years of marriage, we haven't reached the comfortable shoe stage yet. We had a big fight about my taking Danny to the demonstration. Michael claimed I put him in danger. Plus Michael's mother is having trouble accepting the fact that not only was I not Jewish to begin with, but I had the nerve to convert. I think my converting took away her excuse to try to split us up. Michael was supposed to join his father's medical practice and marry the daughter of his father's partner. That was before his father had the fatal heart attack."

"You have to be patient with his mother," Rabbi Deborah suggested. "Remind me, what's her name? How old is she?"

"Lillian. She's seventy-three. She tells Michael she just wants him to be happy, but I think that's only if he does what she approves of. I think she planted a microchip in him at birth that allows her to know all his business."

"Lillian was probably raised with lots of prejudices about non-Jews and women's roles. You and Michael and his mother could have a useful conversation." Rabbi Deborah's voice took on a ministerial tone. "You could begin with a discussion of the Book of Ruth. The story is characterized by a spirit of universalism and acceptance."

"Hmmm, you're sounding preachy, Rabbi." Patricia picked up her paddle threateningly. "I may need to cool you off. Besides, Michael's mother might decide I was showing off my Jewish learning, implying I know more about Judaism than she does. She might be insulted."

"Good point, although many converts in fact have done more formal study of our religion. Sorry, I didn't mean to give a sermon," Rabbi Deborah said apologetically. "Let me know if I can do anything to help."

Patricia put down her paddle and surveyed the huge oaks that sloped toward the river. Their leafy shadows danced across still water. "I think my going to temple and talking with you makes Michael feel guilty he is not more observant. I'll try discussing the issues with him first."

"You know what the author Philip Roth said: Inside every Jew there's a mob of Jews— Jew lovers, Jew haters, Jewish Jews, de-Jewed Jews—that's why Jews are always arguing and badmouthing each other." Brenda patted down her kinking coif.

"That's very insightful," said Rabbi Deborah. "I am glad you are so well read. Roth was one of the best observers of contemporary Jewish life, at least from a male perspective."

"Speaking of which, have you met any interesting men recently?" Brenda nudged the Rabbi's calf with her sandal.

"I wish. It's so difficult to meet people or have a casual date. I'm in a fishbowl. Some congregants monitor my every social contact." Rabbi Deborah paused for a minute to roll up her khakis. "I don't feel comfortable going on those online Jewish dating sites like J-Date or JSwipe. I don't have time to do background checks, and you never know who is really on the other side of the screen."

"Why don't you try one of those speed dating

meetups where you make eye contact with the gender of your choice, sort of real life instant JSwipe?" suggested Brenda. "I'll go if you go."

"Sorry, I'm not good at those minute-timer meat markets. And if word got around the temple, everyone would think I'm desperate. Lenore Weinstein's already offered to fix me up with a Reform rabbi who recently moved to D.C. to work at George Washington University's Hillel. Now that I've gone off the reservation with my support for intermarriage, she's probably having second thoughts. Mrs. Wolfee, the blue-haired widow who heads the Lifelong Learning Committee, has a nephew she wants me to meet. A "very successful" investment banker on his second divorce but no kids."

"Second divorce? Sounds like a guy with commitment issues," Brenda opined.

"What do you both advise? If I go out with the guy and don't like him, Mrs. Wolfee will say I'm too picky. If I do want to see him again and he's not interested, she'll claim I wasn't charming enough, didn't dress right. In either scenario, I'm to blame. As my mother used to say, may her memory be a blessing, if I didn't try harder to meet a nice Jewish guy, I'd have to send my wedding invitation to her at Garden of Remembrance. She was prescient. I'm not married. Not even seriously dating. I miss her. She died five years ago. Breast cancer."

"Garden of Remembrance—that's the cemetery where my father's buried," Brenda clucked. "Rabbi, you need a *shadchan*. A matchmaker, Patricia, for your information."

"I don't have time to invest in a relationship right

now. I've got Rabbi Weinstein to deal with. He's very angry at me about my sermon and Monday's demonstration. Boy, it's hot." The Rabbi blew out a breath and swiped an elbow across her face to wipe away perspiration dripping into her eyes. "Even before last Friday night, Saul's been preoccupied. Bertilla keeps calling and asking him to do more about investigating Roberto's death. Plus he's been busy with phone calls about his autistic son Ethan. There's a problem with the group home where Ethan's living. Poor kid, he's faced so many challenges and he's only twenty-three. Anyone have sunblock?"

"Sorry, I usually carry some with me, I burn so easily. But I put mine on at home today," Patricia said apologetically. "I didn't want to lug my tote down here."

"I've tried to lift that tote of yours," Brenda remarked. "You must have your whole life stuffed in there. Glad you didn't schlep that tote. It could weight down the boat, and we might sink."

Patricia ignored Brenda's jibe. "I agree with Bertilla. The circumstances of the accident were so odd." Patricia silently expressed regrets to the Gomez family for not progressing on her own research.

"Look—over there on the right," Brenda urged softly and pointed.

They all gazed toward the shore. Patricia saw a young doe standing beside the first row of oaks, flanks flickering gold in the sun.

"She's pretty," murmured Brenda.

The deer's narrow face angled toward them, its huge eyes gleaming. Suddenly the doe lifted her head and raced away.

"What scared her?" Brenda asked.

"Good question," Patricia responded. "Deer don't have any predators around here." The question raised an inkling in her mind. "Do you think someone scared Roberto? He mentioned he was afraid of gangs from El Salvador like MS-13. According to the news, the gang is active in the U.S., especially in Maryland and California."

"You think Roberto's death could have been gang-related?" Brenda twisted to face Patricia, sounding a bit breathless. "A hit-and-run in retribution for his refusal to participate in the gang's drug business?"

"Roberto never mentioned anything about MS-13 contacting him," said Rabbi Deborah. "But maybe he was too embarrassed. I'll ask Rabbi Weinstein if Roberto said anything. But why run him over at the temple?"

"Because no one would suspect a gang murder at a temple?" offered Brenda. "Or what if two of our esteemed congregants had a fight over a parking space, and Roberto tried to stop them and got hit."

"At night? In the back lot?" Patricia refused to take Brenda's suggestion seriously.

"It's as likely as a gang killing. How would MS-13 members case out the temple property? They'd stand out like sore thumbs," observed Brenda.

"I haven't heard of any gang-related crime in the neighborhood," said Rabbi Deborah. "Have either of you?"

"No, good points. And I haven't read about any new reports of graffiti or building tags." Patricia rubbed her forehead and brainstormed. "Could Roberto have had a medical condition—a heart attack, a diabetic seizure—that would explain his supposed nap by the garbage dumpster?"

"Hard questions with no good answers," said Rabbi Deborah.

"Rabbi, can you ask Bertilla about gangs?" Patricia could not drop the subject. "Or if he had a fight with anyone? Ask her if she can get into Roberto's Facebook account and check for threats. And ask her if Roberto had any kind of medical condition. What was she told about the official ruling on cause of death from the medical examiner's office?"

"I don't want to upset her," said Rabbi Deborah with a concerned look. "She's coming to the temple tomorrow afternoon to pick up Roberto's extra clothes. I'll question her but gently."

"Please try," Patricia urged. "And did someone tell her that Roberto's death was recognized at services? Has the temple made any progress in setting up the memorial fund for the family?"

"Rabbi Weinstein mentioned to Bertilla that Roberto's name was announced at Friday night services," Rabbi Deborah assured her. "And yes, Saul plans on doing targeted fundraising in the community to raise enough money to ensure substantial support for the Gomez family, for example college tuition, medical bills. The temple doesn't have sufficient funds of its own for that kind of endowment, and Saul's already worried about finances. Brenda, you're looking pale. Are you okay?"

"A little faint. I'm starting to *shvitz* like a pig." Brenda was slumped in the center seat. "Feeling constricted, maybe it's these pants." She unbuttoned the waistband. "How far are we paddling this boat?"

"You're in the middle, Brenda, you're not paddling." Patricia shoved her oar deep into the canal and sprayed Brenda with a froth of whitewater.

"Cut it out. My hair dye will run. I may not be paddling but what if one of you has a coronary? Then I might have to paddle, and we would have to figure out how to switch places. I don't paint walls, iron shirts, or paddle canoes. You ever read about any great Jewish rowers? There's a reason they never let us into those clubs."

"Enough already. We'll turn around." Patricia expertly executed a backward J stroke. "Okay with you, Rabbi Deborah?"

"Not all of us grew up as perfect girl scouts." Brenda shifted awkwardly in her seat and gave Patricia a defensive look. "My overprotective parents wouldn't let me near boats, not that anyone we knew owned one."

"Sorry," Patricia apologized again. "I wasn't criticizing." Or was she? She should be more supportive of Brenda, encourage her to go to the gym. "I need to get back anyways. If I'm too far down the carpool pickup line, Danny worries."

"Sounds like he's already taking after his father." Brenda tried to stretch her legs as the canoe slid close to the rental shed. "And I need to be back for my two o'clock with Marcia Kraus. I don't know how much longer I can stand to operate Brenda's Beautifully Yours. There's a lot of stress involved in the party planning business."

Patricia had heard Brenda's complaints before. Brenda was probably going to tell the Laurie Kraus story. "I'm paddling as fast as I can. Rabbi, dig your paddle in deeper." Maybe they could get back before Brenda had a chance to finish, or maybe the heat was getting to Patricia. If only Brenda wouldn't repeat herself.

"Listen to this craziness." Brenda sat straight up and pounded the metal seat for attention. "Marcia Kraus's daughter Laurie is going to be bat mitzvahed in six months. Laurie wants to send email invites. Marcia wants formal paper invitations. Laurie's insisting on a chocolate fountain flavored with Kahlua, or at least espresso, as one of the desserts, and lilac boxer shorts emblazoned with her name on the butt as party favors. Needless to say, Marcia does not approve. Last time we met, Laurie stopped speaking after ten minutes. Good to know social workers have screwed up their kids as badly as the rest of us."

Patricia backed the canoe up to the small beach and hopped out. She held out an arm to Brenda who grabbed on with one hand and lumbered out of the canoe, holding the remains of her latte in the other hand and trying to keep her sandals dry. Brenda sighed in relief. "Thank God we're finally on dry land."

"Sorry to hear about all your aggravations, Brenda. I really appreciate you and Patricia meeting me here." Rabbi Deborah crouched up and moved toward the middle seat, using the gunwales for balance. "It's so helpful to talk with both of you. We're living examples of Ruth and Naomi, the Bible's model for female friendship. Please don't repeat what we've discussed about Rabbi Weinstein and temple business.

"My lips are sealed." Brenda promised.

"I'm going to stay and meditate." The Rabbi settled on the middle seat. "Have you tried meditation,

Brenda? A few minutes a day can reduce stress and enhance creativity."

"Do you think it would help me stay on my diet?" Brenda asked with a doubtful expression.

"It might. I'll consult with Saul about offering an adult education class on meditation this fall. I'm sure he'll be enthusiastic. Personal contemplation and meditative practices have been traditions in Judaism since the religion's earliest days. For now, I'm going to keep the canoe out and paddle upstream. Who says rabbis can't row?"

"You sure you'll be safe?" Patricia asked. Could Rabbi Deborah handle the canoe by herself? Or was she being paranoid? The idea of Roberto being a victim of gang violence had spooked Patricia.

"Of course. What could happen out here? There are no sharks in the canal. I canoed at overnight camp. I'll be fine."

"Try kneeling on the bottom as opposed to sitting in the seat. You'll be more stable with a lower center of gravity, and your stroke will have more power." Had the Rabbi learned proper canoeing technique? "If you move to the rear seat, you'll be able to maneuver better."

"Listen to our Patricia," Brenda called out from the shore's safety. "She was one of those Bay Watch girls, grew up near water even if it was only the public beach."

"Yeah, thanks for reminding me," Rabbi Deborah grunted as she lowered herself to the canoe floor. "Tough on the knees but I'll get used to it. At the last retreat I attended sponsored by the Jewish Spirituality Institute, we rowed kayaks to the middle of a pond in the mountains of North Carolina and meditated in silence for two hours. No electronics, phones or laptops allowed for the whole five days of the retreat."

"How relaxing and peaceful." Patricia sighed.

"Everyone should go on retreat—helps to clear the mind of distracting aggravations and to focus on spiritual matters." A wistful expression crossed Rabbi Deborah's face followed by her eager smile. "I definitely need to arrange one ASAP." She grabbed the paddle, pounded the canoe floor for emphasis, and waved it in the air at Patricia and Brenda.

"Don't lose that paddle." Patricia kidded halfheartedly. "Will we see you before class on Sunday night?"

"Surely. We'll talk in the next few days." Rabbi Deborah lowered the paddle into the water and started to float away.

****

Early Wednesday afternoon, the phone rang shortly after Patricia had returned home from Danny's preschool pickup. It was Adrienne Blatt, the Temple Executive Director. "Rabbi Weinstein asked me to call. We know you're friendly with Rabbi Zalman, and we're a bit concerned. She had an important meeting with Rabbi Weinstein this morning to talk about the whole intermarriage fracas. I don't mean to blame her but it was her sermon that caused the commotion. The meeting with Rabbi Weinstein had already been postponed from Monday because of the riot, and I'm surprised she would not show up. She's in enough trouble already."

"Wait, Adrienne, have you called her house? Her cell phone? E-mailed? Texted?"

"Of course. There's no answer, no response. We thought we would see if anyone else might know where she is, especially you ladies in the bat mitzvah class."

"Oh dear, this is disturbing. I'll call around and see if anyone has heard from her. It's early but we should contact the police." Patricia knew from her dad as well as her favorite TV crime shows that technically you had to wait twenty-four hours before reporting an adult as a missing person. But given all the controversy surrounding the Rabbi's sermon and the fact that she'd been alone at the canal—except for old man Swain— anything could've happened.

"Now, let's not overreact," Adrienne responded. "I'm sure she'll show up. She may have had a romantic liaison pop up. She seems flighty lately. I have to run to an urgent meeting. Please call if you learn anything."

Patricia hung up slowly. A shiver ran through her. All their joking aside, she and Brenda shouldn't have left the Rabbi by herself at the canal. Rabbi Deborah wouldn't have missed her meeting with Rabbi Weinstein unless she couldn't help it.

Patricia was about to make Danny's lunch and then take him to the library. But she wouldn't be able to concentrate on anything except Rabbi Deborah's whereabouts. Patricia had to get to Swain's Lock and look around. She'd take Danny and make their lunch into a fun picnic. While she searched for clues, she could show Danny the canal and the canoes. The deer or ducks might appear. She'd bring her camera to record anything interesting and take shots of Danny. No way could she leave this mystery alone—first Roberto's death and now Rabbi Deborah's disappearance. What was going on?

Chapter Eight

Wednesday, May 20; Thursday, May 21; Friday, May 22

Patricia's jaunt to the canal was a bust in all respects. She and Danny tried to eat their peanut butter sandwiches at a picnic table under the oaks. But the bugs were biting, and the sun was hot. No ducks were in sight. Fortunately, Mr. Swain was at his usual perch, his hunched figure blending into the petrified wood of the rental shed. Unfortunately, he was not cooperative. And, in fact, old man Swain appeared more sinister than the day before. His forest of gray hair looked even more greasy. The skin on his face and neck was cross hatched with scratch marks. As he picked his teeth with a stick, a spit bubble balanced on his lips.

In response to Patricia's polite questioning, he squinted, coughed up phlegm, then grunted that he kind of recalled three ladies visiting the previous morning. "We get a lot of people coming through here to rent canoes. I can't keep track of everyone," the old caretaker growled. "And nope, no missing canoes. I find 'em stuck in the sand and chickweed. Pull 'em up to higher ground."

Patricia saw no evidence of all those canoe renters, either today or the day before. She checked the canoes beached by the shed. They were empty except for mosquitos, spiders, and stagnant water. Nor could she find any other evidence that would indicate the whereabouts of Rabbi Deborah. The parking lot was vacant with no sign of the Rabbi's yellow hybrid. Hopefully that meant she drove home safely. Easy enough to check if her car was at her place. Or had someone grabbed the car keys and driven off with or without the Rabbi.

Her dad had relied on crime scene photos to reveal evidence in the absence of witnesses. So Patricia took shots of the canoe rental area—in case it became a crime scene. She snapped a few photos of Danny standing by the canal, but he was too tired and cranky to smile after their walk, and the lighting was too bright for good photos. Patricia promised him they'd return and rent a canoe when the weather was cooler. Danny complained the old man was scary, and that Mommy should stay away from him. To allay his fears, Patricia promised they'd make chocolate chip cookies after they got home.

On the way home, Patricia cruised by Rabbi Deborah's place. She'd visited the Rabbi's brick townhouse a few times to study for her conversion. It was located in a newish development with walking paths and recently planted trees. Patricia pulled to the curb and spotted the Rabbi's yellow hybrid parked in its outdoor space. She sighed with relief. The neighborhood seemed peaceful. She and Danny got out and walked up the steps to the Rabbi's townhouse. Patricia buzzed and knocked on the door. No response. The townhouse appeared to be locked up tight.

****

The temple did not wait to report Rabbi Deborah's

disappearance. Despite Adrienne's reluctance, Rabbi Weinstein insisted on calling the police at three p.m. on Wednesday afternoon when Rabbi Deborah had not contacted or shown up at the temple. Because of Monday's controversial demonstration, the police began to investigate immediately. Patricia learned all this when she was contacted by the police on Thursday morning.

The imposing officer who showed up at her door at nine-thirty a.m. looked to be around thirty-five, a year younger than Patricia and a head taller. He was nice-looking with a full mane of red hair, a broad Irish face, and a husky build that demonstrated he took his workouts seriously. The morning light reflected off the aviator-style sunglasses he wore, rendering his eyes invisible.

"Hello, ma'am, I am Officer O'Donnell, Detective, First Class." He took a shiny silver badge from his back pocket. "Please check my identification. I'm here about Rabbi Deborah Zalman's disappearance."

Too bad Danny was at preschool. He would have been thrilled to meet the police officer. "Please come in. I was brewing espresso. Can I offer you a cup?"

Patricia led him to the kitchen table. Taking a seat, he removed his sunglasses, revealing pale blue eyes, what she and her sisters used to call sled dog eyes. Freckles sprinkled across the bridge of his nose, giving him a boyish quality despite his chiseled jaw. He looked familiar. Had she met him before? He resembled guys she and her sisters had dated in high school.

"No thanks. I have a few questions. Adrienne Blatt at the temple gave me your name. When was the last time you saw Deborah Zalman?"

Joyce Sanderly

"Rabbi Zalman, Brenda Gottlieb, and I met at Swain's Lock on Tuesday morning at about nine-thirty. The three of us are friends. We usually meet for coffee at Java Junction. But Rabbi Deborah, that's what we call the Rabbi, said she'd rather go someplace quieter because of Monday's demonstration."

"How long were you at the canal? Did you see anyone else down there?"

"We rented a canoe from the old guy who's the caretaker. Mr. Swain? He and I had a brief conversation." Patricia tried to analyze like a detective but she hadn't been on high alert. She was having too much fun paddling with her two friends. "We were out on the canal for an hour, from about ten to eleven. Then Brenda and I left. I had to pick up my son at preschool. Rabbi Deborah said she would stay a while and meditate. She took the canoe back out. To the best of my memory, I do not recall seeing anyone else around." Embarrassed by her inability to ferret out information, Patricia did not add that she ran down to the canal on Wednesday afternoon in a frustrated attempt to search for clues as to the Rabbi's whereabouts.

"So to confirm," Officer O'Donnell said, "the last time you saw her, Zalman was out in a canoe on the canal by herself?"

Did Patricia detect blame in his voice? Well she deserved the blame. "Rabbi Deborah was in the canoe but floating close to the shore when Brenda and I left. I was worried about leaving her alone, but that seemed silly at the time. The canal was calm, and the Rabbi assured us she knew how to paddle a canoe. I haven't heard from her since. I feel terrible we left her. I called her house and her cell phone and emailed and texted

88

her. I know the temple has as well. Have you found out anything?"

"Nothing, ma'am, but we're doing everything we can." Officer O'Donnell rose and Patricia followed him out to his cruiser in the driveway.

"Please let me know as soon as you hear anything," Patricia called after him, trying not to stare at the broad shoulders of his leather jacket. After all she was the married mother of a four-year-old who would have loved checking out the police car, if not the policeman.

****

By Thursday evening word had spread all over the temple community. In response to police questioning, the caretaker at Swain's Lock said he found the empty canoe that the three women had rented back on shore after his lunch on Tuesday. He figured the ladies left the boat while he was out grabbing a burger on the Pike. Patricia observed that old Mr. Swain's memory improved when he was interrogated by the police. So much for her Ms. nice guy approach to interrogation.

Patricia could barely eat the spaghetti and meatballs she cooked. Michael came home in time for dinner after Patricia phoned him, upset with the news that Rabbi Deborah's disappearance was being investigated as suspicious by the police.

Patricia waited until Danny was done eating before bringing up the subject of the missing rabbi. For once she encouraged Danny to watch TV in the family room while she cleaned up, and Michael finished sucking on a low-calorie frozen fruit bar.

"Michael, it's my fault. I never should have left Rabbi Deborah alone at the canal."

"It's not your fault. You had to pick Danny up

from school. Deborah Zalman is an adult. She started this uproar about intermarriage with her sermon last Friday night. She's probably fine, left town for R and R." Michael rose from the kitchen table and moved behind Patricia, lacing his arms around her waist. "Look, I said stuff I shouldn't have the other night."

He sounded so sheepish. She turned and pushed him back with her wet hands. "You definitely did."

"I apologize. I worry about Danny, about you. But I overreacted." He moved closer and took her wet hands in his warm dry ones. "I was way overprotected as a child. I had to beg my mother to let me ride a two-wheeler. When it came time to learn how to drive a car—it was like World War II. Thank God my father agreed to Driver's Ed after my high school buddy Zach drove us into a ditch one February night. Dad figured I'd be a better driver than my friends. What can I say? I'm a paranoid Jewish guy always expecting the worst. And I agree we don't want Danny raised in the same kind of insular environment that I experienced. We are living in a multi-cultural world. I appreciate your teaching Danny about different cultures and encouraging his curiosity."

"Yes, curiosity is a good thing." She withdrew her hands from his grasp and anchored them on her hips. "That's why I'm going to try to find out where Rabbi Deborah is." Patricia refrained from reiterating her determination to nose around about Roberto's accident. It would only add fuel to the fire.

"Patricia, here we go again. If there was foul play, this nosing-around could be risky."

"Didn't you just say Rabbi Deborah is probably fine, away for rest and relaxation?"

"And that's what I believe is the most likely scenario. Let the police deal with this."

"I agree the police are primarily responsible for the investigation." Patricia was not going to dispute that point. "And you're probably right that she's somewhere safe. The Rabbi mentioned doing a retreat ASAP. Maybe she's in an isolated spot with no cell service? Odd she wouldn't have told someone. Unless she wanted to avoid leaving contact information with all the commotion going on."

Michael put his arm around Patricia's shoulders and pulled her close. "Let's go see what Danny's up to. Stop blaming yourself." As he walked her to the family room's cozy couch, his lips brushed her neck. She shivered.

Curling next to Michael, Patricia leaned her head against his shoulder and eased her hand inside his unbuttoned dress shirt. Thank goodness Michael opted for permanent press. She rested her hand against the velvety fur of his chest and relaxed. Feeling his heart beat strong and steady, she was reassured. Her stalwart sensible husband came through in emergencies, at least if there was no medical crisis at the clinic. But she wasn't going to let herself be lulled into submission. As God was her witness, she was going to do everything she practically could to find Rabbi Deborah. And to figure out how Roberto died. At least starting the next morning.

****

Brenda called on Friday morning. Patricia was in the kitchen cleaning up from breakfast while Danny played with his trucks in the family room.

"I told you we shouldn't have left her there,"

Brenda scolded.

Patricia swallowed her annoyance. "What are you talking about? You couldn't wait to leave and find lunch and flush toilets."

"Well I was thinking it even if I didn't say it. Did that cute Officer O'Donnell come talk to you too? Did you check him out?"

"Yes, he did, and yes, he's kind of cute. He reminds me of my sister Teresa's ex-husband – the cop with the alcohol problem and roving eye. Brenda, I'm afraid something's happened to Rabbi Deborah. Although she was talking about that retreat business. I didn't want to mention the retreat possibility to O'Donnell and give him an excuse to curtail the investigation."

"I tried driving by Rabbi Deborah's townhouse but there's a police car parked outside."

"Danny and I already drove by. Her car's parked in its space. But I'm worried. What if Rabbi Deborah contacted Bertilla about gang threats. What if the gang found out and did something to the Rabbi?"

"That's *meshuggenah*—crazy! When would Rabbi Deborah have had time to talk to Bertilla? She never made it to the temple on Wednesday for her Rabbi Weinstein meeting, let alone for her talk with Bertilla. And why would the gang want to attract attention by hurting a rabbi?"

"Not sure. I'm going crazy. We've got to find out more. What if I volunteer at the temple office? I was considering volunteering anyway now that Danny's in preschool three mornings a week. I can troll for information. About the Rabbi, about Roberto." Patricia left unspoken her hope that volunteering might also be a way to forge a closer connection with the temple community.

"Good idea. I should volunteer too."

"Maybe not such a good idea for you. There's little love lost between you and Adrienne. Didn't you refer to her as the Darth Vader of Executive Directors last week?"

"Yeah, I better watch out for her light saber. Ever since my divorce, Adrienne looks at me funny. I swear she thinks I'm trying to steal her husband, that poor hounded schnook. I flirt with him at services. So what? Who would want to be married to that tight-ass Nazi b-word?"

"Oh, don't use that language. It's so offensive."

"I'll try to control my mouth. Adrienne's the kind of woman who considers every drop of estrogen in the room to be a threat to her marriage. But I guess you're right. I'll coordinate on the outside. I can check out online search engines and list serves for finding missing persons, monitor the Rabbi's Facebook page and Twitter feeds, try to hack into Roberto's Facebook page."

"I'll talk to Jorge. He also mentioned concerns about gangs to me. He and Bertilla can check Roberto's Facebook messages and posts. And I'll ask Jorge about whether Roberto had a medical condition that would account for his falling down outside. Your handling of online research would be great. Harder for me to do that stuff from the family desktop. Michael has the computer set up in his study."

"You definitely need your own computer." Brenda's voice doubled in volume. Patricia moved the phone away from her ear as Brenda continued her rant.

"What if you email an ex-boyfriend or buy yourself a present, like real diamond studs. Your internet history is your own business."

"I'm going to ask Michael for my own laptop as a birthday present next year. No more cookbooks and or silk lingerie."

"Forget diamonds and lingerie. A laptop is a girl's best friend. No sense leaving a financial trail for busybodies, husbands or anyone else to follow. Speaking of financial history, Adrienne gave me such a hard time about my request to reduce my temple dues. So what if I socked my ex with a big support bill. Who knew if he was going to come through and pay the whole darn tab."

"She's not the empathetic type. Let's not get distracted by Adrienne's poor judgment. We need to focus on the Rabbi's disappearance. And Roberto's supposed accident."

"Right, right. We can be the *yenta* patrol. *Yenta*, that's a wise and knowledgeable female of the Tribe who distributes essential information to parties who have a need to know. Kind of a Jewish Facebook."

"Oh, I am honored. No one has ever called me a *yenta* before."

"Welcome to the club," Brenda quipped. "All for one and one for all."

Chapter Nine

Saturday, May 23

On Saturday night Patricia, Michael, and Danny attended the annual potluck dinner at the neighborhood pool and tennis clubhouse. The Potomac Pines Recreation Association sponsored the event every spring before the pool opened. After the meal, candidates running for officers or board members of the PPRA stumped for election, making sincere speeches and extravagant pool-themed promises.

One board candidate who owned a pizza franchise offered free Friday night pizza at the pool. He'd probably write it off as a charitable donation. A developer who was running for treasurer claimed he would give the association a discounted price for pool resurfacing. But hadn't he been sued recently for shoddy renovation at a local restaurant? Patricia supposed hard fought elections were to be expected in a development of McMansions, where everyone strived for success and ever bigger houses.

Through the neighborhood grapevine, Patricia heard that Phillip Haldeman and his wife Christine had run the PPRA as their own private fiefdom for the last five years. This was not the kind of info put on the list serve. Phillip, a WASPY-looking guy whose blonde hair was rapidly receding, had been a tennis pro at an exclusive country club but was let go as his serve slowed and his drinking accelerated. Christine, rumored to be from a wealthy Connecticut family, got her real estate license to supplement their income to pay for their three kids' private school tuitions. Phillip announced he was stepping down to work on his personal issues and endorsed his poker buddy Frank Rowe for president.

Frank, a litigation lawyer with a big firm and not without his own liabilities, was rumored to have a gambling problem. Hard to imagine he'd have time to manage the PPRA. Shirley Wen was running against him. She worked part-time as an accountant and had two elementary school age children who competed on the PPRA swim team. In Patricia's opinion, Shirley was the better choice although some neighbors complained they couldn't understand her English because she spoke with a "Chinese" accent. Shirley was born in Taiwan and immigrated with her parents to the United States when she was eight years old.

Danny spent the evening running around with the pack of neighborhood children, most of whom were a few years older. They played hide-and-seek amidst the glow of fireflies. One of the three brothers from the Lane family helped Danny hide. Patricia and her sisters had played a rougher version, kick-the-can, where the found player had to go to jail unless she beat "It" back to home base. Patricia cherished the memory of those perfect summer evenings without a care for the next day, let alone the "big picture." She wanted to freeze this moment for Danny, hoping he'd remember this evening the same way. Patricia adjusted the focus of her

SLR camera to capture the enchantment on her son's face. As he chased fireflies, she snapped photos. By nine o'clock, he was practically falling asleep. Michael had to carry him home.

A refreshing evening breeze flowed through the family room's open windows. "I loved watching Danny play with the Lane boys." Patricia sank into the couch and shook off her sandals. "It was nice they included him."

Michael, with Danny curled on his lap, sat down next to Patricia. He grabbed *Mike Mulligan's Steam Shovel* from the bookcase and began to read to Danny. It was pure pleasure to watch Michael relax into his fatherly role. He told Patricia that his father had read him the same book when he was Danny's age. Patricia sighed. She wished she could guarantee Danny a happy childhood. But she knew better. She'd have to step back and let him deal with teasing peers and challenging academics on his own. Even quitting her job couldn't insure Danny against loneliness and frustration, especially if he remained an only child. Especially if she ended up being a frustrated suburban mom, career-less outside the home.

After carrying Danny up to his bedroom and tucking him in, Michael returned and snuggled next to Patricia. He gently lifted her left foot and started massaging. She oohed with pleasure as he kneaded her aching foot, his mounded knuckles pressing into her high arch, his fingers probing the delicate pads of her toes. He knew all her pressure points and could release her tension.

"Soon he'll be ready for soccer," Michael murmured.

"Let's not push him."

"I haven't. But he has to develop ball handling skills when he's young. That's how those Brazilian players become great."

Patricia sat up. "Everything around here has to be so competitive. I can't believe how contentious those PPRA elections are."

"If money's involved, things are always contentious. The PPRA collects a chunk of change in dues." Michael reached under Patricia's sleeveless blouse to rub her back. "The two candidates for president clearly have different spending priorities. Frank's kids are grown so it's no big surprise he's campaigning to spend the PPRA's money on shrubs, a shade awning, and new chaises."

"Those are not what our family needs. Shirley's campaigning to spend on more lifeguards and play equipment. According to the neighborhood list serve, Frank's arguing for more lap lanes for adult swim. Shirley wants the pool closed for swim meets on Wednesday nights as well as Saturday mornings." Patricia shifted away from Michael's hands and folded her arms to emphasize her position. "I'm voting for Shirley. She's obviously the better choice."

"Honey, we only have one vote per membership." Michael countered. "You're going to have to convince me." Patricia gave Michael a playful nudge in the stomach with her recently massaged foot. "Our interests are more aligned with Shirley's. Plus she seems more honest and has accounting skills. How can you consider voting for that sleazy lawyer?"

Michael grabbed her ankles. "I'm kidding. I agree with you. Our household can vote for Shirley.

Somebody better be tracking those PPRA funds. I heard the Kenwood Crest rec association is nearly bankrupt because the officers waived dues for so many board members and *friends*."

"That's not the only reason. At tonight's potluck, Shirley said that Kenwood Crest's treasurer is suspected of "borrowing" association funds before moving away to an unknown destination. Definitely bad apples out there, but great so many people who work outside the home are willing to volunteer their time to the recreation association." Patricia looked thoughtfully at Michael. "I've been considering volunteering at the temple a couple times a week. I was already tutoring Roberto once a week. Now that Danny's in preschool, I have all of Tuesday, Wednesday, and Thursday mornings free."

Michael gazed at her suspiciously. "What happened to exercise class? What about your coffee klatch with the temple girls?"

"Oh, I can exercise or drink coffee on one of those mornings. I would like to do something socially useful."

"Why not volunteer at Danny's school? Why at temple? You're not going to try to stick your cute nose where it doesn't belong? Better we attend to our own affairs."

"The preschool has plenty of assistance, and I want Danny to develop independence from me. Besides, I prefer to work with adults. Most husbands would be glad their wives were volunteering at the temple as opposed to spending two hundred dollars having their hair cut and colored."

"You don't need to spend two hundred dollars to

be beautiful. Why don't you take a cooking class? How about lessons in nouveau cuisine? The French Culinary Institute sent me an email about a class."

"You know I don't enjoy cooking. Why don't you take the class?"

"I wish I could, but I don't have time. What if we have a second child?"

"I don't see what's wrong with volunteering at the temple. I would be performing a *mitzvah*. That means good deed, honey. I know more Hebrew than you do."

"I've made a point of forgetting what I learned under forced circumstances. I was subjected to thrice weekly Hebrew classes at our synagogue with a bunch of other bored obnoxious kids who were exactly like me. And nobody's parents ever went to synagogue except on high holidays so they could show off their new outfits. They'd do anything to raise their kids Jewish except go to services. Not that I wanted to spend any more time imprisoned in that bastion of hypocrisy."

"Are you afraid if I volunteer at temple I'll be going over to the dark side? They'll never allow me to escape?"

"No joke—the Jews have all these tribal rituals. Circumcision, crazy food customs. You never know when they might need Catholic blood."

"Michael, that is not funny."

"Sorry. Bad taste. Oops—sorry again."

"And my blood is Jewish now. So you don't need to worry. I'll be able to pick up Danny from school and cook dinner. If we go to family services more often, you won't be so spooked by the temple." How ironic, Patricia contemplated: the ex-*shiksa* trying to convince her Jewish spouse to go to temple. She curled into

Michael. At five feet seven inches tall, she was only a few inches shorter, but Michael's stocky body was a good match for her long frame. She kissed his neck, nuzzled his ear with her nose. She ran her fingertips slowly down his spine, humming "The eensy weensy spider…"

"Ooh, Patsy, that's nice…"

Even Michael could be distracted under the right circumstances. Tomorrow morning she'd run out to Evette's Baguette and buy his favorite *pain au chocolat*. As far as she was concerned, the issue of her volunteering had been resolved. Why should she need Michael's permission anyway? True, they were talking about a second child. She fantasized about having a girl. Plus being an only child seemed so lonely. Despite their squabbles, she and her two sisters had lots of fun together. Given her thirty-six years, she needed to decide soon about a second child. All the more reason to pursue her interests before the arrival of a new baby.

She refrained from telling Michael that volunteering would give her a chance to nose around and check out Rabbi Deborah's office. Had she left any messages? And Roberto's employment files—had he ever been disciplined for falling asleep? Wasn't that presumption a demeaning ethnic stereotype?

Could the two cases be connected? Potential gang involvement? She would start investigative files, like the ones her father brought home to study, what cops referred to as murder books, although there'd been no murder here—had there? She would buy binders and accordion folders along with those croissants.

Michael turned to face her, gently clasped her shoulders with his broad hands. "Patsy, where are you?

You seem a million miles away."

"I'm right here, honey, just tired."

Brenda may have been joking about the *yenta* patrol. Patricia was not.

Chapter Ten

Tuesday, May 26; Wednesday, May 27; Thursday, May 28

Patricia phoned the temple office first thing Monday and offered to volunteer Tuesday, Wednesday, and Thursday mornings. After dropping Danny off at preschool on Tuesday, she arrived for her first tour of duty.

Sunday evening's bat mitzvah class had been cancelled due to Rabbi Deborah's unknown whereabouts. Patricia had not been to the temple in over a week. Before parking by the temple entrance, she drove around to the back lot and surveyed the scene where Roberto's body was found. She had never scrutinized the area before. The lot was used primarily for overflow parking on the occasions of High Holiday services and endless-buffet bar mitzvah parties—the Jewish equivalent of the miracle of loaves and fishes. Now the back lot was devoid of cars. The temple's two-story building bordered the right side of the narrow rectangular space. A high metal fence hugged the shorter far side and left side. A large green dumpster and a blue recycling bin hunkered at the far boundary adjacent to the rear of the building. A double spotlight affixed to the building's top corner illuminated the area at night, but no windows overlooked the lot.

Driving to the front of the temple, Patricia observed that the building's dimensions blocked any view of the back lot from the street. The site of the "accident" would have been invisible to a casual passerby, especially at night. Patricia rang the buzzer next to the locked glass entrance.

Carol Plotsky, temple administrative assistant and discoverer of the body, opened the door, peered around, and motioned Patricia inside. "Come quick. Between Roberto's death and Rabbi Zalman's sermon, we are besieged by photographers, reporters, and stray crazies. I wanted to check no one else is trying to sneak in."

The poor woman looked more disheveled than usual. Her thinning gray hair sprung in wiry strands from a rubber-banded ponytail. Her white shirt, stained with ink and coffee, hung loose over her belly. She must be in her late fifties and had worked in the temple office for forever despite the fact that she never seemed very organized. Whenever Patricia asked for something, Carol had to search through the piles on her desk in a not necessarily successful attempt to retrieve the information. How she managed to last so long in her job was another mystery.

"Thanks, Carol." Patricia set down her heavy tote as she unzipped her sweater. "How's it going?"

"Boy, am I glad to see you. Things are terrible. Someone's put a curse on the temple. Or we've displeased God, too much sin in the city, like Sodom and Gomorrah. Roberto's wife has been calling me. She asked how he looked when I found him and if he was wearing his crucifix. I told her his eyes were open and yes, he had his cross on. I shouldn't have. It must be torture for her."

"She was probably comforted by the fact he was wearing his crucifix," Patricia assured Carol.

"She wanted to know if he looked afraid. Did it seem like he was trying to say something? I said no, but how could I tell? He had a garbage bag in his hand. I didn't say he was partly wedged under the dumpster and his chest was squashed and there was mud and tire tracks around. I'm still having nightmares. Thank God there wasn't that much blood."

"I'm so sorry. Sounds awful." Patricia couldn't bear to hear more at the moment. "Is Jorge around today? I wanted to ask him how Roberto's family is doing."

"He's coming in later. So the police told Bertilla that Roberto had a scrap of paper with a drawing of a train locomotive in his pants pocket. She wants to know why. How would I know? What a tragedy."

Roberto had a scrap with a train drawing in his pants pocket? How weird. Could he have been reading a book about trains for his kids? Patricia was about to press Carol for elucidation when the tap of marching heels grabbed their attention.

"Ah, here comes *Mein Fuhrer* in drag," Carol whispered as she leaned conspiratorially toward Patricia. "I'm sure my boss Adrienne will provide you with plenty of direction and feedback. Like she does for me." Carol straightened and turned toward the tapping. "Hi, Adrienne, I was about to buzz you. Patricia has arrived."

"Obviously," Adrienne snapped.

Carol and Brenda were not the only ones who found the temple executive director to be bossy and rude. There seemed to be general agreement among congregants and staff that Adrienne was overbearing and dictatorial. Adrienne sent out letters when dues were late, threatening to suspend temple membership. She distributed in-demand tickets for High Holiday services – the only occasions when the entire congregation attended to observe the Jewish New Year and Day of Atonement and ask for forgiveness for their sins including not going to services more often. She arranged the scheduling of bar/bat mitzvahs and weddings—a very big deal to most of the mothers. No one wanted to be on her bad side. Even Rabbi Weinstein deferred to her on administrative matters.

Adrienne's grating voice belied her diminutive stature. The joke circulating around the temple was that her cawing would callous your eardrums if you had to listen for too long. "Welcome, Patricia, I assume you're up for this. We could use help. Nothing too exciting or requiring great skill. Copying and filing. Can you type or use a computer?"

As usual, Adrienne's short platinum hair was perfectly coiffed, and she was dressed in a form-fitting pinstripe pants suit. Her tip-tilted nose was identical to Susan Hoffman's. The two of them must have used the same plastic surgeon for their nose jobs. "With Rabbi Zalman *in absentia*, we are all a bit distracted. And now Elaine, Rabbi Weinstein's secretarial assistant, is out for the next couple of weeks. On sick leave. Claims she's too upset to work because of Roberto's death and Zalman's disappearance. What a drama queen!" she snorted, then turned a brilliant smile on Patricia. "Could you sit in the Rabbi's outer office today, answer the phone, and make his appointments?"

Without waiting for a response, Adrienne pointed

to Patricia's black tote resting on the floor near her feet. "I'll show you where to put away that suitcase of yours."

"Yes. Of course." Patricia picked up her tote into which she had slipped an accordion folder holding investigative binders for Roberto and for Rabbi Deborah. She tried to hide her dismay at Adrienne's cavalier tone. Why shouldn't Elaine be upset about Roberto's death?

Hauling the tote to her shoulder, Patricia followed the click of Adrienne's high-heeled boots down the hallway towards Rabbi Weinstein's study. She was determined not to be intimidated by the woman. She'd be cooperative but not obsequious. She'd not lose sight of her investigative missions.

"Here's the Rabbi now," Adrienne announced as she knocked briefly on the study's open door. "Rabbi Weinstein," she barked from the study's outer office, "Patricia Weiss has volunteered to help out. You remember her. She's Dr. Weiss's wife. The one who converted."

Rabbi Weinstein rose from his inner office to greet them. "Of course! That's very kind of you, Mrs. Weiss. May I call you Patricia? How are your husband and son Daniel doing?"

"They're fine, thank you, but we're concerned about Rabbi Zalman." Patricia was impressed the Rabbi recalled the name of her son. Rabbi Weinstein had the elegant demeanor of mature patrician men, although his face looked drawn and ashen under his ruddy complexion. He appeared to have lost weight since she last saw him at the now infamous Friday night Shavuot service.

"I am worried sick," the Rabbi said gravely. "We're doing everything we can. Now please, have a seat at Elaine's desk. I'm working on my sermon for this coming Shabbat. It would be helpful if you answer calls and buzz to let me know who it is."

Patricia was tempted to blurt out her investigative ideas, but she swallowed the urge and nodded. Maybe Rabbi Weinstein would approve of her plans for combing through Rabbi Deborah's office and Roberto's employment file. But maybe not. She'd have to see what she could discover before enlisting help. Better not to disrupt his busy schedule. According to Rabbi Deborah, he had enough on his plate, and Bertilla's calls should keep him on his toes about further investigation into Roberto's death.

And who knew—what if Rabbi Weinstein had something to do with Rabbi Deborah's disappearance? Could he have pressured her into absenting herself until the controversy died down? The way Catholic parents would send away unmarried pregnant daughters until their babies had been born and adopted out. Or was she becoming paranoid again? Best not jump to conclusions without evidence.

Rabbi Weinstein entered his inner office and closed the door, leaving Patricia free to explore. She slowly toured the outer office. Photographs of various family groupings hung on the walls. There was a picture of the Rabbi, his wife Lenore, and the Rabbi's tall handsome older son, Noah, at what appeared to Noah's law school graduation. Another shot showed the Rabbi with both his boys, Ethan as well as Noah, around elementary school age, at a baseball game.

A large-framed portrait of a wedding party was

prominently displayed on the wall behind the desk, presumably from Rabbi Weinstein and Lenore's reception. According to the temple grapevine, the couple had married some thirty years ago. Lenore was from Bethesda, and her father, Jay Katz, had been a successful real estate developer. The reception looked to have been held in the backyard of her parents' spacious home.

Patricia recognized the maid of honor, Lenore's younger sister, Risa—nee Katz—Fleisher, in the portrait. She was also a temple member and a local real estate agent. Her face was plastered all over those Grandview Estates ads as one of their million-dollar sales reps. Based on the wedding photo, Risa had to be almost as old as Lenore, but now she barely looked older than Patricia's thirty-six years. Probably the miracle of laser treatments, Botox, and plastic surgery. The rumor was circulating that Risa was going through a divorce from her husband of twenty-five years. He was a much less successful real estate agent turned restaurant entrepreneur whose latest place, Deli Del Rio, was not doing well. The idea of a Tex/Mex deli didn't excite anyone.

"Patricia, are you terribly busy?" Adrienne's rasp jolted Patricia from her five-minute reverie. She gave a yelp and spun around.

Adrienne stuck her head in the office and rapped on the door jam. "Sorry to startle you. I need copying. If you have time. It's the supplement for the Friday night service. I'll show you how our copy machine works. The machine's state-of-the-art and reproduces colors beautifully. But it's finicky, and you have to be careful."

She then walked to the study door and yelled through the hardwood panel, "Rabbi, I need to borrow Patricia for a few minutes."

"No problem," the Rabbi called. "You're in good hands, Patricia."

Patricia followed Adrienne to the back hallway where the copy machine was located outside the entrance to the temple library. Given Jorge's absence and all this busy work, today would not be a day for snooping around. She'd be circumspect, avoid raising hackles. Patience was a virtue—hadn't Paul said that somewhere in his Gospel?

****

Wednesday afternoon, Patricia and Danny were on their way to Beauty Designs by Bernard at the Pike Center. Brenda had convinced the two to meet her on an urgent matter while she was having her weekly touch-up, blow dry, and mani-pedi.

As Patricia opened the door to the salon, an odorous cloud of cosmetic chemicals and burnt coffee engulfed them.

"Mommy, it smells funny."

"I know, honey. The shampoos and potions these ladies use to make themselves pretty have special perfumes."

"I'm glad you don't smell that way."

"Me too." Patricia bent over and kissed the top of Danny's head, inhaling his fresh scent of childhood. When it came to hair products, her son seemed to have the same preferences as her husband.

"Over here," Brenda waved from the manicure station in the corner. She was seated across from a petite woman of indeterminate age whose dark hair flowed to her waist. "Patricia, Danny, meet Thu, my manicurist. She used to be a princess in Vietnam, isn't that right, Thu?"

Thu gave a slight smile. "No, no, I was the deputy governor's daughter." She whispered softly and pulled out a cherry lollypop from her station drawer. She looked questioningly at Patricia for permission to hand the candy to Danny.

"That's very nice, Thu. Danny, what do we say?"

"Thank you."

"Danny, there's a kid's corner right over there next to the window with trucks and stuff." Brenda pointed to a colorful matted area full of toys.

"Can I go, Mommy?"

"Sure, I'll be right here."

"So what have you found out?" Brenda inquired, leaning close to Patricia.

"Nothing yet, only that Adrienne is a bossy you know what. We shouldn't talk here."

"Thu doesn't care, but I guess you're right. Wave to Bernard over there. We're trying to figure out whether he's gay or not."

"Because he's a stylist and owns the salon? I heard he has a wife and two kids."

"Right, even if he does carry a purse. So what color should I choose for my nails this week? How about Hot Mama Mocha or Ragin Cajun Shrimp?"

"They sound edible."

"Yeah. You could use a manicure yourself. Thu agrees, right? Check out those torn cuticles. And naked nails. My treat."

Patricia shook her head and pleaded no time. Sure, she could paint her nurse's nails a pretty shade of pink, but she wasn't comfortable with surrendering to the superficialities of suburbia's fashion standards. At least not yet. Would Michael even notice?

Brenda shrugged. "I tried. Thu has given me a good idea for the next step in our investigation of Rabbi Deborah's whereabouts. Don't worry, I only mentioned we can't locate our friend. Thu knows a great psychic located up Route 270 outside of Frederick. How about we drive up there."

"That's crazy. Plus I'm volunteering at the temple again on Thursday, and Danny doesn't have preschool on Friday."

"The three of us can go Friday. What do we have to lose? We can take Danny out to the country for fresh air and stop for lunch in Frederick at a great diner I've heard about, with scrumptious pie and homemade ice cream."

****

Thursday morning Adrienne officiously steered Patricia to Rabbi Weinstein's study, as if Patricia might have forgotten the way since Tuesday. Patricia quickly looked around for Jorge but he was not in sight. Since Rabbi Weinstein had yet to arrive, she peeked into his inner office. His diploma from Hebrew Union College hung behind his desk. There were more recent photos of his now twenty-three-year-old son Ethan. In one photo, Ethan seemed to be shelving books at the county library. In another he stood awkwardly in front of a large house with the sign Eden Homes, a Community for Supported Independent Living. Ethan looked more like the Rabbi while his older brother Noah resembled Lenore. Rabbi Weinstein must be about six feet, an inch or two taller than Michael. Ethan was taller and broader, but ungainly. His features were off center, giving him a lopsided appearance. Patricia wondered about the extent of Ethan's disability. She heard he had gone to the Lab School for grades K-12, an expensive private school for children with "intellectual/behavioral challenges." Patricia expected Danny would do fine in public school. He seemed very bright. But who knows. Maybe she should have him tested. Did all mothers, especially Jewish ones, think their children were smart?

Patricia touched the Rabbi's walnut desk. Its polished surface was clear except for a neat pile of papers bordered in soft hues, an oblong crystal ashtray that held the stack in place, and a sleek black phone. The papers looked engraved with a fancy artwork design. The ashtray seemed an anachronism, but did the Rabbi smoke on the sly to reduce stress? What an unhealthy choice. All the doctors agreed that smoking increased the risks of heart disease, cancer, and emphysema.

Patricia was startled by the ringing of the phone. She hurried out to take the call in the outer office and nearly bumped into Rabbi Weinstein. Had he seen her snooping? Smiling as the Rabbi walked past, she lunged for the phone. "Rabbi Weinstein's office."

"Hello? Hello? Who is this?"

"This is Patricia Weiss. Excuse me, may I ask who is calling?"

"This is Mrs. Risa Fleisher. Where's Elaine, his assistant?"

"She's not in today. I am filling in."

"That's too bad. Connect me with Saul, please, I mean the Rabbi."

Fumbling with the buttons on the phone, Patricia

nearly dropped the receiver. Before disconnecting the call completely, Patricia shouted to the Rabbi. "Mrs. Risa Fleisher is on the phone. I am not quite sure how to connect you or use the intercom." How had she ever managed to administer IVs and give injections. Her unsteady hands were out of practice.

"Hang on until I pick up."

"Saul, sweetheart, I have been trying to reach you." Risa's voice resonated in Patricia's ear.

"Thank you, Patricia," the Rabbi interjected. "I've got it."

Patricia hung up. How odd, the Rabbi's sister-in-law calling him *sweetheart*? They must be a close family.

The Rabbi's second line rang. Trying not to panic, Patricia scrutinized the phone's display of buttons. She pushed the flickering one and picked it up. "Rabbi Weinstein's office. May I ask who is calling?"

"This is Lenore Weinstein." Her tone was polite but commanding. "Please connect me with the Rabbi. To whom am I speaking?"

Patricia breathed a silent sigh of relief that she picked up the right line. She explained that she was volunteering, and Rabbi Weinstein was tied up on another call. Truth be told, Patricia wasn't sure how to buzz the Rabbi and tell him Lenore was on the other line when he was already on another call.

Lenore's voice wavered as if she might cry. "Tell him it's important. Ethan's group home is threatening to kick him out. They claim he hit another boy. I don't know why I'm telling you. It's urgent that I speak with the Rabbi." She hung up before Patricia could respond.

"How's it going?" Carol knocked on the open door

to the outer office, then poked her head in.

"Not so good. Mrs. Weinstein called, and she said it was important. But the Rabbi is on another line. I wasn't sure what to do. Could you show me how the phone works after the Rabbi finishes his call?"

"Sure, who's he talking to?

"Risa Fleisher. He's been on a while."

"His sister-in-law. That could be a long one. She shows up frequently. Sometimes crying. We are guessing the Rabbi's doing marriage counseling. Risa makes no secret that she's on the verge of a divorce. After her consult with the Rabbi, she always leaves dry-eyed and happier."

Carol was a talker, a *kibitzer* as Brenda would say, and oblivious as to whether she might be violating anyone's privacy. Carol's proclivity to share might prove useful. Patricia needed Carol to unlock Rabbi Deborah's office and to show her Roberto's employment files. Hopefully next week…

"Call me as soon as he's off. I'll come back and show you how the phone works," Carol offered, then left.

Patricia gratefully thanked Carol and sat in the desk chair. How stressful for the Weinsteins to have an autistic son who might never be able to live independently. Had Lenore Weinstein pursued a career before having children and staying home full time? Did Patricia want that lifestyle for the next twenty years? Doubtful. She was already losing her nursing skills. She should work on her keyboarding. She looked down at the hand-written draft letter that had apparently been left for her on the desk. She had better start typing before the Tiger Lady came to check on her.

"Dear Mr. and Mrs. Adler, thank you very much for your generous donation to the Rabbi's Discretionary Fund in honor of Mark's bar mitzvah. A record of your stock certificates will be maintained at the temple…"

When the Rabbi got off the line with Risa, Patricia gave him Lenore's message. His mouth seemed to droop. Was it her imagination or did tears well in his eyes?

Before the phone could ring again, Patricia hurried out, first of all to find Jorge. She located him vacuuming the social hall and quickly explained her concerns about gang threats and Roberto's health. Jorge promised to consult with Bertilla and check Roberto's Facebook account.

Patricia then found Carol for the offered phone instruction. As the twosome returned to the Rabbi's study, the phone was indeed ringing. Patricia picked it up before it rang again. "Rabbi Weinstein's office."

"Patricia, is that you?" Brenda asked. "Very professional. I've gassed up the car and we're all set for tomorrow morning with Sandi Welz, psychic extraordinaire. I'll pick you guys up around eight-fifteen and you can pop in Danny's car seat. I assume Dr. Mike is gone by then. They'll be saying *"yentas* to the rescue" when we get the goods on Rabbi Deborah."

Given Carol's presence right next to her, Patricia was in no position to argue with her friend. "Yes. See you tomorrow. That's fine." But was it fine? Patricia supposed it couldn't hurt to consult a psychic. Or would this jaunt end up being a waste of time, a big joke?

Besides, Rabbi Deborah's disappearance was no joking matter.

Chapter Eleven

Friday, May 29

Even with Brenda pushing the limits of her radar detector, Friday's drive to the psychic took nearly two hours. Thankfully, Danny fell asleep in the backseat of the SUV. They had started out from Patricia's house at eight-fifteen, after Michael pulled out of the driveway for the office in his meticulously waxed coupe—one of his few indulgences. Patricia cut him some slack, figuring she'd rather have him caressing a shiny sports car than a fresh kosher girlfriend.

Contrary to Brenda's representation, the psychic, Sandi Welz, was located beyond Frederick, closer to Hagerstown. Patricia was annoyed. Was this wild goose chase what underemployed women did with their time? Beyond Frederick, however, the countryside turned pristine with rolling green hills rising to meet the blue of the Appalachians in the distance. Her irritation at Brenda waned, and she began to relax into the hilarity of the situation. Leave it to Brenda to come up with a novel approach.

They drove under a high bridge with a sign reading "The Appalachian Trail." Patricia needed to persuade Michael to do a family hike. Maybe not his family's tradition but a good one to start, especially for a cardiologist who worked too hard. Her father could have used a few more hikes. Maybe his lack of exercise, not her marriage to a Jew, played the major role in his fatal heart attack.

Brenda finally pulled off the highway onto two-lane Route 40. They drove past the Annie Get Your Gun Emporium. "Oy, I have a feeling we're not in Potomac anymore," Brenda observed. "More like Dorothy and Toto's Kansas, not that I've ever been."

"You sure we're in the right place?"

"Yep. Psychic coming up." A straggly group of mailboxes, one of which was marked Welz, appeared on their right. Brenda turned onto a dirt driveway. A big hand printed sign marked "Sandi" came into view over a trailer. An outhouse loomed on the left.

Brenda reassured Patricia. "Don't forget, she only charges ten bucks a visit. People stay in line all night to see her. But that porta potty? Ugh."

One car was already in line ahead of them, and a beat-up van pulled in behind their SUV.

"I'm glad we brought our own toilet paper," Brenda sighed. "This place of business is a little run down."

To the right of Sandi's trailer, two goats were tied to an ancient elm tree with frayed ropes. A rusted pickup with an open hood looked permanently parked next to a dumpster. A large cardboard sign leaning against the dumpster listed Sandi's rules:

1. Put trash in the dumpster. 2. Line up. 3. If you leave your car for longer than 45 minutes, you go to the end of the line.

Patricia checked out the car ahead of them. A middle-aged blond woman had gotten out of a dented brown station wagon and was leaning against its open door. Her hair was tied into a ponytail, and she wore a beige uniform. Off a midnight shift in an all-night diner?

She reminded Patricia of Dee, the owner/waitress at Deelite's Diner where she and her sisters snuck off to after school to meet boys and slurp milkshakes, before calories counted. Patricia imagined her sisters here in line with her. As children, they loved playing with the Ouija board, a present from a black sheep agnostic cousin, to predict the future. Although the Ouija never predicted that Patricia would meet a handsome Jewish cardiology fellow, end up marrying him and move to suburban Washington, D.C., far away from the rest of her family.

Danny woke up with a cry. "Mommy, I have to go to the bathroom."

"I'll take you, honey. And then we can pet the baby goats."

"Mommy, can we feed them? I'm hungry too."

"Sure. Let's go to the bathroom first."

Patricia helped Danny climb out of his car seat that she'd diligently transferred to Brenda's car at the start of the trip.

"Good luck in the porta potty. Don't forget the toilet paper." Brenda tossed the roll. "I am going to try and hold it until we get to the diner in Frederick."

Patricia and Danny followed a narrow path to the porta potty. They were surrounded by tall grass, wildflowers, and bare patches of ground. Patricia inhaled deeply before they got too close to the outhouse and started breathing out of her mouth.

As Patricia and Danny walked back to the car,

Sandi opened the trailer door and waved to the station wagon's blonde. Sandi was short, dressed in a paisley pink knit dress that outlined her prominent stomach and bust line. Her tiny feet were shod in violet high heels. She looked as though she might topple over if she stood too long. She and the blonde quickly moved inside the trailer as if they'd known each other for years.

Patricia unwrapped the crackers spread with peanut butter she'd stuck in her tote for Danny's snack. "Brenda, we're going to feed the goats. Are you coming?"

"I'll sit in the car and read my Slender Ever nutrition magazine. Less chance of being exposed to any diseases. Wait a sec, Danny, would you mind sharing one of your peanut butter crackers with me?" Danny solemnly nodded his head and handed her a cracker.

Twenty minutes later, the waitress exited the trailer, and Sandi waved to Brenda who waved to Patricia and Danny. The threesome entered the chilly, air-conditioned trailer. Sandi planted herself on a worn caned rocker facing the door. Patricia noticed that Sandi's stringy shoulder-length hair, an unnatural shade of black, was thinning in front. She might be in her early sixties, but it was hard to tell. Must be a tough gig, telling fortunes. Sandi didn't charge much, but customers would only return if her predictions were at least partially accurate. Unless she gave those fortune cookie type horoscopes so generic as to be irrefutable, Sandi could luck out some but not all of the time. Or else she was a convincing teller of stories that people wanted to believe would come true.

The psychic pointed to two folding chairs facing

her. Patricia sat down to Sandi's left, with Danny on her lap, and Brenda sat to Sandi's right.

"He's sure a cutie." Sandi winked at Danny and pulled a candy cane from the jar on the table behind her. "Don't worry, Mom. They're not leftovers from Christmas. I bought them at Walmart last week."

"Mommy, can I have it?"

"I guess so. You've followed directions so well on this trip. Let me take the plastic off."

As Danny sucked contentedly, Brenda explained the reason for their visit. "We are looking for our friend Deborah who disappeared last week after we left her in the park by the canal. At Swains Lock. All we know is that she hasn't shown up for work and she hasn't been at home."

Sandi grabbed Brenda's left hand and Patricia's right hand in one of each of her own pudgy mitts. She started speaking quickly. Sandi didn't look at their hands but stared out the door behind them as if she were in a trance.

"You both need lots of loving. You're the kind of women who need to feel needed. She glanced down at Patricia's right palm. "You have a long lifeline. Are you married?"

"Yes."

"I see two marriage lines." Patricia and Brenda glanced sideways at each other. "Did you live with him before you were married?"

"Yes." Patricia remembered what a commotion she'd caused when she moved into Michael's apartment near the hospital in Boston. They were already engaged, and the wedding would be in three months. But her mother Maria urged Patricia to go to Confession and do whatever penance the priest required. This despite the fact that Maria considered Patricia to be practically ready for the convent at the ripe age of twenty-five. And Maria wanted Patricia and Michael to do Pre Cana, the required course for couples preparing to be married in the Catholic church. Patricia had skipped both of the big C's.

"That's why I see two lines. You'll probably outlive him. But stay with him. He's a good man and he'll be able to support you. Be his mistress first and then his wife. You need to drink lots of water. And watch out for spine problems, kidney problems. You've got your father's temper."

Brenda coughed pointedly. "And me?"

Sandi glanced at Brenda's eager face, then examined her palm.

"Do you see two marriages?" Brenda asked hopefully.

"Diabetes runs in your family. Your mother's alive but her cholesterol is over three hundred. Your marriage ended a while ago—am I right?"

"Yeah."

"You're better off without him."

"He was a jerk."

"I see the possibility of a second marriage if you play your cards right, if you don't come on too strong. But stay away from the married ones. They'll only cause you heartache. Like the first one."

"Even the rich ones?" Brenda asked.

Patricia gently shook Brenda's knee. "Excuse me, Ms. Welz, we are here to see if you have any advice about how to find our missing friend."

Sandi set her face with a frown of concentration

and grabbed both their hands again. "She's safe. I am getting vibrations. She's alive, eating well. But the sooner she's found, the better."

Patricia felt a wave of relief but immediately chided herself for magical thinking. She wanted to believe Rabbi Deborah was safe but how could she trust Sandi's statement without any proof? "How do you know? Can you tell us anymore?"

"I sense she's okay for now. I see a medium height man with dark curly hair near her."

"Hey Patricia," Brenda snorted, "sounds like your hubby."

"Brenda, that's not funny." Patricia felt unsettled even by the idea of Michael with another woman. "Sandi, I mean Ms. Welz, can you tell if she's on a vacation or retreat? What do you mean she's okay for now?"

"Just that. She's doing ok for now, but no guarantees. The sooner you can bring your friend home, the better. And call me Sandi."

"What can we do to find her?" Patricia asked impatiently, frustrated by Sandi's omission of specific details. But after all what did she expect from a ten-dollar psychic?

"Follow your instincts," Sandi responded in a soothing tone that sounded well-practiced. "Try to remember everything that happened before she disappeared, what she said, who she talked to, where she was. Then ask yourself if she wants to be found. Trust me. You ladies will figure it out."

Having finished his candy cane, Danny now held out his sticky hand toward Sandi in imitation of his mother. "Do you want to see my hand too?"

Sandi laughed. "Sorry cutie, I don't do kids. The hands are too smooth—no deep lines to read, no secrets to dig up. Would you like a lollipop this time?"

Forcefully shaking her head, Patricia answered no thanks on her son's behalf. Sandi gently took hold of Danny's outstretched hand and placed it in his lap.

Prompted by Sandi's mention of a dark-haired man, Patricia decided she might as well ask about Roberto. "Three weeks ago a friend of ours was run over in the parking lot of the temple we belong to. He was the custodian there. He was taking out the garbage on a rainy night. There's speculation that the garbage truck driver didn't see him and inadvertently hit him. The circumstances are quite unusual. Can you shed any light on things?"

"Sounds like a lot of garbage to me," said Sandi giggling at her own joke. "Trash talkin'. You ladies sure have friends with problems." Sandi glanced out the trailer door window and stood up abruptly. "Gotta long line now. Our time's up. Sorry about your friends' mishaps."

Wobbling on her sky-high heels, she escorted the threesome into the bright sun. Patricia murmured thank you, as Brenda handed Sandi a ten-dollar bill with a five-dollar tip.

Brenda managed to maneuver her SUV past the five cars that had pulled in line behind them. On the way home, the trio stopped at the Treasure Chest Diner in Frederick. Brenda made a mad dash for the bathroom. Patricia and Danny followed her. After being seated in a slick red vinyl booth and perusing the plastic menus, they gave the waitress their orders. Danny played with the miniature silver juke box hung on the wall above the table.

"Well I guess that was worth ten bucks, at least for entertainment value." Patricia sighed. "I understand how Sandi operates now. Since she doesn't give any definitive answers, it's hard to accuse her of being outright wrong. I'm sure she was guessing about Rabbi Deborah but what she said about finding the Rabbi sooner makes me nervous." Patricia felt a small hand shaking her arm.

"Mommy, why was that lady holding your hand? Is she your friend?"

"Not exactly." She looked down at Danny but groaned inwardly. How was she going to explain this visit? "The lady, Sandi, was trying to help us. Rabbi Deborah's away, probably on vacation. We aren't sure when she'll be back to teach our bat mitzvah class."

"Can I see your hand?"

"Of course." She held out her hand. Danny stared at her palm with a confused expression. "It doesn't say anything."

"You're right, Danny. There's nothing there!" Patricia kissed his forehead. Truth from the mouths of babes. She tried to smile. "Sandi and Brenda and I were all having a friendly discussion. And you and I are having a nice day in the country. Here's our food." As the waitress set down a grilled cheese in front of Danny, Patricia thanked the powers that be for the distraction.

Brenda immediately dug into her generous slice of peach pie a la mode. "This pie is pretty good although they didn't use fresh peaches," she opined with a full mouth. "The crust is very flaky. Probably made with lard. Who wants a bite? It's fruit, one of the healthy food groups!"

Patricia took a sip of watery coffee and made a face. "It's not Java Junction. Danny, is your grilled cheese greasy?"

"I like it, Mommy. If I finish, can I get a toy from the treasure chest by the door? Can I pick it out now?"

"Sure. And you don't have to eat all the chips." She watched him run off to the treasure chest. She was relieved. Danny seemed satisfied with her answers, and the discussion was momentarily over.

"How do you think Sandi knew my marriage ended a while ago?"

"Because you aren't wearing a band on your ring finger, and you don't have a tan line there."

"How could she tell diabetes runs in the family?"

"You'd have to answer that one. I don't want to criticize when I know weight's a struggle for you. But what Sandi said about reviewing everything that Rabbi Deborah discussed, everyone she talked to—that makes sense. Not that Sandi needed any psychic powers to offer that observation. It's basic investigative strategy. We were with Rabbi Deborah at the temple and at the canal. She upset people, including Rabbi Weinstein, with her intermarriage sermon."

"But Rabbi Deborah said Rabbi Weinstein was already upset," said Brenda. "His family, Roberto's death, temple finances? Money's always a big issue."

"Isn't it an odd coincidence that Rabbi Deborah disappears a week after Roberto was run over?"

"Definitely." Brenda nodded her head, her curly shag bouncing in agreement. "And what did Sandi mean—we should ask if Rabbi Deborah wants to be found?"

"My detective-dad used to say sometimes people who have gone missing have reasons for disappearing, like debt or insurance fraud or hiding from the cops. Nothing so nefarious in the Rabbi's case—as far as we know. She mentioned going on retreat to escape the pandemonium caused by the demonstration. Wouldn't she have left a message though, or at least notified Rabbi Weinstein?" Patricia wrinkled her forehead and drummed her fingers on the table. "But not if she didn't want to be bugged by Rabbi Weinstein. And maybe she didn't tell us so as not to put us in an awkward situation—having to decide whether to disclose her whereabouts."

"Do you think she went to visit an old boyfriend or that roommate from rabbinical seminary she occasionally talks about?" Brenda raised a forkful of syrupy peaches and crust and popped the dripping load into her mouth. "You're sure you don't want a bite?"

"No thank you." Patricia shook her head. "My mom bakes a delicious peach pie, not that I ever tried to make it or copied the recipe from her." Patricia moved over as Danny returned to the booth. "No way could that pie be as good as Grandma's, right, Danny?"

Chewing the last of his chips, Danny tried to say yumm and instead sprayed crumbs over the table.

"Don't talk with your mouth full, honey. Please, drink your milk." Patricia pushed the plastic container toward him and aimed its straw at his mouth. "My mom served Michael a piece of her peach pie the first time he came over to my parents' house for dinner. That pie may have made up Michael's mind to ask me to marry him. I bet he thought I could bake like my mom. Too bad I never took the time to learn. Brenda, if you eat that whole piece, you are going to have to come to exercise class with me next week."

"You're becoming a nudge, Patricia, like my mother. Very *yenta*-like of you. Are there guys in the class?"

"Only a few old ones, too old even for you."

"I don't mind. Retired's okay as long as those *alte cockers* are living on big bucks from a trust, not social security. *Alte cocker*, that means old man, for your edification. Old farts make a lot of noise about all their investments, but you gotta scrutinize what's liquid."

"Mommy, what's big bucks? What's a cocker?" Danny stopped unwrapping the prize he'd picked from the treasure chest. The cellophane package contained a thin wooden airplane, the kind Patricia remembered from her childhood that had to be pieced together and might glide until it crashed and broke.

"A dog, Danny honey, Brenda may be getting a cocker spaniel and naming him Big Bucks, right Brenda? We'd better start driving before Michael calls and asks where we are."

"And you, my dear Patricia, already have a watch dog."

"Mommy, are we getting a dog?"

Chapter Twelve

Saturday, May 30

It was a beautiful Saturday morning. Not too hot or
humid the way late May in the mid-Atlantic could be.
Patricia missed the cool New England summers of her
childhood when her family had spent whole days on the
beach, racing in and out of the freezing ocean and
flying kites in the stiff breeze.

Michael had taken Danny to watch one of the Lane
boys play soccer. He wanted to sign Danny up for pee-
wee soccer camp in June and hoped the game would
pique Danny's interest. Patricia should be using this
time to clean up from breakfast, run the sleek silent
dishwasher, and go to the market. But the kitchen was
so peaceful and quiet.

Sitting at the kitchen table and sipping espresso,
Patricia acknowledged to herself that she hadn't made
much progress on the investigative files she'd started
for Roberto and Rabbi Deborah. She was keeping the
murder books in her bedroom dresser drawer under the
socks and panties. After she finished skimming the
Post's front section, she'd run upstairs and grab the
binders. Her eyes wandered to the half open bay
window overlooking the forested backyard, which was
small with a minimum of lawn to cut. Low
maintenance, Michael's preference.

She peered over at the counter adjacent to the pantry, her "desk" so to speak. Her bat mitzvah syllabus was stacked on top of a pile of unread *Bon Appetit* magazines. The subscription had been her birthday present from Michael last year. He salivated over the magazine's recipes for gourmet dishes whipped up from unpronounceable ingredients involving animal parts and plants she never considered edible. Her initial reaction to the gift had been positive—how flattering that Michael considered her capable of making these complicated recipes. But the more the magazine stack increased in height, the more she resented Michael's indirect nudge to improve her cooking. He was the foodie of the family. Let him concoct these dishes. She was tempted to transfer the pile of magazines to his desk in the study. But better not to start another argument, not while she had more critical projects to pursue, like these investigations.

Her gaze returned to the bat mitzvah syllabus. Why not do the reading Rabbi Deborah had assigned at the first session even if the class wasn't meeting in her absence? Although she was determined to check out the Rabbi's office and Roberto's employment files next week, Patricia couldn't do much investigating over the weekend. At least she could try to channel the Rabbi's spirit by doing the assignment.

Patricia opened the syllabus and quickly read an excerpt from the first chapter of Genesis. She'd skimmed or at least heard the creation story a hundred times. Funny that Adam was the only creation that God considered incomplete and in need of companionship. She took more time reading an article that the Rabbi had included about modern day perspectives on the creation story. Patricia had never focused on the fact that there were two versions of Eve's creation. In one, Adam and Eve are created simultaneously in God's image and jointly given instructions to multiply. In the other account, God fashions Adam from dust, sets him down in the Garden of Eden, and forbids him to eat from the Tree of Knowledge of Good and Evil. Only then does God create Eve from Adam's rib so she can be Adam's companion.

In both versions, the serpent tricks Eve into eating fruit from the forbidden tree. Eve shares the forbidden fruit with Adam. God tells Eve the consequence of her sin of disobedience shall be painful childbearing, yet she will be attracted and submit to her husband. Isn't that the truth, Patricia chuckled to herself. God tells Adam that because he listened to Eve, his punishment shall be to toil for the rest of his days. Adam and Eve are expelled from Eden. Seems like Eve got the raw end of the deal.

Patricia read on. The article pointed out that Eve came to represent everything about a woman that a man should guard against. Based on the Eve story, the prevalent belief in Western culture was that women are by nature disobedient, deceitful, and prone to temptation. The article came to the depressing conclusion that "the Eve story continued to serve over the centuries as the principal document in support of measures to curtail the rights of women."

Patricia remembered asking her mother and the nuns if she could be an altar girl when she was in fourth grade. Carrying around candles and incense would be more fun than singing in the church choir. But she was informed that her parish priest didn't yet allow girls to serve in that role. Thankfully now both girls and boys are allowed to be altar servers on an equal basis.

However, Catholics had no monopoly on unequal treatment of women. In the course of her conversion studies, Patricia had learned that traditional Jewish custom required women to sit in the back of the bus so to speak, in a separate section of the synagogue. Before the twentieth century, women were not allowed to read from the Torah and were not bat mitzvahed. At least the Reform and Conservative branches of Judaism now allowed women to be ordained as rabbis.

The class material raised so many fascinating questions that Patricia had never considered. If God didn't want Adam and Eve to eat the forbidden fruit, why did He leave them alone with the tree in the first place? Who exactly tempted whom? Why not praise Eve for searching for wisdom? Why not view God's driving Adam and Eve out of Eden as a birth into a life of conscious choices, not as a vertical fall. Wow, this was heady stuff for discussion.

The bat mitzvah class should meet even in Rabbi Deborah's absence. The women could support each other's concerns for the Rabbi and brainstorm about how to help Roberto's family. She would call Brenda. Brenda understood the social hierarchy at the temple, especially the Sisterhood, and how to activate the phone tree. Patricia would volunteer to call Susan Hoffman. As sisterhood president, Susan frequently offered her huge mansion to host temple functions, if only to show off her good taste.

A chorus of "we're starving" terminated Patricia's strategizing. Smiling and sweaty, Michael and Danny marched into the kitchen.

"Our team won!" Danny announced proudly. "Can I have peanut butter crackers?"

"The Lane boys' team won, 3-0." Michael crowed. "Danny loved it. What's for lunch? Did you buy the turkey breast?"

"I'm about to go. I can stop at the deli on the way home from the grocery."

"The soccer team got frozen juice bars for snack. Can we please buy bars?" pleaded Danny.

"You haven't gone shopping yet? We need protein." Michael's voice had that peeved tone of a small boy deprived of immediate gratification.

"Peanut butter and jelly? Or I can pick up Burger Bliss or Mexican?"

"How about tapas from that new Spanish place?" Michael suddenly sounded less whiny.

"It'll take me longer, but sure. Give Danny crackers to hold him. Danny, I'll check out frozen bars." Her son was already showing signs of becoming a foodie like his dad.

Patricia grabbed her keys and rushed out. Guilty as charged, Patricia admitted, as she maintained the max nine miles over the limit so as to avoid capture by photo-enforced speed traps. Guilty, guilty, guilty for shirking her responsibility to provide nourishment for her family. Wasn't "guilt" what all these religions were about? The only difference was Catholics felt good about feeling guilty: that was how they were supposed to feel after sinning at which point if they confessed and did penance, they could be absolved, relieved, and happy. Jews, on the other hand, felt guilty even about feeling guilty. And Judaism had no easy mechanism for relieving guilt. You lived with guilt and hoped it would be character building, a learning experience, and something to be imposed on the next generation. As a Catholic convert to Judaism, Patricia considered herself an expert. She could write the book on guilt and how to be the perfect guilty —choose as many as applicable: Catholic, Jew, mother, wife, daughter, daughter-in-law or other.

Chapter Thirteen

Sunday, May 31

With amazing efficiency Brenda activated the phone tree and convinced the bat mitzvah class members to meet Sunday night. Such a consensus was unusual, but strange times sometimes precipitated better behavior. In response to Patricia's call, Susan Hoffman had immediately offered her home to host Sunday night's emergency meeting.

Now Patricia was running late because of the usual difficulty extricating herself from Sunday's post-supper hour. Michael gave her a hard time about missing the call to his mother again and questioned why the bat mitzvah class was meeting since Rabbi Deborah was *in absentia.* Mumbling an explanation about the importance of being on time, Patricia kissed Michael and Danny and dashed out the door.

Susan did not just live in run-of-the-mill Potomac. She resided in Avenel, one of the poshest neighborhoods in the wealthy suburb. And she didn't just live on any old street in Avenel. Her estate was situated on a private way enclosed with gates that were locked at night by the neighborhood watchman. What was the attraction of such big houses? They were more work to clean and maintain, although Susan must employ a housekeeping staff. As she drove onto Susan's "way," however, Patricia had to concede that the glow of the white stone mansion in the sunset was inviting. She noticed the adjacent tennis court. That explained how Susan stayed so trim.

Patricia lifted the front door's brass knocker in the shape of a tennis racquet and released it gently. High pitched barking pierced the evening air. Susan opened the heavy oak door. Holding a madly yapping miniature dog under her muscular arm, she smiled, revealing impossibly white teeth. She bowed her glossy head, whispered shush to the dog, and then cooed at Patricia. "Dumpling's a Shih Tzu. He's so attached he can't help protecting me."

Dumpling was pure white except for his beady black eyes and squashed button nose. A fan of hair tied with red ribbon sprouted from the top of his head. The dog's silky coat matched Susan's short tennis skirt which she was still wearing, presumably having recently finished a game. Susan's left wrist, barely visible under dog hair, sported a sparkly diamond tennis bracelet. Why was that piece of jewelry called a tennis bracelet anyway? Was the glare of gems supposed to blind your opponent?

Susan ushered her through the marbled entryway into the ceramic-tiled kitchen. Sitting around the huge quartz island, Brenda and half the women in the class sipped and munched. The spread on the island looked like the bar mitzvah brunch Patricia and Michael attended last year for Michael's partner's son. Lox, white fish salad, mini-bagels, cream cheese, mini-Danish. She wished she hadn't eaten dinner. Patricia had to concede that despite Susan's officiousness, she was generous with her wealth.

Susan urged everyone to help themselves. Following directions, Brenda had piled her plate high and gave Patricia a wave. "I didn't have time for dinner. I met with a client, an emergency about changing her daughter's wedding invitation to delete the bride's father who's refusing to attend without his second wife. How many calories could these minis have? Do you think I could take home a doggie bag?"

"I'm not an expert on sisterhood etiquette," replied Patricia as she admired a bouquet of pale-yellow roses decorating the counter. She fixed herself a cup of decaf coffee from silver urn trimmed in gold. "Susan could be Martha Stewart reincarnated as a Jewess except for the fact that Martha is still alive."

"Yeah, she's what's called a *balaboosta* in Yiddish," Brenda said. "A hostess with the mostest."

When seventeen of the twenty class members had arrived, Susan settled everyone on plush leather couches in the great room. She and Dumpling shared a leather armchair as she called the meeting to order.

"Patricia and Brenda suggested we meet tonight. I think it's a great idea. I haven't printed out an agenda. We're all worried about Rabbi Deborah. We should make ourselves available to assist at the temple. We also need to address how to help Roberto's family. Patricia suggested we might even discuss the reading that was assigned for the second session, something to do with Adam and Eve. I didn't have a chance to study it. Did anyone read it aside from Patricia?"

"I've lived that story. I don't need to read it." Brenda bit into her bagel piled with white fish. "Didn't Adam end up blaming Eve for all his troubles? Sounds like my ex."

"I hope you've been able to resolve the issues surrounding your divorce," Marcia Kraus offered in her soothing social worker voice. "We hired your ex-spouse when I had that fender bender with the taxi. He's a good lawyer, but I can see how his aggressiveness would be difficult to live with."

Brenda, her mouth full of fish, nodded vigorously.

"We could have a fundraiser for Roberto's family," suggested Lois Kaplan. "I'd do a special benefit day at the temple gift shop. As manager, I could designate ten percent of the sales as a donation to the fund. Or what about a mahjong tournament or a bake sale?" Lois's smooth well-tanned skin belied her age. She must be close to sixty given that she had two daughters in their late twenties. Being married to a plastic surgeon had its advantages.

"But then we'd have to buy or bake. I work full time and have kids in elementary school with college tuition looming." Benita Schwartz was an attorney for the Justice Department. Patricia didn't know how Benita juggled all her responsibilities. But her husband had his own investment business with flexible hours and wasn't on call like Michael. At least Benita shared Patricia's aversion to wasting excessive time on cooking. And they both wore jeans and tee-shirts, in contrast to the rest of the women who were attired in flowing imported weaves and silks or clingy branded athletic wear, the latest successor to the now less fashionable jogging suits.

"What about a Botox fund raiser? Micro-dermabrasion treatments? We'd raise more money than a bake sale," chimed in Brenda between bites. "Lois, your husband's a plastic surgeon. We could tell people that ten percent of the charge for their Botox injection would go toward Roberto's fund."

"You can't be serious." Lois huffed. "No way would he agree. And everyone does lasers nowadays. Special in-office equipment is required."

Despite her usual serious lawyer demeanor, Benita started to giggle. "Why don't we all get boob jobs while we're at it."

"Some of us don't need boob jobs, we already have too much abundance. Now nose jobs, that's a different story." Brenda pointed to her generous nose. "We could be the Reform Jewesses for Rhinoplasty." Brenda snorted at her own joke.

"You could have breast reduction," suggested Benita.

"They'd have to reduce my whole body to make me proportional."

Wendy Weller, her thin figure topped with a halo of gray streaked ringlets that she called "her Jewish afro," ran a nutrition consulting business and taught yoga. Fidgeting in her yoga pants and matching top, she looked eager to offer an organic solution. "We all had children. But have you considered the benefits of placental vitamins?" With her right hand, Wendy began to massage her stomach in a rotating motion while she held out her left hand and slowly opened her fist – a bud opening? "Placenta Advocates of America have developed a new way to honor maternal tissue by encapsulating the placenta in pill form. The placenta is an endocrine organ and triggers the body's natural production of estrogen, helping to ward off depression. We could sell the pills as a fundraiser." She continued rubbing her stomach as if to demonstrate how tasty the pills were. "They'd be a novel item, great for baby shower presents. You can add the pills to smoothies."

"Oh gross," Brenda, Lois, and Marcia groaned in unison for a change.

"Is the price of delivery included?" Brenda couldn't resist the obvious line.

"Ladies, please let's stay focused." As sisterhood president, Susan acted as if she was an expert at managing meetings, but the discussion was edging out of control. "So we'll do a fundraiser for Roberto's family. Are they here legally? Does anyone know? No? Now, what if anything, can we do about the Rabbi Deborah situation?"

Patricia wanted to jump up and protest. She was pretty sure Roberto's children were born here, and if they were undocumented, so what? They needed help, and Roberto died while he was on the job, although no one knew exactly how. Was it an accident? If not, who done it and why? But Patricia was intimidated by this group of insiders, by their seeming comfortableness with their place in the community. She held her "outsider's" tongue and her seat. Until she gathered evidence, she probably wouldn't be taken seriously. The conversation flowed on about Rabbi Deborah.

"She shouldn't have given that controversial sermon. All I need is my older daughter hearing it's permissible to get serious about her Italian boyfriend." Lois kneaded her forehead as if making sure it was still free of wrinkles. "Sure he's good-looking but what are the chances he'll go into a profession as opposed to his family's real estate development business. He wants her to promise to raise the kids Catholic so they can have a big church wedding."

"Doesn't sound like he'd convert, but it could be worse," offered Brenda. "A friend's daughter went to study in Israel and fell in love with a Muslim boy from Jordan."

"My son doesn't even want to date Jewish girls," chimed in Susan. "He says they are too high maintenance—*meshuggenah*—where'd he get such crazy ideas?"

"We're getting distracted," Patricia interjected. "Whether or not we agree with the Rabbi's position, we should focus on what we can do to locate her."

"Easy for you to say. You're a convert. You obviously agree with the Rabbi," Lois retorted.

Patricia felt her face flush with a combination of embarrassment and anger.

"Aren't we getting too personal?" Brenda looked ready to pounce on Lois.

"We need to respect the choices each of us has made," Marcia interrupted, trying to diffuse the tension.

"I couldn't agree more." Susan stood and held up her hand to signal for attention. "Let's take a vote. All in favor of a bake sale on the last June morning of Sunday school classes?" Everyone's hand went up, including Patricia's and Benita's. Anything to keep the peace. "Once we see how much money we make, we can figure out if we should do a mahjong tournament to raise additional funds for Roberto's family. As far as Rabbi Deborah goes, should we continue class or not?"

"How about if we meet in two weeks and play mahjong in case the Rabbi isn't back. This way we can continue to support each other." Lois smiled apologetically and mouthed "I'm sorry" at Patricia.

"I don't know how to play but I guess I can learn." Patricia figured she should make nice. But she was not giving up on the readings. "And why don't we take turns preparing the first few class assignments and discuss before the mahjong game?"

"Excellent idea. Don't worry, we'll be happy to teach you to play." Susan looked relieved as she sank into the armchair, nearly squashing Dumpling who yelped. "Patricia, would you mind preparing remarks and discussion questions for the first reading assignment? Thanks."

"I'm happy to prepare the first lesson." Susan was always so polite when she delegated tasks.

"The meeting's adjourned. Help yourself to more food. I don't want leftovers. Tomorrow night's Nosh'N'Watch, seven o'clock p.m. at Fresh Farmers Café then the movies."

What was that event all about? Patricia would have to ask Brenda. A mixed pang of hurt and anger shivered through her. She didn't necessarily want to go to Nosh'N'Watch but she definitely wanted to be invited.

Brenda was moving to the kitchen and pulling out a gallon zip bag from her purse. As she packed mini-bagels and Danish, Dumpling followed her and plunked himself down at her feet. His dark eyes appeared to watch Brenda intently.

Brenda stared down at the dog. "What—you have starving relatives in China?"

"Yap, yap, yap…"

Chapter Fourteen

Monday, June 1

Patricia edged her minivan out of the parking space at Fit Force. The next hour's classes began in five minutes. Cars raced around the lot, competing for spots closest to the gym entrance with one or two vehicles the size of Sherman tanks whose drivers seemed to take joy in intimidating those with coupes and compacts.

"You'd think these spandex clad women in their coordinated exercise attire would be strutting their stuff and parading across the parking lot," panted Brenda. Perspiration was visible on her forehead, as she leaned against the passenger seat headrest. "I guess there aren't enough guys around to make it worthwhile. I can't believe I agreed to be your guest at this torture chamber. The teachers are sadists, and these women must be masochists. I'm surprised the instructors weren't wearing leather boots and snapping whips."

"Brenda, don't you feel good now that the class is over? If you keep going, it'll get easier."

"I appreciate the concern, but I should've known better than to take a class called Body Burn. Just the name makes me *shvitz*. I was hoping they'd demonstrate how to grill a steak in class. That Lola woman killed my quads. I may never walk again."

"If you join the gym and make a habit of exercising, your muscles will adapt to the workout, and you'll have more energy."

"Look, Ms. Wonder Woman, I'll never get rid of these flying squirrel arms. No matter what diet I try, I can't drop my thirty pounds of excess padding."

"Sorry, I don't mean to preach, but I worry about you. Not about your arms, but your health. Michael says even losing five pounds can lower blood pressure."

"I never should've asked him about my blood pressure meds. Besides I'll never meet a guy in there with all those buff bodies. The bleached blonde in the front row, she must have had a boob job. No one has boobs as big as hers with those teensy hips. Or else she's a mutant."

"You do get a warped perspective. Some of these women make the gym their career. That must be how they get their gravity-defying butts."

"You should talk. Look at your skinny ass. In these tights, I feel like an ad for the "before" picture. So much for the idea that black is slimming. It's like I'm in high school—big, bloated, and invisible. One of the failed cheerleaders. I didn't even make the first cut. Everyone dismissed me as the funny fat chick."

Patricia sympathized. The women at the gym always seemed to be surreptitiously comparing tummies, butts, and hips, then silently passing judgment and realigning themselves in the pecking order. Brutal business being a woman. Patricia tried offering encouragement. "We're exercising for our health, not for a beauty pageant."

Brenda plowed on. "Yeah, yeah. Did you see those old farts working out with their droopy pecs, withered biceps, and chicken legs? They were only interested in talking up the young chicks. I've decided I'm not interested in meeting any guy worth less than $2 million in net assets. Never sleep with a man whose finances are worse than your own—that's my mantra now. Not that I practice yoga. I'm famished. Didn't Lola say to eat protein within twenty minutes of class? Do we have time for a snack before we pick up Danny from his play date?"

"Probably, but let's drive by Rabbi Deborah's townhouse and see if anything's new. It's on the way to Danny's friend Jake's house. It was nice of his mom to invite Danny over, since the boys don't have preschool today."

A few minutes later Patricia parked in front of Rabbi Deborah's townhouse. She was about to open her door when Officer O'Donnell pulled his police cruiser in behind her car. Coincidence? Or had he been conducting surveillance on the townhouse?

Brenda twisted and stared through the rear window as Officer O'Donnell walked over to the driver side. "He's the cop who talked to us the other week, right? Check out those biceps."

Patricia shushed Brenda as Officer O'Donnell knocked on Patricia's window. She rolled it down and smiled solicitously. "Sorry, Officer, we don't mean to disturb anything. We were checking to see if Rabbi Deborah was back." She shrugged her shoulders nervously, self-conscious in her black leggings and tank top. The officer towered over her. She hadn't realized how tall he was, at least six feet three inches.

"Please, call me Kevin. Don't worry. You're not disturbing anything." He fingered the gold chain around his neck with the small cross. "We're still trying to determine if a crime's been committed. At this time, we have no reason to assume that Miss Zalman went missing involuntarily, let alone was the victim of foul play."

Patricia hesitated, not sure if she was overstepping appropriate boundaries. But she had to know. "Have the police dredged the canal in case…?"

"Yes, of course. We didn't publicize the operation so as not to alarm the public. There was no sign of a body which is not surprising since the canoe was returned to the appropriate spot."

"Hi, I'm Brenda, remember me?" Brenda had awkwardly hopped out the passenger side of the car but not before draping a fuzzy sweater wrap over her gym clothes and applying a fresh coat of lip gloss.

O'Donnell nodded hello. He seemed so accommodating. Patricia figured she might as well be aggressive and take advantage of his presence. "Officer, I've been inside the Rabbi's townhouse for study sessions. Could I take a quick look around inside, see if anything seems out of place?"

"I suppose it couldn't hurt. We were able to gain access to the house with a key from the homeowners' association but found no indication of foul play or clues to Ms. Zalman's whereabouts. Please don't touch anything without my permission." Officer O'Donnell led the women to the entrance, unlocked the door and ushered them into the front hallway. "No suitcases out, no notes, no signs of struggle. Neighbors noticed nothing unusual. The refrigerator was minimally stocked. Doubt that means much since no one cooks these days. Her car's parked in the assigned space. No surprises in the trunk. No messages on her land line. Her cell phone's missing and apparently powered off or dead. No laptop or desktop. We haven't been able to track it."

With Brenda shadowing, Patricia toured the townhouse's interior. As O'Donnell said, everything seemed in order except for a small pile of mail in front of the mail slot. After checking with O'Donnell, Patricia perused the mail but found mainly advertisements and bills. Did the Rabbi receive mail at the temple? Patricia would have to check. She stopped in front of a sepia portrait set on the living room's teak coffee table. During one of their study sessions, the Rabbi had identified the smiling young couple dressed in formalwear as her parents. Her father was in a memory care facility in Buffalo where Rabbi Deborah had grown up as an only child. The Rabbi had described her father as now having the mind of a four-year-old.

Walking through the kitchen, Patricia noticed what looked like a travel brochure by the telephone. She nudged Brenda's arm and put her finger to her lips. The pamphlet announced the "Third Annual Embracing The Spirit Retreat: An Exploration Into The Heart Of Judaism." The Bend of Ivy Lodge, Alexander, North Carolina, May, June, July, August, vegetarian meals, sacred song, mindfulness meditation, time to rest and renew."

Might Rabbi Deborah have attended? Seeing no phone number, Patricia memorized the website. As soon as they returned to her car, she'd write it down in the binder buried in her tote and follow up later to see if Rabbi Deborah might be attending the retreat.

As the women exited the townhouse with Officer O'Donnell, Brenda offered to help any way she could and added, "Kevin, we're going to grab a bite. Can we bring you coffee?"

"Thanks, I'm all set with snacks. I'm going to check around the outside of the townhouse again and make sure everything's secure. Then I'll be leaving. I'll be in touch."

****

"So you think Kevin's too young for me?" Brenda asked as Patricia cut off the driver in the next lane to make a left turn into Burger Bliss. He pounded his horn. "Good move, Patricia." Those male drivers always claim the right of way. Did you notice Kevin wasn't wearing a ring? And he has that police officer aura, clean-cut, serious, like he could give you a good time when he's off duty."

Patricia, too, had noticed the absence of a ring, but she knew not all married men, especially Catholic ones, wore rings. Brushing aside Brenda's questions with an "I don't know" and "we don't have much time," Patricia hurried Brenda into the busy restaurant. While Brenda ordered her egg-and-cheese breakfast biscuit, Patricia pondered whether she dared order one of the fancy espresso drinks. She studied the menu above the slick counter to see if there was a healthy alternative.

"Black coffee, please." Patricia bet on safety. "Maybe he's not married or maybe he is. He might be interested even if he's married." As she foraged in her tote for her wallet, she thought of her sister Teresa's ex-husband, the cop who never came home before ten p.m. Overtime, he claimed. Teresa wasn't the trusting type, but she kept her doubts to herself. Maybe she didn't care to know. He and Kevin were the kind of guys Patricia could have easily ended up with if she'd stayed in Randolph and followed her mother and sister's marital paths—familiar as the boiled potatoes her mother used to serve when her father was in the mood for Irish food.

"Catholic men think sin is negotiable like a loan." Patricia snapped her tote shut. "They borrow and spend extravagantly and then repay the currency through confession and penance. That's how the Kennedy men got serenity as they screwed their way through the typing pool."

"Forget it. I'm not interested in a fling. And no way Kevin's worth two million bucks. You're more his type. Thin and Catholic, at least previously. Did you notice he was wearing a crucifix? He's not interested in an overweight older Jewish woman. No one's going to call me a cougar."

"By the way, I've been meaning to ask," Patricia inquired as she grabbed her coffee, "what's Nosh'N'Watch? Susan mentioned it at the end of the meeting last night."

"You mean they never invited you? It's the sisterhood's version of munch-and-movie night. They eat at crummy restaurants and watch boring movies. I refuse to go. If you'd like to join in, ask Susan or, better yet, I'll drop a big hint. She's such a snob."

"We better take the food to the car. I don't want to be late picking up Danny." Patricia nudged Brenda in front of her toward the exit, debating if Susan hadn't included her because of her convert status, or because Susan simply didn't like her.

Brenda stopped abruptly in front of Patricia, nearly

causing her to spill her coffee. "Isn't that Rabbi Weinstein ahead of us? Who's he leaving with? Is that Risa Fleisher, his sister-in-law? I think she saw me and looked away. Oh, this is choice, the two of them having a *tete-a-tete* at Burger Bliss."

Patricia peered around Brenda, but the couple was out the door. All she could see was the back of Rabbi Weinstein. "Brenda, we don't know for sure who she was or what they were doing here. Let's be discreet."

"Are you kidding? Discreet is my middle name, except my parents didn't give me one."

Chapter Fifteen

Tuesday, June 2

As Patricia drove into the parking lot, she saw Bertilla exiting the temple. Bertilla still wore a black dress, and her face was grim. She carried a large gym bag. Had she come to pick up Roberto's extra clothes, the stuff she was supposed to have gotten from Rabbi Deborah? She stared straight ahead and slid into her car without acknowledging Patricia's presence.

Carol was in the front office sorting mail. Patricia gave her a raised eyebrow of inquiry. Eager to share, Carol whispered that Roberto's wife had met with Rabbi Weinstein who'd then asked Carol for Officer O'Donnell's number. Bertilla was apparently pressuring the Rabbi to push the police to expand their investigation of Roberto's death.

"Good thing Adrienne's out today," Carol added in a louder voice. "Rabbi Weinstein told me on his way in that he's writing a sermon. Adrienne has a fit when he gets interrupted. She's very protective of the Rabbi and hates it when people bother him, unless it's herself, of course. I don't know why I'm whispering. She's not even here today."

Before settling herself in Rabbi Weinstein's study, Patricia searched out Jorge who was cleaning the pantry floor. Jorge said he talked with Bertilla who described Roberto as strong as a horse. "She said there's no way he would've fainted or slept and that he would've lived a long healthy life if the truck hadn't hit him. The police showed her the medical examiner's report. It said cause of death was trauma caused by vehicular impact. Bertilla wants to sue."

Patricia asked if the report specified that a garbage truck was the cause of the trauma. Jorge said he didn't know.

"Did you and Bertilla find any gang contact? Threats?"

"No, nothing. We checked Roberto's Facebook account and phone. No sign of messages or contacts from MS-13 or any gang. The only angry posts were about soccer. Roberto was a ref for El Salvador De Maryland. It's a rec league," Jorge explained. "Not all the players agreed with his calls. He was very strict about the rules and issued lots of red cards."

Hah, the usual male posturing about sports, she thought. Her husband was in good company. She thanked Jorge and walked into Rabbis Weinstein's outer office.

Joking aside, Patricia was frustrated. Her investigations were stalled. Although she tried to follow up on the Embracing The Spirit retreat lead, she hadn't nailed down any conclusive information. When she'd called the contact number on the website yesterday afternoon, the person answering the phone said privacy concerns prevented her from confirming who was in attendance. Explaining that her inquiry was a matter of grave urgency, Patricia insisted on talking to a supervisor. The supervisor would only disclose that no one named Deborah Zalman was currently registered. Could Rabbi Deborah be using an alias? If she wasn't at the retreat, could she be traveling down? Patricia asked about future participants, but the supervisor claimed he had no information about attendees not-yet-checked-in. Very annoying.

The door to Rabbi's Weinstein's inner study was closed, and things seemed quiet. Hoping the Rabbi would stay busy drafting his sermon, Patricia walked to Carol's desk in the front office and explained she needed to see Roberto's employment records. The Rabbi might want addresses for condolence letters to members of the Gomez family in El Salvador. Carol didn't take much convincing and showed her to the main employment files located in a cabinet at the rear of the front office.

Patricia quickly pulled the Gomez personnel file. Not only were there no addresses for family in El Salvador, there were no records of any disciplinary actions or warnings regarding Roberto's sleeping on the job or otherwise not carrying out his duties. In fact, he received several merit pay increases and complimentary evaluations for his conscientious performance. So what had Roberto been doing by the garbage bin? Simply emptying trash? Looking for something or someone? Running away from someone? None of it made sense.

Before the Rabbi registered her absence, Patricia swiftly returned to her desk. She dug deep in her tote and pulled out the Gomez binder to update her notes. But she couldn't concentrate. As she replayed Saturday's late lunch episode with Michael, her shoulder muscles knotted. She supposed she should've managed her time better and gone to the market before

Michael and Danny returned from the soccer game. But if protein was so critical, why couldn't Michael have taken Danny to Burger Bliss?

Later that Saturday afternoon, she and Danny told Michael about Friday's "country" outing. Patricia hadn't wanted Michael to find out "accidentally" and accuse her of keeping secrets. Luckily, Michael assumed Patricia, Danny, and Brenda had simply gone for a fun drive in the country and met a friendly lady with goats. Danny described the stop at the Treasure Chest Diner and asked Michael to help him fly his airplane prize. Patricia emphasized the clean air and the healthful benefits of hiking. Michael countered that soccer was much better exercise for Danny, and mosquitoes had a harder time drawing blood from kids when they were running as opposed to walking. Furthermore, the diner's cuisine was undoubtedly unhealthy. She couldn't disagree with the latter point.

That Saturday night, Patricia informed Michael about her volunteer work at the temple. He was not happy at her determination to become more involved in the "temple's horde of judgmental, kvetching busybodies." An accurate description of her mother-in-law, but Patricia had refrained from sharing her view so as not to fan the flames. She contemplated whether she should have listened to her sister Teresa's warning that marrying an only child—especially a Jewish momma's boy who was used to having his own way and was sure he knew better—was a bad idea.

When he wasn't distracted by his medical practice, Michael could be supportive, sensitive, and affectionate, wrapping his arms around her and attending to her worries. He was her sexy heart doc with his deep brown eyes, full bowed mouth, and a head of silvering curls. Was she attaching too much significance to the physical? Could sex sustain a marriage? Michael did respect her intelligence even if he wasn't enthusiastic about her Jewish studies. He was forthright and honest although her family considered him to be pushy and argumentative. She trusted Michael—trusted that he would be a faithful husband and loving father, that he would provide for the family, and that he would try to make them happy although he might not always understand their needs.

Michael would not slyly hide an affair. Secrecy was not the currency of their marriage, at least not until her recent investigative endeavors. Or was she deceiving herself like her sister Teresa? What had Sandi Welz said about Rabbi Deborah being with a curly haired man? Could she and Michael be having an affair? Ridiculous. He'd never have an affair with a rabbi, given all his conflicted feelings about Judaism. Hard to believe Michael would have time for an affair.

Then on Sunday afternoon, Patricia's sister, Teresa, called to say she was coming to D.C. for the National Association of Realtors Conference at the convention center. Could Patricia please meet her for dinner Tuesday night at her hotel? Teresa's last-minute decision-making was typical, but Patricia did want to see her. Michael promised to be home Tuesday night for Danny as long as she didn't leave before seven-fifteen p.m. for the sisters' dinner. Good that he would spend story time with Danny.

"*Shalom chavayreem*, hello my friend." The melodic bars of the Hebrew song broke into Patricia's obsessing about her weekend. Cantor Max Snyder stuck his round, double-chinned face into the office. In his late fifties, the cantor had been with the temple since its founding thirty years ago. His operatic voice had been the envy of other local congregations, but lately temple members had been complaining that he was forgetting prayers and singing off key. The whispered rumor was that he was going deaf or had the beginnings of dementia. The more unforgiving congregants were starting a movement not to renew his contract. But Cantor Max was always friendly to her.

"Patricia, nice to see you. You're looking lovely this morning. I didn't realize you were working here."

She slid the murder binder into her tote and shoved it under the desk. "Hello Cantor. I'm helping out until Elaine returns from sick leave."

"If you have any extra time, I'm looking for new members to join the choir. Did you see the notice in the temple bulletin?"

"I did. I'm not sure my voice is good enough."

"We welcome everyone with open arms. No offense, but converted Jews are some of our most enthusiastic members. The whole sing along tradition is much stronger in the Christian faith. Reform temples have moved away from congregational participation. Until recently our services tended to be more like performances."

"I will seriously consider it." Patricia remembered singing in the youth choir at St. Joan's, her parish in Randolph. The nuns who directed the choir insisted on putting her in the sopranos section with her older sisters even though she was an alto, a brassy alto at that. Finally the nuns instructed her to just mouth the Latin words "*Tantum ergo Sacramentum.*"

What gleeful revenge if she were to chant Hebrew hymns. "*Ma To Vu*, How lovely are your tents, O Jacob." She imagined the nuns shuddering in their habits, repeating Hail Mary's because Patricia was singing Hebrew, or just singing period.

The overpowering scent of roses wafted into the office. Sniffling noises followed from down the hallway. Patricia and Cantor Max turned in unison toward the study door. The bearer of the heavy perfume waltzed in: Risa Fleisher. A white pants suit showed off her curvaceous figure. Patricia could never wear white—dirty in two seconds no matter how careful she was. Risa's face was tearstained. And very red, perhaps because her visage was framed by shoulder-grazing waves highlighted in bright copper. Or perhaps her blush was a reflection of the violet blouse with the plunging V-neck that peeked from her suit jacket. Or perhaps it was the tanning salon bronze of her chest adorned with a glittering diamond pendant hanging from a platinum chain.

Risa Fleisher kept right on walking past Patricia and the cantor, heading toward Rabbi Weinstein's inner office, without so much as a hello.

"Excuse me, Risa, Mrs. Fleisher, um, let me buzz the Rabbi...."

Risa ignored her, opened the door to the Rabbi's inner office and entered. She slammed the door behind her.

Patricia could hear her crying and the Rabbi trying to calm her. Patricia and Cantor Max exchanged looks. The rumors of Risa Fleisher's impending divorce must be true. Still it seemed odd that she'd been with Rabbi Weinstein at Burger Bliss. More marriage counseling?

"Working at the temple can be rougher than you expect." Cantor Max smiled ruefully at Patricia and shrugged.

As if to confirm his statement, Carol burst in, waving a piece of paper in her right hand. She was gasping for breath. "I was going through the mail and this paper turned up in the pile. I don't know how I could've missed it. I think it's a note from Roberto."

Patricia and the cantor hurried to her side to read the unfolded paper, a white generic eight by eleven-inch sheet, cheap copy grade, with one short typed paragraph:

Dear Rabbi Zalman, please I need to talk with you about some papers I found in the trash. Please let me know when we could talk in private, maybe not at Temple. Sorry for the trouble. Thanks. Roberto.

Patricia grabbed the cantor's arm as he reached for the typed note. The paper might be evidence. Maybe there were fingerprints on the paper. She told Carol not to move or give the note to anyone and asked whether the temple had plastic baggies. Following Carol's instructions to look in the pantry, Patricia returned with several zip bags. Avoiding touching the note herself, she manipulated the paper into the plastic bag and zipped it closed.

The cantor looked ready to explode into a tune, not clear whether in celebration or lamentation. "We can't wait. We have to tell Rabbi Weinstein." Cantor Max strode to the door of the inner study, knocked forcefully, and chanted: "*Oi vey*, we got a note from Roberto today!"

Patricia winced. Over the top. The cantor was living up to his reputation for off key humor.

****

Rabbi Weinstein immediately contacted the police, who requested everyone remain at the temple, preferably in the lobby, not touching anything until Officer O'Donnell arrived. Even Adrienne, who arrived shortly after the note was found, had to stand in the lobby with the commoners.

Officer O'Donnell showed up within ten minutes. His imposing frame seemed out of place in the temple, with so many shortish women. He even made Rabbi Weinstein appear diminished in stature. Did congregants consider her to be Amazonian? At five feet seven inches, she was taller than many.

Patricia noticed the glint of Officer O'Donnell's shiny crucifix above the collar of his shirt, top button undone. In her youth, Patricia had worn her crucifix on a daily basis, to school, to church, and on dates, like a protective talisman. Now when she attended services, she usually put on the delicate gold Jewish star that Rabbi Deborah had given her as a present upon her conversion. Truth be told, Patricia had saved the rose-enameled cross, a tiny garnet at its center, that her mother had given her on her confirmation. She'd hidden it in the bottom drawer of her jewelry box. Nostalgia not so much for the Catholicism of her childhood as for the occasions her family was all together, often connected with religious observances like Christmas or Easter or christenings.

"I want to speak with each of you individually," announced Officer O'Donnell, interrupting Patricia's introspection. He seemed to be handling the investigation in a systematic and professional manner, the way she imagined her father would have. Officer

O'Donnell led Carol into Adrienne's office.

When it was Patricia's turn, Officer O'Donnell asked her to take the seat across from Adrienne's desk as he folded his broad frame into Adrienne's small desk chair. He told Patricia that he managed to elicit from Carol that the note had been in an unstamped envelope stuck in the middle of one of the paper piles on her desk.

"What I can't figure out is how long ago the note was delivered." Suddenly he leaned toward Patricia, both his hands flat on the desk, and continued in an annoyed tone. "When I pressed Carol for a chronology, she started crying, said she'd been meaning to go through the stack of mail where she found the note. Apparently, she'd been letting the stack pile up with what she considered junk mail. She said the note might have been sitting on her desk for a couple weeks. She wasn't sure. Can you shed any light on the situation?"

"No, sorry, I don't deal with incoming mail," Patricia apologized, both for her lack of knowledge and Carol's carelessness. "Carol's not exactly the most organized person and we've had a lot going on. She tries but..."

"Thank you for putting the note in a plastic bag. Carol told me it was your idea," Officer O'Donnell said. "Now, do you have any idea what papers Roberto was referring to in his note?"

"No, so sorry. I wish I did." Patricia was asking herself the same question. She debated mentioning her father's detective career but didn't want to open a personal tangent. Feeling inane, she commented, "All those police procedurals on TV help inform the public about how to treat a crime scene."

Officer O'Donnell snickered and then began what sounded like a well-practiced lecture. "The heavy doses of magical technology on TV crime dramas do not reflect reality. We usually can't rely on fingerprints to solve crimes. If prints are only partial or blurred, identification may be impossible. Even when the fingerprints are entered into the FBI's database, there's no foolproof formula for matching. There are as many as one-hundred-fifty ridge points in the average fingerprint to analyze for a potential match. It takes an expert at least a couple of hours to complete the ID process. Then the FBI usually provides a whole list of potential matches."

Patricia recalled her father complaining that he'd had to wait months for completion of the identification process, but she didn't want to waste time describing the old days to Officer O'Donnell.

Officer O'Donnell plowed on. "I was able to retrieve the envelope from Carol's wastebasket. Plain white business size. We'll examine the note and the envelope on the off chance there are unsmudged prints. I'm not optimistic."

"Had the envelope been sealed? Might there be DNA traces?"

"Smart idea. You know your crime shows. Unfortunately the envelope appeared never to have been sealed. We'll check it out though. DNA's rarely a slam dunk without an exact match to what's already in the system. But you can be my backup at the temple anytime. I didn't realize you worked here."

"I'm volunteering, trying to help out while the temple's shorthanded, with Rabbi Deborah missing and Roberto gone and the Rabbi's assistant out sick,"

Patricia responded eagerly. She couldn't help but be flattered by Kevin's compliment although it was based on a misapprehension of the source of her limited expertise. Relying on his positive view of her "assistance," she ventured a question about Roberto. "Is there any new information regarding Roberto Gomez's death? Has the medical examiner confirmed that it was a garbage truck that hit Roberto?"

"I guess word spreads fast around here. We're looking into the accident in greater depth. The insurance company has requested we investigate to determine whether his death could have been a suicide. In any event, we are trying to confirm no foul play was involved. Roberto's wife insists he never slept on the job. The fact that the toxicology report came back clean—no drugs, no alcohol—supports her position. We're taking a second look at the surveillance tapes of the parking lot. Carol confessed she was confused about whether she located all the tapes for the correct time and date. We're going to re-review notes from the accident reconstructionist who was on scene. It's tough to reconstruct exactly what happened. Could someone other than Carol show me again the route Roberto took to bring trash out to the dumpster?"

"I'm not sure, but Adrienne, the Executive Director, would know." Patricia silently scolded herself for not thinking of the possibility of tapes.

"I'll be speaking to her shortly. If you have a minute in the next few days, I'd like to pick your brain about what you recall from your last visit with Rabbi Zalman. I'll buy you a cup of coffee to make it worth your trouble."

Patricia hesitated. Was this strictly police business?

Officer O'Donnell sensed her reluctance. "If it's a problem I will set up an interview with you here at the temple, but I prefer not to do it on the premises. The best approach would be to retrace your steps at the canal."

Could this be a come on? Or was that wishful thinking on her part. Patricia reviewed her schedule: dinner tonight with Teresa, volunteering at the temple tomorrow morning. She wanted to do anything that might help find Rabbi Deborah. "Sure. I can be available tomorrow morning right after I drop my son off at preschool. I'll let the temple know I won't be in tomorrow."

"Meet me at the Swains Lock parking lot tomorrow morning at ten o'clock. I'll text my cell number just in case." He strode ahead of Patricia out of the office toward the lobby, his broad shoulders blocking her perspective.

Chapter Sixteen

Tuesday, June 2

Even though Patricia had to drive to Shady Grove Metro Station, park the car, catch a metro downtown, and walk to Teresa's hotel, she managed to arrive at the hotel bar before her perpetually late sister. In the humid night air, she could feel her underarms moisten with perspiration. She hoped her sweat wasn't staining the silk blouse she donned for her girls' night out. With cap sleeves and a circle collar, the demure, sea-green top was one of her favorites.

The bar, on the other hand, was freezing cold and dimly lit. She picked a quiet table in the corner and sunk into the plush chair. Thank goodness she brought a coordinating jade sweater which she draped over her shoulders in anticipation of a wait. Teresa always wanted everyone else to defer to her schedule. The behavior must make her feel important. Growing up as the middle child, Teresa had gotten less attention from their parents as well as from male admirers who were always chasing after gorgeous Jeanne. So Patricia was willing to cut Teresa some slack despite their often contentious relationship. On the other hand, Teresa had only herself to blame for her bad choices, *e.g.*, her unplanned pregnancy, her marriage.

Patricia was tempted to order hot coffee from the

young waitress but opted for a seltzer with lime. The coffee undoubtedly would not be freshly brewed. No Teresa in sight, she settled in her chair and meditated on the complicated dynamics among the three Reilly daughters. At five feet nine inches, her oldest sister Jeanne was the tallest. Her legs so long that the plaid skirt of her school uniform never hit the cold floor when the Sisters of Mercy made her take the genuflect test and kneel in the headmistress's office. And that was before Jeanne started rolling up her waistbands. Jeanne joked the nuns were so worried about proper dress, their order should be renamed the Sisters of the Lord & Lacys. She finished in public high school after being caught drinking one too many times with the boys from St. Stephens. Jeanne eventually married John, one of those St. Stephens boys who went to a local law school and now ran his own successful general practice firm. She and John had two teen-aged boys of their own at St. Stephens.

Teresa came along eighteen months after Jeanne. For better or worse, Teresa was Patricia's closest playmate growing up. Three years older than Patricia, Teresa had been way ahead in street smarts. She taught Patricia how to win at gin rummy and how to hide where no one could find her in Kick the Can. They created elaborate wedding scenarios for their Mindi dolls. During a pretend beauty salon appointment, Teresa swiped Patricia's Mindi and cut off her ponytail. Patricia cried to their mother to no avail. Teresa also cheated at Monopoly, but Patricia could never prove it. Eventually Teresa took to borrowing Patricia's clean blouses to avoid doing laundry.

But Teresa was the first to give advice about how

to deal with periods, *i.e.*, explaining the merits of pads versus tampons—yes, even unmarried women could use tampons. Teresa freely shared her experiences with boys and advised which kissing games were safe to play: Spin the Bottle was okay but Truth or Dare no way. She also demonstrated exactly how much beer or rum and coke could be drunk before losing control.

When Teresa got pregnant in college, she married the father, a neighborhood kid who enrolled in the police academy and eventually became a cop like Dad. With all the same problems. His hours too long. His drinking too much. His betting too risky. She was divorced by the time baby Frank was three years old. Once Frank was in elementary school, Teresa took up real estate in Back Bay, selling to the *nouveau* Irish aristocracy, two-income yuppie couples, and gay professionals—the only demographic who could afford to buy in that neighborhood.

When Patricia came along three years after Teresa, her parents were tired. Patricia was able to convince them to let her switch from Holy Child to a regional public academic high school. She had been the only daughter to pursue a professional career.

Jeanne was the only practicing Catholic among the Reilly sisters. Swinging single Teresa claimed her religion was "raised Catholic." Teresa complained she'd been discriminated against because no priest had hit on her. She raised her son Frank without any formal religious affiliation, unless you counted Anti-Catholic. Patricia was proud that she had been the true independent, not only not practicing Catholicism but adopting a new faith.

Glancing across the room, Patricia saw her sister

sashay into the bar. Teresa wore a deep blue suit tailored to flatter her fit figure and blow-dried brunette highlights. The straight skirt, slit five inches up the side, revealed her shapely calves. Teresa must be working out. Shod in indigo heels close to three inches high, Teresa sauntered over to Patricia. Several business-suited middle-aged men sitting at the bar followed Teresa's moves with their eyes. Patricia considered whether she would have attracted more notice if she dressed in stilettos and a tight skirt. Would she want the attention?

"Italian," pronounced Teresa in response to Patricia's admiring gaze. "Thanks, sis, for meeting me. It was a last-minute decision to come to the convention. I wasn't sure I could get away."

An Italian designer—that was beyond Patricia's fashion knowledge. "You look great," Patricia obligingly complimented.

"I bought it cheap at a samples sale, a real steal now that I can fit into a size ten. Not as skinny as the rest of you but skinny for me. Not bad for thirty-nine, never going on forty," Teresa proudly declared.

"How's the real estate biz?"

"Terrific." Tugging down the hips of her straight skirt, Teresa angled her recently toned backside into the chair. "Sorry I'm late. I had to take a call from a client who's putting an offer on a condo." She waved over the waitress and ordered a glass of chardonnay for each of them. "You wouldn't believe how hot the market has gotten in Beantown, what with the tech industry exploding and hospitals and universities expanding."

Patricia recalled the Boston of her youth as slower paced, not dominated by either technology or the health industry. "Thanks, sis. Contributing to my sobriety as usual. How's Mom?"

"Mom's doing okay. Jeanne helps with cooking and housekeeping."

"Thank God for Jeanne," Patricia exclaimed as the waitress set down their drinks.

"You aren't kidding," Teresa nodded vigorously, although not a hair of her sprayed coif budged. "She and John have the model Catholic marriage. The whole family goes to mass every week, and John hardly drinks. Let's have a toast to Jeanne, the role model we can never live up to!"

Patricia clinked her glass with Teresa's and asked what Teresa's son was up to.

"Frankie likes working at the computer store, but I don't think he has a future there. These millennials have it tough. In a couple months, he'll probably end up moving home so he can stream movies from my account. Good thing I didn't convert his bedroom into my home office yet. Why don't you guys come up this summer? You can visit family and I'll have a chance to see Danny. I don't have time to go out to your place in the burbs this trip. But if you drive up, I'll clear my schedule, and we can all hang out together at the beach."

Patricia said she'd been considering coming up to the Cape but hadn't had a chance to discuss the idea with Michael.

"So how is the Doc? And Danny? And the little Jewish mother?"

"Michael is as busy as ever, and Danny's great. He loves pre-school. My mother-in-law continues to be a pain in the butt."

"Yeah, I hear they always are. But I wasn't referring to Michael's mother. I mean you. How's the new Jewess doing?"

"Well, if it's a contest between communion wafers and matzah, I'll take matzah every time."

"Ha, ha. Me too. I always thought of communion as ritualized cannibalism—all that talk about ingesting the body and blood of Christ. Remember how we were supposed to let the wafer dissolve on our tongue, not chew it? Not that any priest would let me have a taste of wafer if I managed another marriage. Matzah's that dry crackly stuff that comes in a box, right?"

"Yes. We eat Matzah at Passover. The holiday commemorates the exodus from Egypt, when Jews could not wait for bread to rise before they fled."

"Yeah, I know Passover. Don't tell anyone but I went on J Date a couple of years ago. I met a nice Jewish guy, but it didn't work out. He decided he could only get serious about a Jewish girl—or at least his parents decided. So Ma tells me you're studying for this bar mitzvah thing. What exactly do you have to do?"

"I am. I meant to tell you. For girls, the ceremony is called bat mitzvah, "daughter of the commandment." Patricia proceeded to explain the adult bat mitzvah process. "But the big news at our temple is that Rabbi Deborah Zalman has gone missing. She was the one who helped me through my conversion, and she's leading the adult bat mitzvah class. At least she was before she disappeared."

"Wow, that's right up your alley. Remember when Mom kept losing her keys, and you'd be the one to find them dropped behind the sugar canister or under the clothesline. Do you think there was foul play? Or she met a guy and took off for Atlantic City?"

"Good questions. We've been trying to figure out where she is." Patricia didn't feel like going into detail. She wanted to relax and enjoy her night out with her swinging single sister. "What about you? Are you dating anyone?"

"Only casually. Remember that boy Joey I had a crush on in eighth grade? I was putting in confirmation hours at the rectory to help with the food drive. My confirmation number was forty-four and his was forty-three. I was wearing that ugly uniform—the knee-length navy plaid skirt, gray knee socks, and a blue-collared shirt. I rolled up my skirt to make it a mini like Jeanne used to do. We were kind of sluts in training." Teresa recrossed her legs and smoothed her skirt. "Then I spilled grape juice on my skirt to attract Joey's attention. That skirt wasn't protecting much of anything by that point. All Joey did was blush. I had to run to the girl's bathroom and try to wash out the stain. I ran into Joey at his dad's restaurant in Worcester. Carl's Clawhouse. Joey helps his dad manage the place. We've gone out a couple times but who knows."

Patricia sighed. "Sometimes I think a religion that tried so hard to instill chastity spurred us kids to be more interested in the opposite sex than we otherwise might have been. Remember how the Sisters warned us never to slow dance or at least keep enough room for the Holy Spirit between us and the boys."

They laughed. Patricia got a guilty kick out of dissing their conservative Catholic upbringing with Teresa. She felt compelled to elaborate. "Maybe if we'd spent more time concentrating on scripture instead of boy-chasing, we would have a greater appreciation for the religion. I'm sure there are plenty of respected Catholic theologians we could be reading up on to better understand the issues facing the Church."

"Hard to say." Teresa sounded uncharacteristically hesitant. "I have a hard time taking the whole confession thing seriously. Kneeling in a spooky confessional, tell all to the priest, then pay the penance, like a tax on any fun you had."

"Really—talk about extracting penance." Patricia winced. "Remember how we used to make up sins to tell the priest?"

"Eventually I had to get creative about what not to say. And how convincing is the Virgin Birth and the Immaculate Conception?"

"Mary's pregnancy isn't the only miraculous one in the Bible. All religions have their myths. Abraham's wife Sarah didn't give birth to their son Isaac until she was supposedly ninety," Patricia responded.

"By the way, did I mention our old alma mater, Holy Child, went bankrupt? Enrollment fell and the city of Randolph's taken over the building. The powers that be may convince investors to open an indoor multi-use mall with restaurants, a movie theatre, and condos."

"Sounds like progress. I brought my good camera. Let's ask the waitress to take our picture." Patricia eagerly pulled out her digital SLR and waved the waitress over who obligingly took a shot of the two sisters smiling harmoniously. Then Teresa ordered a bottle of pinot grigio. After the two had consumed nearly the entire bottle, Patricia managed to stop worrying.

It took the same amount of imbibing for Teresa to regress to adolescent older sis. "So isn't it about time for you guys to have a second kid? What's the holdup – Mikee having performance problems in bed?"

Reverting to her role of picked-on youngest sister, Patricia raised her chin and glared, ready for a fight. "Shut up, Teresa! Michael's fine in bed, great if you really want to know, not that you have any need to know."

"And you'd be comparing Michael to who now?"

"Jesus Mary and Joseph! You should talk, with your history of dysfunctional relationships," slurred Patricia. A picture of Kevin O'Donnell's tall figure and broad shoulders flashed through her mind. No no no, she chided herself and shook her head as if trying to dislodge the image.

"Uh oh, sis, you're bringing out the big guns. I don't want to be responsible for your lapsing back into the Church. I surrender. Anyways, you've hit the proverbial nail on the head. I haven't exactly had the greatest luck with men. Do you know any nice doctors you can fix me up with?"

"Seriously?"

"Yeah, I need a doc to support the lifestyle I want to become accustomed to. Back to my first question— are you going to have a second? I love being Danny's auntie."

"I'm pretty sure I'd like another child. Not politically correct to express but having a girl would be nice. I'm not sure I'm ready. Danny's about to start kindergarten, and caring for an infant would be a lot of work. Michael's busy, and I'm in the middle of bat mitzvah study." And trying to investigate the Rabbi's whereabouts and Roberto's accident, she added silently to herself. "But being an only child is lonely, and

Danny's going on five."

"Your hubby's a perfect example of why you should have a second. He's a bundle of only-child neuroses." Teresa laughed loudly.

"That's unfair," Patricia snapped, pushing her glass away and grabbing her sister's arm. Although a bit true, she conceded. "Michael's not a saint but he's a real mensch as they, I mean we, say. A good provider, an affectionate husband, and an involved father, even if he's not around enough."

"And he's a perfectionist, a picky eater, and a control freak with an overbearing mother. I'm surprised he hasn't called to ask when you're coming home."

"You only see Michael when he's with the whole family and has to fight to get a word in."

"You mean get in his take-out order for Chinese food? I'm kidding. Don't get all huffy. The three of us kids did have a good time growing up together."

"Except when you cheated at gin rummy, borrowed my clothes without asking, stole my diary and tried to blackmail me."

"At least I never stole your boyfriends."

"They were too young, too nice for you."

"And too neurotic…"

Chapter Seventeen

Wednesday, June 3

Officer O'Donnell was waiting for Patricia as she pulled into the Swain's Lock parking lot promptly at ten o'clock a.m. He did look handsome, leaning against his police cruiser. His short-sleeved navy shirt hugged his muscled biceps. Bronzed chest hair curled from the neck of his shirt. He was conversing with a bicyclist prepping a fancy road bike for a ride.

"Sorry, Officer, I didn't mean to delay you," Patricia said, trying to catch her breath as she hurried toward him. She had dressed more carefully than usual in black pants and a mint-green blouse instead of her usual jeans and T-shirt. Was it Teresa's influence?

He gave her a broad smile. "Please, call me Kevin. Thanks for meeting me here. As we discussed, it might be helpful if we walked through the events of Tuesday, May 19, the last time you saw Rabbi Zalman."

Patricia and Officer O'Donnell retraced the route that the three women had taken on their canoe outing. She and the officer walked the tow path as far as the women had paddled which turned out to be not very far at all, much to her chagrin. He peppered her with questions. Had Patricia seen anyone watching them? Was Rabbi Zalman romantically involved? Did she take drugs? Did she associate with anyone who had a reputation for violence? Had she received any threats of physical harm? As far as Patricia knew, the answer to his questions was no. But did she really know the Rabbi well enough to be able to answer with certainty?

"Rabbi Deborah gave a controversial Friday night sermon in support of interfaith marriage," she told him. "There was a demonstration at the temple the following Monday, the day before she disappeared.

"Oh yeah, we were called out for that fracas. Gotta control the religious kooks," Officer Kevin declared. "They nearly caused a riot. All over a sermon. Crazy."

"She did say people were angry with her. Including temple members. She never mentioned any threats of physical harm."

"You indicated you have no idea why Roberto's note said he wanted to talk to Rabbi Zalman? Or what papers he was referring to?"

"Correct. I do not know." Patricia did have a few speculations that she'd better keep to herself. Could Roberto have found a love note from Risa Fleisher to Rabbi Weinstein? Could the two of them actually be having an affair?

Patricia considered whether Rabbi Weinstein suspected he'd been found out by Roberto. Had he become sufficiently angry with Roberto to physically harm him? Dubious. She never observed him losing control of his temper. He had more efficient ways to deal with an off-the-reservation employee, like threatening to fire him.

"Did you hear Rabbi Zalman's sermon? Do you agree with her views on intermarriage?"

Whoa, this question was out of left field. Patricia

stopped walking and studied the officer. "Why do you ask?"

"Well, you don't exactly look like a Weiss," Kevin stammered.

"Since you asked, my husband is Jewish. So, yes, I heard the sermon. Yes, I agree with her position."

"I figured."

"Excuse me?"

"Sorry, I didn't mean to offend. It's just with your auburn hair and emerald eyes and Nor'easter accent, you look like a nice Catholic girl, maybe Boston?"

"You guessed it." Patricia started walking again, unsettled by the ease with which Kevin had managed to zero in on her origins. Of course he was a detective. She was fairly sure she knew the answer to her next question. "How about you?"

"Oh, I'm a good Catholic boy from Massachusetts myself. Seekonk, near the Rhode Island border."

"I know exactly where that is." Patricia's sister Jeanne had dated a fireman from Seekonk.

"My whole family lives up there. Two brothers in the family business. We own a couple of gas stations. They have a bunch of kids. I visit the nieces and nephews all the time. Stay with my parents. My mom cooks for me. She makes a great fish fry, corn beef and cabbage, and Brunswick stew. How about you?"

A mama's boy. An Irish mama's boy this time. Patricia smiled to herself. She must attract them before they realize she couldn't cook.

"What's so funny?"

"I was thinking of my mom, my two sisters," she said, stifling her laughter. "They still live in the Boston area. My dad was a police officer, a detective. My mom

Maria is Italian. Also an excellent cook. Her lasagna is to die for."

"So your dad was a cop. Funny coincidence. How'd your mom like being married to a cop?"

"It was tough on her. My dad worked long hours. He died of a heart attack after he retired." Patricia refrained from mentioning her father's gambling habit. "As a kid, I liked hearing about his investigations. He demonstrated his handcuffs on us, showed us how to search his jacket pockets. We used to play pretend pat-down and arrest."

"Did you learn how to pop door locks?"

"Hardly."

"So what brought you to the area?"

"We moved down here for my husband's medical practice. And you?"

"My wife. That is, my ex-wife. Actually, my almost ex. We're separated. She got a job down here as a teacher. It paid well, but she didn't like the D.C. scene, too competitive, too congested." Kevin raised his arm to swat a mosquito at the nape of his neck. "And she didn't like the hours cops keep or the salary. And I guess she didn't like me enough to stay. She moved back to her parents' house in Seekonk about a year ago."

So his separation must be how he justified not wearing a wedding ring. Debatable. "Had you known each other long?" Patricia asked as she watched his substantial bicep flex. Her nostrils filled with the scents of musk and vanilla—his deodorant?—and sweat. More exotic than Michael's soapy smell. She felt an odd tug of arousal, then shame. Was Kevin trying to trap her with a seductive pheromone? Was she projecting?

"That was part of the problem. We were high school sweethearts." Kevin continued in a resigned tone. "I was the football player. She was the cheerleader. I blame Hollywood. Life is one big romance."

Until the traits that attracted us in the first place become annoying, Patricia thought. Growing increasingly uncomfortable, she kept her opinions to herself. As they walked silently along the canal, she contemplated her sisters' marriages: Jeanne's traditional Catholic one, Teresa's unannulled marriage because of Frankie. Without that mystical Papal dispensation, Teresa couldn't remarry in the church, although she claimed she could care less.

Patricia wanted to believe her parents had forgiven her for marrying a Jew. She suspected her mother believed she should atone for her sin by raising Danny in the Catholic faith. Every Christmas and Easter, Maria gave Danny presents and told Santa Claus and Easter bunny stories. After Patricia converted to Judaism, her mother must have realized there was never going to be a baptism. Now Maria's big complaint was that her youngest grandson lived so far away, and she didn't see enough of him.

"Anything else you recall?"

Patricia shook her head as if to clear memory's cobwebs. "I wish I could remember more about that Tuesday. Nothing seemed out of the ordinary. Rabbi Deborah was enjoying the canal. We all were."

"Something might come back to you in the next few days. Don't look so worried." Kevin raised his hand and pointed. "Look at that bird on the canal."

"Oh, I see it. Beautiful. Is it a heron or a swan?"

"Could be. Have you heard the one about Leda and the Swan?" Kevin began to recite in a sonorous voice:
'A sudden blow: the great wings beating still
Above the staggering girl, her thighs caressed
By the dark webs, her nape caught in his bill,
He holds her helpless breast upon his breast.'
"That's all I remember."

"Yeats, I believe. Such a lovely poem, but violent." Patricia couldn't remember Michael ever reciting a poem to her. She felt herself flush, and wished she'd applied deodorant herself that morning.

"Yeah. My dad used to recite it to my mom."

Patricia was definitely detecting a flirty vibe. Time to refocus on Rabbi Deborah. "Have you been to Rabbi Deborah's house since Roberto's note?"

"As a matter of fact we rechecked her townhouse. No suspicious papers. We repeated the standard tests. No blood spatter. Took a stab at dusting for prints but she's not in the system for starters, and no matches turned up. As far as you or anyone else remembers, she was following her usual routines. No activity on her bank cards, which is unusual. Did she like wilderness hiking?"

Relief washed over Patricia at the good news about no blood. She did feel obligated to disclose to Kevin that Rabbi Deborah occasionally enjoyed spiritual retreats but didn't elaborate lest she discourage the search effort. Taking advantage of Kevin's sharing, or rather over-sharing, mood, Patricia asked if the police had uncovered any new information about Roberto's accident. "Did the surveillance tapes show anything?"

"I can't say too much. The surveillance camera didn't catch the back area of the lot where the garbage dumpster is located. The tapes showed two cars parked out in the front lot that night. One was Roberto's. We are in the process of determining the second car's owner. He or she may have been in or around the building and seen or heard something. Seems unusual for a car to be parked there so late. I am not at liberty to say more."

Combing her memory for other details of the accident, Patricia said, "Carol told me that Roberto had a scrap of paper with a train drawing in his pants pocket. Do you have any clue as to why?"

"Yep, Roberto was found with the paper. And nope, we have no clue as to why."

Did Kevin's curt response indicate his annoyance at her question? Or his reluctance to concede ignorance? Patricia might as well go ahead and suggest the theory she had come up with. "Did I mention that I tutored Roberto in English? It's just a thought, but perhaps he was practicing his reading skills with a book about trains, one that belonged to his kids? Did you locate anything like that?"

"Good idea about the book. Unfortunately the garbage truck had already picked up the trash before the body was found. So far, we've been unable to determine the source of the paper. But if you have any more insights, please let me know."

"Has there been confirmation that the garbage truck was involved in Roberto's death?"

"We've confirmed that Roberto's injuries were in all likelihood a result of vehicular impact. There's no forensic evidence that definitively links the garbage truck to Roberto's death. None of his clothing or blood or tissue was found on the truck. The techs are still studying the casts of the tire impressions from the lot. Unfortunately the ground was very muddy."

"I assume you talked to the driver of the truck?"

"Of course. He said he pulled into the temple lot and emptied the dumpster at approximately ten-thirty that Thursday night. He was running late because of the storm. It was raining hard, and visibility was poor. He said he did not see Gomez or anyone else in the parking lot."

"What happens next? How will you proceed?"

"We are going to survey local garages for cars brought in with damage consistent with hitting a body. Speaking of surveys, what's it like to be married to a Jewish guy? A friend said he met a nice Jewish girl on J- Date. I'm interested in meeting new people."

Kevin clearly wanted to move away from Roberto's crime scene and onto personal matters. Was he concerned he'd disclosed too much info? Had she trod on his professional boundaries? He was certainly treading on her personal boundaries. But if she wanted him as a police source, she needed to stay on good terms.

"Is there a chance you might get back together with your wife?" she asked. She did not object to divorce on principle, but she was not interested in aiding and abetting adultery. Too many people got badly hurt when spouses cheated. So what if the patriarchs had multiple consorts—she refused to accept or encourage that behavior.

"No way. My ex has no interest. I offered to try counseling, although I don't believe in that stuff. She refused."

"Too bad. But better to resolve issues in a marriage

earlier rather than later. Before children arrive." Patricia understood why his wife might not want to rejuvenate the marriage or add a child to the mix. She remembered her father's unexplained hours out of the house, and Teresa's ex as well. In her father's case she was pretty sure it was "only" gambling at the track.

"Definitely better to split up before kids. Speaking of kids, how are you raising your son? Does your husband want you to go to temple all the time?"

"I converted, and we are raising Danny in the Jewish faith." She left it at that. Kevin's simplistic view of a husband's role would be funny except for its serious repercussions in a marital relationship.

"Wow, you converted?" Kevin stopped walking and faced her. "That must have been scary. Did you have to get dunked? Shave your head?"

Patricia was appalled. "That's not the way it works," she replied stiffly. Thank goodness she hadn't elaborated on her family's religious challenges. Kevin seemed clueless.

"I'm kidding. Didn't mean to offend. I'm all in favor of having choices. Oo—big mosquito about to bite on your right. Don't move." A wide plane of palm shot out and brusquely brushed the insect off her arm, then hovered above her shoulder.

Patricia moved out from under the shadow of his hand and mumbled thanks. Despite the day's warmth, she shivered with goosebumps.

"Variety's the spice of life. I'd like to date a Jewish girl."

"Really?" Trying to regain her composure, Patricia lamely offered, "My friend Brenda is interested in meeting new people, too." She realized the idea of their dating was absurd, and she was skeptical of Kevin's blarney about meeting Jewish women. Even if he dated a nice Jewish girl, she doubted if he'd ever marry one.

"Brenda of coffee and doughnuts? I'm not sure she's my type."

Suddenly he grasped her shoulder, pulled her close. "Whoa—watch out for the geese shit!" His substantial jaw grazed her forehead, smooth, not bristly like Michael's.

Patricia's face flushed as she grabbed onto his arm to keep her balance. Kevin's bicep was granite hard.

As if to steady her, Kevin held on to her shoulder. Patricia pushed away—decisively. That six seconds of contact was at least three seconds longer than necessary for her to avoid the poop. "I'm sorry," she apologized. But to who? Kevin? Michael?

"I'm the one who should be apologizing. Excuse my French." To his credit, Kevin did appear embarrassed, taking his turn at burning the deep flush of Irish redheads. After a momentary loss for words, he continued with his quest. "What was I saying, oh yeah, I really would like to date a Jewish girl. You'd be perfect. Nice Catholic girl who's expanded her horizons. But I guess you're taken?"

This conversation was still headed in the wrong direction. "I assume you're joking," she replied coolly, trying to sound nonchalant. That she was married might provide an attractive challenge for these Irish boys who were commitment phobic. Corral those fillies into the fold. If she wasn't careful, she would be stepping into a big pile of poop and making a mess of her marriage. She checked her watch. With a combined sense of panic and relief, she realized time had gotten away from her.

"Oh dear, I have to run. I'm afraid I'm going to be late for preschool pick up."

"Then let's run!" Kevin took off ahead of her at a fast jog. She watched his long legs slide into action, his taut butt move in a smooth rhythm. She had to stop this train of thought. Beware what you wish for. Guilty, guilty, guilty again. She imagined holding her mother's pearl rosary: one hundred Hail Marys and twenty Our Fathers, smooth beads slipping through her sweaty fingers.

Chapter Eighteen

Thursday, June 4

Seated in the executive director's office, Patricia tried to pay attention to Adrienne's lecture about the temple's business accounts. Patricia couldn't stop obsessing over her goose poop epiphany the day before with Officer O'Donnell, or Kevin, or whatever she should call him. Had she encouraged his inappropriate behavior? Where was Rabbi Deborah? What had the surveillance tapes shown?

Adrienne, thankfully, seemed oblivious to her lack of focus. "Morris Mizchek, the temple's bookkeeper, needs our help. I swear he's going deaf and blind. The guy's at least in his seventies. He's been here for years and has no idea how to use the computer. We need to replace him, but no one will take me up on my recommendation. The board feels sorry for him. His wife died of cancer two years ago. No kids. The guy can barely see. He almost smashed up my new car the other day with his big gold convertible when he was searching for a parking space. Left a big scrape on my side door. I swear the State of Maryland needs to establish stricter driving requirements for the elderly. Make these *alte cockers* take a driving test to renew their licenses! *Alte cocker* – that means old guys."

"Thank you. I know that Hebrew expression."

"No, not Hebrew, dear. It's Yiddish slang, a much more colorful tongue. The national language of nowhere. But be careful how you use Yiddish and with whom. There are a number of words not for public utterance. For example *shmuck* is one to avoid and *shvartze*."

"I have heard those words."

Adrienne bulldozed on as if Patricia hadn't spoken. "Shmuck means penis in the literal sense, jerk figuratively. Shvartze means black, the color, but can be used to refer to a black person. Sometimes in a derogatory way. Or Negro or African American. I am not up on the latest politically correct terminology. We do have a few black congregants, converts I assume."

Stung by Adrienne's dismissal of converts and minorities, Patricia felt compelled to respond. "I hope they feel welcome in our congregation." She had the urge to quote the line from Exodus that Rabbi Deborah had cited, about not oppressing strangers because the Jews had been strangers in the land of Egypt.

"Of course they do. Why wouldn't they?" Adrienne's voice rose in volume as she leaned forward over her glass desk. She jabbed her finely-honed, scarlet-tipped index finger at Patricia. "Where was I—ah, yes, the executive committee directed us to update the temple's accounts. We need to put all the accounts on our computer system. That includes donations made to the temple over the last ten years. We have paper records. Letters from donors, typed lists of contributions to various temple funds. And we have documents in the safe. For example, stock certificates. Morris doesn't know how to do a spread sheet and refuses to learn. So I would like you to start a spread sheet in Microsoft Excel."

"I've never done a spread sheet," Patricia started to apologize.

"I'll show you how." Adrienne barreled on. "Enter each donation with a brief description including who it's from, the value, and the temple fund it was contributed to."

Adrienne pointed her saber of nail in the air toward an imaginary target. "I'll bring you the contents from the safe. Please inventory and enter the amount of any old stock certificates or bonds. We can run the total contributions to each fund over the ten-year period. Then the bookkeeper can tally the amount actually in the funds to see if the figures match up. Not that I trust Morris's ability to reconcile accounts. I doubt if the guy can still count. I don't know why we even keep that cubicle in the library reserved for him. We'll need to double-check the figures. Can you do this? It's complicated."

"I'll try my best." Patricia was impressed with Adrienne's computer expertise. Adrienne was certainly bossy, although Patricia didn't like to use the "b-tch" word to describe such women—too sexist. But Adrienne was definitely organized and computer literate. Patricia had done basic word processing, but dealing with temple accounts was more challenging volunteer work than she expected. Plus it was kind of exciting that Adrienne trusted her with the task.

"Our treasurer Jonathan Kripke is busy dealing with dues assessments, the capital plan, and this year's budget. He's a volunteer, too. With his law practice, he doesn't have time for tracking the nitty gritty details, especially the ancient history stuff. I'd ask our secretary, Carol, but we are so shorthanded with the Rabbi's assistant out and the business with Rabbi Zalman and the investigation going on into Roberto's death, although it was clearly an accident. I don't understand why the cops are pursuing it." Unlike her usual curt self, Adrienne was rambling. Patricia sensed she must be overwhelmed or nervous.

An hour later, Patricia sat studying the screen of the computer terminal that had been newly installed in Rabbi Weinstein's outer office with a list of funds and donations. Adrienne had also left a colorful pile of stock certificates from the safe, joking she kept the gold bricks and diamonds for herself. Not often that Adrienne cracked a joke. At least Patricia assumed it was a joke. Adrienne had set up the spread sheet to get Patricia started. She was grateful for the guidance.

Rabbi Weinstein was not in yet. On her way from the Ladies, Patricia noticed Adrienne exiting out the front door of the building. Now was the perfect time to enlist Carol's help to search Rabbi Deborah's study. Once again, it wasn't difficult to convince Carol to assist. Patricia suggested the two of them might notice something that the police had missed. After all, they knew the Rabbi so much better.

The first hurdle was finding the master key. "It's got to be here somewhere. I haven't had to use it for a while." Carol bumbled through her desk drawers, pulling out magazines, mini-chocolate bars, and wrinkled candy wrappers. "Aha, got it." She held up the key in victory.

The two scooted down the hall. Carol unlocked the study and switched on the light.

"Wow," Carol observed, "Rabbi Deborah has more piles of books and papers covering her desk than I do."

Patricia refrained from commenting that Rabbi Deborah's piles looked neater and more organized. Walking toward the bookshelves on the right, she began a systematic survey of the study. "Carol, why don't you start on the left side of the room."

"Sure thing." In her haste to move left, Carol's substantial hip brushed against the desk. A stack of what turned out to be extra syllabi for the bat mitzvah class hit the floor along with a copy of the late, great Nora Ephron's autobiography. Was that book going to be part of the curriculum?

Patricia and Carol hastily knelt down to pick up the mess. "While we're on our knees, let's check out what's down on this level," suggested Patricia. They peered under the desk and chairs and into the two wastebaskets. There was no evidence of recent human or animal habitation. Not even any dust balls. "Jorge's doing a good job."

The bookshelves held the expected volumes of Torah, Talmud, and other biblical commentary. An examination of Rabbi Deborah's desk drawers led to a few surprises: a Koran and an old copy of the King James Bible in the top drawer. Was the Rabbi studying comparative religion? The middle drawer contained brochures for tours of Israel and Jordan, maybe twenty of them. Rabbi Deborah must be seriously considering a trip. Stuck in between the brochures was literature from an organization opposing Israel's occupation of the West Bank. The bottom drawer was crammed with personal items: pantyhose, a blow dryer, tampons, high-heeled pumps, unopened cans of Diet Coke, and packages of chocolate covered candies.

"Yum, now I know where to go when I run out of chocolate," Carol joked.

"We should try restocking the Rabbi's desk with healthier snacks. Nuts, dried fruit, and protein bars. Carol, how about trying a substitute for chocolate?"

Carol rolled her eyes. "We better get out of here before the dragon queen gets back and starts breathing fire." Quickly straightening up the room, they agreed the search was their secret. Too bad they hadn't found anything to disclose Rabbi Deborah's whereabouts or to explain why Roberto wanted to meet with her.

As they returned to their desks, Patricia asked Carol if she had heard anything about the contents of the surveillance tapes. Carol said she was clueless.

Back in Rabbi Weinstein's study, Patricia had no choice but to confront her spread sheet assignment. As she stared at the computer screen, Patricia tried to recall the conversations she heard between Michael and his partner Richard and their office manager, Helene, about reconciling the medical practice's books. She could call and ask Michael or Helene, but she didn't want to bother him, and she sensed the office manager disliked her. The officious Helene always acted like Patricia was creating a disturbance when she called Michael. Helene probably wanted to marry a doctor herself or at least have her daughter marry one. Perhaps Helene thought it was a waste that Michael wed a skinny Catholic girl, taking a Jewish doctor out of the Tribe's gene pool. Patricia was thankful Helene was fiftyish and overweight. She heard too many stories about fortyish docs running off with their young secretaries or nurses.

She urged herself to concentrate. It was crazy that

Adrienne had given her this task. She knew nothing about balancing accounts or spread sheets. She perused the list of funds. Unbelievable, how many there were. The temple attempted to appeal to every possible interest in order to raise enough donations to support its activities. There was Rabbi Weinstein's Discretionary Fund, the Cantor's Choral Fund, the Religious School Fund, the Adult Education Fund, the Repair the World Fund, the Battered Women's Shelter Fund, the Torah Acquisition Fund, the Fine Arts Fund, the fund honoring the temple's founding rabbi, and funds in memory of almost every wealthy member who had died and left money to the temple. She perused the stacks in front of her and shook her head. Ugh.

Perhaps she could start with a listing of the old stock certificates that Adrienne had removed from the safe. The certificates were like artworks with their engravings and intricate borders. Adrienne had explained nowadays companies are loath to issue paper certificates. Almost everything was electronic to save time and money and for better tracking. Companies might still issue a paper certificate upon request and for a hefty fee. In the days before computers, email, and cell phones, companies had taken care with their paper stock certificates, imprinting them with elaborate designs. Some older certificates had become collector's items. Adrienne warned Patricia that she'd better treat the paper stock certificates with "utmost care" because they were like cash – "that's why the temple keeps them in the safe."

Patricia had never seen a paper stock certificate before. Her father had made a point of never buying stock. She remembered how much he hated those guys he called fat cats who made tons of money on Wall Street. When one of the neighborhood kids managed to snag a summer internship with a Boston investment company and walked down the street attired in a pin-striped three-piece suit, her father had mercilessly yelled out jokes about his slick princess outfit.

Her father hadn't owned a suit decent enough to be buried in. Patricia's mother had to plead with her and her sisters not to put him in one of his worn-out checkered double-breasted get-ups. She said she wouldn't be caught dead going out with him in one of those outfits. The girls ended up burying their father a nice gray suit that matched his hair so at least he could be "stylin" in the hereafter.

Patricia shuffled through the stack of multi-hued stock certificates. The industry names were prominently displayed and included computer firms, utilities, airlines, auto and train corporations, even the publisher for a men's magazine. The 1971 certificates from the men's magazine featured a barely clad woman labeled as the centerfold from that year. The picture would have made a great decoration for a bachelor's party.

"Ahem."

Patricia looked up, startled. Embarrassed, she turned over the certificate. "Oh Rabbi Weinstein I was uh about to start typing the list …."

"Ah, I see Adrienne has put you to work computerizing our records. Don't worry, I've seen all those certificates. Some are quite entertaining. We used to have some temple members who were real jokesters. That Mr. Krinsky thought it was a riot to donate stock from men's magazine publishers. Shows how times have changed. I'm just dropping off materials. I need to run an errand. Please tell anyone who calls, my wife, my son, I'll be back shortly."

Patricia assured the Rabbi she would transmit the message and resumed her study of the stock. The certificates for the train company, Union Central Railroad Trust, featured a detailed drawing of a powerful looking locomotive in several hues, red, blue and green. Very impressive.

She should suggest to Michael that they buy some stock for Danny. Danny adored that cartoon show about the British tank locomotive and friends. He would probably love the idea of owning a share in a train company. It would be a way to teach him about finances, a lesson she could've used. Michael could persuade his mother Lillian to contribute. She could certainly afford it. According to Michael, his parents had had plenty of investing experience. Michael's father had done well in the real estate market before it crashed, and his mother had stocks in a trust that should be Danny's someday.

But…better not to count chickens before they hatch and get back to the spreadsheet. She could list the stock name, but how much was each certificate worth? What was this number $.01 printed on the train trust certificate? Could that be the correct value?

And – wait a minute – the train trust certificate was imprinted with a drawing of a locomotive. Where else had she recently heard about a drawing of a train locomotive? Carol had said Bertilla told her that Roberto had a scrap of paper with a train drawing in his pocket. Kevin confirmed that Roberto was found with the train drawing in his pocket. Was the train drawing in Roberto's pocket similar to the train drawing on the trust certificate? Identical? Was this a wicked coincidence or did the train drawings originate from the same source? Patricia closed her eyes and pressed palms to forehead. Had a train trust certificate been discarded—because it was expired or damaged or replaced? Could Roberto have picked up a train trust certificate and pocketed it? From the trash? From a desk? Accidentally? On purpose?

Patricia opened her eyes. Her brain had not been flooded with insights. What she needed was physical evidence. She had to compare the locomotive drawing on the train trust certificate to Roberto's scrap of paper. Could she convince Kevin to allow her to inspect the scrap? She had to talk to him but not until she followed the trail of evidence, figured out the facts before casting aspersions. Until then, she'd keep the "coincidence" to herself. Even taking Brenda into her confidence was one person too many.

Now all she could do was to progress with her accounting project. If she tallied up the donations, she might be able to determine what, if anything, of value might be missing.

She examined a tech company certificate with a lovely, green-tinted picture of the world embossed on its face. But she had the same questions. What was the stock worth? Where was the value printed? Both Adrienne and Rabbi Weinstein were unavailable. Who to ask? She could make a copy of the certificate on the new high speed copy machine. Should she get permission from Adrienne first? Maybe she should leave Adrienne a voicemail message asking her to call. In the meantime, Patricia left the value column blank and typed in the stock name and the fund to which it had been donated. Most of the certificates seemed to have been directed to Rabbi Weinstein's Discretionary Fund, whatever that was used for.

Patricia wanted to demonstrate she could master this assignment, show she was a valuable temple member, convert or not. Yes, she was going to prove that times really had changed, that women could handle stocks, not just decorate them like the nearly nude girls on the men's magazine certificates.

The phone's buzzing interrupted her internal pep talk. Patricia grabbed the receiver. "No, Mrs. Weinstein, he's not in. He said he'd return soon. No, he didn't say where he was going. No, he didn't mention whether he was meeting you at an appointment with the Rockville Disabled Adults Division. I don't know why he isn't answering his cell phone. I'm so sorry. I will give him the message as soon as he's back." The connection abruptly clicked off.

Patricia recalled Lenore Weinstein's calm, composed Friday night greeting of *Shabbat Shalom*, Good Sabbath. Now her practiced warmth had been replaced by alternating demands and pleas that Patricia could not satisfy. Before she ended the call, Lenore had sounded as if she was trying very hard not to burst into tears.

Patricia massaged her forehead again. Lenore's anxiety about her husband's whereabouts echoed Patricia's mother's and sister's complaints about absent spouses. And what about absent rabbis? And tooting trains? A smiling locomotive cartoon flashed through her mind. A pain throbbed behind her eyes. She felt a migraine coming on. Maybe things haven't changed much after all.

Chapter Nineteen

Friday, June 5

Patricia perched on the edge of the stone bench in Cabin John Park, poised to jump up in case Danny needed help climbing the jungle gym. Towering oaks shaded the playground, making it bearable in the warm afternoon.

The playground was a perfect match for the skills of a going-on-five-year-old boy. After complaints from parents in the litigious Potomac community, the Park Service had removed all play equipment that was deemed dangerous, *i.e.*, challenging. Elementary school kids didn't come to the park anymore. Too boring. Danny enjoyed the playground and tried to do everything himself.

Patricia watched Danny crawl up the low plastic slide. She had tried to call Adrienne that morning only to be informed that Adrienne was gone for the weekend. Then she called the cell number that Kevin had texted her. Again no answer. Just as well since she had not yet framed how to broach the train drawings issue to Kevin.

Her immediate crisis was what to make for Sabbath dinner tonight. She could run to the market, buy and roast a chicken. Who knew what time Michael would arrive home on a busy Friday, last day of appointments before the weekend? Or she could drive to Finger Lickin' Chicken and pick up a prepared bird. So much easier, and at least as good as her cooking. Michael cared less about the Sabbath than the taste of the chicken. Better to do take-out. If she put the chicken on the good china from Michael's mother and threw away the containers, she might be able to pass it off as her own.

"Mommy, watch me go down the slide."

Patricia waved at Danny and another boy around his age who were taking turns on the slide. She dug her cell phone out of her tote and shot a picture, wishing she'd brought her good camera with the zoom lens for action shots. Her tote bag was already so heavy, she hadn't felt like *schlepping* the bigger camera. Hah, here she was *kvetching* in Yiddish. Maybe she'd start dreaming in Yiddish soon.

She and Michael were lucky that Danny was such a sweet child. She did want another child soon, especially because, at age thirty-six, her biological clock was ticking. According to her Catholic upbringing, she was supposed to be having more kids, not using birth control to prevent conception. Her mother Maria would enjoy another grandchild. From the beyond, she could hear her father's eager voice urging her to hurry up, it wasn't rocket science to have another kid, especially with a husband who was willing and able to support the family.

Plus Danny liked company, although sibling relationships were complicated. If the baby was a little sister, Danny might resent the new addition less. If the baby was a boy, Danny and his brother might initially compete. Hopefully they'd become buddies, wrestle, and pretend-play cops and robbers. She admonished herself. Girls play those games now too. If she raised a daughter, she would have to guard against inculcating the sexist traditions she'd been brought up with. All the kids played video games now too. Thank goodness Danny wasn't there yet.

As they were getting ready for bed last night, she and Michael had again had The Second Child discussion. Michael expressed his desire to have another child. Patricia made clear she would only agree to a second child if Michael promised to come home earlier and take more responsibility for childcare and household duties. Michael conceded that he was too involved with his medical practice and should be spending more time with her and Danny. As usual, he blamed his compulsive work ethic on his guilt-tripping parents who were overinvested in their only son. He recounted the pressure to follow in his doctor-father's footsteps and the gift of a real stethoscope his mother had given him on his bar mitzvah.

Patricia had heard it all before and couldn't agree more. But she refrained from catty comments. Instead she pressed him for a commitment to help with a variety of household duties even before they tried for a second child, including cleaning up from dinner, grocery shopping, and spending at least one weekend afternoon with Danny. Only if Michael fulfilled his commitment would she agree to stop birth control measures and try for a baby. She had been religious about taking her little yellow birth control pill every day, positioning it on her tongue as carefully as if it were a communion wafer.

As Michael tried to entice her into bed, she

admonished him that spending time with Danny meant he had to focus on his son and not multi-task, respond to emails, or take calls. The mention of calls suddenly reminded Michael that Adrienne had phoned several hours earlier when Patricia was reading bedtime stories to Danny. Adrienne said something about returning Patricia's call. Michael apologized sheepishly for forgetting and said he didn't want to prolong the conversation because Adrienne started to ask for advice about her husband's high blood pressure.

Emphasizing how important it was for her to get messages, Patricia announced she was putting a message pad right next to the landline to ensure Michael would write down who called and the number, and not in the illegible script he used for prescriptions. Michael's compliance would be another way to demonstrate his resolution to focus on the importance of their family.

"Mommy, Mommy. I'm going inside the tube tunnel and then to the big slide, the orange one."

Patricia pulled herself back to Potomac and raised her cell phone to take another photo of Danny. He did love the freedom to run around and challenge himself on the play equipment.

If Patricia and Michael were seriously considering adding a second child to the mix, maybe the family needed a vacation first, an outdoor one that Danny would enjoy. Another trip up to Cape Cod? The Irish Riviera, her father had called the Cape. They could hang with her family on the Dennisport beach. Her mom could babysit Danny, and Patricia and Michael might be able to sneak off to the Whale Watch for a night. The inn, a lovely old place near Nauset Beach, was where they had spent their first weekend together as an engaged couple.

She would ask her mom to teach her how to make peach pie and lasagna. That might sell Michael on another Cape vacation. Otherwise, he might not be so keen on the idea. Her sisters made fun of Michael. He was too picky about what he ate and too worried about Danny. Because of shark attacks reported at the Cape, he only allowed Danny to wade in the ocean surf. Michael lectured everyone on the dangers of sun exposure and insisted no beach time for his family before two o'clock p.m. None of this endeared him to the Reilly family.

The negative feelings extended to brothers-in-law and boyfriends. Last summer, the Reilly family had gathered at a Dennisport cottage that Patricia's mom had rented from a Randolph neighbor. The house was two blocks from the beach and had a wide deck out back. In the early evening Patricia and her sister Jeanne were helping their mom prepare dinner. Teresa ran out to buy wine. Danny was inside with Jeanne's boys who were trying to figure out which cable stations they could get on the TV and ignoring requests to set the table for dinner. The adult males were on the deck.

Teresa's boyfriend of last summer, Tom, was relaxing on the lounger in jeans and a wife beater undershirt, his sunburned biceps not quite outweighing his abundant belly. Yet another Irish American guy who'd been born and raised in Worcester, Mass, he drove one of those World War II style amphibious landing vehicles for Boston duck tours.

Michael had been dressed in a scrub top left over from his intern days and cargo shorts, the pricey brand he loved with numerous pockets. He was standing with Jeanne's lawyer-husband John whose crew-necked shirt was neatly tucked into khaki pants. John had taken charge of cooking steaks on the gas grill. All the men, including Michael, were drinking beer, a local lager, toast of Boston, and talking trash.

Tom asked Michael if he'd ever heard the joke about Jewish porno movies. "One minute of sex and six minutes of guilt. An old Irish joke. Ha ha."

Michael asked Tom if he'd heard the obits were the Irish sports page and advised, "If you keep drinking and adding to that gut of yours, you're going to be on that page soon."

Tom scowled and addressed John. "Do you know the difference between a porcupine and a limo full of lawyers? The porcupine has its pricks on the outside and the limo has 'em inside." John turned his back to Tom and fired up the grill ever higher.

Michael checked out the steak. "Aren't you charring the meat? The char is a carcinogen. Not what you want to eat too much of."

John had looked annoyed. "I like my steak seared on the outside and raw on the inside. That's how Jeanne likes it, too."

Patricia, running in and out of the screen door to serve hors d'oeuvres of bluefish dip and crackers, had heard enough. "Do you gentlemen need the kids out here to control your language?"

Another cry of "Mommy, Mommy, watch me," brought Patricia out of her reverie. After snapping a few more shots, she saw the text message icon alight. She took one more photo and opened the text:

—*Having great time in the Promised Land.*

Spreading bliss and happiness. Assume you got my message. I missed meeting with Bertilla. Can you talk to her. More later. Hugs. Rabbi D—

Patricia's hands started to tremble. She shivered, suddenly cold all over despite the afternoon heat. She looked up to check on Danny. Tears of relief sprang to her eyes. She blotted her cheek with the crook of her elbow before Danny could notice. She punched in Brenda's number.

Brenda answered immediately. "Have a ball with Brenda's Beautifully Yours."

"It's me. You aren't going to believe this. Rabbi Deborah just sent this weird text." Patricia summarized the message.

"Bliss spreading in the Promised Land? Is she in Israel? Did she want to get away? Why didn't she tell us? What message?" Brenda was whispering in an uncharacteristically low voice.

"I have no idea. Does she realize the police are investigating her disappearance? Should we tell Rabbi Weinstein and everyone that she's on a trip? Brenda, I can barely hear you. Is someone with you?"

"Nah. I guess I don't need to whisper. What if Rabbi D didn't write the text?"

"Good point. Could someone be impersonating her? What if she's injured or worse?" Patricia stopped and gulped air. Feeling faint, she put her hand to her forehead.

"Yeah, although she mentions Bertilla. I can hear you're hyperventilating. Don't panic. The *yenta* patrol's gonna sleuth this under control."

"I'll text her back. See if she'll confirm her location and what's going on."

"Let's meet and brainstorm. Keep this to ourselves for a day. When can you get away?"

"Not before tomorrow. Danny and I are in the park, and then we have to pick up Shabbat dinner. Michael takes Danny to soccer on Saturday morning while I go to the market."

"Drive to the market. I'll swing by and pick you up in the parking lot. We can grab a bite at Corky and Benny's. It's the only decent deli around. My car knows the route by heart."

Chapter Twenty

Saturday, June 6

Patricia and Brenda sat at a chipped laminate table in a corner booth at Corky & Benny's. The deli didn't exactly offer gracious dining. The aroma of overheated meat and sweaty men emanated from the kitchen. The ill-lit dining room was packed.

Patricia surveyed the scene. "Management must keep the lights low so customers won't notice the grease splatter on the walls."

They'd requested a quiet booth. They had not, however, requested the worn-weary waitress who hovered over them. The ancient server seemed to be graying along with her nondescript uniform. She hunched over and jabbed a pencil against her pad, impatient for their order.

Brenda scrupulously examined the large rectangle of plastic menu. "Hmm, the blintzes look good, but it's been a long time since I've had a Reuben sandwich." The waitress started to walk away.

Patricia spoke up. "I'll have a plain bagel with the cream cheese on the side." She smiled at the waitress and tried to communicate support. Standing for hours on a hard floor was not easy. "Do you have espresso?"

The waitress stared at her without responding, as if Patricia had spoken gibberish.

"Never mind, I'll have a cup of regular," Patricia demurred. "Black. And a glass of ice water and utensils. Thanks. Brenda?"

"That's all you're ordering? Not very adventurous."

"Deli food's not my thing. Too greasy. Not that I'm a fan of Irish cuisine—boiled, bland, boring as my Italian mother used to say."

"Don't listen then. God forbid, you might gain a few pounds." Brenda stared up at the waitress. "I'll have the Reuben but with pastrami instead of corned beef, and extra Swiss cheese and Russian dressing. Could you please bring hot mustard?" She pointed at the menu. "And a chocolate egg cream. I might order more later."

The waitress scowled at Brenda and moved to the neighboring table without putting in their order.

"I'm glad to see this deli has authentically rude service," Brenda quipped.

"Is it odd there's a menu section entitled Jewish specialties?" Patricia puzzled. "I thought the whole idea of a deli was Jewish dishes."

"Yeah, that used to be true. Corky's has expanded the menu since I was here last. Paninis, chorizo, breakfast quesadillas. Didn't used to have those exotic items. I hear a Dominican family bought out the deli's original owner."

"I noticed lox and nova on the menu," Patricia commented. "What's the difference?"

"Lox is for working class Jews. Very salty. Nova is also smoked salmon, but more expensive with a subtler flavor—for Jews who made it to professional school. Sable is even pricier and smoother, like the fur. For

Joyce Sanderly

those who inherited family money."

"And what are kishkes?"

"If you have to ask, you don't want to know. Jewish soul food. Kishkes are stuffed cow intestine filled with liver, bits of unidentified meat, and flour. Add onion, garlic, and paprika. Mix it all up with *shmaltz* and whatever odds and ends can be scraped together. Delicious." Brenda licked her lips, smearing the edges of her coral-colored mouth.

"Your lipstick matches the lox," Patricia joked.

"Ha, I'll tell the cosmetic company to name the color Loxa Love."

"And *shmaltz*? That's like shortening, right?"

"Chicken fat. You can buy it in the store. Boy, this place is packed. Reminds me of my New Jersey childhood in West Orange. My dad sold furniture six days a week in Trenton. Then every Sunday, my dad and I went to the neighborhood deli to pick up lox, corned beef, and warm rye bread sliced while we waited. We brought the goodies over to my *bubbe's* apartment and feasted on the *forshpeiz*, the appetizers."

"Remind me, where was your grandmother from?"

"My *bubbe* made it over from Poland before the war. She and my dad talked in Yiddish. I sort of understand the language but can't speak it except for a few words here and there. I was as tall as *Bubbe* and almost as wide by the age of seven. After she died, we started celebrating any Western holiday involving food: Christmas with all the trimmings including ham and Easter with chocolate bunnies. You can see why I have food issues. My family's religion was really Foodish. Speaking of family, did you have a problem getting out of the house?"

Patricia shook her head. "I actually told Michael I was meeting you for lunch, that you were having a personal crisis on the anniversary of your divorce. I promised him I would bring home take-out. Michael and I had our own little crisis the other weekend when I didn't make it to the market while he and Danny went to a soccer game. I didn't want a repeat so I decided I'd better be honest in case we ran late."

"Thank you for remembering my anniversary. It's been eight years since my divorce was final. The divorce was really cause for celebration. The worst thing about the whole process was having to admit to my mother she'd been right. My ex was not the man of my dreams."

When their waitress reappeared at the table and slapped down plates and drinks, Brenda requested a basket of rolls. The waitress informed her there would be a two-dollar charge, because she hadn't ordered an entrée.

"That's ridiculous. Tell Corky or whoever's in charge."

Patricia raised her cup and sipped the black coffee. Cold and bitter. She considered asking for a fresh cup but it wasn't worth the trouble. "So Rabbi Deborah has not responded to my texts. Maybe she's in the mountains? Mount Carmel? No cell service?"

"It's possible. Or the text isn't legit."

"If we tell Kevin, I mean Officer O'Donnell, about her text, the cops may stop investigating her disappearance."

"True. I don't see the cops devoting much effort to her disappearance anyways. Your buddy Kevin doesn't even believe a crime's been committed."

"I'm not sure what he believes." In more ways than one, Patricia thought to herself. "It's odd Rabbi Deborah didn't notify Rabbi Weinstein. Did she not want him to know?"

"Or maybe she tried and there was a glitch. Look, her text implies she sent you a message and you didn't get it."

"What should we do?" Patricia's forehead creased with tension, and she massaged her temples. "Please not a migraine. King Solomon I'm not. Should we wait a few days and hope she returns or sends another message? God, I pray she's not in danger."

"I second that. Buys us some time so we can talk to Bertilla."

"Right. I'll try to arrange a meeting. I can ask her if Roberto was threatened by anyone, like those soccer competitors Jorge mentioned."

"Yeah, and we can ask her if she knows why Roberto wanted to meet with Rabbi Deborah. Maybe Bertilla knows what papers he found. He could've discovered a love note and confided to Bertilla that Rabbi Weinstein was having an affair with his favorite Burger Bliss dining companion."

Found papers, papers—the scrap of train drawing in Roberto's pocket, the railroad trust stock certificate. Patricia didn't want to exclude Brenda, but she hesitated to bring up her theory about a possible connection. It was so far-fetched and speculative at this point. And complicated to explain.

"Can I come to the meeting? Who knows, maybe Roberto found a copy of a memo from Adrienne to Rabbi Weinstein trying to convince him to dump Rabbi Deborah because of the demonstration. Adrienne never liked her. She was a threat to Adrienne's autocracy over the bureaucracy."

"I didn't realize you were a conspiracy theorist," Patricia joked. She could apply that label to herself. "I'll ask. I hope Bertilla agrees to talk with us. Do you think she realizes I was the one tutoring Roberto? I'm worried she'll feel intimidated by us. We have to be careful not to upset her or step on the cops' toes."

"We'll question her with kid gloves." Brenda held up her closed fist and Patricia raised hers to meet it. They bumped fists in a solemn pact.

"To the *Yenta* Patrol," they chanted together.

Patricia stood up. "I'm going to order Michael's takeout."

She walked to the deli's long counter covered by stacks of bagels and seeded rye. The counter crowned a glass case filled with pop-eyed whitefish, chopped liver, and vats of greasy chicken soup afloat with matzo balls. Marbled hunks of corned beef, pastrami, and brisket waited to be sliced by grizzled men aproned in blood.

A diminutive older lady in an olive sweater approached the counter and studied its contents as if about to make a major investment. She pointed at the vat of soup with her cane and asked for a quart. She hemmed and hawed about adding a pound of brisket to her order, interrogating the deli man as to whether the meat would be too tough to chew with her dentures.

A couple, at least in their mid-eighties, lined up next. They were dressed in matching outfits, he in checkered pants and she in a plaid skirt. Both looked well-fed and annoyed at the delay. "We need to eat to keep up our blood sugar," Checkered Pants announced, then faced Patricia. "No cutting in line, young lady. Don't take advantage of seniors."

When the old man was done barking, Patricia apologetically explained she was simply admiring the abundance.

A raspy male voice from behind Checkered Pants yelled out, "Syd, leave her alone. We need more pretty young faces around here. See how thin she is, she's the one who needs to eat."

Patricia turned to see who her rescuer was. A short elderly gentleman had squeezed in behind the matching couple. His face was shadowed by dark glasses and a tweed fedora. The hefty figures of Checkered Pants and companion blocked Patricia's view.

Her rescuer continued his disembodied admonition: "Don't pay any attention to Syd. He's crabby because he lost a couple bucks when we played pinochle last night. Go ahead and buy a nosh, don't just window shop."

Patricia smiled and called out thanks to her rescuer. Not wanting to attract any more attention, she hurried to the table and shrugged at Brenda in frustration. "Too many old people buying deli. I'll wait a minute. I see you got your basket of rolls."

Patricia's cell rang. "Michael? Yes, we're at the deli. Yes, I'm about to order the takeout. Yes, a pound of Nova, half a pound of sliced turkey breast, half a dozen whole wheat bagels if they have them. Bye."

"Hah. I thought you'd asserted your independence when you informed Michael we were meeting here. I bet your hubby had a plan all along. You can take the doctor out of the deli, but you can never take the deli out of the doc. Bring him a Reuben sandwich and a slice of cheesecake. He'll inhale it."

"He'll blame me when his cholesterol shoots up."

"You can't win. You shoulda married a nice Catholic guy. He wouldn't have guilt-tripped you all the time."

"I don't know about that." Patricia explained her theory about the difference between Catholics and Jews when it came to guilt: how Catholics feel good about feeling guilty because that's how they are supposed to feel but Jews feel guilty about feeling guilty because they know they must have done something wrong at some point in the past. "The Jews may have invented guilt, but the Catholics perfected it."

Brenda snorted. "So the Jewish mother gives her son two neckties for his birthday. She invites him over to dinner, and he shows up wearing one of the ties. "What's a matter?" she asks him. "You didn't like the other one?"

"You could be describing Michael's mother."

Patricia was glad they could kid around. It was a relief knowing Rabbi Deborah appeared to be safe, at least for the time being, at least that's what she wanted to believe. She prayed the Rabbi texted again soon. "I guess I can't win this one either. We'd better ask for the check. I'll order Michael's takeout on the way out."

"Let me gather my spoils." Brenda opened her purse, pulled out a plastic bag, and dumped in the remaining rolls. She raised her hands as if to ward off criticism. "We paid for these rolls. And didn't we read about Ruth scavenging for leftovers in a field? The restaurant's not supposed to re-serve the rolls. Waste not want not. Isn't that one of the Torah's six hundred commandments?"

Chapter Twenty-One

Tuesday, June 9

Patricia was second in line for Danny's preschool drop-off in an effort to arrive at temple as early as possible. When she pulled into the lot, she noticed Rabbi Weinstein's older black sedan and Adrienne's newer silver coupe already parked in their reserved spots. Patricia sighed with relief. She could get answers to her stock certificate questions. And she could ferret out why Adrienne had gone to the trouble of calling her at home last Thursday night. Then she'd have a couple hours to concentrate on her accounting project and make progress toward resolving discrepancies, even those she might not want to discover.

She also needed to contact Bertilla to set up a meeting to ask if she knew whether Roberto was threatened by anyone or why he wanted to meet with Rabbi Deborah or what papers he found. And Patricia had neglected the assignment for the next bat mitzvah class. Although she'd planned to do it over the weekend, Michael had proposed they spend Sunday at the art museum's annual kite festival on the mall. It had been a glorious June day with a stiff breeze and not much humidity. Michael and Danny had made a special trip to Toy Palace and bought a red diamond-shaped kite with a long tail. Danny loved helping Michael fly the kite. They had a wonderful afternoon. Michael was growing into fatherhood. Maybe he meant what he said about making more time for family.

As Patricia entered the temple lobby, the full force of Rabbi Deborah's absence hit her again. Should she notify Rabbi Weinstein or Officer O'Donnell about the text message? She'd received no further communication from Rabbi Deborah. If the rabbi suffered a terrible injury or worse, Patricia would have only herself to blame.

She collapsed into the chair in front of her desk. Patricia was indebted to Rabbi Deborah who had supported her through the conversion process, and shown her the beauty of the Jewish religion, its encouragement of debate, and its acceptance of life's uncertainties.

Patricia fondly recalled her conversion ceremony last year, both the temple service and her visit to the mikvah, the ritual bath. Rabbi Deborah had encouraged her to try a dip in the purifying waters of the mikvah, even though the ritual was optional for Reform conversion. The day before the conversion ceremony, Rabbi Deborah had accompanied her to the mikvah at a nearby Orthodox synagogue where Patricia descended seven steps into a windowless enclosure tiled in a sea of blue. Under the guidance of an elderly matron, she bared her nakedness and took the plunge into the mikvah's warm crystal waters. She immediately felt her worries release. She floated peacefully in the shallow pool, buoyed by a mysterious presence, perhaps a divine spirit? Afterward she resonated with a quiet energy and sense of purpose.

The mikvah had been a sanctuary, and the world

outside hardly seemed to exist. If only Patricia could immerse herself in the calming waters of the mikvah now.

For the moment all she could do was enter the temple's brick and mortar sanctuary. When she had a chance, she would meditate before the luminous stained-glass windows and pray for guidance as to what to do about Rabbi Deborah's message, and about Roberto. While she was at it, she might as well ask God's forgiveness for being tempted by a good-looking Irish cop who'd probably turn out to be a jerk as a husband. Rabbi Deborah had told her the now discredited Sotah story. In ancient times, a woman suspected by her husband of adultery or otherwise straying, was forced to drink bitter waters, a potion of water, dust, and ink dissolved from a parchment scroll inscribed with an oath of faithfulness. If the woman sickened from drinking the mixture, she was guilty of adultery and was cast out by her husband and society. Thankfully, the sages had abolished the Sotah ritual.

How could she, a devoted wife and mother of an almost five-year-old, fantasize about a romance with a man other than her husband? Did the tendency run in the family? She suspected Teresa had been involved with another man during her short-lived marriage. From what Teresa said the other week at the hotel, she was playing the field.

So why not fix her sister up with Kevin? And why hadn't it occurred to Patricia sooner? True they lived in different cities, and Teresa was a few years older. But Kevin could use a more mature woman of independent means. Plus, they each had their Catholic upbringing in common.

Rabbi Weinstein's low bass interrupted Patricia's internal debate about playing cupid. Through the closed study door, Patricia could hear a heated telephone conversation but couldn't understand the words. She powered on her computer and pulled up the listing she had started of the donated stock certificates. Time to visit Adrienne.

As Patricia knocked on the half open office door, Adrienne slowly lowered the Wall Street Journal she'd been reading. "Enter. We've been playing phone tag. I was about to go find you. I didn't realize you finally arrived."

Choosing to ignore the implied insult of tardiness—after all she was only a volunteer, Patricia began asking her questions about how to value the stock certificates. She wasn't going to let Adrienne's pettiness derail her.

Adrienne scratched her head, mussing her coif with an unusually flustered tousle. "Yes, yes," she acknowledged, "I did ask you to assign a value to the certificates. The face value marked on the certificate, that's the par value, does not reflect current market value. That's what we need for the listing. I usually rely on my broker for that information. I'd say call Morris but given his half senile state, why don't you try Jonas Schwabstein, the broker who handles the temple's investments. He deals with sales of stocks donated to the temple. Occasionally the temple has extra funds, and Schwabstein finds the best way to invest the money and maximize the profit. I'll give you his number but first talk to Rabbi Weinstein. I hate to have you disturb him, but he and Morris have spent more time reviewing the certificates than anyone else. They seemed to get a kick out of looking at all those pictures. I'll get the stack out of the safe for you again. Hope they're there. Just kidding."

Was she really joking about the whereabouts of the certificates? Patricia pondered. Adrienne must have heard about Roberto holding the train drawing. Did she know why? Patricia refrained from raising the issue until she could compare the train drawings. She returned to her desk. She'd call Kevin after she talked with Rabbi Weinstein.

Hearing no sound of conversation, Patricia knocked lightly on the Rabbi's study door, now half open. "Excuse me, Rabbi. I had a few questions about the temple's donated stocks."

"I'm so glad you're volunteering," he said. "I'm expecting a congregant for an appointment. Can this wait?"

"One quick question. Adrienne asked me to describe this railway trust stock for the computerized listing, and I don't know how to determine the value. I have the same problem with the other stock certificates. Adrienne suggested I talk with you before calling the temple's broker."

Rabbi Weinstein's ruddy complexion paled. He rubbed a hand over his silvery pompadour. "I can't quite remember exactly how the temple handled the donated stocks. Why don't I check with our bookkeeper. Morris isn't here today but he'll know. One of us will get back to you."

"Thanks. Do you have Bertilla Gomez's contact information? I was going to see how she was doing."

"What a nice idea. I must have it here somewhere." The Rabbi pulled open a desk drawer. The scent of roses filled the office. "Ah, here's my appointment."

Risa Fleischer brushed past Patricia. She looked unhappy, despite her meticulously made-up face and the crimson silk scarf tied elegantly around her neck. The Rabbi ushered her into a chair then showed Patricia out and closed the door.

Patricia bit her lip to keep from saying damn in frustration. No swearing in the temple. Carol must have Bertilla's contact information. She'd check. From inside the Rabbi's study, she heard Risa crying and imagined black mascara running down her bronzed cheeks.

A rush of footsteps made Patricia spin around. The Rabbi's wife, Lenore, marched into the office. "Where is she, where is my sister? I followed her car here. I smell that awful perfume of hers. She's in the study with him, isn't she?"

Before Patricia could answer, Lenore pushed open the study door, then stopped in her tracks and grabbed the door jamb. Patricia peered around Lenore. The Rabbi had pulled his chair next to Risa and had his arm around her, unclear whether to comfort or embrace her. Whatever was intended was too much for Lenore. Her sobbing accusations pierced the air like an injured animal.

Rabbi Weinstein rapidly dropped his arm, pushed back his chair, and stood. Patricia could see his forehead crease with deep furrows as if carved by a spurned wife's knife. Risa, eyes scrunched shut and revealing a fan of wrinkles, slumped in her chair.

"You always thought she was more attractive. You married me because I was older and more available." Lenore's sobs increased in pitch, finally morphing into a desperate wail sounding like a cat in heat. "Sure, she looks good. She doesn't have an autistic man-child to deal with. You know she's had work done. A little lift here, a lot of liposuction there." Lenore pointed to her sister's curvy thighs. "So are you sleeping together?"

"Lenore, let's not have this discussion here."

"Where then? You're never home. When you're home, you're too tired. You don't show up for meetings about your son, Ethan. Did you tell her how much money we've spent on his care? I want to know what's going on, now."

"Lenore, let's talk about this like civilized people. I have apologized for forgetting to put that one meeting in my calendar." The Rabbi reached out his hands as if in supplication and took a step forward toward Lenore. "Your sister's going through a difficult time with her marriage and needs counseling."

"Civilized? You should talk about civilized," Lenore spat. "You hypocrite. You're civilized like a cave man. If you could, you'd have a harem like those Muslim sheiks you're so critical of. Of course all that screwing around would probably give you a heart attack. Did he tell you, Risa, he has heart problems? You're getting a prime specimen, Risa. You can have him."

Heart problems? Patricia wavered, unsure whether she should intervene between the Rabbi and his wife. Before she could make a move, she watched in shock as Lenore yanked off her gold wedding band and threw it at the Rabbi. Lenore ran out of the office, and the Rabbi raced after her. Risa was left sitting by herself in the study. Tears and mascara trickled silently down her cheeks.

Patricia ran into the inner office. She bent down over the floor where she guessed the ring had landed. Quickly locating the golden gleam, she retrieved the ring for safe keeping. She turned toward Risa, abandoned in her seat and now snuffling loudly. "Would you like coffee, Rachel? Oh, I mean Risa. Excuse me." Freudian slip, Patricia chided herself. Too much Torah study about sisters Rachel and Leah. Rabbi Deborah had said how stressed Rabbi Weinstein seemed. Maybe it wasn't only his autistic son and Roberto's death. Now his marriage was blowing up.

"Excuse me," Risa struggled through her tears. "I'll take that coffee you offered. Decaf if you have it with cream and sugar."

"Let me check the pantry to see what's brewing. We should have milk in the fridge." Patricia felt sorry for Risa, regardless of what was going on with Rabbi Weinstein. Sharing was hard, especially sharing a man. Was Rabbi Weinstein like Jacob? Was he deceiving his wife and having an affair with Risa? Was Lenore his Leah – the woman who raised his children and Risa his Rachel – the woman who captured his heart? And not a very strong heart at that, according to Lenore. Had Roberto or Rabbi Deborah suspected an affair?

As she rummaged around in the pantry's fridge looking for cream, Patricia worried where they were all heading. As the Catholics and Jews both preached, just as he or she deceives, so shall he or she be deceived? And where should Patricia put this ring?

Chapter Twenty-Two

Wednesday, June 10

The next day, Patricia could only pray the morning would be calmer than yesterday. Rabbi Weinstein had yet to arrive. He undoubtedly had more on his mind than talking to the bookkeeper about Patricia's project. Adrienne had given her the number of the temple's broker, Mr. Schwabstein, after Patricia explained that the Rabbi said he couldn't remember how the temple handled the donated stock. Patricia then gave Lenore's ring to Adrienne for safekeeping and called Kevin but had to leave a message.

Carol had given her Bertilla's contact info, and Patricia had called last night. Thank goodness Bertilla had agreed to meet with her and Brenda. Bertilla wanted to meet on her lunch hour on Thursday. Patricia apologized that she would have Danny with her. Bertilla said she didn't mind. Patricia suggested they meet in Cabin John Park so Danny would be occupied. Plus the park was convenient to the assisted living facility where Bertilla worked.

After taking a long sip of her skim grande latte, Patricia called the broker. Mr. Schwabstein answered but insisted on calling Adrienne to confirm Patricia's identity. He apologized but said "you can't be too careful these days."

When he called back, he put Patricia on hold for close to ten minutes while he looked through his files. Returning on the line, he sounded puzzled. "Those stock certificates you're asking about were sold or cashed out approximately five months ago.

"Even the Union Central Railroad Trust shares?"

"Yes. Perhaps there's a mistake. You have to speak with Morris, the bookkeeper. He's the one who's been keeping closest track of the temple's stocks."

Unbelievable—everyone shucking responsibility for the stock and shooing her to the mysterious Morris who was nowhere to be found. After getting his number from Adrienne, Patricia called Morris repeatedly but kept getting his voicemail. He must be a solo practitioner. For the time being, she'd continue to type her computerized listing of donations.

Despite the wide range of temple funds, most of the donations, especially the stocks, seemed to have been placed in Rabbi Weinstein's Discretionary Fund. Letters had apparently accompanied some, but not all, of the donations. She was having a hard time matching letters to donations, because the letters were kept in a manila folder and filed separately from the donations.

Given the amount of donations, the Rabbi's Discretionary Fund seemed low. She supposed some of the donations in check form might have been cashed out over the years, and the monies used for various purposes. Were there limits on how the fund's resources could be used? She'd have to ask Adrienne or Morris. Perhaps the Discretionary Fund's low balance reflected careless accounting, which would only serve to confirm Adrienne's low opinion of Morris.

As she sorted through documents, Patricia kept

replaying yesterday's confrontation between Lenore and Risa through her mind. She'd called Brenda yesterday afternoon to recount the drama. The fight was hardly a secret, more like a scene from a Greek tragedy or a soap opera. Carol, Adrienne, and everyone else in the temple had watched or heard Lenore's despairing wails.

In their phone philosophizing about marriage, Patricia and Brenda debated whether something had gone terribly wrong in the Rabbi's relationship or whether he had messed up this once. One bad year over the course of a long marriage might not be fatal. But was the Lenore/Risa fight a reenactment of the Rachel/Leah sibling rivalry? Had the Rabbi wanted to marry Risa, the younger sister, as Lenore had claimed?

Of course falling in love with a new person was intoxicating. A path one could easily slip down as Patricia recognized too well. Had Risa come to the Rabbi for marital counseling? Had things gotten out of hand? Had the Rabbi needed relief from the responsibilities of dealing with a dependent adult son and the temple's financial problems? And Risa was attractive.

Who else suspected their relationship may have crossed boundaries? Had Roberto found a love note from Risa in the garbage? Lewd photos? Were these the "papers" that Roberto wanted to discuss with Rabbi Deborah? Patricia and Brenda hoped Bertilla might have some answers.

Brenda and Patricia had concluded yesterday's call with the wisdom that it was unrealistic to expect a spouse to fulfill every need. Search for all the qualities you want from a partner—sexual chemistry, fidelity, conversation, intelligence, parenting skill, respect, support— and you might find three, maybe four if you're lucky. Only in the movies do you end up with the perfect someone. What the movies didn't show was that aftermath: in about ten years you discovered what qualities your spouse lacked and how his family screwed him up, for better or worse. And it took that long to realize you couldn't significantly change your spouse. Like when you bought shoes that were too tight, thinking you'd break them in to fit perfectly. It never happened.

"You just got bunions," Brenda commented. "Or he throws you into the closet for a newer style. Can you believe my ex asked me for a divorce while we were in the middle of watching season three of Bad Breakups. What a jerk – how could he break up with me in the middle of the season?"

Patricia rested her hands on the computer's keyboard and assessed her relationship with Michael. Was there anything seriously wrong with their marriage? Sure they argued but mostly about mundane things like cleaning up, babysitting, in-laws, the usual administrative headaches of a shared life. Their sex life was good. Sometimes even great. She shivered, remembering Michael's wide palms spanning her back and running slowly down her body. They might not have the same temperament or come from the same background, but they treated each other with respect and worked things out, most of the time.

"I see you are being your usual efficient self." Patricia turned and flinched as she saw Kevin leaning in the office doorway.

"Sorry. I didn't mean to startle you," he boomed in

his deep baritone.

"I've been trying to contact you," she said, trying to calm her breath and tone down the whininess. After all, it wasn't like Kevin was an unreliable date who'd failed to call as promised. She had serious business to discuss with him about stock certificates. Should she mention Rabbi Deborah's text?

"Got your messages but I was up in Seekonk for my nephew's birthday. Didn't want to get distracted by work or whatever business. I'm here to follow up with Adrienne on the Gomez case. Thought I'd stop by." He sauntered over and draped his butt against her desk, crossing his long lean legs in front of her.

Clearing her throat, Patricia proceeded to give a detailed description of how she'd been making a list of stock donations to the temple and noticed that the Union Central Railroad Trust stock certificates were decorated with drawings of locomotives. "We'd discussed that Roberto was found with a scrap of paper printed with a train drawing. It seems like a good idea to compare the scrap of paper to the railroad trust certificate." She tried to sound deferential but determined. "I'd like to examine it. Would you be able to arrange that?"

Kevin stood up and hovered over her. "You may be onto something. We're already re-examining evidence in the Gomez accident. Better if our forensic experts do the comparison. They're professionals. They'll do a thorough job although it may take a while given the evidence backup. I'll get Adrienne to make me a copy of the certificate."

Patricia flushed with annoyance and pushed away from her desk, away from Kevin. She'd lost any leverage her newly discovered information had given her. She couldn't fault him for insisting that his experts do the comparison. But why was he practically standing on top of her. "What else are you re-examining in Roberto's case?" she asked, grabbing her coffee cup as a defensive weapon.

"Our forensic experts are comparing the tracks adjacent to the body with the garbage truck tires. There may be inconsistencies in the width of the treads. We're investigating who else may have been working late that Thursday and continuing to review the surveillance tapes. That's probably more than I should be telling you. But if you think of anything else…"

"Yes, yes, of course." Patricia hesitated. Should she mention yesterday's Weinstein family fireworks or Rabbi Deborah's text? She didn't want to spread what was still gossip and her own speculation.

"Anytime you come up with something I'm happy to hear it. You know me, coffee and donuts anytime, anywhere."

Better than he realized, thought Patricia, then reminded herself of her no-flirting vow. "I'm sorry. I need to make a few phone calls before I leave to pick up my son."

Apologizing for the interruption, Officer O'Donnell turned and left abruptly.

So much for sharing. Had she offended him? Patricia hated having people mad at her. Neither parochial school nor nursing school had prepared her for conflict. Was there a recommended protocol for ending a flirtation? Could there be a novena for absolution for an inappropriate dalliance? She might have to borrow her mother's rosary after all.

Patricia tried Morris's number again. Miraculously a male voice answered, rumbling "Mizchek Monetary Mitzvahs."

"Mr. Mizchek? This is Patricia Weiss. I've been volunteering to help computerize the temple accounts. Adrienne suggested I call you because we need your expertise."

Morris seemed flattered to be asked for help although he had no immediate plans to be at the temple. Patricia agreed to schedule an appointment at his office for the next morning between preschool drop-off and pickup. She'd inform Adrienne in case she didn't trust Patricia to handle the meeting by herself. And what were monetary mitzvahs anyways? She'd ask Morris tomorrow. First an interview with Morris, then Bertilla. Tomorrow would be a busy day.

Chapter Twenty-Three

Thursday, June 11

Morris Mizchek's office was in one of downtown Rockville's nondescript glass rectangles, fronting Wisconsin Avenue. Patricia took the elevator to the eighth floor and followed his instructions for locating the accounting firm of Berman, Beeman, Dewey, and Cheetem. Claiming she had a conflict, Adrienne seemed happy to permit Patricia to conduct the meeting by herself.

She had dressed in black pants, ivory silk shirt, and a tailored gray jacket to give herself a professional aura. The young blonde receptionist sitting behind a fortress-like desk in the spacious entryway made a sour face when Patricia said she had an appointment with Mr. Mizchek. Ten minutes after the receptionist buzzed him, a frail elderly man ambled out, limping slightly.

"Hello, how are you? Please, call me Morris." Mizchek stuck out a gnarled hand. "So nice to be visited by a pretty girl in the morning. Sorry for the delay. I got bad knees. Old joints."

Morris fulfilled every stereotype Patricia had of a bookkeeper. He was overweight, shortish, about an inch taller than herself. His wispy zebra-streaked hair was combed over a significant bald spot. Did he use cheap black hair dye to create that unusual skunk-like effect?

Thick glasses framed his hooded eyes. His sport jacket and corduroy pants needed pressing. His collared shirt was unbuttoned over his ample pot belly and was coming untucked from his pants. To say his appearance did not inspire confidence was an understatement. Maybe a pair of green eyeshades that accountants stereotypically wore to protect their eyes from strain would have made him look more professional. He seemed naggingly familiar, or he fit her archetype for aging bookkeepers.

Before Patricia could place him, Morris grabbed her elbow and guided her down a corridor leading to a warren of interior offices. Nearly breathless by the time he stopped in front a door bearing the brass numbers 36, he pulled out a key ring and unlocked a thick door.

As Patricia watched, Morris touched the small, tarnished mezuzah affixed to the doorpost. She was impressed with his observance of the custom. The silver ornament contained a miniature scroll inscribed with the *Shema* prayer, Hear O Israel God is One. As she'd learned in her studies, the mezuzah designated a home as Jewish and symbolized God's watchful care over the home. She'd bought a mezuzah for their house at the sisterhood Hanukah mart last December. She repeatedly asked Michael to affix it to the front doorpost. He kept delaying, claiming the whole world didn't need to know they were Jewish. She did not understand his paranoid reluctance. Morris Mizchek was proud to be identified as a Jew even in his place of business.

Morris opened his office door and ushered her in. "Welcome to my hole in the wall. Number Thirty-six for good luck—a multiple of eighteen which signifies "life" in Hebrew. I sublet the space from one of the big shot accountants, Larry Berman. His father and I were partners in the bookkeeping business. He passed a few years ago. Too bad, such an honest guy, too honest for his own good. No one ever wanted his advice. He was such a stickler on taxes."

Patricia stopped on the threshold before she could bring herself to follow Morris into the windowless room. The office looked as though it hadn't been cleaned in years. Even without windows, dust glinted in the air as the older man switched on the floor lamp. The odor of rotting garbage permeated the room, as if a creature had died and lay buried under all the papers. Bookshelves lining the walls bulged with accounting tomes and a number of ancient-looking parchment scrolls.

Morris squeezed behind a battered wood desk and pointed to an upholstered chair set diagonally across from him. Stuffing erupted from the chair's beige fabric which was covered with dark fur of an unidentifiable origin.

She picked her way through towers of folders piled on the floor. After inspecting the chair, she hesitated. Morris stood up with effort and grabbed a Kleenex from the box on his desk. "Let me dust that chair off. Don't worry, it's only Marilyn, my kitty. She's shy with strangers. I guess I'll have to let the janitorial staff in here for a once-over." Morris emitted a phlegmy cough as if to confirm his intent to clean up his act. "I keep the office locked up tight. Security, confidentiality, can't be too careful nowadays."

Wasn't that exactly what Mr. Schwabstein had said to her? Must be the mantra now among financial professionals who preferred to delay sharing information. Hand-fanning dust away from her nose, Patricia thanked Morris and sat down on the edge of the chair. As if on cue, a faint meow emanated from under the desk. A mud-brown cat, its fat belly sagging to the floor, crept out and immediately jumped onto Patricia's lap, forcing its muzzle into her stomach. Patricia gasped.

"Marilyn likes you. Isn't that cute. You don't look so comfortable. Marilyn's gotten a bit heavy. Kitty, get down. I know Patricia's a very attractive woman, and she's sitting in your favorite chair, but we want our guests to feel welcome."

Patricia encouraged the cat's departure with a gentle push. Not that she didn't like animals, but she preferred not to have her pants covered with cat hair. Plus she wondered exactly where Marilyn had been hanging out. The cat smelled funky.

Taking her time, Marilyn leapt down and stalked over to one of the folder towers. When she raised her hind leg and peed, Patricia gave another gasp and tried not to gag.

Morris shrugged. "I named her after my favorite actress, Marilyn Monroe. Ah, what a woman. Marilyn converted to Judaism before tying the knot with Arthur Miller. Did you know?"

Patricia murmured in assent. Trying to make nice, she asked Morris how long he'd had Marilyn.

"Nine years since she was a kitty. Wouldn't you know, after a year, I discover she is a he. I don't see too well even with these overpriced trifocal lenses." He adjusted his glasses over his rheumy eyes. "I suppose I should have changed his name to Monroe, more neutral, but I like Marilyn better. I always wanted a little girl.

My wife and I were never able to have children." He sighed and cleared more phlegm from his throat. He sniffled and grabbed a Kleenex. "Sorry, allergies. So what can I do for you?"

A transgender kitty—what next? Patricia again explained her task of making a computerized listing of donations to the temple. "I have a few quick questions about the stocks. I'm confused about how to value certificates and whether or not they may have been sold."

Morris's hand jutted out from behind the desk and gave her knee a squeeze. Patricia whipped her legs around, as far from him as possible in the cramped space. Thank goodness she'd worn slacks. What a lech—was she giving off signals to attract wayward hands?

Oblivious to her repulsion, Morris ruminated with a *non sequitur*. "Quick, quick. Everyone's in a hurry these days." He leaned back in his desk chair, appearing in danger of falling over backwards. "Adrienne's such a nice girl. She's doing a remarkable job, keeping everything together at the temple with all the *meshuggenah* stuff going on—Rabbi Zalman's disappearance and poor Roberto's death. By the way, any news?" He popped upright, giving Patricia a lascivious grin, the tip of his tongue sticking out between his teeth, or were they dentures?

Patricia shuddered and responded with a simple "No. The police are continuing to investigate both matters."

"Yes, yes, that's good, I guess. Can I offer you tea?"

Before Patricia could decline, Morris swiveled to

the right and switched on an electric kettle sitting on top of the bookshelf next to him. How long had the water been stagnating in the pot? Assuming there was water in there.

Determined not to be distracted by tea or lechery, Patricia sat upright and faced Morris directly. In a crisp, businesslike tone, she presented the issue. "Adrienne suggested I call the temple's broker, Mr. Schwabstein. He told me that the stock certificates I was examining had been sold. He advised I speak with you."

"Were the certificates in the safe? I always lock up the certificates after I've inspected them. For bookkeeping purposes, of course. Only Rabbi Weinstein, Adrienne, and I have keys to the safe." Morris pointed an index finger at Patricia's nose, as if aiming a gun. "How did you get your hands on them?"

"Excuse me," Patricia responded huffily. "Adrienne entrusted me with those certificates for the specific purpose of recording their value and their status."

"Well, I don't see how the stocks could have been sold," Morris declared, as if stating the obvious. "They've been in the safe all this time." He peered over his trifocals at the steaming kettle. "Ah, the water's hot. What kind of tea would you like?" Opening the desk drawer, he pulled out two desiccated tea bags that looked as if they'd been resurrected from an archaeological dig. "I have Lipton's or lemon. My grandmother enjoyed tea, a Russian tradition." He opened another drawer and pulled out paper hot cups and napkins swiped from Java Junction.

Hoping the cups were unused, Patricia agreed to Lipton's, then pushed on. "Do you have any idea how we can confirm the status or value of the certificates? Especially the railroad trust certificates, and the other certificates donated to the Rabbi's Discretionary Fund?"

Ignoring her questions, Morris leaned over the side of his desk and pulled out a bottle from a tattered leather briefcase. "Fine Russian vodka. Spices up the tea. And medicinal too— cures whatever ails you. I never leave home without the stuff. Can I add a shot to your cup?" He poured a generous shot into his own cup.

"No, no, plain tea please." She grabbed the offered cup before Morris could doctor her drink then repeated her questions in a louder voice.

"I'm a bookkeeper, not an accountant. Mainly I keep track of what the temple spends. The accountants are the *ganza machars* nowadays, the big shots who use these financial models to value stock." Running stubby fingers through his zebra-streaked strands, Morris managed to dislodge his comb-over. Patricia noticed his nails were ragged and bitten to the quick. He glanced sideways at Patricia and flashed a grin. "Not that I can't perform, and my years of experience count for a lot. I can do that stuff." He waggled his eyebrows.

Ugh, was he flirting? Despite the close air and lack of circulation in the office, Patricia shivered. "Whatever you can find out would be very helpful. We'd like to reconcile our records as soon as possible."

"Let me check. Maybe there's something in one of these files." He gestured vaguely toward the folder-covered floor where Marilyn had recently relieved herself. "It's going to take me a few days to dig out any info."

Patricia surveyed the grimy stacks and repressed an

urge to cover her mouth and nose with her wadded napkin. "Thanks for meeting with me. I await your response. Can I phone you in a few days?" Morris was going to need nudging, as Brenda would say, to dig through his files. If she limited their contact to the phone, Patricia could avoid his creeping hands.

"I always enjoy receiving calls from beautiful women. We need more pretty young faces around here. And look how thin you are, we can grab a bite to eat next time we meet."

Where had she heard that gravelly voice speaking those lines before? All at once Patricia realized where she must have glimpsed Morris. He sounded like her mystery savior at the deli. "Were you at Corky's last Saturday? We may have met there."

"Yes, yes. I was your defender against that old fart Syd." Morris fidgeted in his seat, coughed, cleared his throat and then spit into the wastebasket under his desk. He smiled sheepishly. "I recognized you when you walked in today, but I didn't want to bring up our previous meeting, because I wasn't sure you remembered me."

"I definitely remember you now. Are you sure that vodka's enhancing your health?"

"Yeah, it's strong stuff."

"Do you go to Corky's often?"

"Sure, all my buddies do." Morris reached out and tapped her knee which she had inadvertently let slide towards the desk. "If you have a minute, let me tell you about the new project I've been spending most of my time on."

As Patricia quickly moved her knees out of groping range, Morris stood and eased out from behind the desk. She noticed he was in his stocking feet, a hole in the toe of one sock.

He puttered over to the shelf full of scrolls and ran his fingers tenderly along the cylinders, as if caressing a woman's spine. "A rabbi in Israel has recovered Torah scrolls that were hidden in Eastern Europe during the Holocaust. He's been bringing them to me at the request of various congregations and individuals in the Rockville area who are interested in buying them. It's a *mitzvah*, a good deed, to be saving these Torahs and bringing them back to life, so to speak."

Despite her reservations about Morris's overreaching behavior, both his groping and bookkeeping, Patricia was impressed. "Fascinating. I meant to ask about all the scrolls."

"That's why I call the business Monetary Mitzvahs. Here, let me show you one." As if cupping a child's head, he gently placed his palm around the top of one of the parchment scrolls and began to pull it out.

A loud meow suddenly filled the room. Marilyn ran toward the corner of a nearby bookshelf, ready to pounce. A large black bug, a roach or a beetle was slowly crawling up the side. Patricia, already feeling ill from the tea, stood up quickly. "I'm short on time now. I need to pick up my son from preschool. I will definitely be in touch."

"I look forward to hearing from you. Today's Thursday, and I don't answer the phone on Shabbas. So next week? When we go out for a bite, we can talk more about these precious scrolls. Say, aren't you the one Adrienne said converted so you could marry the cardiologist? I have questions for the doc. I'm having heart palpitations."

Chapter Twenty-Four

Thursday, June 11

The carpool pickup line seemed to take forever. By the time Patricia and Danny finally pulled into the Cabin John parking lot, Patricia could see Bertilla already sitting on a shaded park bench. Instead of black, she wore a blue uniform-like dress, probably a requirement of the assisted living facility where she worked. Her hair was pulled into a neat bun. Grabbing the tote containing Danny's peanut butter sandwich and water, Patricia hurried over to Bertilla. Danny ran to the jungle gym.

Patricia extended her hand. "I'm glad to finally meet you."

Bertilla shook it solemnly. "Roberto really appreciated your tutoring. He said it was a big help with his computer class. And with the kids' homework."

"He was a fast learner." Patricia sat down next to Bertilla. "I am so sorry." She was relieved Bertilla knew about the tutoring. Maybe she would consider Patricia's questions less intrusive.

"Yes, he wanted to get a job in computer tech. But now ...." Bertilla's eyes misted over. "Please, why do you want to talk to me. Are you helping the police? Are you here on behalf of the temple?"

Good questions. How could Patricia explain her involvement? Had she and Roberto been friends? Compatriots in arms struggling to find their way in a land they weren't born into? "I'm volunteering at the temple. The congregation has an obligation to support your family. It's important that we figure out what happened to Roberto because…"

"Sorry I'm late," Brenda gasped. Catching her breath she hovered over the bench, unsure where to locate. "I see Danny's enjoying himself."

The three women waved at Danny who waved back from the slide.

Relieved to be rescued from her inarticulateness, Patricia introduced Brenda to Bertilla. "Brenda and I are working together on this." Patricia hesitated. Was "this" an investigation?

"Nice to meet you, Brenda. I don't care whether you ladies are official or not. I need help, especially with the insurance company. Roberto did not kill himself," she stated forcefully and moved closer to Patricia to make room. "Please, Brenda, sit. What can I tell you?"

"I understand you have questions about the accident, about the circumstances of Roberto's death," said Patricia.

"It wasn't an accident. Roberto would never fall asleep on the job. He was targeted. Someone must have been watching him, waiting." Bertilla's voice rose with anger. "And when he went out to empty the trash, they hit him and ran."

"Who would target him? Who wanted to hurt him?" Patricia asked. "Jorge mentioned that some players in the El Salvadoran soccer league had threatened Roberto."

"No. I know those families, those men. They are big mouths, boasters." Bertilla shook her head emphatically. "But no way would they use violence against a countryman."

"What about gangs? MS-13?" Brenda asked. "They sure don't honor national loyalties."

Bertilla crossed herself. "Thank God. No gangs. Roberto never mentioned any gangs, and he would have said, because the kids and I could have been targets."

Patricia suppressed an urge to mimic the familiar move. "Did the police tell you they are investigating whether another vehicle, not the trash truck, hit Roberto?"

"No. But Officer Kevin told me when they found Roberto, he had a scrap of paper with a drawing of a train in his pocket. Can I ask you a question, Patricia? Why did he carry that paper? Did you give him a train book to practice his English?"

"No. I was going to ask you. Did he buy a book about trains to read to your children?"

"No. Javier and Anna have so many books to read for school. Roberto didn't buy extra."

"Did the police tell you that Carol at the temple found a note on her desk from Roberto to Rabbi Deborah?" Patricia asked. "He said he wanted to talk with her privately about papers he found in the garbage. Do you know why Roberto wanted to meet with Rabbi Deborah? Or what papers he was talking about?"

"Officer Kevin asked me the same question. I said I didn't know. But I'll tell you my suspicions." Bertilla looked hard at Patricia and Brenda. "This is just between us. I don't want to get in trouble or ruin

Roberto's honor."

Patricia and Brenda nodded in unison.

"A couple days before his passing—" Bertilla cleared her throat "—Roberto told me he found papers in the wastebasket in the hallway at the temple. They looked important. Some kind of financial records. Roberto's good with numbers. He kept the books at his father's mini-mart in St. Theresa and tracked the customers who owed money or who had a credit. Roberto wasn't sure the temple papers should be thrown out, maybe there'd been a mistake. It was late. The only person in the building was that old man, the bookkeeper. What's his name?"

"Morris," clarified Patricia.

"Yeah. So Roberto talks to Morris because Morris may know if it's a mistake. Morris says something about the temple not needing to keep old records, and not to worry about them. Morris rips up the papers, hands them back to Roberto, tells him to dump them in the garbage. Roberto wasn't sure he believed Morris. That's all I know."

"Did Roberto describe the papers?" asked Patricia.

"No." Bertilla shook her head vehemently. A few wisps of hair fell loose from her bun.

"Why did Roberto want to talk to Rabbi Deborah?" queried Brenda. "Why not Rabbi Weinstein? He's the head rabbi."

"Roberto always liked Rabbi Deborah. The tutoring was her idea," answered Bertilla. "Plus I'm guessing, Roberto didn't want to worry Rabbi Weinstein. Roberto told me a while ago that the Rabbi had problems with his older son, the autistic one. And the Rabbi was seeing too much of his sister-in-law, not in a good way. But I don't want to spread rumors."

"Roberto probably never got a chance to meet with Rabbi Deborah." Brenda sighed. "Too bad we can't ask her."

"Where did she go?" asked Bertilla. "Are the police looking for her?"

Patricia and Brenda exchanged a glance.

"We think she's away on a trip," said Brenda. "The police say they haven't found any evidence of criminal activity and believe she left voluntarily. They aren't putting a lot of resources into a search."

"Mommy, Mommy, I'm hungry." Danny raced into Patricia's lap. "Can I sit next to you?"

"Of course." Patricia made room for Danny on the now crowded bench and pulled out the peanut butter sandwich. "This is Mrs. Gomez."

"Nice to meet you." Bertilla nodded at Danny and then at Patricia. "Let's talk about something else. Don't want to upset anyone. Roberto said you used to be Catholic? Do you miss it?"

"I do miss the beautiful traditions in the Catholic religion, Christmas Eve services with candles and bells and Easter's high mass. We celebrate Christmas with Grandma, right Danny?"

"Grandma buys me presents and sends me cookies," Danny said in a serious tone between bites of sandwich.

"And the rituals of holy water, saints, and relics make the concept of God more palpable," added Patricia. "They provide a lot of comfort to people." On the other hand, Patricia thought to herself, it was hard to appreciate a religion that had been stuffed down her throat at home, in school, and at church. She was coming to understand Michael's ambivalent attitude towards his own conservative Jewish upbringing with its rigid expectations imposed on young men. He had described his bar mitzvah as his last good religious experience and that probably had more to do with the elaborate party and presents than with spiritual enlightenment.

"My church community at St. Rose's has been a great source of strength for my family. Especially now that Roberto is gone." Bertilla's eyes started to mist up again.

"The funeral service at St. Rose's was beautiful," Patricia said, in an attempt to be supportive.

"Danny, you are welcome at our house next Christmas," Bertilla offered as she blotted her eyes with a handkerchief from her pocket. "You can help us make cookies."

"What a nice idea. Right, Danny?" These religious issues were too complicated to discuss here, and Patricia did not want to offend Bertilla. Better to change the subject again. "Bertilla, did I see you at the demonstration at the temple two weeks ago?"

"Yes. Please don't spread that around. I don't want to get fired. I'm part of an organization that is trying to organize domestic workers, health aides, and nursing aides. Domestic Workers Alliance. We meet at St. Rose's church. We are fighting for improved working conditions, better pay, and limits on hours. Speaking of which, I need to get back to work." Bertilla rose.

"Thanks for taking the time to talk to us," said Brenda.

"Yes, thank you so much," added Patricia. "We will keep you in the loop. The temple's trying to arrange a memorial event and raise money for the kids."

"Yes. Rabbi Weinstein told me. I just want justice for Roberto. Please." Bertilla waved and walked toward the parking lot.

"So Roberto suspected Rabbi Weinstein was having an affair with Risa," said Brenda, leaning back with a grunt. "Was he going to blackmail Weinstein?"

"Blackmail? No way. Roberto wouldn't do that."

"I'm brainstorming. Your response isn't exactly objective."

"True. But many people already suspected an affair. Rabbi Weinstein didn't seem like he was trying to hide anything, or even be discrete."

"Now everyone knows something's up. Not so a few weeks ago. Roberto could have threatened Weinstein with outing him. Weinstein can't pay up what with expenses for his son's care. Weinstein arranges to get Roberto whacked, make it look like an accident."

"Sounds like an episode of a TV crime show. Kevin says the cops are investigating what vehicle hit Roberto, if not the trash truck. That should lead somewhere. I wonder if those papers Roberto found in the garbage are connected to the scrap in his pocket and if the scrap is connected to stock donated to the temple." Patricia proceeded to explain about finding the railroad trust certificate in the course of her volunteer assignment and her conversation with Mr. Schwabstein, the temple's investment broker.

"Whoa, that's critical. My ex tried to sneak off with stock in his 401(k). Took me years and a chunk of change on lawyer's fees to get the percentage I was entitled to. Who deals with temple donations,

Adrienne? Rabbi W? Morris? Let's text Rabbi D and tell her we met with Bertilla. That might elicit a response from her."

"Good idea," said Patricia as she pulled out her phone. "And I need to find out if Kevin's experts have finished their exam and confirmed a connection between the railroad trust stock certificates and Roberto's scrap of a train drawing."

"Mommy, can I watch the train show on your phone now? Who's Blackmail? Is he a bad guy or a good guy?"

"Danny, sometimes it's hard to tell the good guys from the bad guys," explained Brenda. "The train show sounds like a good idea. Right, Mom?"

"Definitely. I hear tooting," responded Patricia as they all left the park bench.

Chapter Twenty-Five

Friday, June 12

Perspiring profusely, Patricia tried to steer the massive garbage truck around the Temple Israel parking lot. Sitting next to her on the edge of the passenger seat, Roberto Gomez directed her to drive the truck toward the road. He was explaining patiently in Spanish, but Patricia couldn't understand a word of his instructions. Despite her desperate pull on the heavy steering wheel, the truck continued to speed forward. Through the windshield she saw Rabbi Deborah knocking on the temple's locked entrance. Kevin towered over the Rabbi. He was raising his baton as if about to strike. Roberto yelled and pointed, and Patricia realized the truck was heading straight towards Rabbi Deborah and Kevin.

Patricia jammed her foot on the brake, but the truck accelerated. A crash exploded in her ears, and Patricia was thrown forward. She cried out.

Suddenly she was twelve years old and on the beach with Jeanne and Teresa. All three sisters were crying. They had brought their father's best deck of cards to play gin rummy. Decorated with green and gold Celtic knots, the deck was the one he used for good luck at his Friday night poker game. The wind had blown the cards all over the beach and into the water. Patricia raced around and gathered up the cards, now soggy and sandy, except she couldn't find the king of clubs. The sky darkened and the moon rose. Patricia was coated with sand, and she was lying on a beach blanket. Michael was kissing and caressing her matured body, peeling off her bathing suit. Patricia was afraid to move. From behind the dune, she heard a conversation in Spanish. Bertilla arguing with Rabbi Deborah? Then that fat cat Marilyn ran onto the blanket with a fish in his mouth and peed. Patricia could feel the wetness seeping into her.

With a start, Patricia's eyes popped open. Lying flat on her back and soaked in her own perspiration, she scratched at her thighs, exposed below her hiked up nightgown. Where had she gotten these itchy bug bites? The park, the shore? She hadn't been to the beach recently. The dream sequence flashed through her mind: the garbage truck, the cards, Michael on the blanket. Had they ever actually made love on the beach? She was so confused.

Turning her head to check the time, she saw three-thirty a.m. glow blue on her digital clock. She turned her head the other way. Michael was sound asleep, snoring lightly. Curled on his side facing her, he'd wrapped his arm around her waist. Patricia felt a tingling charge from his skin like the static air before a thunderstorm at the shore. She was wide awake. No point trying to remain immobile next to Michael.

Slipping slowly out of bed so as not to wake him, she tiptoed over to her dresser. She eased open the second drawer from the top and pulled out her investigative files buried under her socks and underwear. Michael stirred but didn't wake up. She crept out, pausing a moment at Danny's open bedroom door. Calmed by the sound of his soft breathing, she stealthily descended the stairs into the kitchen.

Using the dimmer switch to spotlight the kitchen table, Patricia sat down and spread out her files. She removed the Gomez murder book from its accordion folder and perused the pages. How would her father have approached the case? Follow the facts to rule out alternatives. According to the temple's personnel records, Roberto had never been caught sleeping or drinking on the job. On the contrary, he'd been a hard worker. It was unlikely Roberto had fallen asleep against the dumpster. She hadn't heard from Kevin about the results of the document comparison, but how had the train drawing scrap ended up in Roberto's pocket? Had he found a railroad trust stock certificate in the garbage? Was this paper what he'd shown to Morris? Had Roberto kept a portion of one of the certificates? Had he found shreds of another certificate in the garbage? God forbid, had he stolen it? Was this paper what he wanted to discuss with Rabbi Deborah?

Kevin had said the tire tracks next to Roberto's body probably didn't match those of the garbage truck. Had Kevin figured out who else worked late that Thursday night? Whose car was parked in the lot? Maybe Adrienne? Morris? Rabbi Weinstein? They all had keys to the safe. Was Roberto's death accidental? Or intentional? Who would benefit by his death?

Pushing away Roberto's file in frustration, Patricia moved the Zalman binder in front of her. She had copied down the wording of the Rabbi's text. Rabbi Deborah stated she was in the Promised Land. A reference to Israel? Rabbi Deborah mentioned missing her meeting with Bertilla. The text sounded authentic. But why hadn't the Rabbi responded to Patricia's latest text about meeting with Bertilla? Patricia had sent it yesterday afternoon. With the time difference, maybe the Rabbi hadn't had a chance? And why hadn't Rabbi Deborah informed anyone about her plans? What message was the text referring to?

Patricia stifled a yawn. If she closed her eyes for a minute, perhaps matters would clarify, solutions would appear. She put her head down on her arms and felt the coolness of the glass table against her skin.

"Mommy, Mommy," Danny's voice resonated down to the first floor. "I wet my bed."

Patricia bolted awake and upright. The dawn sun streamed into the kitchen's bay window. The wall clock read six o'clock. She grabbed her files and surveyed the kitchen quickly. Her glance fell upon the long-untouched pile of *Bon Appetit* magazines that she'd shoved into a corner of the counter next to the pantry. The stack of seldom opened issues should be a safe hiding place. She stuffed the folders into the middle of the stack. After Michael left for work, she'd stash them in her dresser drawer. She hurried upstairs to Danny.

****

On Friday evening, Patricia breathed a sigh of relief as she heard Michael's car pull into the driveway at six-forty-five. Another long day. The morning had begun with bathing Danny, stripping his bed, and washing the sheets. Michael had helped remake the bed and joined them for breakfast at the kitchen table. Gulping down a bowl of oat bran with skim milk before his rush to the office, he sympathized with the wet bed and Patricia's poor night of sleep which she attributed to her concern over Rabbi Deborah.

"You shouldn't stress about the Rabbi. I don't want you to get sick because you're losing sleep." Michael stood up, kissed Patricia gently on the forehead, and hugged Danny in his booster seat. "I'll try to get home early tonight," he promised as he put his bowl in the sink.

Patricia smiled wearily and began the process of brewing a double shot of espresso. An hour later she and Danny left for the preschool story hour and Lego playdate at the Rockville library. They arrived the requisite half hour early to get one of the limited number of spots for the popular program. Given the homogeneity of her immediate Potomac neighborhood, Patricia was always pleasantly surprised by the diversity of moms, dads, and nannies who brought preschoolers to library events.

Patricia watched Danny offer to share blocks and build a tower with another boy. He'd be a kind older brother and enjoy the company of a sibling. Having a new baby could be fulfilling—although overwhelming without support. Michael would have to help a whole lot more.

At the end of the hour, Patricia and Danny checked out an armful of picture books and beginning readers from the library. They walked to the nearby Mellow Munchies for lunch. Danny always chose the kid's peanut butter and jelly sandwich. She ordered the Caesar salad with the dressing on the side. As she picked at her lettuce, she debated what to do about yet another Friday's Shabbat dinner.

Relying on Michael's promise to come home early,

Patricia decided to attempt cooking a chicken from scratch. Why not reward his good behavior—assuming the chicken came out bronzed and juicy like her mom's. She let Danny help her choose an organic roaster at the supermarket along with broccoli and fresh corn, first of the season, and two pints of ice cream, coffee for her, and low-fat cookies and cream for Michael and Danny. She hurried into the kosher bakery next to the grocery and bought challah bread to honor the Shabbat.

Confronting the raw poultry on her kitchen counter, Patricia wished she had watched her mom Maria more closely when she roasted a chicken for the family. On her next visit, she would insist her mom write down the directions. How hard could roasting a chicken be? She rinsed the bird. Then she and Danny seasoned the chicken with plenty of salt, pepper, and garlic powder. Because she knew Michael liked his food spicy, they added a healthy dose of red pepper flakes. Calculating the cooking time according to the package directions at two hours, she put the bird in the oven at four-thirty. Coming home early for Michael meant no earlier than six or six-thirty. Safer to assume the latter. At five-thirty, she peeked into the oven. The bird looked pale and raw. Despite the package directions, she raised the heat from three-fifty to three-seventy-five degrees, since underdone chicken could cause salmonella.

Michael pulled into the driveway at six-forty. Only ten minutes later than anticipated. She and Danny had set the kitchen table. Unsure how much Jewish ritual Michael would appreciate, Patricia, with Danny's assistance, lit Shabbat candles and recited the blessing. As Michael settled into his seat, Patricia proudly placed the platter of crispy chicken at the head of the table. Danny announced that he had helped Mommy make it. Michael carved and served.

As Patricia watched, Michael brought a forkful to his mouth and began to chew—then cough. He grabbed for his glass of water and swallowed a mouthful. Patricia tasted a bit of meat. Oh no—too salty and way too spicy. Her eyes filled with tears.

"Great, really a great effort. The chicken looks good but maybe a bit overboard with the spices, especially the salt and that's red pepper, right?" Michael smiled encouragingly at both of them as he set down his fork.

"I'm sorry. Now the chicken's ruined." On the verge of a teary breakdown, Patricia felt overcome with exhaustion. She had tried so hard. How had she made such a mess? Danny started sniffling.

"No permanent harm done. We can remove the skin and wipe off the meat. The chicken will be fine, if a little overcooked. I take part of the blame since I was later than I meant to be." Michael assiduously peeled the skin from the breast and leg on his plate. "You might check out one of these recipes." Michael bounded up and over to the stack of *Bon Appetit* magazines. "Marinades are a safe and tasty method for tenderizing chicken. How do you like my French chef imitation?"

With horror, Patricia realized that in the bustle of the day's activities—laundry, library, shopping, cooking, preparing for Shabbat—she'd forgotten to return the investigative files to her dresser drawer. Rising out of her chair and waving her arms as if to freeze Michael's movement toward the magazines, she cried out, "I'll ask my mother next time we talk. Not necessary to check another recipe."

Too late. Michael already started to rifle through the magazine stack, his hand stopping at the bump of accordion folders. "What's this, a folder of your mom's favorite recipes you've been keeping secret?" He skimmed through the binders and then looked up at Patricia with a puzzled expression.

"No, no." Patricia blurted, too upset to improvise a last minute fabrication. "Those are my investigative files, my notes about Roberto Gomez's death and Rabbi Deborah's disappearance." Didn't the Bible say the truth would set you free? Probably the New Testament, maybe John? Regardless of who said it, the path of truth was the only way for her to travel now. She needed resolution with Michael. Enough sneaking around. Her tears dried as she prepared to defend herself, to make her case.

Putting his hands to his head, Michael groaned. "Haven't we talked about sticking your nose into dangerous police business, putting the family at risk?"

"No, we haven't talked about it. You have opined and passed judgment. I never said I wouldn't concern myself with Roberto Gomez's death and Rabbi Deborah's disappearance."

Readying for a fight, Patricia stood as straight as possible, her hands resting on the kitchen table doubling as her lectern. "I know Rabbi Deborah as well as anybody in this town, and I empathized with Roberto's cultural newcomer status. Their fates are important to me, and I want to use my analytical skills to try to figure out as much as I can about what happened to them. So what if I'm not the best cook. I would rather spend my time coddling you and Danny than eggs and potatoes or whatever foods are supposed to get coddled."

"What's coddle?" Danny asked from his seat at the table. "Can I have another piece of challah? Please?"

"Coddle means to treat tenderly, the way we're careful with the Shabbat challah and special toys and good friends," Patricia explained, toning her voice down a notch. "Yes, you may have another piece of challah. Thank you for saying please."

Looking surprised, Michael stepped towards her, his arms outstretched. "I didn't realize this was so important to you, that you cared that much."

"Because you haven't been listening. I admit I haven't been as forthcoming as I should have been. I don't completely understand my compulsion to investigate. You blame your mother for your personality quirks. I blame my father. It's his influence. I inherited his detective gene. Being the youngest of three sisters, I was always trying to find out what was going on so I could join in or protect myself—my learned survival mode. Mom and Dad were busy and tired, and I was left alone to fantasize and follow Dad's footsteps. For whatever reason, I have to find out what happened to Roberto and to Rabbi Deborah."

"Mommy, Daddy, why is everyone standing up? Is dinner done? Can I have dessert?" Danny started to wiggle out of his chair. "I promise to coddle my ice cream and my toys."

Patricia and Michael exchanged glances and smiled at Danny's comment. With the magic of marital telepathy, they silently agreed to continue the discussion later. Sitting down, Michael proceeded with the chicken's desalination, and Patricia settled Danny into his chair in anticipation of dessert.

After Danny was tucked into bed, Patricia sank into the family room couch. Exhaustion washed over her, but she was determined not to back down. Michael finished loading the dishwasher, a new behavior, and joined her. He reached for her feet, ready to massage. Not wanting to be distracted, Patricia curled her feet beneath her.

"I may not solve Roberto's mysterious death or locate Rabbi Deborah before she returns but I'm trying to make a contribution. By the way she did text me a few days ago. I didn't mention it because her text was a little vague and I'm unsure about its authenticity. She said she's in the Promised Land, spreading happiness. Brenda and I think she's in Israel on some kind of goodwill tour."

"I told you she left voluntarily. And she's safe. She is a little flakey."

"Please don't judge. We don't know the circumstances. She said she left me a message, but I never received it."

"At least you can stop aggravating yourself. Not to change the subject, what about a new sibling for Danny?" Michael asked softly. "We were waiting until I wasn't so tied up with establishing my practice. Now we're behind schedule, and not getting any younger. I promise I'll try to be home and help out more."

"Even though I would like a second child, I don't want to be totally defined by motherhood. I voluntarily gave up my nursing position, because Danny is my first responsibility. I don't want to be one of those parents who's always arriving, always leaving, never there. But

I need to have some time to pursue my own projects. For starters, these investigations. And I want to keep volunteering at the temple and studying for my bat mitzvah."

"Can you handle the stress?" Michael voiced his concern in his serious doctor tone. "You acknowledged you haven't been sleeping well."

Patricia nodded. "Yes, I can. But I need your support. You and Danny are my anchors. I should have told you about all this investigating up front. By the way, I'd like my own laptop. Maybe an early birthday present?"

"Now that I can easily accomplish." Michael laughed and laid his head in her lap.

She gazed down into his eyes, their irises tinged with flecks of amber in the fleeting evening light. Her auburn hair swung over his face. With both hands, he grasped her shoulders, and they rolled off the couch onto the indigo and aquamarine rug that cushioned the hardwood floor.

Falling onto him, she pressed her cheek against the solid ground of his chest. Michael rolled on top of her. Fumbling with the buttons of her jeans, his fingertips traced the contours of her hips and thighs. Electric currents rippled across her skin. Her hands fluttered as if she were treading water. Michael caught them in his and pulled her to him. As he kissed her, her arms circled his neck, her legs twining around his waist. Patricia felt as if they were afloat in the ocean, breathing rhythmically, moving gently with the tugging waves. The tide flowed slowly around them, washing away the day's worries. This lovemaking was definitely not a dream.

Chapter Twenty-Six

Saturday, June 13

Michael and Patricia sat at a small table in the courtyard of Iron Bolt Inn. The evening air was warm and welcoming. Torches sat in big pots on the stone-tiled patio and cast soft shadows. How handsome Michael looked when he was able to relax. The restaurant—nouveau, fusion, or whatever—had been his choice. He snagged a reservation after a last-minute cancellation. She was willing to go anywhere. She could hardly believe they were out by themselves on a Saturday night, especially after their blow-up yesterday.

This morning, Michael had expressed his desire to have an early Father's Day celebration, just the two of them. Patricia interpreted Michael's unexpected request as his effort to make amends and demonstrate his heightened consideration for the needs of the family, in particular his wife, future bearer of the second child. She'd take what she could get. She needed a break. Happily, she was able to find a babysitter, a neighborhood teenager who Danny liked. Michael assured Danny he would spend the actual Sunday of Father's Day with him and maybe with *Bubbe* Lillian, who was threatening a visit.

Patricia perused the Iron Bolt menu. The restaurant's specialty seemed to be mystery ingredients:

foam, ash vinaigrette, antler mustard, whipped pig's tail, kelp laver. Who knew people ate this stuff. Her stomach twinged. Clearly her palate was not refined enough to appreciate the pricey dishes.

Patricia's thrifty Irish father would have passed out at the prices: two week's salary for a dinner that probably would leave you hungry. Years ago, Patricia and Michael offered to take her parents to one of Boston's fanciest restaurants. Her father was so upset at the cost he refused to go, said he couldn't enjoy a meal at those prices. Her mother claimed her father felt too guilty to enjoy good food because his family had fled Ireland during the potato famine.

For her big night out, Patricia had donned a turquoise wrap that set off her hazel eyes and emphasized her slender waist. The dress was a designer copy she had bought with Teresa on a Boston shopping excursion. Patricia's auburn hair fell in waves around her face. Michael watched her across the table.

"You are as beautiful as ever," he declared. After she murmured thanks, Michael began to study the complicated menu in earnest. She imagined this was how he reviewed pathology test results for a critical patient.

They debated whether to order the four, six, or eight-course tasting menu. There was a ten-course alternative, but they might have to break into Danny's college fund for that prix fixe, especially because Michael was ordering the wine pairing. He settled on the six-course "deal."

Patricia decided on four courses. For her first course, presumably the appetizer, she ordered mixed greens, shaved fennel, garrotxa, and lavender vinaigrette after confirming with their server that garrotxa was a kind of cheese. "Made from organic goat's milk," the rail thin young waiter attired in black officiously informed her.

Michael ordered lamb tartare topped with hen's egg yolk and pickled sunchoke. Was it healthy to eat raw meat and eggs? Michael assured her at this caliber of restaurant, the ingredients were safe. How out of character for Michael not to worry given his normally cautious approach to nutrition and novelty.

Before the first course, the wraithlike waiter arrived with complimentary *amuse bouche*, little tastes. Radish and aioli. The waiter was so skinny Patricia wondered how he'd be able to carry the heavy main course plates.

When the appetizer/first courses arrived, they were the size of quarters. She began to appreciate the significance of "tasting" menu. Unlike her Cape Cod waitressing days, it did not appear that the starved wraith—he of the single digit body mass index—would be required to shoulder weighty trays.

Patricia cautiously chewed a leaf of her greens. Not bad, sweet with the lavender dressing. Michael dug into his tartare with gusto and proclaimed it delicious. He scooped up a thimbleful and held it out to her.

She held up her hand. "No thank you. I'm sure it's good. I remember when Reilly family funds were low, and my mom served us SPAM. I see a resemblance."

Michael laughed then shook his head as if to deny any similarities. "We have to go out more often before a second child comes. Danny is growing up fast." Unclipping his phone from the holder on his waist, Michael pulled up a photo of Danny that Patricia had texted him. She'd taken the shot that Saturday when they flew kites on the mall. "Great picture, Patsy. Look at Danny, he's such a little man. I never considered what it would be like to raise children. Maybe because I was an only child. It's much more fun and rewarding than I expected. And you are a wonderful mother."

Patricia debated whether to re-raise his comments about Jewish mothers. Since they seemed to be airing unresolved issues, she forged ahead. "So you've forgiven me for taking Danny to the demonstration at the temple?"

"I still think it wasn't the best idea, but I can understand why you went. The scene may have been a learning experience. I mean what I said about your being a terrific mom. You read to Danny and take him to all sorts of educational places while I'm at work. You deal with doctors' appointments and carpools and meals. You relieve me of the humdrum boring stuff."

Patricia smiled. "Thanks. It's nice to feel appreciated. Promise me you'll come home earlier if we have a second. Two is more than double the work. Danny won't be happy initially about competing with a new addition."

Before Michael had to respond or commit, the wraith appeared with the next course. He set a small plate down before Michael and announced the ingredients: "beef cheeks in broth with pickled turnip, lap chong sausage, shitake mushroom, bok choy and chi raka."

A small plate appeared before Patricia. The wraith intoned "roasted Amish chicken breast, fried thigh, dandelion greens, lentils *du puy*, butternut squash." At least she recognized most of the ingredients even if she hadn't ever tasted them.

As the wraith walked away, Patricia commented that the young man should be putting his memory to better use. "He's probably working as a waiter while he tries out for roles at the local theatres," she whispered to Michael who chuckled.

Michael slurped his broth and offered a taste to Patricia. She declined again, not sure from what portion of the cow beef cheeks originated. He asked how her dish was, his code for "can I have a taste."

She pushed her plate toward him. Michael came from a family of over-sharers and not only with regard to food. She smiled, recalling the old joke about how to tell the difference between Wasps and Jews at a Chinese restaurant—the Wasps weren't sharing.

"I may not express it, but I am happy we are raising our son Jewish. My med school friend Max and his wife are trying to raise their children in two religions. Remember Max, the doc who lives in Newton? He's Jewish. She's Catholic, too."

"I'm Jewish, honey."

"Right. Well, you used to be Catholic. Anyways, he emailed me how their two kids have both been christened. His family celebrates Christmas with a tree and Hanukah with candles. They alternate where the kids go to Sunday school, one weekend at church and the next at temple. The kids keep asking what religion they are. They're going to be a holy mess."

"Or Unitarians," Patricia joked.

The wraith silently floated to the edge of the table with the next course, Michael's marrow mousse, pickled turnip, and celery leaves, and Patricia's spinach tortellini, cauliflower ala Romano with locally foraged watercress, white wine, and pine nuts.

As Michael lifted a fork to his mouth, his cell phone buzzed. He audibly groaned. "I forgot to mention I'm on call for Dr. Plotkin tonight. He's out of town. He asked if I'd cover for him as a favor, and he'd cover for me next time. He promised no emergencies expected." Michael stood up to take the call out front in the entryway.

Forgot? How could he forget, Patricia mused as she toyed with her pasta. Probably easier for him not to mention he was covering and hope he wouldn't get a call. That was her Michael, always efficient and multitasking. Be a good doc and a good husband at the same time—her marital blessing and curse, not sure which came first. She had actually been looking forward to sipping the Italian small-batched espresso listed after the menu's "Happy Endings" dessert course section. The desserts themselves were unusual: black sesame/coconut/yuzu or mango/pistachio/smoked celery root/mascarpone. She could skip those concoctions although the chocolate hazelnut/nitro milk stout/nanaimo bar might be tasty if she could figure out the last two ingredients.

Michael hurried to the table. In the shadows cast by torch flames, his face appeared carved with creases. "I'm sorry. Let's ask them for my next two courses to go. I have to get to Shady Brook Hospital. Believe it or not, Rabbi Weinstein is one of Dr. Plotkin's patients, and he's in the hospital. The ER doc said he may have had a heart attack."

Patricia dropped her fork in shock. This was not a time for petty disagreements. Setting aside her irritation at the interrupted evening, she realized she couldn't stay mad. Michael motioned to the wraith who cruised over and reluctantly agreed to have the kitchen pack Michael's sour cream and beer yeast meringue topped with caviar, and his whipped pigs tail with dehydrated cabbage and mustard seeds.

The wraith joked that it was a good thing Michael had decided not to order the bouillon of pastured animals, smoked beef fat, and lobster. "That would have been a bitch to pack. Oops, sorry," he glanced at Patricia and apologized.

Patricia doubted his sincerity, but she remembered the rule from her adolescent waitressing days: always end on a positive note with the customer so as to increase the probability of a big tip. She'd never worked at a fancy restaurant like this one, but she'd definitely been more polite.

Thank goodness she'd only ordered four courses and not Michael's six. For Michael's "happy ending," they both agreed on the summer berry dish: blueberries and black raspberries from Earth'N'Eats Farm served with buttermilk cake and classic egg white vacherins baked until dry and crunchy. The wraith assured them it would carry well minus the mulberry and strawberry sorbets.

They rushed out of the restaurant past the potted torches and patio. As if trying to lighten the heavy mood now suffocating the evening's romance, Michael joked he was relieved to be out of range of their waiter's chanting. "I was beginning to feel like I'd gone to a seder hosted by Actors Equity."

Then he turned to Patricia, framed her face with his hands and kissed her, long and hard on the lips. She inhaled the scent of him, soap and sweat, and touched his cheek. Apologizing for the truncated evening, Michael raised his arm and grabbed the first cab to the hospital. Hungry for a peanut butter sandwich and a mystery novel, Patricia drove home alone.

Chapter Twenty-Seven

Sunday, June 14

Patricia would not have felt comfortable visiting Rabbi Weinstein at Shady Brook Hospital but for the fact that Michael was the cardiologist on call. Michael and the hospitalist doctors had decided to admit the Rabbi for observation, monitoring, and more testing.

On Sunday afternoon Patricia and Danny accompanied Michael to the hospital when he went to check on Rabbi Weinstein. Patricia held Danny's hand as the threesome rode the elevator to the third-floor cardiac unit. They walked through a cheerful lobby with a play area where a young girl was sitting on a woman's lap. Danny wanted to stop, but Patricia pulled him along as they proceeded to the Rabbi's private room.

Michael knocked on the door and strode into the room. Patricia and Danny followed behind him. The sun streamed through the window blinds, brightening the beige dreariness. Rabbi Weinstein was propped up in bed, Lenore seated at his side. A tall young man, broad shouldered and bushy haired, stood next to Lenore. He was well over six feet, wore a red Nationals baseball T-shirt, and looked down at the floor. Patricia recognized him from the photos in the Rabbi's study.

Rabbi Weinstein was attached to various fluids and beeping monitors by way of tubes and wires. Danny hid behind Patricia, afraid of all the whirring machinery.

Lenore stood up shakily and smiled. "Please come in. Nice to see the doctor and his family. This big guy here is our younger son Ethan. What's your son's name?"

Patricia made introductions. "This is Danny. Mrs. Weinstein is Rabbi Weinstein's wife. Remember the Rabbi from tot Shabbat services at temple? And from Purim when everyone wore funny costumes?"

Danny murmured hello.

"Nice to meet a handsome young man like you." Lenore offered her hand to Danny and looked to Patricia. "How about if I take him out to the lobby for a few minutes? I saw some books out there my boys enjoyed. Dr. Weiss can talk with my husband, and you can visit."

Patricia and Danny nodded their assent.

"Come on, Danny. We'll read a story. Ethan, Saul, I'll be right down the hall if you need me."

After the two left, Rabbi Weinstein issued a low sigh. "This has been hard on her."

"Let's focus on you," said Michael in a soothing bedside manner. "How are you feeling?"

"Better. I wish I could eat something solid, a corned beef sandwich on rye? I'm kidding, sort of."

"We may need to run additional tests. As a precaution we have you on a restricted diet. We've also added a blood thinner to your medications which we have to monitor. The electrocardiogram and the echocardiogram showed the potential for arterial blockage. The good news is that the blood enzyme tests did not reveal any major damage to the heart. We're going to rerun those tests later today. Tomorrow you and Dr. Plotkin will discuss whether having an angiogram to pinpoint the location and extent of the potential blockage is the best approach. We have a variety of new medicines and stent procedures to treat your condition and to minimize the risk of future problems."

"Thank you, Dr. Weiss. I didn't think anything was seriously wrong at first. I've been faithful about taking my blood pressure pills. Ethan and I were throwing a baseball around after lunch yesterday at the house. I started feeling pain in my left shoulder but assumed it was because I was out of throwing practice. When the pain started shooting down my arm, we got scared. Lenore called Dr. Plotkin's answering service. They told me to go to the hospital immediately."

The Rabbi's recounting was interrupted by Ethan's hoarse chanting. "It's my fault, it's all my fault." He was nearly crying. "If I hadn't thrown the ball so hard at Dad, he wouldn't have gotten sick."

Patricia wasn't sure what to do. She felt sorry for Ethan, his long arms hanging limply by his sides, his tear-clouded eyes angled downward as if in shame. Michael moved directly in front of Ethan and looked up at him, trying to catch his gaze. Ethan continued to stare at the floor. Michael spoke quietly but forcefully as Ethan rocked back and forth.

"Ethan, your father's illness is not your fault. Your dad has a minor arterial blockage that can be treated with medicines and safe surgical procedures. Your father's condition is probably due to a combination of genetics, environment, and lifestyle. For example, years of eating corned beef sandwiches and watching hours of baseball on TV. Not that I don't enjoy baseball myself. We should all be exercising more and eating less."

"I shouldn't have thrown the ball, I shouldn't have thrown," Ethan repeated, hunching his shoulders and hugging himself.

Michael reached up and put his hand lightly on Ethan's shoulder. Ethan flinched but didn't move away as Michael continued in a calming voice. "This event may be a blessing in disguise by getting your dad into the hospital so we can diagnose and treat his problem before it becomes more serious. You can be a big help to your dad by encouraging him to live a more active life. Once he's recovered, he needs more physical exercise, not less. Walking and playing catch are great activities. And no more corned beef sandwiches for your dad. Do you think you can help your dad with his diet and exercise?"

Ethan gazed slightly to the right of Michael's face, looking relieved. He nodded in agreement and asked, "No more corned beef ever?"

Michael laughed. "On special occasions, birthdays, bar mitzvah, anniversaries."

Now it was Rabbi Weinstein's turn to look relieved. "Gee Doc, I'm glad you're willing to entertain the possibility of dietary exceptions for corned beef."

"Let's all shake on that nutritional commitment," Michael said. He held out his hand first to Ethan and then to the Rabbi. The men all shook hands.

"Dad, can I go down to the cafeteria and grab a sandwich?" asked Ethan. "This talk about food makes me hungry. I know where the cafeteria is. Maybe Mom and the little boy will go with me."

Rabbi Weinstein nodded in assent.

"Fine with me," Patricia chimed in. She was impressed and proud of her husband, Dr. Michael. It had been a long time since she'd seen Michael in action with patients and their families. He was a good caring doctor.

"Speaking of a healthier lifestyle," Rabbi Weinstein began to speak in a low voice. "I'm glad you are here today, Patricia. I want to talk with you about a few matters. Please sit next to me." The Rabbi struggled to sit upright as he spoke. "Doc, you listen too. I assume everything we discuss is between us. Doctor/patient confidentiality and all."

Surprised, Patricia moved forward and sat in the chair recently vacated by Lenore. Suddenly the room seemed over-air conditioned. She shivered and clasped her hands in front of her to keep them from trembling. Michael walked over and stood behind her, resting his hands lightly on her shoulders. Patricia felt reassured by his touch.

"This illness has put things in perspective for me." The Rabbi spoke in a somber tone. "I am sorry, Patricia, you had to witness that scene at the temple last week. Lenore and I had a long talk this morning. We agreed that it would be better for all of us, our families and our congregation, if Lenore's sister, Risa, sees an independent mental health professional for marriage counseling. I want to clear the air."

An embarrassed flush spread up Patricia's neck despite the room's chill. She was not used to playing the role of confessor. What would her priest have offered? Better yet what would Rabbi Deborah advise? "I have two sisters. I understand how intense and complicated the relationship between sisters can be. Referring Risa, I mean Mrs. Fleisher, to an outside counselor is a wise decision." Patricia bit her tongue so as not to add that Rabbi Weinstein and Lenore might also benefit from marriage counseling.

The Rabbi nodded and continued speaking. "The hospital's social worker, Betsy her name was, visited me this morning. We talked about how important it is to manage stress in our lives, not only for personal health, but for our ability to lead and to help others. Betsy lifted a glass of water sitting on my tray table and asked how heavy I judged the glass to be. Before I could answer, she explained that the absolute weight didn't matter. What matters is how long I hold the glass. Holding for a minute's not a problem. Holding for an hour or a day causes aches, pains, and medical emergencies. If we carry our burdens with us all the time, sooner or later the burdens become too heavy to allow us to carry on with our lives in a meaningful way. Only when we put down our burdens, can we be refreshed enough to determine how to handle our problems."

Patricia thought the rabbi was sounding a little preachy from his sick bed. Before she could respond, Michael chimed in. "Betsy gave you excellent advice. Stress negatively impacts our health and affects how well we recover from illness. And how quickly you can return to work."

"Thank you, Dr. Weiss." The Rabbi slowly raised his hand toward Michael as if to utter a blessing. Then his hand dropped. "In that vein, I want to put down my burdens. Patricia, you were asking about donations to the temple. I want to share with you and Dr. Weiss, in confidence, that my Discretionary Fund may be low. Once he turned twenty-one, Ethan no longer qualified for free government programs. He needs a special kind of support to help him function to his full potential. We are paying an arm and a leg for Ethan's care at Eden Homes. It's a community for young adults on the autism spectrum. I needed a loan to pay Eden's fees. I discussed it with Morris, and he approved the short-term borrowing from the Discretionary Fund."

Straightening, Patricia focused on Rabbi Weinstein. In a soft but firm voice, she asked, "Do you know how Morris obtained the cash from the fund?"

Michael moved to face her with a questioning look. "I don't understand. What's going on with temple donations? A discretionary fund?"

Taking Michael's hand, Patricia told him she'd explain later and reiterated her question to the Rabbi. How did Morris obtain the cash?

"I'm not sure." The Rabbi's breathing quickened, and he began to perspire. "Morris said it wasn't a problem because I was going to pay back the money ASAP. Plus there's flexibility as to how the Discretionary Fund can be used. I see now the inappropriateness of what I did, even if it was technically kosher and for a good cause. Immediately upon my release from the hospital, I'll repay the loan, even if we have to borrow from Lenore's family trust."

"Did you tell anyone else about the loan?" Patricia asked. "Adrienne maybe?"

"No, no one else. Patricia, I know you and the Doc understand and can keep this between us, patient confidentiality and all." The Rabbi slumped against his pillow, pale and exhausted after his sermon-like confession.

Patricia wanted to ask more but the Rabbi was growing short of breath, and his eyes were closing. Michael put a hand on the Rabbi's forehead as if to confirm her evaluation. The noise of the door opening caught their attention. Adrienne and Carol, the temple staff contingent, barged in without knocking.

Michael turned and admonished Adrienne: "I believe the hospital's cardiac unit allows patients only two visitors at a time. The Rabbi has to rest."

"Oh, it's only us. There won't be a problem," Adrienne assured Michael, who rolled his eyes.

"I'm fine, Dr. Weiss." The Rabbi's voice barely rose above a whisper. "I'm glad to see Adrienne and Carol. Thank you for coming."

Carol was carrying a box from Mandel's Bakery. "Rabbi, we have a treat for you. Your favorite bakery was on the way to the hospital. How could we not stop?" She opened the box and offered a Danish to the Rabbi who was struggling to sit up into a more dignified position.

Michael stepped between the pastry box and the Rabbi's bed. "Rabbi Weinstein is not allowed to eat Danish today. He's undergoing tests. In fact we should all be staying away from pastry."

"Well, I already bought them. I'll have this small cherry-cheese Danish. Does anyone else want one?" Carol moved the box in front of Patricia who demurred and then Adrienne who helped herself to a prune Danish. Carol pulled out napkins, but crumbs spilled onto the floor as she munched.

"The nurse will clean it up," Adrienne announced to the room as she moved closer to the bed. "Rabbi, you look lousy. What are they doing for you? You must feel like crap." She turned to face Michael. "Can't they give him something to make him feel better?"

Without waiting for an answer she barreled on. "My husband keeps complaining about chest pains. He doesn't look as bad as the Rabbi. Dr. Weiss, how can we tell if he's having a heart attack? I don't trust his internist, Dr. Hoenig. Have you heard of him?"

"I don't know him personally, but Dr. Hoenig has a fine reputation."

The door opened again. Lenore entered with Danny and Ethan in tow. The two boys were talking baseball although Ethan's gaze quickly focused on the Mandel's box.

A nurse followed them in. Michael directed her to check the Rabbi's vital signs. After ascertaining the measurements were stable, Michael announced he, Patricia, and Danny were leaving. He asked the nurse to assist the other non-family visitors with their goodbyes to the Rabbi. Michael stared pointedly at Adrienne and Carol.

As she exited the room, Patricia recalled another joke of Brenda's about the difference between Gentile, the generic term for non-Jews, and Jewish guests. "Gentile guests," Brenda had said, "leave and never say goodbye. Jewish guests say goodbye and never leave."

Patricia hoped the nurse could convince Adrienne and Carol to depart quickly. The Rabbi looked very fatigued despite putting down his burdens. Now, Patricia had a few more of her own burdens to put down. She owed Michael an explanation of the shenanigans going on with the temple's stock donations. It was going to be a challenging afternoon.

271

Chapter Twenty-Eight

Monday, June 15

Gathering up the ten books she and Danny had taken out of the library, Patricia perused the kitchen table and her desk. Satisfied she'd caught any strays, she stacked the volumes: books about trucks, cars, and construction sites; a beautifully illustrated collection of fairy tales with scary plots; books with bear characters that taught lessons about too much TV and messy rooms—her attempt to convince Danny to start cleaning up after himself as opposed to following his father's example; and a couple of fun Dr. Seuss books—the only ones she recalled from her childhood.

Patricia made an effort to read to Danny at least thirty minutes a day, longer if he was interested. She wanted to give him a good foundation for learning to read on his own, maybe before kindergarten. Her own parents never concerned themselves with the ages at which their daughters started to read. Who knew which was the better approach.

Perhaps because of Rabbi Weinstein's health crisis or because of their weekend heart-to heart, Michael had been surprisingly receptive to Patricia's recounting of her discovery of apparent inconsistencies in the temple's donation records. He said he was impressed with her sleuthing into the temple's accounting issues. Could he be turning over a new leaf and reconciling himself to her puzzle-solving obsession?

A knock on the screen door startled her. She walked then ran toward the noise. Her heart pounding, she cried out, "Hail Mary, Mother of God, thank you Jesus" and threw open the door. "Rabbi Deborah, thank God. I'm so glad to see you." Patricia bent over and threw her arms around the woman.

"I see you're covering all your divine bases." Rabbi Deborah laughed, putting down the stuffed laundry bag she was carrying, and returning the hug.

"Come in, come in. Sorry, old habits die hard." As Patricia's pulse slowed, she noticed Rabbi Deborah looked bronzed and hale, a bit rounder. She was dressed in cargo pants and a blue T-shirt imprinted with a white dove and the logo, Israel Peace and Love.

From the family room, Danny ran into the kitchen. He stood behind Patricia and waved at the Rabbi.

Rabbi Deborah smiled broadly and waved back. She motioned behind her. The point of a tapping cane crossed the door's threshold followed by a diminutive older woman. Hobbling in and wearing a powder blue pants suit, she resembled a wizened bird. "Oy, such a nice house," she chirped in a thick Yiddish accent. "The Rabbi tells me you're married to a doctor?"

"Patricia, let me introduce you to my new friend, Channah Berman. She's originally from Grovno, Poland."

"I came in 1937 with my mother and sisters," Channah said. "Our father was already in New York City, working in a sweat shop. The aunts, uncles, cousins who stayed behind—they were killed by the

Nazis. I need to sit." The elderly lady tottered over to the kitchen table and plopped into a chair before continuing. "The Jewish people must stick together and make sure the next generation doesn't forget. That's why I was so aggravated about my grandson Jason and his *shiksa* girlfriend. I feel better now, after discussing with the Rabbi. She knows what she's talking about, even if she's still single. I told my grandson all about the Rabbi's Israel trip. Jason and the girlfriend want to go on the next one."

"Rabbi, what's Channah talking about? Were you really leading a trip in Israel?" Patricia stared in confusion at the Rabbi. She tried to keep the hurt out of her voice. "Why didn't you tell anyone? We were worried. Why didn't you answer my texts?"

"Wait—you didn't get my message? Morris never called you? I left a note with him to give to Rabbi Weinstein, too. I kept meaning to text but things were so hectic and the cell service was erratic."

"I didn't get any message from Morris."

"I don't understand what happened." Rabbi Deborah gave Patricia a pleading look and reached up to touch her shoulder. "That Tuesday after the canal, I went home to change. I had an urgent message on my phone from Channah. She wanted to talk to me about intermarriage, because her grandson had announced his engagement to a Methodist girl. I had free time that afternoon, so I drove over to Channah's apartment. While we were discussing, I got a call on my cell from Love Milk and Honey Style. They said the rabbi who was supposed to lead their impending trip to Israel had come down with a serious case of the flu and asked if I could step in."

"Love Milk and Honey Style?" asked Patricia.

"Yes, it's a wonderful program. Love Milk and Honey Style, LMHS for short, takes interfaith couples on tours of Israel. The program's open to committed partners, married or not, regardless of sexual orientation, as long as one of them is Jewish. The idea is that the couples will be encouraged to incorporate Jewish values and traditions into their lives. And the trips are cheap because LMHS is foundation subsidized. I've been in contact with them for over a year, because I was interested in leading a tour."

"Sounds great. I wish the trip had been around when Michael and I were younger. Why didn't you tell us where you were going? Why keep it a mystery? We were so worried."

"Mommy, are we going on a trip?" Danny piped up from behind Patricia.

"Sorry, Danny, no kids allowed on this trip." The Rabbi wrung her hands in a contrite gesture. "Sorry about causing all the worry. After I explained the LMHS program to Channah, we called her grandson Jason, who's interested in the next one. Then I drove home, packed some clothes and my passport. I ubered to the temple to pick up a few things from my office. Morris was the only person around by then, sitting at his desk in the library. I ran in, told him what was up, and wrote a note for him to give to Rabbi Weinstein about my plan. Morris said he'd find the key, unlock the Rabbi's office and leave the note on his desk. I gave him your phone number and asked him to call you. He promised he would call ASAP."

"He never called," said Patricia, shaking her head in frustration. After all the worry and aggravation she had put herself and Brenda through, Patricia couldn't believe the Rabbi's unexplained disappearance was the result of crossed signals. But was Morris's dropping the ball a simple misunderstanding? Or did he do it on purpose? She felt her cheeks start to flush in anger.

"I meant to text you, but I was in a big rush. I raced to the airport and just made my flight," Rabbi Deborah apologized. "By the time I thought about texting, I was on the plane and didn't have service."

"Morris never called. Apparently, he didn't leave a note for Rabbi Weinstein. Unless the Rabbi was faking his concern this whole time."

"I don't get it. Why didn't Morris leave the note or call you? Could he have forgotten? Been confused? Please don't be upset with me," Rabbi Deborah said contritely.

"I have my suspicions. There's lots going on here I have to tell you about. My guess is Morris wanted to create a fracas about your absence and divert attention from misappropriated temple donations." Patricia gave Rabbi Deborah a hard gaze, still not ready to grant forgiveness. "But if you hadn't been so secretive, we could have avoided some of the uproar. Brenda, me, Rabbi Weinstein, the police—we were all trying to figure out where you were, if you were in danger, if you'd been kidnapped!"

"I was afraid my leading the LMHS tour would create more of an uproar. Adrienne ordered me to leave the temple grounds. After the demonstration, she screamed at me for giving the temple a bad rep and instructed me to keep a low profile. Like hide in a cave. What better place for caves than Israel. I bet she wasn't all that concerned about my absence."

"Come to think of it, you're right. But the rest of us were frantic—me, Brenda, Rabbi Weinstein."

"There's another reason I had to get away and clear my head. Rabbi Weinstein's counseling his sister-in-law was making me ill." Rabbi Deborah exhaled deeply, sounding like a punctured balloon. "I was beginning to suspect they were having an affair. I was afraid that if I raised the issue with him after the demonstration, he'd think I was trying to distract him from the interfaith marriage furor, even blackmailing him to lay off my case." Rubbing her forehead, Rabbi Deborah suddenly paled beneath her Israeli suntan.

"Events may have superseded your concerns. Rabbi Weinstein is in the hospital. He had a mild heart attack, but he is recovering with no permanent damage. Not to worry, his attack was probably not due to the demonstration," Patricia reassured her. "He has bigger problems. Among other things, I have to catch you up on the Lenore-Risa-Rabbi triangle. The situation may be resolved, although who knows how far down the track that train might have traveled."

"Thank God Saul is going to be okay. I want to hear all about it. He's been my mentor and supported me at the temple—except for my stance on intermarriage." Rabbi Deborah shook her head and continued. "*Mea culpa.* First I will apologize to him for disappearing, for causing so much trouble. Would you ask Dr. Michael to tell Saul I've returned safely? I'd like to stop by the hospital for a visit this afternoon. I don't want to shock Saul into cardiac arrest."

"Good idea. Will do. I'll call Michael, and Brenda too, to let them know you're home. The police will have to be informed." Patricia paused for a breath.

"And we have to confront Morris about why he never delivered the messages. We need to be careful." Patricia was about to jump in and detail the potential stock certificate mystery. "Listen to what I've discovered about stock donations to Rabbi Weinstein's discretionary fund."

"Wait one minute," Rabbi Deborah interrupted her. "Let me introduce my LMHS co-leader." Rabbi Deborah turned and motioned once more.

Patricia noticed someone waiting patiently by the door.

"This is Amir Faryad. He's originally from Baghdad by way of Cambridge, England, where he studied philosophy and religion." Rabbi Deborah was beaming. "Now he's a medical technician and studying for a business degree. He's interested in the topic of interfaith marriage from the Muslim perspective."

An attractive dark-haired man strode through the door. Patricia observed that he was a few inches shorter than Michael and very fit, lean to the point of wiry. A black polo shirt and designer jeans hugged his body. He smiled in greeting. Patricia held out her hand. Amir's hand remained at his side.

"Amir doesn't touch women with whom he does not have a familial relationship." Rabbi Deborah explained.

"I am pleased to meet you, Mrs. Weiss. Deborah has talked about you. I was honored to accompany Deborah on the Israel trip." Amir bowed slightly toward the Rabbi and continued in a melodious voice. "Not only is Israel rich in culture and history. It is a powerful place to consider questions of religion and identity no matter your views on Israel's government.

We visited sites important to many religions: the Baha'i Gardens and Shrine of the Bab, the Beit Hagefen Jewish-Arab Culture Center, and Bethlehem's Church of the Nativity."

"And we explored the Jewish, Muslim, Christian and Armenian quarters of Jerusalem's old city and paid our respects at the Dome of the Rock and the Al Aqsa Mosque, the Temple Mount and the Western Wall, and the Church of the Holy Sepulcher," Rabbi Deborah elaborated. "We meditated at Jerusalem's Neve Flow Yoga Center. Jews, Christians, Muslims— everyone can share the universal experience of breathing with intention."

"Oy, hearing about all this traveling and breathing makes me tired and thirsty." Channah coughed as if to remind everyone of her presence. "My throat is parched. Mrs. Patricia, you have anything to drink?"

"I apologize. Would you like a hot or cold drink? I have coffee, tea, ice water or juice?"

"Coffee would be nice. With cream and sugar. Do you have a sweet to go with the coffee? Rugeleh? A Danish? Is he your son?" Channah pointed her cane at Danny. "He looks hungry."

"Mommy, can I have a snack?"

"Channah, please meet my son, Danny. Sorry, we don't have Danish. We do have Oreos. Danny, you can have one cookie, but let me serve our guests first."

Luckily Patricia hadn't yet spilled out the remains of her recently brewed coffee. She poured a cup for Channah and asked the Rabbi and Amir what they'd like. Rabbi Deborah took a seat and asked for a glass of water. Amir remained standing and declined any refreshment.

"Channah, I hope we're not tiring you out. Thank you for helping us out," said Rabbi Deborah. "I didn't want to take a taxi straight home from the airport. I wasn't sure what might be going on at my place. More protestors? Amir and I took a cab to Channah's apartment. Since it wasn't too far, I asked her to drive us here."

"I'm fine. Don't worry about me." Channah grabbed an Oreo from the plate Patricia had set on the table and stuffed the cookie into her mouth. She chewed and talked, spewing cookie crumbs. "Jason's such a smart boy. He was talking medical school. All of a sudden, he decides he wants to be some kind of investment guy. It's his *shiksa* girlfriend's fault. She wants him to make money quick. When they announce they're engaged, I ask if they're going to raise the kids Jewish. Jason tells me they don't know if they'll have kids. He says it's so expensive now to raise kids and the world is such a mess. No kids? Who ever heard of such a thing? What else do they have to spend their money on?"

Rabbi Deborah gently placed her smooth hand on top of Channah's deeply furrowed one. "Channah, we discussed how your grandson and fiancée need to make their own decisions with regard to having children and how they'll be raised. By going on the LMHS trip, we hope Jason and his fiancée Brook will feel welcomed into the Jewish community and be encouraged to participate."

"Yeah yeah. I'm trying to be open-minded. Brook—who ever heard of a girl named Brook? Now she says she's interested in converting. I'll buy her a nice gold necklace with the Hebrew letter *chai* sign as an engagement present. I'll explain *chai* means good luck and to life. Making new lives. Children. I'll tell her the magic works better if you're Jewish."

"The necklace would be a lovely gesture," affirmed Rabbi Deborah.

"The Rabbi needs to be fixed up," Channah announced to the room. "Don't you agree, Amir? Amir seems like a nice man. Too bad he's a Muslim."

"Ah, but under Islamic law, a Muslim man is permitted to marry a non-Muslim woman provided she is from among the People of the Book, in other words, a female Jew or Christian," said Amir. His face maintained a serious expression, but he seemed to have a sparkle in his eye. "So that would not be a problem for me. Although Muslim men are allowed to have up to four wives if they can all be treated justly. That might present a problem for the lovely and learned Deborah." He broke into a smile as he nodded toward the Rabbi.

Was it Patricia's imagination or was Rabbi Deborah blushing?

Seeming to want to divert attention to a more academic subject, Rabbi Deborah described how she and Amir had an interesting discussion about her sermon on the Ruth story and that he disagreed with her analysis.

"Yes, let me explain." Amir spoke up again. "In biblical times, women were treated as chattel, and their religious affiliation was irrelevant to the religion of their children. Religion was inherited along patrilineal lines. Not until the Middle Ages did inheritance of religion begin to proceed along matrilineal lines."

"Even if we don't agree, I am willing to concede

that Amir is very knowledgeable about world religions," Rabbi Deborah commented approvingly. "We've discussed developing an interfaith dialogue group between Jews and Muslims in the greater Washington D.C. area. We both agree that Islam and Judaism have many kindred religious traditions. For example, both Muslims and Jews are spiritual descendants of Abraham."

"Yes, and both Abraham's sons, Isaac and Ishmael, came together to bury him," added Amir. "The Jewish patriarch and the Muslim patriarch joined forces."

Rabbi Deborah nodded and rolled on. "Both traditions encompass a religion and a culture that cannot be completely captured in the written liturgy. Not the Torah nor the Koran. More on this later," she concluded as she scratched her scalp. "Now I need to go home and shower. Patricia, can you and Danny give Amir and me a ride to my townhouse? We can confirm everything's calm before you drop us off. This way Channah can drive home to her apartment. I can give Amir a ride to the Metro. He lives in Columbia Heights."

"Wait a minute, I haven't finished my coffee." Channah made a loud slurping noise. "Coffee's a *bissel*, a little too strong for me. I could use a warm-up. And a few more of those cookies? More cream?"

Giddy with relief, Patricia practically skipped to the coffee pot. "More coffee, cookies, and cream coming right up. Of course Rabbi, we can give you a ride home."

Thank God Rabbi Deborah had returned safely, although Patricia wasn't sure that the Rabbi was sufficiently contrite about all the anxiety her unexplained absence had caused. In the glow of her Israel adventure and newfound companion, she probably couldn't fully appreciate the shadow her disappearance had cast over the lives of Patricia, Brenda, and the temple community. At least Patricia could close one of her investigative files.

But the troubles for the temple, for the rabbis, for Roberto's family, were not over.

Chapter Twenty-Nine

Monday, June 15

As she sped along the road with Rabbi Deborah next to her in the front seat and Danny and Amir in back, Patricia tried to keep her pent-up anxiety from spilling over. "I can't believe you walked into my kitchen this morning. We are so glad you've returned, right Danny?"

"Mommy and I looked for you."

"I missed you and your mom. Thank you for looking for me."

"I didn't tell anyone about your text message, except Brenda and Michael," said Patricia. "Keeping the secret was making me crazy. How did Channah get your number in the first place?"

"Channah knows Morris Mizchek, the temple's bookkeeper. They're both in a widower's support group at the Jewish Community Center. Morris heard about my sermon. Of course, who hadn't? He gave Channah my phone numbers, at temple and at home. My contact information is publicly listed. I want to be available to temple members or whoever else in the community needs support, especially about interfaith marriage."

"I met with Morris," interjected Patricia. "I haven't had a chance to tell you. In your absence, I started volunteering at the temple. Adrienne assigned me the task of computerizing the temple's donations. I had to talk to Morris about bookkeeping irregularities. He comes across as a pathetic old man, but there's something unsavory underneath the surface." Patricia shivered remembering Morris's gnarled hand reaching out to grab her knee, and Marilyn peeing in his office dungeon.

"Wait, first tell me what's happening with the investigation of Roberto's accident." asked Rabbi Deborah, leaning toward Patricia as if trying to check the speedometer. "Speaking of which, aren't you driving too fast?"

Patricia shrugged and maintained her speed. "Trying to get you home ASAP. I'll slow down if it makes you nervous." She was tempted to floor it, give Rabbi Deborah a taste of her own medicine. But Patricia forced her foot to release. Not very Christian or Jewish to act on her anger. Plus Danny was in the car. "The police are continuing to investigate. They found discrepancies between the tire tracks in the lot and the garbage truck."

"What's that mean?" asked Rabbi Deborah.

"The discrepancy leads to a conclusion that the garbage truck may not have hit Roberto after all. And maybe it's not an accident. But no resolution yet. A couple days after you left, Carol discovered a note from Roberto in one of her piles. It was addressed to you. Roberto wanted to talk privately with you about papers he found in the garbage."

"Oh no, I wish I had had the chance to talk with him. What papers?"

"Everyone's asking the same question," responded

Patricia. "Brenda and I met with Bertilla and asked about Roberto's note. She said a couple days before Roberto died, he'd found some kind of financial records in the wastebasket. He wondered if they'd been thrown out by mistake and went to talk to Morris. Like you said, Morris hangs around the temple at night. Morris says no mistake because the records are old, rips them up, and instructs Roberto to put the papers back in the trash. That's all Bertilla knows."

"I can't believe this. What is going on?"

"Here's my guess. Morris and Rabbi Weinstein are caught up in some kind of loan fraud with the temple's donations." Struggling to keep her eyes on the road, Patricia summarized the Risa-Rabbi-Lenore blow-up, the Rabbi's health crisis, and the Rabbi's loan confession. "By conveniently not delivering your messages about the Israel tour, Morris managed to distract everyone from the borrowing scheme he and Rabbi Weinstein cooked up."

"That's awful. *Mea culpa* for leaving you with all this."

"The good news for you is that Rabbi Weinstein has much bigger problems to deal with than your sermon and mysterious disappearance."

"Let's hope." Rabbi Deborah rolled her eyes at the irony of the situation. "I guess whatever occurred in that love triangle has been resolved, at least temporarily." Rabbi Deborah's voice took on a serious tone. "And Saul is going to make a full recovery?"

"Assuming some lifestyle changes that's the preliminary prognosis." Patricia explained how Michael ended up being the cardiologist on call, how they visited Rabbi Weinstein at the hospital, and that his heart had not suffered extensive damage.

"Thank God for that," Rabbi Deborah exclaimed as she relaxed into the passenger seat.

Amir murmured, "*Alayhi as-salaam*" from the back seat and explained to Danny the Arabic phrase means "peace be upon him." Danny asked Amir to teach him the words.

"Now Michael and I are debating what to do about Rabbi Weinstein's admission. He confessed to us that the Morris "approved" loan was from the discretionary fund and was for Ethan's care. The Rabbi said he was sharing in confidence. Michael says there's no medical confidentiality for financial fraud." Patricia threw up her hands for a second in frustration and grabbed the wheel again.

"Ethan's nice," Danny piped up from the backseat. "He is going to teach me to play baseball." Patricia hadn't realized Danny was listening so closely. Oh dear.

"Ethan is a good baseball player. I've watched him play softball at the temple picnic," said Rabbi Deborah, turning to smile at Danny. "I hope you and your mom and dad will come to the picnic this summer."

"We definitely plan on going." Patricia reached around and grabbed one of the library books she had thrown on the floor of the back seat. She pushed the book toward Danny to redirect his attention to the pictures. "Frankly, I don't see how Morris had authority to approve or in any way facilitate a loan. Wouldn't the decision be up to the temple board?"

"Yes, of course," Rabbi Deborah confirmed. "It's highly questionable whether money from the discretionary fund could be loaned to a rabbi for personal reasons, even for a sympathetic family situation. Although there are no written guidelines for the fund's use. As best I remember, the fund's description simply says donations can be used for congregational needs as determined by the rabbi. I can't say I'm surprised. Saul was so preoccupied, even before Roberto's death and my sermon."

"What should be done about the loan?" asked Patricia.

"In my role as clergy, I'll take responsibility for dealing with Saul's loan. I'll talk with him first and then with the temple's officers and board of trustees. I'll explain to Saul that you confided in me as your spiritual advisor. Isn't that kind of communication legally protected?"

Patricia exhaled a grateful sigh of thanks. "Yes, I remember my dad talking about the clergy confessional privilege that witnesses invoked. Let's pray there's a resolution before anything gets as far as a trial."

"Assuming the loan's repaid, I'm fairly certain the temple won't pursue the matter in court," Rabbi Deborah assured her. "The board will likely try to keep the matter in-house, to minimize negative publicity."

"Now what do we do about Morris? The Rabbi says Morris approved the loan. Sounds like Morris didn't have the authority to approve. Plus there's the issue of why Morris never delivered your messages."

"We should talk with Morris and hear his side of the story. I don't understand why he never left my messages. Maybe he thought he had authority to approve the loan under extenuating circumstances. He could have a good excuse for at least some of his actions."

"Or not." Patricia shook her head. "We have to tread carefully. Morris also seems to be mixed up in some kind of stock scam. He may have sold stock donated to the discretionary fund and generated cash for the Rabbi's loan. And for some of his own purposes, this Torah scroll business. Roberto could have found evidence of the scam. I haven't been able to confirm yet."

As they approached Rabbi Deborah's neighborhood, Patricia quickly summarized the potential connection between the railroad trust stock certificates and the train engraved scrap found in Roberto's pocket. "We should contact the police. I'll consult with Adrienne and Officer O'Donnell. We need to set up a meeting with Morris."

"That's advisable, as much as the temple will hate to involve the police in its business."

"Will the temple really let this loan hanky-panky go away? Not press charges? Against either Rabbi Weinstein or Morris?"

"Yes, as long as there's no permanent harm. On the positive side, forgiveness is a mitzvah, a divine command, in Judaism," Rabbi Deborah opined. "The Torah, in Leviticus, explicitly forbids us to take revenge or to bear grudges. Look at Joseph. His brothers sold him into slavery. After he miraculously interpreted the Pharoah's dream and predicted a famine, he became viceroy of Egypt. When his brothers came to him dependent on his power and mercy, he forgave them."

"Thanks for the mini lecture. Forgiveness via confession and penance," Patricia said. "Sounds familiar."

"I certainly would prefer the forgiveness route,

including for my own insensitive conduct. I want to expend my energies on pursuing an interfaith forum, not on a punitive court case. Amir and I might eventually offer seminars and counseling. The goal is to make Jews more open to embracing people of other faiths and cultures, and to accept differences within the Jewish community itself."

"And my goal is to build bridges among Muslims regardless of whether they are Sunni or Shia," added Amir from behind. "Islam, like Judaism, values debate and free exchange of ideas. The history of hostilities between the Islamic sects is shameful."

"What will Rabbi Weinstein think—you'll both probably give him another heart attack," Patricia joked. She could be mistaken but Rabbi Deborah seemed infatuated and not only with her interfaith dialogue project. After all, Amir was smart and handsome.

"We'll begin slowly. We may start with an evening of exploration to promote understanding among religious groups. I don't see how Rabbi Weinstein can be against that," said Rabbi Deborah.

"You'd be surprised," Patricia said dryly.

Rabbi Deborah didn't seem to hear. "The demonstration at our temple showed what a critical need the interfaith dialogue would fill. I also plan to put together a roster of rabbis who perform interfaith weddings. Besides, Rabbi Weinstein will want my support when he informs the temple about his borrowing. In Judaism a prerequisite to God's forgiveness is correcting the damage done and asking for forgiveness from the one who suffered. Saul will have to ask for forgiveness from the congregation and repay the loan."

"To be continued. Here we are." Patricia pulled in front of the townhouse. "The coast is clear. No protestors."

As Amir and Rabbi Deborah stepped out of the car, Danny waved goodbye. "Mommy, when can Amir teach me more words?"

"Soon, soon," said Patricia, impressed by her son's curiosity. Hadn't she read that to be a Jewish child is to learn how to question? Was she succeeding in raising Danny with Jewish values? Had she herself been born with an old Jewish soul in a previous incarnation? Always questioning instead of complying with dogma?

"Mommy, we passed by the Burger Bliss. I'm hungry."

Patricia smiled, glad that Danny had been distracted by food. He definitely took after his father. "You've been very patient during all the grownup discussion. What a busy morning. We deserve a treat." She pressed on the gas and headed toward the fast food.

Chapter Thirty

Tuesday, June 16

Patricia sat at what she now considered her desk in Rabbi Weinstein's outer office and pondered how best to confront Morris about the stock certificates, his loan approval, his conversation with Roberto, and his failure to deliver Rabbi Deborah's messages. Rabbi Weinstein was recovering from his heart episode and not back to work. She couldn't question him further about the status of the stock certificates. Besides, his previous responses had been vague and uninformative. At least Rabbi Weinstein had admitted why his discretionary fund was low. Thank goodness, Rabbi Deborah had offered to deal with ramifications of the loan confession.

Rabbi Deborah had notified the temple, aka Adrienne, yesterday afternoon that she'd returned from an unexpected trip due to a "last minute situation," and would explain in more detail today. Adrienne was left to speculate.

First thing this morning, Adrienne whispered to Patricia that Rabbi Deborah might be trying to kick an addiction. Or she'd flown off on a romantic fling with an inappropriate beau and been dumped. Or she'd been on a spy mission for a radical organization. Then

Adrienne deposited a pile of certificates and donation letters from the safe on Patricia's desk to add to the not-yet-completed computerized listing.

Rabbi Deborah arrived late, carrying two huge boxes of Danish and donuts, her peace offering and bribe for the temple staff. She was meeting with Adrienne at this very minute to inform her about the true nature of the mystery trip. Patricia mused. Was the Rabbi apologizing profusely and groveling? Or claiming she was only following Adrienne's orders? Probably some combination thereof. The LMHS tour would not enhance her reputation with Adrienne who already blamed her for causing the demonstration and contributing to Rabbi Weinstein's heart attack. Would Rabbi Deborah decide this was an opportune time to inform Adrienne about the loan? Did Adrienne suspect, although Rabbi Weinstein claimed he never told her?

Adrienne had notified the police of Rabbi Deborah's return on Monday afternoon. This morning Adrienne informed Patricia that Officer O'Donnell would be over to talk with Rabbi Zalman and other staff before he closed the case.

Running her fingers through her thick hair, Patricia removed an elastic from her tote and twisted her locks into a ponytail. She surveyed her desktop littered with a mess of colorful certificates. After spilling some of her grande skim cappuccino on one of the folders, she positioned the partially empty cup on the other side of the phone and away from the documents. In Rabbi Weinstein's absence, the phone rarely buzzed. She had no excuse for not focusing on the task at hand.

What exactly had happened with the railway trust and other stock certificates sitting at the center of her desk? Mr. Schwabstein, the broker, said they'd been cashed in or sold. Had these physical certificates inadvertently fallen off the grid? Patricia sipped her lukewarm cappuccino and drummed her short nails against the computer keyboard.

Since Adrienne had approved her previous request, Patricia decided to make copies of the certificates in question. She'd ask Adrienne to schedule a meeting with Mr. Schwabstein. They'd bring him the copies, and he'd figure out the problem. By then Kevin's experts would certainly have ascertained any connection between the railway trust certificates and the train-engraved scrap.

Until she had the relevant background info, Patricia didn't want to question Morris. If she put him on alert, he might destroy documents or abscond with ill-gotten gains. Once she coordinated with Kevin, they'd set up a meeting to confront Morris about the status of the certificates as well as the loan approval, the Roberto conversation, and why he never delivered Rabbi Deborah's messages.

For the moment, Patricia took the path of least resistance and headed toward the copier with a folder full of certificates. She was thankful she had mastered the operation of the temple's fancy copy machine standing outside the library. As Adrienne had advertised, the machine did make beautiful color reproductions.

Following Adrienne's detailed instructions, Patricia carefully removed a railway trust certificate from the folder, this one tinted blue. She lifted the machine's cover and slid the certificate onto the glass surface. She pushed various buttons. After humming and beeping, the machine's side vent spewed forth a copy of the certificate into the plastic tray. An identical copy. Look at that blue locomotive faithfully reproduced in all its detail. Patricia lifted the original from the glass surface with her right hand and picked up the copy with her left. She held the papers up for comparison. The copy was so exact she was hard-pressed to tell which certificate was the original. She'd have to be careful not to mix them up. Amazing how well the color reproduced. She copied another certificate, this one tinted red and then a third tinted green.

An inkling teased the edge of her mind. "Analyze like a detective!" Patricia admonished herself. Aside from the stock certificates piled next to the copier, where else had she seen colorful papers like this? The temple's shower curtain covering the ark? Danny's crayon creations at home? Bright kites soaring over the mall?

The hunch arrived in a rush: multi-hued paper stuffed in trash bags that she'd laughed about with Roberto that Thursday evening before his death. Why this rainbow of wastepaper? Imperfect copies not good enough to pass as originals? Made by someone who had easy access to the copier? In fact, maybe none of the colorful certificates in her hands were originals. Were the railway trust certificates stored in the temple's safe merely copied placeholders to avoid detection of the sale of the original certificates? Patricia carefully separated the copied pages from the "original" certificates, gathered up the two piles, and raced to her desk.

If the original stock certificates had been copied before they were sold, who was the likely perpetrator of this switcheroo shell game? Only Rabbi Weinstein, Morris, and Adrienne had keys to the safe. Adrienne had the expertise with respect to using the copier. But Rabbi Weinstein and Morris had the motivation since they needed a chunk of cash to cover the Rabbi's loan and potentially some of Morris's other projects like those Torah scrolls.

Had Roberto recognized the nature of the colorful trash as he emptied the temple's wastebaskets? Were those the papers that Roberto had shown Morris in case they'd been thrown out by mistake? Were those papers what Roberto had wanted to discuss with Rabbi Deborah? Was that why Roberto was found with the train-engraved scrap in his pocket? Had Roberto saved part of a certificate to study further? To protect himself? With good intentions? With questionable intentions?

"Ms. Patricia, can we speak a minute?"

She jumped, quickly shifting her focus from the stock certificates to a deep voice she recognized. Speaking of the devil. "Hello Kevin, I mean Officer O'Donnell."

He approached her desk. "Sorry, I didn't mean to startle you."

Patricia felt his bulk looming over her. "Would you like to sit down?" She pointed to the chair on the opposite side of her desk.

"No thanks. I've been informed Rabbi Zalman has returned so we'll be able to close the case. As we surmised, her absence was voluntary. Can you enlighten me as to its nature?"

"Yes, it's wonderful that Rabbi Deborah's back but you'd best talk with her."

"Zalman's in with Adrienne. I will definitely be speaking with her when she's out."

Prime time for a subject change, and Patricia needed information from Kevin. "Has there been any progress in the investigation into Roberto's accident? Have your experts done the comparison of the railroad trust stock and the scrap found in Roberto's pocket?"

"I'm waiting to hear on that. As a matter of fact, I wanted to ask you about that Thursday evening, May seventh, when you spoke with Gomez. The temple's surveillance camera does not show the back lot where the garbage bin is located and where Gomez's body was found. The camera's range is limited to the front parking lot. That night's surveillance footage shows two cars remaining in the lot as of about nine o'clock, Roberto's blue compact and a gold Cadillac convertible we have identified as belonging to Morris Mizchek. Adrienne told me Mizchek is the temple's bookkeeper. As I may have mentioned earlier, the tire tracks adjacent to Gomez's body did not match those of the garbage truck. The tracks do appear to match those of the model of car owned by Mizchek. Have you met him?"

Patricia's stomach churned from shock and too much caffeine. She fanned her flushing face with one of the files littering the desk. Her suspicions had already been raised about Morris's involvement in the stock scam. Could this old guy be so nefarious as to have also played a role in Roberto's death? He seemed so pitiful, no family, in poor health. Now was the time to tell Kevin what she had discovered. She confirmed that she had met with Mizchek to inquire about the valuation of the temple stock.

"Do you recall if you saw Mizchek at the temple on the evening of May seventh?"

"No. I did not see him although that was before we had ever met, and I only got as far as the main office that night. So the police are seriously considering the possibility that Roberto's death was not an accident?"

Kevin nodded in assent as if to avoid acknowledging the possibility out loud.

Trying to control the anxiety in her voice, Patricia hurried on. "I do recall when Roberto and I spoke, we talked about his computer class and paperless offices. Trash bags stuffed with tinted paper were leaning against the wall. My son Danny started scribbling on a sheet. I'm not sure how relevant this is, but it's possible the trash bags contained discarded copies of stock certificates that had been donated to the temple."

"Whoa, slow down," Kevin said. "I'm not following you."

Patricia's thoughts and words were racing. No more of those grande cappuccinos for her. She took a deep breath. "Someone with access to the certificates may have made copies of the certificates and then taken the originals and cashed or sold them. That person may have replaced the original certificates with copies so no one would notice the originals were missing."

"How did you figure this out?" Kevin sounded astonished but willing to listen.

Patricia described the discrepancies regarding the status of the stock certificates in Rabbi Weinstein's Discretionary Fund, and the broker Schwabstein's determination that the certificates had been sold.

"Whoever substituted fake certificates for authentic ones would possibly have a motive for killing Roberto, particularly if that person feared that Roberto had discovered the forgery by examining the discarded copies in the trash. Adrienne, Rabbi Weinstein, and Morris all have keys to the safe where the certificates are stored. Roberto's wife Bertilla said that a few days before his death, Roberto had found what appeared to be financial records in the trash. When he asked Morris if they'd been discarded by mistake, Morris told him no, no mistake. Morris then ripped them up and told Roberto to throw them away. Robert left that note for Rabbi Deborah about papers he found in the garbage."

Patricia stopped to catch her breath again. She hesitated to jump to the heinous conclusion. Had someone—likely Morris—been cashing in temple stock not only to loan to the Rabbi but for his own enterprises? That Torah scroll business? Had Morris waited for Roberto to take out the garbage? Run him over?

Kevin's lips set in a thin line, and his nostrils flared as if ready to sniff out a criminal's trail. Stretching to his full height and patting the gun at his side, he addressed Patricia in a no-nonsense tone devoid of any hint of jokiness. "We have to speak with Mizchek. Given that his car was on the lot, he had access to the stock certificates, and he had contact with Roberto, he is definitely a person of interest. I'll tell Adrienne to set up a meeting ASAP. It's not standard practice, but I want you to be at the meeting. You're familiar with this stock business, and your presence may exert pressure on Mizchek to be more forthcoming. If we question him in his office, we might catch him off guard. Other than Adrienne, please not a word to anyone before we meet with Mizchek. I don't want to spook him or give him time to prepare or, in the worst scenario, flee the jurisdiction."

"I'll be there," Patricia said without hesitation.

She was thrilled to be included in the meeting. Officer O'Donnell was a professional and was asking for her assistance. He had accepted her certificate-copying theory as credible. Her father would be proud. All fingers were pointing to an old man with a mission and bad eyesight.

Chapter Thirty-One

Wednesday, June 17

With Patricia in the back seat, Officer O'Donnell up front in the passenger seat riding shotgun, and Adrienne at the wheel, the threesome sped to Morris Mizchek's office. Kevin didn't want to drive his squad car to avoid attracting attention. He had, however, worn his uniform, Patricia assumed, for the intimidation factor. And he did look imposing.

After their discussion the previous day, Kevin and Patricia had outlined their discoveries to Adrienne. Adrienne agreed to set up the meeting with Morris but insisted on being present. "I knew that guy was losing it. He can barely see, scraped up my car with his big convertible when he was trying to park in the lot. I have no idea what he's doing with the temple's donated stocks. That's why I asked Patricia to do an inventory."

Adrienne shook her head and twisted the heavy gold bangle adorning her wrist as if she could tune into a garbled truth. Looking close to tears, she blurted out the stream of conscious confession in her raspy voice. "To think I was stupid enough to trust the guy. Or stupid enough to think he was too stupid to be up to something. Boy, did I underestimate his sneakiness. As far as loans go, no one told me anything. I should have suspected a problem. The Rabbi was having a rough time with his family. He and Morris were constantly consulting in whispers late in the day. I guess I didn't want to know."

Patricia had never heard Adrienne sound so chagrined and remorseful.

Adrienne hadn't been able to reach Morris until late yesterday afternoon, so the Mizchek meeting was scheduled for this morning at ten. Thankfully, Danny had preschool. Kevin had instructed Adrienne not to mention he would be in attendance, leaving the old man with the impression that only Adrienne and Patricia would be dropping by for a chat.

Yesterday morning, Adrienne and Patricia had had a conference call with the broker, Mr. Schwabstein, who informed them that the certificates in question appeared to have been sold five months earlier, and their value at the time of sale was approximately eighty-five thousand dollars. He also stated that the stocks' value had substantially appreciated in the intervening period since the sale.

When Patricia, Adrienne, and a police officer walked into the accounting firm's lobby, the receptionist uttered a surprised "Oh no, I paid my parking fines!" After Kevin explained they were there to see Morris Mizchek, she exhaled a sigh of relief and immediately buzzed Morris.

Rather than wait for Morris's slow amble to the lobby, Patricia led Adrienne and Kevin down the narrow corridor to Lucky No. Thirty-six. Morris was locking his door just as they arrived. Was he wearing the same stained corduroys she'd had last seen him in?

"Everybody's in a hurry nowadays. I was on my

way to pick you girls up. Ah, I see you brought a police escort. I have a reputation as a lady's man, but no way am I dangerous. Who's our friendly officer?"

Patricia introduced Officer O'Donnell. Morris's hand trembled as he fumbled for the key and unlocked his office door. "Can't be too careful with financial records and Torah scrolls," he said to the threesome.

Kevin looked at Patricia and raised a questioning eyebrow, she assumed in response to the Torah scrolls reference. Patricia mouthed she'd explain later.

Morris's cramped office stunk even worse than the previous week. Apparently, the janitorial staff had not yet been allowed inside to clean. As Morris rearranged boxes and chairs, he wheezed apologetically to Patricia. "Sorry I haven't gotten back to you. So many files to go through. But you didn't need to sic the police on me. Ha ha – just kidding."

Morris's physical exertion brought on a coughing fit. He stopped to catch his breath before continuing. "Three's a crowd. If I'd known you were all coming, I'd have baked a cake or at least provided peanuts. Adrienne says you want to talk about the books. I guess not prayer books. Ha ha, a joke, a joke."

Morris moved behind his desk and collapsed into his chair. He expectorated phlegm from his throat, spitting into what was presumably a wastebasket behind the desk. Adrienne pulled a tissue from her purse, brushed fur from the infamous upholstered chair leaking reams of stuffing and sat down. Patricia perched on a stack of boxes. She surveyed the room for Marilyn, but the cat was nowhere in sight. He/she was probably stalking prey behind the boxes.

Kevin remained standing and started the

interrogation in a curt official voice. "I'm here on another matter, Mr. Mizchek."

"Call me Morris. We're all friends here, right? Should I call my lawyer?"

"That's up to you. I have a few questions. We examined the temple's surveillance tapes for Thursday night, May seventh, the night Roberto Gomez was run over. As you're probably aware, the temple's surveillance system is out of date. The cameras show only the front parking lot."

"We've been meaning to replace or at least update the system," Adrienne interjected in an apologetic tone. "We haven't had the funds to buy new equipment."

"Surveillance systems are an expensive proposition," Mizchek confirmed. "I advised the Rabbi against such a major outlay while he was worried about finances."

Kevin forged on. "The surveillance tapes show that at approximately nine p.m., Thursday night, May seventh, two cars were parked in the lot. One was a blue compact that has been identified as belonging to Mr. Gomez; the second was a gold Cadillac convertible. We have a partial license plate for the car: MM4U. The cameras record footage on the hour and half hour for ten minutes. By ten-thirty, the convertible was no longer parked in the lot."

"That's your car, right, Morris?" Adrienne scowled at him.

"Was the car gold?" Morris inquired.

"The footage's black and white. But it's your car, Morris. I recognize your car. The tape's focus was blurry. Was it raining that night?" asked Adrienne.

"Adrienne, make your point," Kevin said sternly.

"Your car's got that dent on the front bumper where you scraped my car. Don't think I've forgotten. I had to pay close to two thousand dollars to have my car fixed."

"It was a nudge, a love tap. You shouldn't have let the garage scalp you for that much dough. Not my responsibility."

Kevin impatiently interrupted their back and forth. "Was that your car in the temple parking lot on the night of May seventh?"

"I'm a senior—who remembers? If you say you saw my car on the temple's surveillance tape, then it must be."

Kevin's tone deepened, became more intimidating. "Were you in the temple building that night and, if so, where? What was the nature of your visit?"

"I must have been in my office cubicle in the library working on the temple's books. That's what I do. I'm a bookkeeper, ha ha."

"What time did you leave the temple?"

"Well, Officer O'Donnell, I can't say I remember exactly. I often arrive late in the day, after business hours at my office. If Saul's there, we kibbitz and consult. We go way back. I finish up late, after everyone else has gone home. Occasionally I pull an all-nighter. Although for a guy my age that usually means not having to get up for a pee all night. Hah. I haven't been back lately. Too busy with my new business rescuing Torah scrolls. What's the big deal if I was at the temple that night?"

Kevin moved to loom directly in front of the old man, fixing him with a pointed stare. "The tire tracks next to Mr. Gomez' body do not match the garbage truck as was originally anticipated. They do match the tire tracks for the make of your car parked in the temple's lot the evening of May seventh. How do you explain the fact that the tire tracks next to Gomez' body match your car's tire tracks?"

Morris seemed to shrink into his chair. Perspiration beaded his forehead. "I don't know. I don't see too good." Sweat dripped into his eyes, and he took off his thick trifocals. He wiped them across his wrinkled dress shirt, its armpits already stained with sweat circles, and then carefully centered the spectacles back on his generous nose. "I usually back my convertible out of the parking space then turn the car around in the rear parking lot so I can head out, front end forward, into street traffic."

"Is it possible your car made contact with Roberto Gomez' body on the night of May seventh? Why didn't you come forward and disclose your presence at the temple that night?"

"I don't know, I don't know. It never occurred to me it mattered if I was at the temple. I suppose anything's possible. I told you I don't see good, especially at night. Oy, that's terrible. You think my car might have bumped Roberto?"

"I'd like you to come down to the station," announced Kevin in a commanding voice.

Morris sat up at attention. "Am I under arrest?"

"Not at this time," responded Kevin.

Not yet, Patricia silently whispered to herself.

"Then I'm staying put. I'm not obliged to go with you. I know my rights." Morris's response sounded awfully practiced to Patricia's ear. Had he been in this situation before? He began to cry, then wheeze, then cough. "I want to talk with my lawyer."

Crocodile tears or not? How much of this wily old guy's coughing and bumbling was an act? Regardless of whether his tears were fake, Morris was genuinely in distress and coughing hard now. Was he having an asthma attack? Patricia's nursing experience warned her to proceed cautiously.

On the other hand, this might be her only chance to pursue her line of questioning regarding the stock certificates, the loan, the undelivered messages. Playing hardball was part of being a detective as her father said when he shared troublesome cases with her mother. Patricia also knew that Kevin could not continue interrogating Morris about Roberto's death once Morris requested a lawyer. Otherwise Kevin risked compromising evidence that might solve the crime, what her father referred to as fruit of the poisonous tree.

"Can I run out and get you a glass of water from the drinking fountain?" Patricia offered.

Morris declined with a shake of his head.

Although he still looked agitated, his coughing eased. Patricia decided she could proceed, although Morris's guard must be up. Trying to sound authoritative, Patricia did her frosty nun imitation. "Last time we met, I told you I was putting together a list of stocks donated to the temple. I had questions about whether the Union Central Railroad Trust stock and some other company stocks had been sold or cashed in. Yesterday, I examined certificates that Adrienne gave me from the temple's safe. Whether they are copies or originals is open to debate. Let me show you a couple." Patricia pulled a Union Central Railroad Trust certificate from a folder stuffed into her purse.

"Oy, you shouldn't be carrying around those certificates. They're valuable."

"These are copies, Morris."

"Really?" His tears miraculously evaporated. His head swiveled back and forth. Was he looking for an escape route? Or a comforting rub from the mangy Marilyn?

"Yes. Mr. Schwabstein, the temple's broker, has confirmed that the originals of these certificates were, in fact, sold. So what I am showing you are copies of copies." Patricia was theorizing about the "copy of a copy" scam. But her father had described how skilled interrogators had to slant questions and guide suspects toward the truth. "Can you explain, Morris?"

He started with the bumbling again, the "I don't knows" and the bad eyesight lines. "I gotta get a shot," he muttered as he leaned over the briefcase behind his desk. Patricia saw Kevin's hand move toward his sidearm and hover.

"Anyone else want a drink?" asked Morris as he pulled up a half-empty vodka bottle. "Officer? Ladies? It's the finest Russian vodka there is."

Kevin's hand relaxed. "No thank you. I'm on duty."

"Yeah, I can see that." Morris commented sarcastically. "No takers? I have tea."

Patricia and Adrienne shook their heads. Morris poured a generous vodka shot into a chipped cup sitting on his desk.

"Allow me to spark your memory," Patricia offered politely but firmly. Another piece of her father's advice: if you want the suspect to talk, you have to ask the same questions over and over again, and sooner or later he'll slip up. "Rabbi Weinstein has confessed that he asked you for a loan from the Rabbi's Discretionary Fund, and you approved the loan."

"He told you that?" Morris's eyes popped wide-open, magnified by his thick glasses.

"Yes. When he was recovering in the hospital, he made a full statement. Can you describe how you obtained the funds for the loan?"

Morris looked cornered like that roach Marilyn had been about to pounce on the other week. Feeling like a predator, Patricia reminded herself of Morris's complicity in the loan scheme and potentially in Roberto's death.

"Well, the Rabbi needed a loan. He has a son with major physical and mental health problems, both quite expensive problems. Saul and I are old friends. His kids are like my kids. I was trying to help him out." Fresh beads of sweat erupted from Morris's shiny forehead. "He promised to pay back the loan when he had the cash. So I sold a couple of the stock certificates in the Rabbi's Discretionary Fund. No harm done. Nothing says how the money in the Discretionary Fund has to be spent. *Discretionary* means no strict limits. Get it? So yeah, I cashed out a couple of certificates. About fifteen or twenty K. Nothing illegal about that. It was for a good cause. Saul's going to pay it right back. For all I know, maybe he has already."

"Did anyone else know about the loan?" asked Patricia.

"No. We thought it best to keep the transaction between the two of us, under the radar so to speak. We didn't expect the loan to be outstanding very long." Wheezing again, Morris gulped a slug of vodka and unbuttoned his yellowed shirt collar as if trying to ease the flow of oxygen or evasion. "It was maybe a month or two ago. We agreed Saul would have to repay the value of the certificates when they were sold plus any additional appreciation and interest during the loan period. Then we'd, I mean the temple, would be fully compensated. I made copies of the original certificates to keep track of the transactions. I must have gotten confused, mixed up the copies with the original certificates."

"Mr. Schwabstein has informed us that the certificates were sold five months ago, and their value was eighty-five thousand dollars at the time of sale. However their value has appreciated."

"What's a couple of months, a couple thousand dollars among friends?" Despite his boastful posturing, liquid nutrition, and loosened collar, Morris started to wheeze more heavily. "Bookkeeping's lonely work. Maybe I'm overindulging in vodka. Makes me fuzzy."

Morris was suffering. Should Patricia keep questioning him? What was her motive? Interrogating an old man to show off her detecting skills? Rabbi Weinstein had already admitted to the loan scheme and Morris had conceded he sold the stock to cover the loan. But what about Roberto? She couldn't stop without getting the whole story. Patricia pushed on.

"Did you use the entirety of the proceeds from the stock sales for the loan to Rabbi Weinstein?"

"Funny you should ask." Morris grimaced in a fake smile. "Turned out he didn't need the whole amount for his son's medical expenses. So I took a *bissel*, a little for my Torah rescue business. No point in letting the money sit. I'm performing a *mitzvah*, helping distribute these precious Torah scrolls rescued from the Holocaust. The Orthodox communities have parades when they ferry the scrolls down the block to their synagogues. Some Torahs are stained with blood. They've been rescued from the barracks at Bergen-Belson concentration camp."

Morris reached over to the nearby shelf and started pulling out scrolls. "Saul expressed interest in buying a scroll on behalf of the temple. When funds become available, of course."

"Don't count your shekels," Adrienne sneered.

Patricia remained focused on her interrogation. "Do you know Channah Berman?"

"Channah and I are friends from the Jewish Community Center. We're in a surviving spouses group. I'm still grieving my wife. A wonderful woman. I'm lost without her."

"Did you advise Channah to consult with Rabbi Zalman about her grandson's engagement to a young woman who is not of the Jewish faith?"

"How should I remember every conversation I've had with Channah. So what if I did?"

"What were you doing at Corky & Benny's when I saw you there on Saturday, June sixth?"

"Eating. What's wrong with being at the deli? We all gotta eat."

A dead-end diversionary tactic. Patricia switched up her interrogation to the real issue. She knew she was treading on tricky legal territory. Morris had not been given Miranda warnings about self-incrimination and his right to a lawyer. So she didn't want to ask directly about Roberto's death for fear of tainting evidence. But she had to know what Roberto had discussed with

Morris about the certificates. "Did Roberto Gomez ever approach you about papers he found in the temple's trash?"

"What? What do you mean 'approach'?"

"Did Mr. Gomez ever ask you anything about papers that had been thrown out in the trash?"

"You mean did he ask if he could empty my wastebasket? No. Why would he ask me about garbage?" Morris acted insulted by the question.

"Did Mr. Gomez ever mention or ask you anything about stock certificates?"

"No way. What would a poor uneducated Mexican beaner know from stock?"

"Mr. Gomez was from El Salvador," Patricia clarified in an icy tone and pushed on. "Did Mr. Gomez ever ask you if any papers at the temple had been thrown out by mistake?"

"Enough with the questions. I want my lawyer!" Morris made a show of zipping his mouth closed which only exacerbated his breathing difficulties, then defiantly folded his arms over his chest.

"One more question, why didn't you deliver the messages that Rabbi Deborah left with you on her way to Israel?"

"She's a loose cannon. The Rabbi, the real one, agrees. I don't recall any messages, and I'm not a secretary. I'm done talking."

Kevin seemed to have heard enough. "Mr. Mizchek, don't leave town."

"Of course not. Where would I go? The temple's my only family, especially since my wife died. By the way, Adrienne, don't we have an indemnity agreement whereby the temple agrees to indemnify its employees for legal fees arising from temple business? I certainly qualify."

"Chutzpah, what nerve! You have got to be kidding," Adrienne barked. "Morris, you are such a *schnorrer.*"

Patricia knew chutzpah but *schnorrer*? She'd have to ask Adrienne later what that meant. But she recognized dissembling criminal behavior when she saw it. Dear Father, how was anyone going to elicit the straight truth from this sick, slippery senior?

As if on cue, a whiskered dun triangle of a head popped out from under Morris's desk. Had he kicked Marilyn from behind as a fitting distraction to conclude the interview? A thick hair hung out of the cat's mouth. Or was it a wire? Or a tail? Was it wiggling? Ugh. Trying to wiggle away? Like Morris, like Marilyn, masters of mendacity?

Chapter Thirty-Two

Thursday, June 18

The Thursday morning sun and her friends' companionship warmed Patricia as she relaxed with Brenda and Rabbi Deborah at a Java Junction patio table. She had given herself special dispensation from Thursday duty at the temple for her sorely missed coffee klatch.

"First, let me say how much I'm enjoying the three of us being together again. We missed you, Rabbi." Patricia sipped her iced espresso. "I'm sorry you two couldn't be at Tuesday's meeting. I was sworn to secrecy by Officer O'Donnell. Morris wept crocodile tears every time he was asked a crucial question."

"What a sleaze bag," exclaimed Brenda.

"Watching Officer O'Donnell and Morris maneuvering—it was a regular cat-and-mouse game," said Patricia. Figuratively and literally.

"I assume Kevin was the cat and Morris the mouse," said Brenda.

"Definitely. Morris practically admitted to running over Roberto," Patricia confirmed.

"Are they going to throw the book at him?" Brenda asked eagerly. "Murder, in the first degree?"

"Too much TV, Brenda. With no independent,

third-party witnesses, I don't know if the police will ever be able to determine, let alone prove, if the supposed accident was intentional or not." Patricia took another sip of espresso and frowned. "Morris is the only eye-witness alive who could give an accurate account. He claims he doesn't understand what happened. Blames his poor eyesight, impaired memory, bad weather, and vodka-drinking."

"Morris should suffer the consequences if he ran over Roberto. Even if it was an accident as Morris claims," announced Brenda. "It's not fair to Roberto's family."

"I agree," Rabbi Deborah affirmed. "Regardless of his age or his physical condition, Morris needs to take responsibility for his actions. The temple is cooperating with the state prosecutor and is hoping for an expeditious conclusion of the matter. I'm not sure what's going to happen."

"As far as criminal charges, the State may be able to prosecute Morris even if he claims no intent," Patricia stated with authority. "He could be charged under the vehicular manslaughter statute. Thank goodness the police experts finally confirmed that the scrap found in Roberto's pocket is a piece of a copied railroad trust stock certificate."

"Meaning what?" asked Rabbi Deborah.

"The connection supports the theory that Roberto found copies of railroad trust certificates in the trash, suspected something suspicious was happening, and asked Morris to explain. Roberto probably wanted to meet with you, Rabbi, about the same issue. The nexus gives Morris a motive: to prevent his scheme from being discovered. If intent can be implied, Morris could be charged with criminal homicide. I bet Morris and his lawyer are engaged in heavy-duty plea bargaining right now."

"And you learned all this how, Patricia?" Brenda quizzed.

"I googled the State of Maryland's criminal code last night. Also Kevin, I mean Officer O'Donnell, called last evening," Patricia admitted. "He was checking in case I had additional information about Morris's spending habits. Officer O'Donnell was speculating whether Morris's "borrowing" on behalf of Rabbi Weinstein was motivated by gambling or personal debt. From what I observed, Morris didn't spend much on himself or anyone else. His clothes were worn out and his office was decrepit. On the other hand he's running this dubious Torah scroll business."

Patricia's thoughts strayed to Kevin and how exciting she'd found the stock certificate investigation and her interrogation of the cunning Morris. She started to flush. Then she reminded herself how cruel she felt going after the asthmatic old man, purposely trying to confuse and mislead him.

"Did Morris explain why he never delivered my message for Rabbi Weinstein and why he never called you?" asked Rabbi Deborah.

"He claims he doesn't remember your leaving any messages with him," responded Patricia, omitting Morris's gratuitous insults about the Rabbi. "He's a crafty guy. Adrienne called him a *schnorrer*. She said it's Yiddish for a chiseler who makes pretensions to respectability, a moocher with *chutzpah* and resourcefulness for getting money from others."

"That's a good one," Brenda laughed. "A perfect

description of he who feeds at the trough. The old *chazzer*, that's Yiddish for pig, Patricia, never kosher, for your information. Morris is more evil than that."

Rabbi Deborah hushed her friend. "Brenda, we should be more sympathetic to Morris. He's alone and not in good health. He was trying to help Rabbi Weinstein."

"I'm alone, Rabbi. You're alone, too," Brenda responded. "That tan looks good on you. I need a trip to Israel, or at least a bit of bronzing." She raised her face toward the sun and pushed up her flowered tunic's loose sleeves.

"I can't say we solved your disappearance." Patricia pulled down on the wide-brimmed straw hat she wore to shield her fair skin from sun. "But I do think the *Yenta* Patrol's sleuthing skills contributed to uncovering the stock certificate mystery and the loan scheme."

"*Yenta* patrol?" Rabbi Deborah asked with a puzzled expression as she lifted thick curls off her neck. "Anyone have an elastic?"

Patricia rummaged in her black tote, found an elastic, and handed it to Rabbi Deborah. "While you were away, Brenda made me an official member of the *Yenta* Patrol." Patricia explained how she and Brenda had formed their own squad to investigate the Rabbi's absence and Roberto's accident.

"To repeat, I am so sorry for causing you guys all the worry," said Rabbi Deborah. "I am touched by your concern and honored to have been the impetus for creation of the *Yenta* Patrol."

"We are just glad you are safely back," said Brenda. "So what's in store for Rabbi Weinstein at the temple?"

"Everything's going public now," Rabbi Deborah assured Brenda and Patricia. "Saul was released from the hospital yesterday and will meet with the temple board next week. He's written an open letter to the congregation apologizing for his poor judgment in taking a loan from his discretionary fund. He asks for forgiveness and recounts the entire episode, including his son's medical needs and how he will repay the loan in full, including appreciation and interest, by the end of the month."

"How's he gonna do that? Didn't he claim he had no money?" asked Brenda.

"Lenore has a family trust. She and Saul are making a special application for the release of funds," said Rabbi Deborah. "Some of the principal has to be sold. Saul should have gone to Lenore in the first place, but I guess he didn't want her to know how bad their finances were."

"Did he spend too much on a diamond pendant for his sister-in-law?" Brenda joked.

"Let's not encourage rumors," Rabbi Deborah scolded. "In his letter, Saul offers to resign from his position if that's what the temple board and/or the congregation want him to do. The letter will be released on Monday, but he's already given me a courtesy copy. He's sending the letter snail mail. You should be receiving yours soon."

"Rabbi, do you think the temple will accept his resignation?" asked Patricia.

"A congregational meeting will be scheduled to discuss the issues, and the board will also make a recommendation. My prediction is Rabbi Weinstein will survive the scandal. After all, the temple will be made whole financially, the Rabbi is beloved, and his son's situation is sympathetic."

"What about Morris the Moocher?" Brenda slurped up the dregs of her frozen cappuccino. "By the way, have you heard Java Junction has come out with mini-fraps? It's a great idea. I can have two different flavors of minis and not have to choose between java chip and s'mores."

"Brenda, take it easy," Patricia admonished. "They all have whipped cream and tons of sugar."

"Thanks for the advice, Ms. Nudge. You're becoming a real *yenta*."

"This is on the QT," Rabbi Deborah spoke softly. "From what I understand, the temple would just as soon close the affair regarding the sale of stock certificates without any more negative publicity. If the temple went after Morris, the Rabbi could also be implicated. It wouldn't be fair to let Morris take all the blame. Morris, however, has been relieved of his bookkeeping duties at the temple."

"Rabbi Deborah's correct," Patricia confirmed. "If the temple pursued prosecution of Morris, then Rabbi Weinstein could be considered a co-conspirator and held jointly liable."

Rabbi Deborah nodded in assent. "The temple board will be establishing a fund for the Gomez family. The amount depends on how much money can be raised. Pending the outcome of the criminal investigation and an arrest, Adrienne is pressuring for Morris to perform custodial duties at the temple."

"Hah, that would certainly be well-deserved community service," Brenda quipped. "Adrienne would make a dynamite taskmaster. I can see her in black boots with a whip. That must be how she keeps her husband on such a tight leash."

"I'm skeptical about Morris's housekeeping skills. His office was a dump." Patricia shivered as she pictured Marilyn's peeing and preying.

"Morris would be under Adrienne's close supervision, of course," Rabbi Deborah assured. "She promised she'd watch Morris like a hawk to prevent any funny business."

Patricia focused her gaze on Rabbi Deborah. "What are your plans for the future at the temple?"

"Good question. The congregation seemed to find my sermon in support of interfaith marriage more offensive than Saul's dubious loan arrangement. I'm serious about starting this interfaith dialogue group. We may organize a community forum or seminars. Amir and I are meeting for coffee next week."

"You mean the Muslim guy you met? Is that safe?" asked Brenda.

"Brenda, not every Muslim is a terrorist. That's an insulting stereotype. In fact only a few members of the Islamic faith have radicalized and turned to violence. Similar to the percentage of Jews represented by extremist groups." Rabbi Deborah shook her head and took a swig from her cup. "But I promise to report in after my coffee with Amir. We've had fascinating comparative religion discussions. For example, under Jewish law if you sin against another person you must ask forgiveness from that person. In Catholicism, the sinner can confess to a clergyman who grants penance as part of the forgiveness process. Islam encourages forgiveness between believers but allows revenge to the extent of the harm done."

"I admit it," conceded Patricia. "Penance was a convenient way to deal with guilt. One hundred Hail Marys and all's right with the world. Plus there were indulgences, sort of get-out-of-jail-free cards. My mom would give my sisters and me a quarter to plop into the donation box to buy them. Like paying in advance for sins under a layaway plan—part of the Church's accounting system for salvation. Too bad I've given up those paths to absolution."

"An Eternal Revenue Service, hah! Hope I'm paid up," Brenda commented. "My shrink always tells me I shouldn't blame myself for anything. I never have to ask for forgiveness. My shrink's Jewish but I consider him my atheist priest."

"I have to reflect on that concept, Brenda. Anyways it's hard to say how the temple will react to the interfaith extra-curricular activities I'm proposing, especially once Saul realizes that a Muslim man is involved," Rabbi Deborah continued. "In the meantime since Saul is on leave, I'm giving the sermon at Shabbat services tomorrow. On a non-controversial topic, of course. Maybe Father's Day. Please come?"

"Of course we'll come, right Brenda? Rabbi, I hope you are planning to continue teaching the adult bat mitzvah class?"

"Yes, of course. We'll meet next Sunday night. I'll send out an email today."

"Great, I don't have to prepare anything then." Patricia explained how the bat mitzvah class had met to brainstorm about what to do in Rabbi Deborah's absence, and Patricia had agreed to make a presentation.

"I'd appreciate any insights you'd like to contribute regarding the next reading. What about you, Brenda? What are your plans?"

"All this excitement has me reevaluating whether I should continue with Brenda's Beautifully Yours. I've been party planning since my last husband."

"I didn't know there'd been more than one?" Patricia asked.

"I'm kidding about the husbands, not the business. All that stressing over invites and party planning seems silly. Last month at a bar mitzvah at a country club, a bunch of kids crowded into the handicapped bathroom and flushed my customized yarmulkes down the toilet. Disgusting. I'm considering alternatives. A friend who's a certified bra fitter represents a brand at high-end department stores. Imagine all the lacey push up bras, matching panties, and silk teddies I could buy at a discount." Brenda made a show of raising her palms and pretending to lift her bust line.

"On the other hand who would appreciate my new boudoir attire?" Brenda dropped her hands to her drink. "But I could do a bra-fitting fund raiser for the sisterhood. I heard Wendy Weller, the bat mitzvah class's own Miss Organic Foods, is promoting moisturizing creams made from breast milk. Could be a big seller."

"I bet there's a market. Several congregants who are nursing mothers have asked me about breastfeeding in the sanctuary," mused Rabbi Deborah. "There was an uproar about nursing at another temple. I don't see why it's not permissible, although I suppose I should bring the issue before the board."

"Yeah, you don't want to drown in any more hot

water." Brenda waved a finger. "Of course I'll never meet any men if I pursue the bra fitting or a moisturizer line. I'll have to start reading the obits to see if any rich guys have been recently widowed."

"Brenda, that's an old Joan Rivers line," said the Rabbi.

"You'd win the Jewish comics category on one of those TV quiz shows," confirmed Brenda. "Seriously, I've been considering starting a new on-line dating service: IF Only which stands for InterFaith Only. Or I could name it the Non-Kosher Meet Market. Anyone who's interested in relationships with someone of a different religion, faith, philosophy, whatever, could join. Sort of a new spin on J-Date."

"That's a great idea. I prefer the first name, very clever." Rabbi Deborah clapped her hands and gave Brenda a high five.

"We'd do activities that attract a broad crowd – a sushi Shabbat dinner or a foreign film event."

"How about a Shabbat *schvitz*-fest?" Patricia joked. "You could meet at the gym and encourage people to do a ten-station circuit, like the Ten Commandments or a condensed version of Stations of the Cross."

"I'm being serious. Don't make fun of me."

"I'm not. I love hearing your creative ideas." Patricia reached over and squeezed Brenda's hand. "IF Only would be a terrific innovation."

"Patricia, what are your plans? Have you considered studying for a private investigator's license?" Rabbi Deborah suggested.

"It was fun investigating the missing stocks. But the more I think about it, the more uncomfortable I am with witness interrogation techniques," Patricia mused, touching the Jewish star on the chain around her neck, her conversion present from Rabbi Deborah. "A certain amount of deception and cruelty accompanies the job of being a detective. I'm afraid I'd have to betray the truth before I could obtain the truth—if finding out the truth is even possible or the best outcome. It's not like being a firefighter when everyone's happy to see you with a hose to put out the fire. No one's glad to see a detective with a warrant for a loved one's arrest or an intrusive search."

"You're a regular philosopher," said Brenda.

"Plus, Michael wants us to have another baby. I'd like a second child too, but not without more support at home."

"I'm not surprised he's nudging you about a second kid. Make him promise to help more. Believe me, two is more than twice the work. I speak from experience."

"Thanks, Brenda, for the advice. I've told him, and he is promising to be home more and take more responsibility for childcare and household chores."

"You're not going to let your excellent analytical skills go to waste, are you?" Rabbi Deborah asked.

"For now I'll concentrate on solving the mysteries of Torah and Talmud in bat mitzvah class. I plan to keep volunteering at the temple. And, your interfaith forum and Brenda's IF Only have inspired me. What if I start a support group for interfaith couples at the temple?"

"Excellent idea. I second that," affirmed Rabbi Deborah. "Do you want me to run it by Saul?"

"Yes, thank you, although we'd better wait until he recovers," said Patricia. "I've also been practicing my photography. I might sign up for a class in advanced camera techniques. The study of Torah and photography feel connected. The Torah's like a zoom lens, starting with Genesis' panoramic view of the world's beginnings and ending with a close up shot of Moses and his last days."

"Very perceptive." Rabbi Deborah nodded enthusiastically. "May I use that line in one of my Torah study sessions?"

"Of course, I'd be flattered." Patricia grinned but then turned sober. "Speaking of the Torah, does anyone know any details about Morris's Torah scroll business? He claims the scrolls were rescued from the Holocaust but how does he confirm their authenticity?"

"You've heard the old adage," Brenda opined. "It takes two to create a fraudulent scheme: one to lie and one to listen. But good question, Patricia. In your official capacity on the *Yenta* Patrol, you'd better investigate. At least before the second kid arrives. Can you guys wait here for a minute? I'm going to try the s'mores mini-frap to cool off. Part of my observance as a gastronomic Jew. I'll be right back."

"You've convinced me, Brenda. I'll go with," said Rabbi Deborah. "I want one too. My treat. Patricia, can I tempt you?"

"I succumb to peer pressure. I've been tempted. Can you ask the barista to add an extra shot of espresso? Thanks." Patricia was glad she could share concerns and caffeine with her two friends. But she couldn't shake her doubt that Morris was never going to pay for all his sins, certainly not with interest or appreciation. She needed to keep her eye on Morris and she needed that extra shot of caffeine.

Chapter Thirty-Three

Friday, June 19

Hand in hand, Patricia and Michael walked into the sanctuary at Temple Israel. The sun was setting, and the stained-glass windows glinted with bejeweled light. Brenda stood at the sanctuary's back, deep in conversation with Officer O'Donnell who looked very official, dressed in his police uniform. After a moment's hesitation, Patricia led Michael up to the twosome. "Officer O'Donnell, I didn't expect to see you here. This is my husband, Dr. Michael Weiss."

The two men shook hands solemnly, without smiling. "Adrienne contacted the police and asked for extra security," Kevin explained. "Now that Rabbi Zalman's returned, Adrienne's worried about repercussions from the intermarriage sermon." Kevin turned to face Michael. "So you're the doc, huh? I've heard a lot about you."

Michael gave Patricia a questioning look before observing "I'm glad to see no demonstrators tonight."

"I second that sentiment." Kevin nodded heartily. "Brenda here is telling me about IF Only, her new online dating service. I'm definitely interested, but Brenda's giving me a hard time." He chuckled.

"Kevin wants to join but I explained NO

MARRIED PERSONS in capital letters!" Brenda spoke in an adamant tone that Patricia rarely heard her use.

"I've been separated for over a year now." Kevin pleaded his case. "Why shouldn't I be able to sign up for IF Only?"

"No deceptions allowed on this website. Open eyes, Open hearts. No Rachel/Jacob/Leah mix-ups. You must be available for a serious relationship. If a casual connection develops, okay. But there should be at least the potential for longer-term commitment, even matrimony. Look, here's Rabbi Deborah. What's your opinion?"

Rabbi Deborah, in her flowing white robe and embroidered *tallit*, had paused by the entourage on her way to the *bimah*. "You raise a complicated question, Brenda. What about that situation in Silver Spring's ultra-Orthodox community where the husband refused to give his wife a Jewish divorce, although he was cheating on her? According to biblical law, a married couple is released from the bonds of matrimony only if the husband agrees to grant the wife a bill of divorce. The document's known by its Aramaic name, *"get."* The Silver Spring husband fled town five years ago without agreeing to a get. How would you handle the wife's request to join IF Only?"

Brenda shrugged in frustration and sarcastically thanked the Rabbi for her advice.

"How else are you going to limit the website?" Michael seemed eager to put his two cents into the debate. "Would an atheist be able to sign up? Does atheism count as a religion? What about Orthodox Jews who are interested in meeting Reform Jews? Would they qualify?"

"Yeah, and what about gays?" Kevin interjected.

"Of course the website will be open to gay people," affirmed Brenda.

"Rabbis, at least Reform ones, will marry a gay couple, both of whom are Jewish, before they'll marry a Jew and a non-Jew," Patricia informed the group. "What about transgendered persons?"

"I haven't dealt with all those details." Brenda sighed. "I guess IF Only will be open to men and women of all races and sexual orientations. But I insist online photos will have to be taken within the last two years."

"That means ten years in online dating time." Kevin spoke with what sounded like the voice of experience. "Are men allowed to wear toupees in their photos?"

"Of course. Although the self-summaries are more significant than the photos. The summary should disclose profession, favorite pastimes, and whether you'd be willing to be an emergency contact. Also whether you have pension benefits or investment income. And any alimony obligations or other indebtedness. And any criminal history."

"What about willingness to convert?" Patricia said, half joking. This debate could go on forever. She took Michael's arm and made a move toward the sanctuary's seating. "Brenda, join us when you're ready."

Organ music played softly. Patricia led Michael toward the front of the sanctuary where half of the beige wall behind the ark was finished with a handsome sandstone design. The other half of the wall was plain, symbolizing that the full history of the Jewish people had yet to be written, and that man—and woman—was still striving for perfection. For this reason, a temple always left some element undone. Patricia found the plain wall comforting neutral territory upon which she might be able to work out issues in her own life and marriage.

"Do we have to sit so close?" Michael whispered.

"You sound like Brenda. You'll enjoy the service more if we sit up front. There will be fewer distractions, and congregants will have a harder time asking you medical questions." Patricia gazed fondly at Michael. He was wearing a new charcoal sports jacket cut to flatter his broad shoulders. He was an attractive man, more substantial, more mature than Kevin.

She recalled last night's heart-to-heart about a second child, family responsibilities, and religion. Michael promised to share more parenting duties and housework and to arrange his schedule around kid activities. He'd take Danny on special outings once a week, soccer or hiking or fishing. Patricia was dubious about the fishing. Did Michael know how to fish? He promised to go to the market every other week. That chore she could see Michael actually performing, given his interest in gourmet cuisine. He also agreed to attend services with Patricia and support her bat mitzvah studies. By agreeing to a babysitter and accompanying her to temple tonight, Michael had started off on the right foot.

After last night's talk, they made love, and she hadn't swallowed her little yellow pill for the first time in a long while. Michael wrapped his strong arms around her long torso, and she held on until the entire world was encompassed in their embrace. His voluptuous lips on her mouth, the chafing of his rough beard on her face, their legs intertwined—the moves were sweet and familiar. They made the quiet love of two people who trust each other. After the sex was over, they rocked each other to sleep.

Patricia blushed at the memory and looked around to make sure she was unobserved. Michael was surreptitiously checking his cell phone for messages. Rabbi Deborah had slipped from behind the sanctuary's alcove onto her seat on the bimah.

After their Thursday morning coffee, the Rabbi had emailed Patricia readings on marriage, including the seven blessings recited at a Jewish wedding ceremony. One of those blessings described a married couple as loving and beloved friends. A rabbinical scholar had defined love as sexual friendship and a relationship of honesty and mutual respect. Perhaps if Patricia and Michael kept supporting and encouraging each other, they could live up to that description of passionate friends for life.

A squeaky plunk of the adjacent seat ended Patricia's reverie. Brenda wiggled close to Patricia. "I'm glad I had that conversation with you all. I hadn't considered the complications raised by an online dating service. In the meantime, who can we get to occupy this empty seat next to me? If you have nothing good to say about a person, then come sit by me. Or as my *bubbe* used to say 'if you can't say something nice, say it in Yiddish.'"

"I'm not sure I want to learn that Yiddish adage," said Patricia.

"You're too nice." Brenda craned her neck around. "On the other hand, after coffee yesterday, Rabbi Deborah emailed me an article about gossip. Did you know Judaism teaches that speaking negatively of others or listening to gossip is sinful? I'm turning over a new leaf, starting tomorrow."

The organ music grew louder. Rabbi Deborah and Cantor Max rose and stood before the pulpit. They began to chant *Hineh Ma Tov*, the hymn from Psalm 133. "Behold, how good and how pleasant it is for brethren to dwell together in unity." Patricia heard Michael tentatively begin to murmur the Hebrew as if resuscitating the words from some buried vein of memory. She breathed deeply and joined Rabbi Deborah, Brenda, and her husband in song.

Epilogue

Brenda opened her online dating service four months later. One of her sons, a web designer, provided technical support. She charged a minimal fee to avoid putting ads on the site. As part of her leaf turning, she returned to her healthy choice nutrition class at the Jewish Community Center and met a retired senior citizen, a widower looking for mature female companionship for *kibitzing*, otherwise known as conversation; *kvetching,* also called complaining, and *kvelling,* or beaming with pleasure or pride especially with respect to children's and grandchildren's perceived accomplishments. They *kugeled* together—the making of kugel, a traditional Jewish pudding of noodles, potatoes, matzoh, or other heavy ingredients, often on the sweet side—and dined out. Brenda said they were going to take it slow and not combine finances ever. He didn't have much stock but had accumulated a safe government pension after a long career as a government lawyer. Plus he still had his hair and drove.

Adrienne and her husband eventually divorced. She signed up for IF Only and may have met someone. She was not telling, concerned she might compromise her position at the temple by dating a gentile. With the temple board's approval, Adrienne hired an independent outside auditor who was a Certified Public Accountant to handle the temple's financial records.

After a contentious temple board meeting at which Rabbi Weinstein apologized profusely for his poor judgment and threw himself on the mercy of the officers and trustees, the board voted to continue his contract. The congregational meeting also resulted in a vote to support the Rabbi's return. Rabbi Weinstein remained as Senior Rabbi at Temple Israel for the foreseeable future. Using funds from Lenore's family trust, he and Lenore established a foundation to support research and interventional treatments for adults with autism spectrum disorders. Lenore took on administrative and executive responsibilities for the foundation.

Lenore's sister, Risa Fleishman, divorced her husband, moved to Boca Raton, and started earning more than a million dollars as one of the most successful real estate agents on Florida's east coast. Rumor had it that she was dating an attractive fundamentalist minister associated with Messianic-Jews-for-Intermarriage.

Morris pled no contest to a charge of negligent manslaughter and gave up his driver's license. He was sentenced to ten years of imprisonment. He was serving his sentence in a minimum-security prison with many of the comforts of home except for Marilyn, the tabby. While incarcerated, Morris cornered the chocolate market in the lockup by buying up candy bars from the commissary and selling them for a profit in the yard. Morris hoped that he would eventually be released on parole due to his age, asthma, and good behavior.

Morris's business of selling rescued Holocaust Torah scrolls, however, was under investigation for fraud. His representation that several scrolls had been recovered from a barracks at Bergen-Belsen concentration camp had been challenged by a Holocaust survivor who remembered that the British had burned down the barracks in 1945, due to a typhoid epidemic. Morris's defense was that he'd been duped by his Israeli contacts who sold him the scrolls.

After soliciting donations from the congregation as well as from the community at large, Temple Israel was able to establish a substantial fund to support Roberto's family. The insurance company also came through with its payment to the Gomez family. After extensive discussions with her priest and a gratis evaluation of Morris's finances by the temple's new accountant, Bertilla Gomez decided not to pursue a civil case against Morris. In exchange, Morris committed to teaching on-line bookkeeping classes from prison to low-income high school students, many of whom were from families where English was not the first language spoken at home. In Bertilla's view, it was only fair that young people from low-income homes be given the same opportunities to learn financial skills as wealthier teens. Bertilla also decided to pursue a nursing degree in a part-time program at Montgomery College.

Three months after she returned from her LMHS trip, Rabbi Deborah announced she would be leading a second LMHS tour the following summer. Channah's grandson Jason and his fiancée Brook participated. Seven months after that second trip, Rabbi Deborah officiated at Jason and Brook's wedding at Valley Gardens with Channah in attendance. Brook wore the Chai necklace that Channah had given her.

After two more years at Temple Israel, Rabbi Deborah left to pursue various interfaith coalition building activities. She started a local chapter of Caravan for Religious Reconciliation sponsored by Clergy Beyond Borders.

The Caravan gave presentations at synagogues, churches, mosques, and other public venues to educate communities about preventing religious and racially motivated hate crimes. She blogged for a liberal American Jewish lobbying group that supported a two-state solution for Israel. She and Amir held several dialogues and day-long seminars to discuss interfaith issues. Their relationship remained ambiguous even to themselves.

In the fall, Patricia's sister Teresa attended another realtors' convention in Washington, D.C. Patricia introduced Teresa to Kevin. The two dated long distance for several months. However, Teresa decided she was too mature for Kevin or at least at a different life-stage.

After the break-up with Teresa, Kevin signed up for the Sledgehammer Workout at the local gym where he met a nice Catholic girl, a blonde in hot pink spandex. Kevin and his new girlfriend suffered and sweated together as they hoisted sledgehammers overhead and slammed them down on tires. Kevin informed Brenda he no longer needed to join IF Only and joked that working out was his religion, grueling enough to offer physical atonement. It was unclear if the hard-bodied blonde knew Kevin was technically married.

In the spring, Kevin was promoted to sergeant on the Rockville police force after he cracked a case involving oxycodone tablets stolen from an oral surgeon's office. Turned out the oral surgeon's son had "borrowed" the meds and brought them to parties, charging five bucks a hit. The parents were influential, and the boy received probation and community service after which his record would be wiped clean so as not to sully his chances of being accepted at an Ivy League college.

In August, Michael surprised Patricia by leaving three tickets for a family trip to Israel on the kitchen counter. In October, Michael added a new cardiologist to his practice so that he would have more time to spend with his family. He continued to attend services with Patricia at least once a month. He took Danny to tot Shabbat services and coached Danny's soccer team. Michael signed up for cooking lessons at *L'Academie de Cuisine* and prepared gourmet meals bi-weekly. He and Patricia invited his mother down once a quarter. Michael also agreed to marriage counseling so that he and Patricia could learn how to disagree and debate like thoughtful and caring adults.

Patricia's nightmarish dreams about crashing garbage trucks and preying cats eventually abated. Although Morris was serving jail time, Patricia did not consider his punishment to rise to the standard of Old Testament biblical justice. Not exactly Deuteronomy's "eye for an eye." But she and Rabbi Deborah discussed that the Biblical phrase was more of a limit on punishment, rather than an authorization for retribution and revenge. Reform Judaism had been moving toward a more humane jurisprudence that replaced the Torah's literal language. Rabbi Deborah also pointed out that regardless of whether an individual has been brought to justice, the Torah teaches that all people should love their fellows. Patricia would have to reflect upon that lesson. But she was determined to keep a *yenta*'s eye on Morris to confirm he was fulfilling his commitments.

Patricia and Michael continued to try for a second child over the summer. She stopped taking her little yellow pills and became pregnant in September just after the Israel trip. She had a miscarriage two months later. When she, Michael, and Danny joined her mother and sisters for Thanksgiving, Patricia learned how to make peach pie, using her mother's canned peaches.

Patricia completed her bat mitzvah studies with Rabbi Deborah. She, Brenda, and the rest of the class were bat mitzvahed in a group ceremony in May of the following year on Shavuot. Patricia invited her mother and sisters as well as Michael's mother Lillian. Everyone graciously attended. In honor of Shavuot, Rabbi Deborah recounted the Ruth story again, reminding congregants that "we all have the ability to blossom and grow, and there is bravery in leaving behind all we've ever known for the spark of future potential."

Patricia became pregnant again after the May bat mitzvah ceremony. Squeaking in under the wire, as her mother commented. Since Danny had started elementary school, Patricia decided to train as a lay clergy person at the temple to assist with services, b'nai mitzvahs, funerals and counseling. She also started a support group for interfaith couples at the temple with Rabbi Weinstein's blessing. Apparently, Rabbi Deborah had convinced him that the group would attract well-to-do young families to the congregation.

Patricia began tutoring Roberto's son and daughter in math as well as English. She was also instrumental in convincing the temple to declare itself a sanctuary congregation committed to protect immigrant families and other vulnerable groups who face workplace discrimination, bigotry, or deportation.

On a lovely September afternoon, when Patricia was four months pregnant, she and Michael reaffirmed their vows under a flowered *chuppah* in Temple Israel's sanctuary. Rabbi Deborah, still officiating, performed the commitment ceremony with all the traditional rituals. Cantor Max, still chanting, sang the *Sheva Berachot*, the seven marriage blessings. Wine was drunk, and glass was broken. Brenda read from the Song of Songs. Danny recited a poem that Rabbi Deborah helped him write and memorize. Patricia delegated the catering responsibilities to Brenda who, with Michael's approval, hired Corky & Benny's and Frostings Bakery to provide refreshments. A good nosh and good time were had by all.

A word about the author…

Joyce Sanderly is a Pushcart-nominated poet and a lawyer. She retired as a Senior Counsel from the U.S. Securities and Exchange Commission. Her poetry collection, The Shomer, was a finalist for the Blue Lynx Prize and semifinalist for the Elixir Press Antivenom Award and for the Codhill Press Poetry Award. Her poetry has recently been published in Atlanta Review, Folio, Delmarva Review, Peregrine, Another Chicago, PANK, Ekphrastic Review, Women's Studies Quarterly, Sow's Ear, Lilith, Common Ground, and CALYX, among others. She was awarded first place in the 2022 Dancing Poetry Festival, received an honorable mention in the 2019 Ginsberg poetry contest, was shortlisted for the 2018 O'Donoghue Prize, and was awarded first place in Poetica's 2016 Rosenberg poetry competition.

She has lived in Washington, D.C. and Montgomery County, Maryland for the last forty years where she raised her family and practiced law for the federal government. *Wild Irish Yenta* is her debut novel.